A QUAINT CUSTOM

When Lord Robert Andreville lay down beside Maxie, she knew she should be wary. But the night was cold, and he was warm.

"This is like bundling." Maxie said.

"Bundling?" asked Robert.

"It's a custom in America," Maxie explained. "Couples share a bed, both wearing clothing to keep matters from getting out of hand. Often the bed will be divided by a board."

Robert chuckled. "I'm sure that neither board nor clothing stop determined people."

And as Maxie felt his arm tighten around her, she realized how far she was from America—and how close to temptation. . . .

MARY JO PUTNEY was graduated from Syracuse University with degrees in eighteenth-century British literature and industrial design. She lived in California and England before settling in Baltimore, Maryland.

THE ROGUE AND THE RUNAWAY

by

Mary Jo Putney

A SIGNET BOOK

SIGNET
Published by the Penguin Group
Penguin Books USA Inc., 375 Hudson Street,
New York, New York, 10014 U.S.A.
Penguin Books Ltd, 27 Wrights Lane, London W8 5TZ, England
Penguin Books Australia Ltd, Ringwood, Victoria, Australia
Penguin Books Canada Ltd, 2801 John Street, Markham, Ontario,
Canada L3R 1B4
Penguin Books (N.Z.) Ltd, 182-190 Wairau Road,
Auckland 10, New Zealand

Penguin Books Ltd, Registered Offices:
Harmondsworth, Middlesex, England

First published by Signet, an imprint of Penguin Books USA Inc.

First Printing, July, 1990

10 9 8 7 6 5 4 3 2 1

To the memory of Georgette Heyer:
seldom equaled, never surpassed

With special thanks to Theresa Jemison, for letting
me use her Mohawk name, Kanawiosta.

Dear Carolyn,

Thank you for
your kind words —

Best wishes,

Prologue

The great estate of Wolverhampton graced the Vale of York like a royal crown, its placid majesty dating from the late days of the seventeenth century. The mansion had been built by the first Marquess of Wolverton, whose grand taste in architecture had been matched by his eye for heiresses; in his long life he had married and buried three of them.

In the century and a half since its completion, Wolverhampton had been visited by the great and notorious of every generation and had provided a splendorous setting for a succession of worthy lords and ladies. The Andrevilles were the first family of northern England, its members known for unimpeachable honor, conscientious management, and sober behavior. At least, most of them were.

It would have been more suitable to hire a post chaise, but Robin preferred to ride through the English countryside after so many years away. Though the weather was dry and relatively warm for early December, there was a hint of snow in the air, the hushed stillness that heralds a coming storm.

The ancient Wolverhampton gatekeeper had recognized him and rushed to open the gates, almost falling over himself to be hospitable. Robin had given a brief smile of greeting but not lingered to say more. The mansion itself was almost a mile farther, at the head of a wide elm-lined drive. He reined to a halt in front, temporarily unobserved, and scanned the vast granite facade. It was not a homelike place, but nonetheless Wolverhampton had been his home, and it was here that his weary spirit had demanded to return when his duties in Paris were finished. He should have notified his brother that he was coming, but had chosen not to. This way, there was no chance to be told that he was unwelcome.

A footman espied him and bustled out, and Robin dismounted and wordlessly handed his horse over before climbing the steps to the massive ten-foot-high double doors. The footman who crossed the marble-paved foyer was new to the household and didn't recognize the newcomer until his eye fell on the calling card.

"Lord Robert Andreville?" the servant gasped before recalling that aspirants to butlerdom must learn to control their reactions better.

"In person," Robin said mildly. "The black sheep returns. Is Lord Wolverton receiving?"

"I shall inquire." The footman's demeanor was under control. "Would you care to wait in the drawing room, my lord?"

"I can find my way there on my own," Robin remarked when the servant started to show the way. "I was born here, after all. And I promise I shan't steal the silver."

Coloring, the footman bowed, then disappeared into the depths of the house.

Robin strolled into the drawing room, knowing that he was overdoing the casualness; anyone who knew him well would realize that he was nervous. But then, he and his elder brother did not know each other well, not any more. While they had been friends as boys and had maintained a tenuous contact over the years, it had been fifteen years since they had lived under the same roof, four years since the last brief meeting in London.

The drawing room was brighter and pleasanter than it had been; Versailles softened with a touch of English coziness. Probably that was Giles' doing; he had never had much patience with pomp. Or perhaps the redecoration had been done by the woman who had briefly been Giles' wife. Robin had never met her, did not even recall her name.

Robin paced the drawing room restlessly. His left hand and wrist ached from the long ride, not yet fully healed from being broken earlier in the autumn. It was hard to be comfortable when he could almost hear the echoes of old rows with his father rebounding from the silk-clad walls.

Above the carved mantel hung a portrait of the Andreville brothers, painted two years before Robin had left Wolverhampton for good, and he paused to study it. A stranger would not know the two youths were brothers without reading the engraved plate; even their eyes were different shades of blue. Giles was tall, with a muscular build and brown hair, and even at twenty-one he had worn the grave air that came from knowing the burdens he would some day carry on his broad shoulders.

In contrast, Robin was no more than average height, slightly built, and brightly blond. The portrait painter had done a good job of catching a mischievous twinkle in his azure eyes. Superficially Robin knew that he had changed very little, though he was now thirty-two instead of sixteen. Ironic that he retained that boyish look when he felt so much older than his years, from having seen and done things better forgotten.

Pausing by the window, he looked across the rolling green velvet grounds, immaculate even in late autumn. What was he doing here? A scapegrace younger son didn't belong at Wolverhampton. But then, Lord Robert Andreville didn't belong anywhere else, either; that was the whole point.

Behind Robin the door opened, and he turned to find the Marquess of Wolverton poised in the doorway, slate-blue eyes scanning the room as if doubting the footman's announcement. Robin had to suppress an involuntary shiver at the sight of his brother; Giles' stern, handsome face was all too reminiscent of the late marquess. The resemblance had always been there, but it had strengthened with years and responsibility. His whole demeanor was that of a man of solid power and authority.

Robin had braced himself for this encounter by remembering that it was Giles who had taught him to ride and shoot, who had tried—with little success—to keep peace between formidable father and recalcitrant younger brother. But that had been a lifetime ago; now there was every likelihood that the marquess would regard his younger brother with anger or cool contempt. While Giles had an easier disposition than their father, his brief letters over the years had made it clear that he believed Robin belonged in England, behaving as an English gentleman ought, rather than skulking about Europe on dubious business.

Their eyes met and held for a long moment, wary azure to controlled slate. Using his lightest tone, Robin said, "The prodigal returns."

At his words, the marquess's face lit with laughter and he swiftly crossed the drawing room, his hand extended. "The wars have been over for months," Giles said, his voice rough with emotion. "What the devil took you so long?"

With relief so powerful that it was an ache, Robin clasped his brother's hand in both of his and shook it fiercely, knowing that this at least was all right, that Giles was as glad to see him as he was to be here. "The fighting might have ended at Waterloo, but my special brand of deviousness was useful during the treaty negotiations."

"No doubt," Giles said with a hint of dryness. "But what will you do now that peace has broken out?"

"I'm damned if I know," Robin replied wryly. "That's why I've turned up on your doorstep, like a bad penny."

Giles laughed again and clapped the younger man on his shoulder, the sternness so reminiscent of their father entirely gone. Once more he was the tolerant big brother, and Robin was passionately grateful for that fact.

Lord Robert Andreville, rebellious younger son, master spy, black sheep, and survivor, tried to keep his tone light, but he found that his voice broke when he said, "It's good to be home."

With so many blank years to fill in, the brothers talked all afternoon, through dinner, and into the night. As the hour approached midnight, snow fell in silent drifts outside and the level of the brandy decanter slowly declined. As the conversation lulled, Giles watched his brother with a slight frown, misliking the younger man's fine-drawn air. The signs were subtle, but he suspected that Robin was on the edge of mental and physical collapse. Hardly surprising, considering the vital and dangerous work he had been doing for so many years. It was a miracle that he had physically survived; uneasily, Giles was aware that the question of mental survival might still be in doubt.

Hesitantly the marquess asked, "I realize that this is premature, but do you have any plans for the future?"

"Trying to get rid of me so soon?"

"Not at all. But I think you will find Yorkshire rather tame after all of your adventures."

Robin sighed and tilted his gilt head back in the corner of the wing chair. In the flickering light he seemed fragile, not quite of the mundane world. "I found adventures to be a deucedly tiring business. Not to mention dangerous and uncomfortable."

"Are you sorry for what you have done?"

"No, it was needful." Robin paused for a sip of his brandy. "But I don't want to spend the second half of my life the same way I spent the first half."

"You are in a position to do anything you wish—scholar, sportman, politician, man-about-town," the marquess said, disturbed by the bleakness in his brother's voice. "That's more freedom than most people will ever know."

"Yes," Robin agreed softly. "The problem is not freedom, but desire."

After an uneasy silence, Giles said, "Since you were occupied on the Continent and communications were chancy, I didn't notify you at the time, but Father left you Ruxton."

"What!" Robin was so startled that his injured left hand jerked, splashing his brandy. "I assumed I would be lucky to get a shilling for candles, particularly since Uncle Rawson had made me his heir." He shook his head in amazement. "If I recall correctly, Ruxton was the best of the Andreville estates after Wolverhampton. Why on earth would he leave it to me?"

"He admired you because he could never force you to do anything you didn't want to do."

"That was admiration?" Robin asked, incredulous. "He had a damnably strange way of showing it. We couldn't spend ten minutes in the same room without quarreling, and it wasn't all my fault."

"Nonetheless, it was you Father boasted about to his cronies." Giles gave his dry, characteristic half-smile. "He used to say that the blood had run thin in me, and that it was a pity his heir was such a very dull dog."

Robin's face tightened. "I'll never understand how you could be so patient with the old curmudgeon."

"I was patient because the only other choice would have been to leave Wolverhampton, and that I would never do, no matter what the provocation."

Robin swore softly and rose from his chair, crossing to the

fireplace to poke at glowing coals, which didn't need attention. After coming down from Oxford at the age of twenty-one, Giles had taken over most of the hard work of running the huge Andreville estates. He had always been the reliable one, quietly doing the difficult tasks with no reward or recognition. "Entirely typical of Father to be so insulting when you were making his life so much easier."

"It wasn't really an insult," Giles said matter-of-factly. "I *am* a dull person. I find crops more intriguing than gaming, the country more satisfying than London, books more amusing than gossip. Father may have gotten some satisfaction from knowing that his heir was reliable, but that didn't mean that he liked me as a person."

Robin searched Giles' face, wondering if his brother was genuinely detached about such painful insights. "People are interesting because of what they are, not what they do. Only a fool would find you boring."

Giles shrugged as if the comment must be brotherly politeness, then changed the subject. "I imagine you'll want to visit Ruxton. I've been keeping an eye on the estate, and it's doing well."

"Thank you for looking after it for me." Robin watched a log break apart and send sparks dancing up the chimney. "Between Ruxton and Uncle Rawson's fortune, I'll have more money than I know what to do with."

"Get married. Wives are excellent at disposing of excess income." There was a distinct note of bitterness in Giles' voice. He halted, then continued more smoothly, "Besides, Wolverton needs an heir."

"Oh, no," Robin said with a faint gleam of amusement in his eyes. "Producing an heir is your job, not mine."

"I tried marriage once, and failed. Now it's your turn. Perhaps you'll be more successful."

The flat comment made Robin wonder what the late marchioness had been like, but the expression on his brother's face did not invite questions. Robin sighed, stabbing the poker into the fire again. "I'd like to oblige, but I've only ever met one woman I thought I could live with, and she had more sense than to accept me."

"You refer to the new Duchess of Candover?"

Robin lifted his blond head to give his brother a hard stare. "Apparently I am not the only one in the family with a talent for spying."

"Hardly spying." The marquess made an impatient gesture. "Candover is an old friend of mine, and when he returned to England, he knew I would be interested in news of your welfare. It took no great powers of deduction to realize that there must be more to the tale than what he told me." His voice softened. "I met the new duchess. A most extraordinary woman."

"She is indeed," Robin agreed in an unforthcoming tone. Then he sighed and ran his hand through his fair hair. This was his brother, not a gossipy stranger—no need to poker up. "If you've met Maggie, surely you understand why the idea of marrying a bland English virgin is so unappealing."

After a pause, Giles agreed. "I take your point. There can't be another like her." He smiled faintly. "Well, if neither of us is willing to do our duty by the family, there's always cousin Gerald. He has already sired a whole string of little Andrevilles. In the meantime, do you intend to stay at Wolverhampton long?"

"Well," Robin said tentatively, fearing that speaking the words aloud might invite a rebuff, "I had thought through Christmas, or perhaps longer. If you don't mind."

"I should like that very much." Giles' voice was warm. "This is your home, and you can live the rest of your life here if you choose."

Robin shut his eyes for a moment, not wanting to show just how moved he was by his brother's welcome. Then he returned to his wing chair and settled in again, the peace of Wolverhampton beginning to dissolve tensions so old that he had thought they were part of him. Giles was right that Robin was unlikely to spend the rest of his days rusticating in Yorkshire; Lord only knew what he *would* want to do. But for the time being, it was indescribably good to be home.

1

The moors of Durham were very different from the forests and farms of America, but they had their own kind of peace. Since her father had died two months before, Maxima Collins had walked the hills every day, absorbing the wind and sun and rain with mindless gratitude. She would miss these barren hills more than anything else she had found on this side of the Atlantic.

After two hours of walking, Maxie settled cross-legged on a hillside, absently nibbling a tender stem of wild grass as she absorbed the bright spring sunshine. It was time she returned to America. Her uncle, Lord Collingwood, was kind in a distant way and had even talked of presenting her in London, but the rest of the household regarded the American guest with feelings that ranged from dubious to downright hostile. Maxie could understand their position—she was an oddity who never should have set foot in an English country house—and she suspected that the English fashionable world would be equally unwelcoming. No matter, she had no desire to find out.

In her own country, there was more room to be different. The major deterrent to the practical plan of returning was that she had less than five pounds to her name, but surely Lord Collingwood would lend her the fare to America, plus a little extra to support her until she was established.

His lordship would probably balk a bit at first, worrying whether he was doing his duty to his late brother's only child. Proper English girls would not want to go off on their own; the correct behavior was to live on someone else's charity, and Maxie had no doubt that Lord Collingwood's sense of duty would allow her to live at Chanleigh indefinitely if she so chose.

However, Maxie was neither proper nor English, as had been made clear in a hundred subtle and not-so-subtle ways in the three months since she and her father had arrived on these inhospitable shores, and she did not chose to become one of her uncle's dependents. Even if his lordship proved recalcitrant, he couldn't prevent her from leaving; Maxie had just turned twenty-five and had been taking care of herself and her father for years. It would take her longer to return to Boston if she had to work in England for the passage money, but sooner or later she' would return to her native land.

Her decision crystallized, Maxie rose to her feet with an unladylike athleticism, brushing crushed grass from the skirt of her black dress. The mourning gown was a concession to the sensibilities of her English kinfolk; she herself would have preferred trousers and no outward display of her loss. Well, it would not be for much longer.

Half an hour of brisk walking by a direct route brought her back to the manor house. Unluckily, as she cut through the gardens, she came upon her two female cousins languidly engaged at the archery butts. Portia had just managed to miss the target entirely from a distance of no more than a dozen paces, and there was a note of malice in her voice when she glanced up and saw Maxie. "Maxima, how fortunate that you have come by. Perhaps you can show how to improve our skills. Or is archery one of those fashionable occupations that you have been deprived of?"

Portia was eighteen, pretty, and petulant. Even at the beginning she had not been friendly to Maxie, but after Maximus Collins' death caused Portia's London debut to be postponed, her attitude had become positively hostile, as if Maxie herself was personally responsible for the disappointment.

Maxie hesitated, then reluctantly joined her cousins on the archery range, unwilling to feed Portia's prejudices by being openly rude. "I have done some archery. As in most things, it is practice that refines one's skill."

Portia's lips thinned as she managed to find insult in the remark. "Then perhaps you should practice your hairdressing skills," she said with a significant glance.

The skill that Maxie had been practicing lately was ignoring gibes. "You're right," she said mildly, "my appearance is quite disgraceful. I had hoped to slip into the house unobserved." Even at the best of times her hair was too long, straight, and black for fashion, and at the moment she was windblown and disheveled from her walk. Portia and Rosalind, by contrast, were as bandbox neat as when they received callers in their mother's parlor. They also towered over the smaller American, but then, almost everyone did.

Sixteen-year-old Rosalind had the grace to look uncomfortable at Portia's bad behavior. She was a quiet girl, but had shown signs of amiability when her older sister was not present to frown her down for being civil to the unwelcome cousin. "Would you like to use my bow?" she offered in an attempt to warm up the atmosphere.

Maxie accepted the bow and expertly drew it several times, testing the degree of flex. She had not done any archery in some time, but her muscles remembered the old skills.

Behind her, Portia said *sotto voce*, "I should have realized that archery was a skill for savages long before it became fashionable."

For some reason, this remark penetrated Maxie's cultivated calm as nothing else had. She swung her head toward her cousin with such a flash in her brown eyes that Portia involuntarily stepped backward. Nonetheless, Maxie's voice was soft as she said, "You're quite right, it is a skill for savages. Move back out of the way."

As her cousins hastily retreated to a tree well away from the range, Maxie scooped up a handful of arrows and stepped back until she was four times as far from the target. She shoved all but one of the arrows point-first into the earth near her right hand, then nocked the first shaft. Drawing the bow, she focused her mind not merely on the act of aiming but also on sensing what it was to be an arrow seeking a target.

Then she released the shaft to flash the length of the range before burying itself in the exact center of the circle. With a blindingly quick economy of movement, she pulled the next of the arrows that was ready to hand and sent it on its way. In less than a minute, five quivering shafts were clustered in the bull's-eye so closely that several touched. Nocking the final arrow, she turned in the direction of her cousins, who watched in paralyzed horror as Maxie let fly.

The arrow neatly clipped the lime tree that the sisters stood under, and Portia yelped as a severed branchlet fell into her hair, rendering it much less neat than it had been. Stalking back to her cousins, Maxie returned the bow to Rosalind. Still speaking softly, she said to Portia, "And since I am a savage, as you are so fond of pointing out, I have a talent for mayhem and violence. You would do well to remember that."

Then Maxie turned on her heel and continued her interrupted path to the house, head high and pulse pounding. It had been foolish to lose her temper with Portia, but there had been an undeniable satisfaction in it. Fortunate that she would be leaving Chanleigh soon, or she might well become the savage they thought her.

Inside the house she paused at the end of the hall that passed Lord Collingwood's study, wondering whether she should visit him now or make herself presentable first. He might be more willing to see the back of her in her current state of dishevelment. The decision was taken out of her hands when one of the footmen entered the far end of the passage, escorting a burly man with a battered face to the door of the master's study. Maxie was in shadow and neither of the men saw her, so she slipped away to her own bedchamber.

Having an indecently comfortable room all to herself was the single best aspect of life at Chanleigh, though Maxie would also miss the luxurious hot baths and the library, which contained over a thousand volumes, most of them sadly unread. But she would miss little else, most especially not her cousin Portia.

An hour later Maxie sat on her window seat, her dress brushed and her hair arranged in a demure chignon. Less demurely, her knees were pulled up and her arms looped around them as she gazed out. Then her attention was caught by a figure emerging from the side door of Chanleigh. It was the same rather danger-ous-looking man who had come to see Uncle Cletus earlier, and as the visitor mounted a dusty horse, she wondered idly what business brought such an improbable person to the wilds of Durham. She shrugged; her uncle had a wide variety of business interests. What mattered was that Lord Collingwood should now be free to talk to her.

Maxie stood and reflexively checked her appearance in the mirror. Hard to say why she bothered; mourning blacks did not become her. While she was much neater than when she had returned from her walk, her appearance was still hopelessly un-English. Her expression, however, had returned to its normal determination after two months of drifting. Fervently she hoped that her uncle would grant her request for a loan. Squaring her shoulders, Maxie left her bedchamber and headed downstairs.

Just outside her uncle's study, Maxie heard her Aunt Althea speaking within. She halted and considered, then decided that pleading her case in front of Lady Collingwood would be an advantage. While her ladyship had always been civil to her husband's niece, there had never been any genuine warmth or welcome. Surely she would endorse Maxie's request as a way to be rid of an unwelcome guest.

Maxie's hand was poised to knock on the paneled door when Lady Collingwood's sharp voice said, "Was that horrid man worth what you paid him?"

"Don't begrudge the money—it isn't easy to find anyone who will undertake that sort of unpleasantness. Though Simmons may be unprepossessing, he's most efficient at what he does, and he did take care of the business about Max very well." Uncle Cletus' deep voice was harder to understand than his wife's, but after missing a few words Maxie caught the phrase, ". . . Can't let it become public knowledge how Maximus died."

Maxie froze. Her father had had a previous chest spasm before dying suddenly on his trip to London. His body had been brought back to Durham and he had been buried in the family plot with all due respect. Maxie had been concerned about his health for some time; though she was grief-stricken, she had had no reason to believe his death was unnatural—until now. After glancing around to ensure that she was unobserved, shamelessly she pressed her ear to the oak door.

Her aunt was saying, "What if Maxima does find out how her father really died?"

"There would be trouble if she learned the truth" he acknowledged in a heavy voice, "but with luck she never will."

"When she learns about the inheritance, she will probably put two and two together. The little heathen isn't stupid," Lady Collingwood said waspishly. "Then the fat will be in the fire."

"Control your tongue, madam, she is my brother's child. And remember that the inheritance is by no means assured." Then, dryly, "Would you be so hostile if your own daughters were as pretty as she is?"

"The idea!" Althea sputtered. "As if I would want my girls to look like Maxima. They are well-bred young English ladies, not dusky little savages."

"Well-bred they may be, but no one will notice them if their cousin is in the same room."

"Of course men notice her, just as stallions notice a mare in heat. No real lady wants to draw that kind of attention," her ladyship said, adding viciously, "I'll never understand how your brother could bring himself to marry a Red Indian. That is, if he did marry the creature. And the effrontery of him, bringing his half-breed daughter here."

"I'll have no more of that, Althea," Cletus snapped, his raised voice clearly audible through the door. "Max might have been a wastrel, but he was a Collins and Maxima is his daughter. I have seen no deficiencies in either her manners or her understanding. Indeed, she has been far more of a lady to you than you and your daughters have been to her."

"How dare you speak so to me!" Lady Collingwood said furiously. "Why, not an hour since, she threatened Portia with a bow and arrow. I live in dread that she will run mad and murder us in our beds. It is time and past time she left. And if you won't get rid of her, I will."

Lord Collingwood replied with equal anger, but his voice was blurred, as if he was moving away from the door, and his wife's next words were unintelligible. Even if their speech had still been audible, Maxie had heard more than enough. Stunned and shaking, she turned and retraced the route to her room, forcing herself to walk slowly. Locking the door of her bedchamber, she curled up in a tight, shuddering ball on the brocade sofa while she tried to make sense of what her aunt and uncle had said.

First and foremost was the clear implication that her father had not died naturally. Could he have been killed in an accident, or perhaps murdered by footpads? But if that was the case, there would be no reason to keep the facts secret. Instead, he had

died in a way that her aunt and uncle wanted to conceal. Try
as she would, the only interpretation Maxie could find was that
someone had killed her father deliberately. But why would
anyone want to murder her charming, feckless father?

She tried to analyze the question as a simple problem in logic.
Money and passion were the probable reasons for murder; since
Maximus Collins had scarcely had a penny to bless himself with,
no one should have murdered him for gain, but lethal jealousy
seemed even more unlikely. Her father had not been of a
womanizing disposition, and he had been so long out of England
that it was unlikely ancient feuds were still smoldering.

Lady Collingwood had mentioned an inheritance. Maximus
had been disinherited by his own father, but perhaps he was
heir to some distant relative, and he had been killed to prevent
his claiming his legacy. If so, was Maxie in danger since she
was her father's heir? She shook her head in disbelief; such
things belonged only in melodramatic novels, not real life.

There was another possibility, tawdry but more believable.
Maxie cast her mind back to the last time she had seen her father,
just before he left for London. Maximus had been a trifle flown
and had told her with his incurable optimism that their financial
problems would soon be at an end and she could be a lady and
have the life and grand husband she deserved. It was not the
first time he had made such statements in his cups, and Maxie
had laughed indulgently before kissing him good-bye.

Could he have made money from some mad scheme, then
been murdered for it? Maxie found that her fists were so tightly
clenched that the nails bit into her palms. She had loved her
father dearly, but was well aware of his failings; it was not
inconceivable that he had attempted some genteel extortion.
Perhaps he had discreditable information about some long-ago
schoolmate and had threatened to reveal it. If so, his intended
victim might have decided that it was easier to eliminate a black-
mailer than to pay. After all, who would miss an impecunious
reprobate? Except, of course, his daughter.

It was all horribly farfetched, but then, so was murder. If
her father had resorted to blackmail, could it have been been
aimed at his own brother? Certainly family secrets would be
the most easily come by. If Max had done such a thing, could

Lord Collingwood have had him killed? Perhaps that villainous-looking man from London was a hired assassin.

Maxie closed her eyes tightly as she wondered if she were going mad. She had always had a vivid imagination—lurid, according to her father—and since she lacked the data for informed conclusions, that imagination was running riot. Perhaps there was a simple, noncriminal explanation of what she had overheard. If so, she could not guess what it was. She could ask her uncle what he had meant, but that did not seem a prudent course, not when she was under his roof and entirely at his mercy. Difficult though it was to think of Uncle Cletus as a danger to her, under the circumstances it would be madness to risk finding out. And even if he was not dangerous, it was unlikely that he would tell her a truth that he was going to so much trouble to conceal.

For all his faults, Maximus Collins had loved his daughter as much as she had loved him. Now he was dead and she was alone in an alien land. Maxie had known that Lady Collingwood did not like her, but even so she was appalled by the depths of antipathy revealed in that overheard conversation: "heathen . . . dusky little savage . . . half-breed."

At least Uncle Cletus had defended her right to exist, but he had also wanted to conceal the facts of her father's death, whatever they might be. Therefore, she could no more trust him than her aunt. She bit her lip as her mind moved inexorably on through grief and confusion. Only two things seemed sure: her father had not died naturally, and she herself was *persona non grata* in her ancestral home.

The two facts clicked together into a decision. Maxie had intended to leave Chanleigh, and now she would do so as quickly and secretly as possible. But she would not return tamely to Boston—not, at least, until she had gone to London and discovered the truth about how her father had died. She had the address of the hotel where he had been staying as well as names of several old friends he had intended to call on.

The only question was how to get to London. Maxie swung her feet to the ground, the need to plan clearing her tumultuous emotions. While she had a few pounds, it was not enough for a coach ticket, so she would just have to walk. The distance must be about 250 miles, but that was no great challenge to someone who had spent half her life traveling the back roads of New England.

This time, however, Maxie wouldn't have her father's protection, and she was in a strange country. While traveling as a lone female would be foolish, the solution was easy. She had never deliberately masqueraded as a male, but the rough roads of America had made it advisable to dress as one much of the time and she had brought her masculine attire to England. With her breasts bound, her hair under a hat, and a loose shirt and coat, she would appear to be a nondescript young boy. And if someone wanted to investigate too closely, she had her knife.

It took only a few minutes to sort through her wardrobe. Besides her male clothing, she would need one respectable female outfit for London. Her mother's silver cross was always around her neck and she tucked her father's gold watch and her harmonica inside her coat. She needed nothing else. Certainly she wouldn't mind abandoning the two black dresses her aunt had insisted on providing after Max's death.

Maxie had accumulated very little in the way of possessions in a quarter of a century of living, and she spent a moment considering whether that was good or bad. Then she shrugged and concentrated on packing a small soft bag that could be slung across her back as a knapsack. Since she had no choice, she might as well consider traveling light to be a virtue.

Maxie would leave this very night, after the household had gone to sleep; the sooner she was away from Chanleigh, the better. Indeed, she could not even face her aunt and uncle at dinner, so she sent down a message that she had the headache and requested a meal in her room.

The hardest task proved to be writing a note. Having been a guest in the Collingwood home for months, it would be very shabby to disappear without a word. Odd how manners remained even when she was deeply suspicious of her aunt and uncle.

Maxie gnawed on the quill pen for quite some time before inspiration struck and she wrote that she was going to visit her Aunt Desdemona. Desdemona Ross was the much-younger sister of Cletus and Maximus, and a widowed bluestocking of ferocious and unbridled opinions. Since she was cordially loathed by Lady Collingwood, she did not often visit the family home in Durham. Maxie had never met Lady Ross, but they had corresponded, so it was simple to say that Desdemona had invited her niece for a visit to London.

It was a perfect solution, and Maxie bent to the notepaper with satisfaction. While it would be considered rude and eccentric to leave at night with no warning, no one would be so surprised or offended as to pursue her, and that was what counted. She doubted anyone would even bother to wonder where she had gotten the money for coach fare.

In fact, it was such a good idea that she decided to actually visit Aunt Desdemona, whose letters had always been amiable and witty. With sudden longing, Maxie thought that it would be pleasant to discover some member of her father's family for whom she might feel kinship.

Leaving Chanleigh proved to be as easy as Maxie had hoped, and she was delighted to don her boy's clothes again after too many months in skirts. Among her mother's people, women wore leggings, and Maxie was more comfortable in them than in the constricting white man's dresses. The farewell note was left in her room; with luck it would not be found until well into the next day.

She made a stop in the kitchen for cheese and bread and a slab of ham, which would spare her limited funds at least until Yorkshire. After some hesitation Maxie also took a map of the road to London. Since her uncle had a newer map, she assuaged her guilt over the theft with the reflection that he wouldn't need this one.

Maxie let herself out a French door. Here in the country, leaving it unlatched was unlikely to endanger the household. It seemed a good omen that the skies had cleared after an evening of intermittent rain. The night air was still damply chill, but she drew it into her lungs eagerly, already feeling happier and freer. She was used to the life of the road and would feel far more at home on this journey than she had at Chanleigh.

Her practiced stride took her swiftly down the drive, but she stopped for a last glance at the manor house, dark under a waxing quarter-moon. Maximus had been glad to return to his family home, and doubtless wherever his spirit was now, he was pleased to know that his bones rested here. But while Chanleigh had been her father's home, it was not Maxie's, and it was unlikely she would ever return. She had been the merest discordant ripple on the surface of a deep pool of Englishness, and like a ripple she would soon be forgotten. Turning, she began her journey with no more backward glances or thoughts.

Maxie covered six or seven miles before the moon set. She could have continued in the dark, but it would be wiser to set an easy pace at first. London was about two weeks away, and in spite of her impatience to investigate her father's death, a day or two would not make a difference.

Shortly after Maxie decided to seek shelter, the silhouette of a small building appeared against the starlight, and she picked her way across a soggy field to a storage shed. Scent and touch identified remnants of the previous year's hay inside, and she made a nest for herself, her pack serving as a pillow and her cloak as a blanket. The hay was soft and fragrant and she settled in with reasonable comfort. This was not the first night she had spent in a barn, and it was unlikely to be the last. It was, however, the first time Maxie had been entirely alone; in the past her father had always lain an arm's length away.

The thought produced an ache deep inside her, a pain that was both grief for her father and sorrow for her own total aloneness. Her fingers curled around her mother's silver cross, and there was comfort in the touch. Maxie was a Mohawk, an American, and a Collins, and she would not feel sorry for herself. But as she drifted into sleep, her last conscious thought was to wonder bleakly if, now that her father was dead, she would always be alone.

Lady Collingwood's private parlor was full of choice little *objets d'art*, but having come nearly three hundred miles, Desdemona Ross wasted no time in admiration. "What do you mean, Maxima has gone to London to visit me?" she inquired, her thick auburn brows rising. "I am not in London, I am here in Durham. Against my better judgment, I might add."

Lady Collingwood gave her sister-in-law a frosty glance, then reached into her escritoire. "If you don't believe me, read her note for yourself." She handed over a folded sheet of paper. "The ungrateful chit decamped in the middle of the night three days ago."

"Maxima says I had invited her for an extended visit, which simply isn't true." Desdemona frowned as she read. "I came north to meet her, with the idea that she could return with me if we got on well, but I had not suggested that in writing."

"It did seem odd, but Maxima is a most unaccountable creature, not at all civilized or gently bred." Lady Collingwood gave a bored shrug while she evaluated her sister-in-law's clothing. Really, Desdemona had a talent for dowdiness that amounted to genius; doubtless looking attractive went against her bluestocking principles. Then again, perhaps Lady Ross was wise to go about swaddled in dark concealing bonnets and cloaks; her red hair was hopelessly ungenteel. And her figure . . . there was no way that figure would ever be fashionable either.

Lady Collingwood yawned delicately behind one languid hand. "Bolting off at midnight to catch a coach at a crossroads is exactly the sort of thing one would expect of the girl. For that matter, so is lying. Really, Desdemona, you are fortunate to have missed her. It still amazes me that Maximus dared bring her to Chanleigh. She belongs back in the forest with her Red Indian relations."

"As opposed to staying with her savage English relations?" Desdemona paused, then added with lethal sweetness, "Her mother may have been a Red Indian, but at least her family wasn't in trade, like some I could mention."

Althea Collins had spent years attempting to forget where her father had made his money, and she flushed furiously at the gibe, but her retort was forestalled by the entrance of her husband.

"Dizzy," Lord Collingwood said, his long face lighting up with pleased surprise. "You should have written that you were coming. It's been too long since you visited."

In spite of the twenty years' difference in age and no physical resemblance whatsoever, Desdemona and her brother were fond of each other, and she rose to give him a quick hug, feeling him flinch at the demonstrativeness. She had known he would flinch, just as he had known that she would hug him anyway. It was long-established family tradition. "Apparently I should have arrived three days ago, Clete."

His lordship flinched again; he didn't like the nickname any more than Desdemona liked her own childhood nickname of Dizzy. Formalities completed, she favored her brother with a scowl. "I came to see how my niece was faring, only to be told that she has run off with some whisker about visiting me."

Collingwood frowned as he realized the implications of his sister's presence in Durham. "Why aren't you in London waiting for Maxima?"

"Because I didn't invite her," Desdemona snapped. "Apparently the poor girl was so miserable here that she ran away in the hopes that I would treat her better. What kind of care have you been giving your brother's only child?"

"Maxima is not a child; she's a woman grown, only a few years younger than you," her brother said defensively. "And she did not consult my wishes before vanishing."

"I'm surprised she even had money for the coach fare," Desdemona continued. "I thought that Max was virtually penniless when he died."

There was a sudden silence while Lord and Lady Collingwood exchanged glances. "You're right, she didn't have much money," her ladyship said, a crack showing in the languorous facade. "I had to pay for her mourning clothes when Maximus died. We have been looking out for her, though she showed precious little gratitude."

"If she was expected to be grateful, no wonder she left." Desdemona swung around to face her brother again. "She may be a woman grown, but she is a stranger to England, and anything could happen to her, particularly if she is walking to London."

"Good God, she would never attempt such a thing," Lord Collingwood said. Then he halted, his face reflecting uneasiness. "This morning I noticed that an older map of the London road was not in my desk, but I thought someone must have borrowed it."

"Apparently that is exactly what happened. Since she and Max spent much of the year roaming the wilds of New England, a journey to London must have seemed quite tame." Desdemona had been attempting to hold her temper in, but now she exploded. "You should be ashamed of yourselves! Surely Max had a right to believe that his daughter would be properly cared for at Chanleigh. Instead, you drove her away."

Collingwood flushed. "I thought Maxima was happy here. I like the girl, and she is welcome to stay as long as she wishes."

"Did you ever tell her that?" Desdemona demanded.

Her brother shifted uneasily. "I suggested presenting her in London with Portia, but never pressed the issue. It didn't seem appropriate to decide her future until she had recovered more from the loss of her father."

Desdemona fixed her sister-in-law with a gimlet eye. "And did you make her welcome too, Althea? No snide little comments about her background? Did you order a proper wardrobe for her, introduce her to the young men of the neighborhood?"

"If you were so concerned about the little savage, why didn't you do something yourself?" Lady Collingwood said with the anger of the guilty. "You could have visited anytime these last four months, but all you did was write an occasional letter."

"We've been working for an act of Parliament that would protect apprentices, and since we were finally making progress, I was unable to leave London." Desdemona's expression was troubled. "You are right, I should have done more. But I thought she would be safe here until I had time to come north."

"There's no point in recriminations," Collingwood said, hoping to head off a major altercation. "The important thing is to get Maxima back here safely." After a moment's thought, his face brightened. "I know just the man to send after her, and he's in Newcastle now. With luck, she'll be home in no time."

"Send for your man if you wish, but I'm going after her myself," Desdemona said, her teeth gritted. "Someone in the family should care enough to try. What does she look like?"

Lord Collingwood started to say that his sister was being absurd, that such matters should be left to those with experience, but a glance at Desdemona's set face made him decide that it was easier to let her go. After all, his sister was an independent and worldly widow, attended by her servants—what kind of trouble could she get into?

2

The two men shared breakfast in peaceable silence, broken by the occasional flutter of paper as one of them turned a page. The news, however, was uninspiring as well as several days old, and eventually the Marquess of Wolverton laid his *Times* aside. "Do you have any plans for the day, Robin?"

"I thought I might take a stroll through the west woods," his brother replied, glancing over his *Gazette*. "That's the only part of the estate I haven't reacquainted myself with."

Giles shook his head. "I still can't believe what a tame life you're living. I keep expecting you to vanish."

Robin smiled. "It could happen. But don't worry if I go missing. It would just mean that I found something interesting like a tribe of gypsies in the west woods and couldn't resist going off with them. I'd return eventually."

Giles nodded without comment. He would be delighted if Robin did find something interesting enough to lure him to unpredictability. Certainly his younger brother looked far better than he had the previous December. He was the perfect guest, amiable, charming, and good-natured, ready to talk, be silent, or participate in the neighborhood social rounds. He could even laugh and make jokes.

Nonetheless, Giles still felt that something was gravely wrong. Robin's most vivid characteristic had always been a joyous zest for life, an enthusiastic desire for new experiences. Even in leading strings he had been like that, and his vitality had been undiminished through youth and the dangerous years gathering information on the Continent. Or at least, four years earlier, when Giles had last met his brother on a fleeting trip to Whitehall, there had still been that joy. Now it was gone.

The marquess wondered sometimes if the blame should be laid on the woman who was now the Duchess of Candover, or if the reasons were deeper and less easily defined. Whatever the cause, he felt that something in his brother had been broken, perhaps past mending, and he grieved for that, for his own sake as well as for Robin's.

Giles suppressed a sigh, wishing there was something he could do. They had been on easy terms over the winter, but friendship, even blood kinship, had its limits. Rising, he said, "I have a magistrate's session that will occupy me all day. I'll see you at dinner, unless you've gone with the raggle-taggle gypsies, ho."

Robin smiled a response before making his way to the kitchen to request food for his expedition. Then he headed across the hills to the west woods. The woods were really a forest and had been a royal hunting preserve in earlier times. Too dense for easy riding, the area was best explored on foot, and walking suited his mood.

Though the marquess had done a noble job of not plaguing his guest, Robin knew that Giles was concerned about his younger brother's state of mind, and with justice; Robin was concerned himself. He had hoped that the peace and familiarity of Wolverhampton would heal whatever ailed him, and up to a point it had. There was nowhere he would rather be, and that in itself hinted at what was wrong: in the past, Robin's usual problem had been deciding what interesting activity should be attempted next.

Now, for whatever reason, he was submerged in a gray melancholy unlike anything he had ever experienced, a weariness of the soul rather than the body. Worse, in the last month or two he had begun to experience undercurrents of restlessness. With a flash of the dark humor that came easily these days, Robin thought that it was unfair to be both restless and too lethargic to do anything about it. Apart from a duty visit to Ruxton, Robin had done little for six months but ride, tramp the countryside, and catch up with his reading and correspondence, yet nothing else really interested him.

Avoiding the lures of various wellborn maidens of the district could also be considered an occupation, he supposed. The two eligible Andrevilles had been much in demand at winter social gatherings. While Giles had the title and the superior fortune, he was generally considered unlikely to remarry, so more feminine wiles had been exercised on Lord Robert, with his blond good looks, dashingly mysterious past, and more than adequate assets. That the younger brother might well inherit the title added to his allure.

Robin sighed and hitched his bag of provisions over his right shoulder. It was all exactly as he had told Giles last December: he would not have objected to falling madly in love, but it was impossible to imagine marrying one of the vapid innocents he had met in the great houses of Yorkshire. It wasn't just that they had been raised to have a narrow view of the world; far worse was that none of the eligible females he had met had had an unconventional bone in her pampered body. He had not known Maggie when she was a proper young lady, but even at seventeen she would not have been so bland.

The day was warm, and after an hour of steady walking it was pleasant to reach the shady forest. Robin had worn his oldest and most nondescript clothing, so he was unconcerned about the snagging undergrowth as he explored the winding paths made by deer and other wildlife. The sun was high when he reached a little clearing by one of the streams that ran through the forest. As a child, he had come here to daydream about the world beyond Wolverhampton, and he was pleased to find the spot again.

He stretched out on the grass in the shade of a bush, crossing his arms beneath his head as he gazed absently at the tree above and considered his future. Gracious a host though Giles was, Robin could hardly stay the rest of his life at Wolverhampton. Perhaps he should go on a journey; he knew Europe like a mother knows her child's face, but he had never seen the Orient or the New World. Or perhaps he should try political journalism; he had no shortage of opinions on public affairs, and journalists were a rowdy and irreverent lot. He should fit in well, if he recovered his rowdiness and irreverence.

His thoughts circled in the same vague paths as they had for months, striking no sparks of enthusiasm. Since the sun was warm and the grass scents sweet, it was easier to slide into sleep.

Maxie scowled at the road, really no more than a track, that ran through the thick woods. She had been avoiding the highways in favor of smaller, quieter roads where a lone boy would attract little attention. Unfortunately, she suspected that the farmer who had given her a ride on his wagon this morning had also given her poor directions. Supposedly this track would connect with a southbound toll road, but it looked more like a private estate road.

It didn't help that she had run out of food the day before, and her stomach was feeling ill-used. Well, there had been no signs of habitation for quite some time, so she had best carry on. Eventually this track should lead to a village or farmstead where she could buy food. In America she could have lived off the land indefinitely with no more than a knife, but England's ferocious game and property laws made her wary of doing the same here. Though if she got hungry enough, that would change.

The sound of hoofbeats and wagon wheels made Maxie stop and cock her head. A heavy vehicle was coming along the track behind her, and on the whole she would rather not meet anyone in such a remote spot. Scrambling up the bank into the underbrush, she went deeper into the forest, swinging away from the track.

In the distance she heard the jangle of harness and the steady thud of hooves as a dray rumbled by. No danger appeared, so Maxie relaxed, turning her attention to an unfamiliar birdsong as she made her way quietly through the shrubbery on a course parallel to the track. One of the pleasures of England was discovering new creatures and plants.

In three days of travel she had experienced no difficulties at all; indeed, except for rides with two taciturn farmers, she had not so much as spoken with another person.

Lulled by the tameness of the country, she exercised a lamentable lack of caution, but even Old World forests can have unexpected hazards. A small clearing lay behind the bush she was skirting, and she paid no attention to her feet as her gaze searched the treetops in an attempt to locate the unknown songbird. Maxie's carelessness caught up with her when she tripped. Off-balance, she was unable to recover her footing and fell heavily. What she descended on, however, was not the cool forest floor.

Gasping for breath, she found herself sprawling across the warm body of a man who had been sleeping in a sunny spot between bush and tree. They were virtually nose to nose when he opened his eyes. Mere inches away, Maxie saw that those eyes were vividly blue, with startled alertness showing in the depths. The fellow had excellent reflexes, because even as he was abruptly woken up, he had immobilized her by grasping her upper arms.

For a moment they were both locked in position, strangers as close as lovers. Then, as the man comprehended what had come crashing down on top of him, amusement replaced shock in the blue eyes. "I apologize for being so clumsy as to get in your way," he said, his mouth curving into a smile.

"Sorry," Maxie said gruffly, breaking his grip to scramble to her feet. Caution decreed vanishing into the forest, where she could travel faster than most men, but she was short of breath from the impact of her fall. Also, a clear look at the man whom she had tripped over temporarily immobilized her with aesthetic admiration. He was quite possibly the handsomest man she had ever seen, in a very blond and utterly English way. Moreover, his expression was amiable and unthreatening as he pushed upright, propping his back against the tree trunk.

"I admit that females have thrown themselves into my arms a time or two before, but not usually quite so hard," he said, a suggestion of twinkle in his eyes. "However, I'm sure we can work something out if you make a polite request."

Maxie tensed at his words. "You haven't woken up yet. My name is Jack and I am not a female, much less one interested in hurling myself into your arms." Her voice was naturally low and could easily belong to a young boy rather than a female.

The blond man raised his brows. "You can pass as a lad at a distance, but you landed with considerable force, and I was quite awake enough to know what hit me." A sapient gaze surveyed her from head to toe. "A word of advice: if you want to be convincing, find looser trousers. I've never seen a boy shaped quite like you."

Maxie colored at the remark, grateful for the hat that shadowed her face. She was turning to escape when the man raised a disarming hand. "No need to run off. I'm a harmless fellow. Remember, you assaulted me, not vice versa." Then, coaxing as if she was a fey forest creature, he went on, "It's time for a midday meal, and I have far more food than one person needs. Care to join me?"

For a moment the issue wavered in the balance. Maxie knew that she should put some distance between herself and this too-handsome fellow. But he was friendlier than most of the English she had met, and he seemed innocuous. Her decision was made when he dug into the pouch lying on the ground next to him and pulled out one of the meat-filled pastries that the natives called Cornish pasties. It must have been baked that morning, for a fresh, delectable scent wafted through the clearing.

Her stomach would never forgive her if she refused. "If you are sure you have enough, I would be pleased to join you." She lowered her knapsack to the ground, then settled on crossed legs just beyond pouncing distance, in case young Apollo proved less harmless than he appeared.

The blond man handed over the pasty, then rummaged further in his bag, producing another pasty, cold roast chicken, several bread rolls, and a small jug of ale. Uncorking the jug, he set it midway between them. "We will have to share the ale."

"I do not drink ale." She did, however, eat pasties, and it took some effort not to wolf hers down; the crumbly crust and well-flavored shreds of beef and vegetables deserved savoring.

The blond man chewed and swallowed a bite of his own pasty before saying in a reflective tone, "In most circles, it is considered rude to eat with one's hat on."

Maxie was reluctant to expose herself to the other's gaze, but could not ignore the appeal to manners; the acceptance of hospitality imposed obligations. Raising her hand, she removed the shapeless hat, keeping a wary eye on her companion.

For a moment he stared, an arrested expression in the blue eyes, but he refrained from foolish or vulgar comments. Instead, after a long moment, he swallowed and said, "Care for some chicken?"

Maxie relaxed and accepted the drumstick offered. "Yes, thank you."

"How do you come to be trespassing in the Marquess of Wolverton's forest?"

"I was walking on what appeared to be a public track. When I heard someone coming, I decided that being unobserved was the better part of wisdom. What is your excuse, poaching?"

He gave her a wounded look. "Do I look like a poacher?"

She finished the chicken leg and licked her fingers. "I admit that you don't look like a poacher, or at least, not a successful one," she said, trying not to smile at his comical expression. "On the other hand, you don't look like the Marquess of Whatever, either."

"Would you believe me if I said that I was?"

"No." She cast a disrespectful eye over his clothing, which was well-made but far past its prime.

"A young woman of excellent judgment," he said with approval. "As it happens, you are right. I am not the Marquess of Wolverton any more than you are British."

Wariness returned. "What makes you say that?" Maxie asked, thinking that her host was altogether too perceptive.

"Your accent is almost that of the English gentry," he allowed, "but accents are something of a speciality of mine." The blue eyes narrowed in thought. "I would guess that you are American, probably from New England."

"A reasonably good guess," Maxie allowed with a grudging nod and no further elaboration.

"Is your name still Jack?"

"You certainly ask a lot of questions." She made no attempt to keep the irritation from her voice.

"Asking is the easiest method I know for satisfying curiosity," he said with perfect logic, "because it often works."

"An irrefutable point." She hesitated a moment longer, but saw no reason not to tell him. "My real name is Maxima."

"You look more like a Minima to me," he said promptly, examining her scant inches.

Maxie laughed. "You're not precisely Hercules yourself."

"Yes, but I'm not named Hercules, so I'm not trying to deceive anyone."

"My father was named Maximus and I was called after him," she explained. "No one thought to wonder if I would grow up to fulfill the name. Since I didn't, my father thought a diminutive was appropriate, so I became Maxie." Her brows arched in question. "If your name isn't Hercules, what is it?"

"It isn't a lot of things." He took a swig of ale, and she could see him weighing what to say. Maxie thought cynically that the blond man was probably a wayfaring rogue who had had so many names and identities that he probably didn't remember himself what he had been christened. "I have been known by a great many names over the years," he said, confirming her guess. "Lately I've been using Lord Robert Andreville."

Startled, Maxie asked, "Are you really a nobleman?" In spite of his worn clothing, he did have an air about him. Then she frowned. "You're hoaxing me, aren't you? My father explained titles to me once. A real peer does not use Lord with his Christian name." The explanation was obvious, and she chided herself for almost believing him. "I reckon that Lord Robert is a pretend title that you invented to impress people."

"And here I thought I could hoax someone from the colonies," he said mournfully. Then he grinned. "You're quite right, I'm a commoner, not the least bit noble. My friends call me Robin."

Whatever his name, the man had a marvelously expressive face. Perhaps he was an actor rather than a swindler. Of course, he could be both, but still Maxie found herself smiling back. "In that case, you should offer something to your namesake for luck." She gestured at a small bird that had been hopping closer and closer as they ate.

"A good idea." He broke off a piece of pasty crust and tossed it to the bird, who grabbed the morsel and flew away. "One should always offer to the gods of luck."

Considering the bright-eyed English robin, she decided that her companion was aptly named. "The American robin is quite different—larger and heavier and with more orange on its breast. More like your thrush, I think."

"I expect the early colonists were homesick and put familiar names on any New World creatures that had some resemblance to what they were used to." He found more food fragments and tossed them to two more robins that had replaced the first one. Then he delved into his food pouch again. "Care for some shortbread?"

He had a marvelously engaging grin, with the charm of a man who could sell you a dozen things you didn't need. Maxie and her father had met more than one such charming wastrel on their travels, and the self-proclaimed Lord Robert was undoubtedly another of that breed. Actually, Max could have been considered one as well. Perhaps that was why his daughter had a taste for beguiling rogues.

She accepted two pieces of the butter-rich shortbread with pleasure, thinking that it was the best meal she had had in a very long time. After finishing, she went to the stream to wash her hands and drink some of the cool water.

As she returned, Robin asked, "Do you have a long journey ahead of you?"

"London. Speaking of which, it is time I was on my way again. Thank you for sharing your food." She bent over to pick up her bag and hat.

"London!" Robin was seriously surprised by the casual answer. "Do you intend to walk that whole way alone?"

"London is only about two hundred miles from here. I'll be there within a fortnight. Good day to you." She settled the hat back on her head, tugging it over her eyes.

Robin wanted to tell her not to put the hat on, not before he had memorized that lovely, exotic face. When she had first crashed down on him, her soft curves had made it clear that she was female, but he had thought her a mischievous young tomboy in a brother's clothing.

Then she had doffed her ridiculous hat and he had briefly forgotten how to speak or breathe. While the delicate features might have been English, the smooth dark complexion and subtle modeling of the bones were definitely not. Her eyes were a clear rich brown, lighter than the glossy black hair suggested, and even in her shapeless boy's clothing she was beautiful.

But Robin had met other beautiful women and not been so strongly affected. What set Maxie apart was a quality of focused directness as strong and true as a blade, a still strength that showed in every word and gesture she made. Their brief conversation had proved that she also had wit and education, and under any circumstances he would have been intrigued by her. In his present drifting state, she drew him like a magnet.

Sweeping the remnants of the meal into his bag, Robin stood also, slinging the bag over his shoulder. For the first time since Giles had welcomed his brother back to Wolverhampton, he had a passionate desire: to know this unusual female better.

As Maxie turned and entered the forest, he fell into step beside her. "The distance to London is not insurmountable," he admitted, "but the roads are not safe for a young woman alone."

"I have had no trouble so far," she replied. "No one except you has realized that I am female, and I will not be so careless as to trip over anyone else."

"A young boy could be equally in danger." Looking down at Maxie, Robin realized how small she was, scarcely over five feet tall, but so perfectly proportioned that it was hard to judge her height unless standing next to her. "In fact, some of the gentlemen of the highway would probably prefer a lad."

The brown eyes looked askance; a proper young lady would not have understood the remark, but Maxie did. Another point to her credit; perhaps she was not dangerously naïve.

"Here in the north the roads are fairly safe, but the closer you get to London, the greater the hazard," Robin continued as they emerged back on the grassy track and turned south.

"I am quite capable of defending myself." Her patience was beginning to erode and her voice was snappish.

"With that knife you carry?"

That gained him a hard, narrow-eyed stare. He explained, "You did land on me rather hard, and the haft of a knife feels quite different from a human body." Especially from a soft, rounded female body.

"Yes, I have a knife, and I know how to use it," she said with a definite note of warning.

"It won't be enough if several highwaymen attack you."

"True. However, I don't intend to get involved in any pitched battles."

"One doesn't always have a choice," he said dryly. They walked in less-than-companionable silence for some time, Maxie studiously ignoring his presence and Robin thinking hard. Even though he had only known her for an hour, he knew better than to attempt to persuade Maxie from her hazardous journey; this was not a female easily swayed from her course. Traveling alone, she might reach London without incident, but more likely she would run into trouble along the way. Even if he hadn't found her appealing, Robin would have been very reluctant to let a young woman continue alone. The conclusion was inescapable.

As the woods began to thin, he said reflectively, "There is really no help for it. As a gentleman, I shall have to escort you to London."

"What!" Maxie sputtered, coming to a stop in the middle of the track to stare at him. "Have you run mad?"

"Not in the least. You are a young woman alone in a foreign country. It would be quite dishonorable to let you continue alone." He stopped also and gave her his most trustworthy smile. "Besides, I have nothing better to do."

"And what qualifies you as a gentleman of honor?" Her face reflected both outrage and amusement at his presumption.

"Gentlemen do not work. Since I do not work, therefore I must be a gentleman," he said with the air of Socrates discoursing to his pupils.

Maxie began to laugh helplessly. "You are the most absurd creature," she gasped. "That logic wouldn't convince a babe in arms. Besides, even if you don't work, surely you can't just take to the road on impulse, and I have no intention of waiting for you to settle your affairs."

"But I can just go off on impulse," Robin replied. "In fact, I have already done so."

"If you will forgive the observation, you appear not only harmless, but downright ineffectual," she said acerbically as she resumed walking. "I am more likely to have to protect you than vice versa. I have spent much of my life on the road and know how to take care of myself. I most certainly do not want an escort, no matter how good your intentions."

Surreptitiously she surveyed her companion. Robin was no more than average height, and while that made him almost a head taller than she, his light, elegant frame did not look designed for brawling. On the plus side, he was quite glorious to look upon, as well as good company, but she did not need more complications on her journey. "For all I know, I would be in more danger from you than from hypothetical highwaymen."

An offended expression crossed his mobile face. "The lady doesn't trust me," he said sadly.

"I can't think of any good reason why I should." Maxie almost laughed again. "Are you an actor? You are constantly performing, and actors are often without work."

"I have played many roles," he admitted, "but never on a stage."

After another moment's thought, she asked, "Have you ever done anything useful, or are you purely a lily of the field?"

Robin considered her question solemnly. "That would depend on your definition of useful."

Maxie shook her head. "I see there is no getting any sense out of you." She tried another tack. "If you have enough money to buy us coach tickets to London, I might reconsider, but I can't afford to feed you and myself both."

That gave Robin pause for a moment. Then he brightened. "I am not in funds at the moment and my banker, alas, is in London." He reached under her hat and produced a shiny shilling. "However, I can conjure money from the air when necessary."

Maxie blinked. He must have gotten the shilling from his pocket, but she hadn't seen him do it. If she had not been familiar with such legerdemain, it would have been easy to believe that he had indeed conjured the coin. "Not bad," she allowed, "but sleight of hand is not in the same class as turning lead into gold."

"Sleight of hand!" He looked offended. "We are speaking of magic, not mere trickery. Give me your hand."

Amused, she stopped walking and did as he requested. He placed the shilling on her right palm and folded her fingers around it, his clasp warm and strong. "Make two fists and I will magically move the shilling to your left hand."

Obediently she did as he asked, and he made several graceful passes in the air, murmuring unintelligible words as he did. "There, the shilling has moved," he said after a final flourish.

"Sorry, I still feel it in my right hand." Maxie opened her fingers as proof, then gasped. Lying on her palm was not the single coin he had given her, but two. "How did you do that?"

"Very well." He grinned, dropping his showman's manner. "I admit that it is only sleight of hand, but I'm fairly good at such things, and I've often earned dinner and lodging for the night when my pockets were to let."

Her companion was definitely a shiftless vagrant, albeit an entertaining one. Maxie handed back his two shillings. "This has been very pleasant, but why don't you return to your nap in the forest and leave me alone?"

"The roads are public." He pocketed the coins. "Since I have just decided to go to London, you can't stop me."

Maxie opened her mouth, then closed it again. What he said was quite true. Unless her unwanted escort actually assaulted her, which didn't seem imminent, he had as much right to the road as she did. And if he chose to walk the same road at the same pace, what could she do about it? She was reminded of the dogs that sometimes followed her and her father for a few miles. Like a dog, no doubt Robin would soon get bored and leave her, since the average charming wastrel had a span of attention somewhat shorter than that of the average mongrel.

The miles and the afternoon rolled by, but he did not flag from the brisk pace she set. Occasionally Robin made an entertaining comment on the passing scene and they would converse a bit; sometimes he whistled, very skillfully. Maxie privately admitted that his presence made the miles go more quickly.

They left the forest behind them and joined a wider road with occasional traffic. It was coming on to suppertime when they entered a small village built entirely of the gray local stone. Robin gestured at a small inn called the King Richard that stood to the right of the road.

"Shall I buy you dinner? Anything you like as long as it costs less than two shillings."

Maxie gave him a cold stare. "You may stop if you wish, but I intend to continue. Have a pleasant journey, Mr. Anderson."

"Andreville," he said, impervious to snub. "Anderson is too common to impress anyone. Are you sure you don't want to stop? While I have enough food for another day, the air is cooling and a warm meal would help us through the night."

"There is no us, Mr. Andreville," Maxie said in a doomed attempt to maintain formality. "We are two individuals who have chanced to travel the same road for a few hours."

"You still don't take me seriously, do you?" Her companion seemed unfazed by the observation. "People seldom do, so you're in good company. Very well, cold food it is."

"Oh, for heaven's sake," Maxie said, exasperated as she walked past the inn and Robin stayed at her side. In spite of his charm, the man was becoming a blessed nuisance. Then an idea occurred to her. If she agreed to stop for dinner, she could surely find an opportunity to slip away from him, and with a few minutes' lead, she could be down the road and gone. The next day she would cut across to a different southbound road and he would never find her. "You're right, a hot meal would be welcome, but I will pay for my own."

His blue eyes danced, and she had the uneasy feeling that he had guessed her intentions. They entered the inn together and found seats in a smoky taproom so dark that no one would notice that Maxie didn't remove her hat. There was no choice of meals, and they were each served a plate of food described by the barmaid as griskin and potatoes. At Maxie's questioning glance, Robin explained, "Griskin is from the loin of a bacon pig. It's not bad."

Maxie took a bite and chewed it thoughtfully. "You're right. It's not bad. On the other hand, it isn't good, either."

"True, but it's hot, and it tastes better than one would expect anything named griskin to taste."

She covered up her smile with another forkful of food. She had eaten far worse in her travels, and at a shilling, the meal was a bargain. She finished quickly, then stood, casually taking her knapsack in hand. "I have to use the necessary."

Robin nodded, his attention concentrated on his plate. Crossing the taproom, Maxie entered the courtyard behind the inn, then turned left into a lane that ran behind the buildings that fronted on the main road. The food had been paid for when ordered, so there was no account to settle and she could leave with a clear conscience.

Her sense of satisfaction was short-lived. The lane was only half a dozen buildings long, and when she returned to the main road, she almost collided with Robin, who was leaning against a wall, his arms crossed on his chest as he waited for her.

"Your opinion of my intelligence really is low if you believed that I am so easily eluded," he said with undiminished good nature.

Maxie stared at him, for the first time believing that the imbecile man really meant to accompany her all the way to

London. "The issue is not your intelligence, but your presumption," she snapped. "I do not want your escort, your company, or your free meals. Now, leave me alone!"

She turned and started stalking down the street, but was not surprised that Robin stayed at her elbow. Whirling angrily, she faced him. "I have warned you. Believe me, I am quite capable of defending myself."

She was about to say more when he cut her off with a sharp gesture of his hand. "People are coming. If you want to maintain your masquerade, don't make a scene here. Or at the very least, lower your voice."

Several approaching locals were watching them curiously, but Maxie would still have exploded with fury if she hadn't been caught by Robin's gaze. His blue eyes had measureless depths, the eyes of a man who had walked on the dark side of life as well as in the sunshine. He was also older than she had thought. She had guessed him as near her own age, but now revised that upward, past thirty. The realization that her self-appointed guardian was far more complex than she had supposed was not a comforting one, but it stilled her protests while she revised her assumptions and strategy.

Taking Maxie's arm in a casual-looking but unbreakable grip, Robin started walking again, guiding them along the village street toward open-country. As they passed the interested group of villagers, an elderly woman said in a broad Yorkshire accent, "Say, Daisy, isn't that gent—"

"No, it isn't." Robin's cultured tones cut across the woman's sentence. His interruption was accompanied by a dazzling smile that made the woman's mouth go slack with delighted admiration. Leaving a murmur of voices behind them, he marched Maxie down the road before anything more could be said.

Fuming, she considered calling to the villagers for help, but that would require endless explanations and she was sure that Robin could talk his way out of any accusation she could make. Besides, she did not feel physically endangered by him; on the contrary, at the moment he was in more danger from her than vice versa.

Maxie waited until they rounded a bend and were out of sight of the village. Then she stopped and jerked away from Robin, who released her arm and waited for the explosion. "If I had any doubts about traveling with you, they are resolved," Maxie said furiously. "You arrogant, egotistical . . ."

She was reaching for her knife when Robin caught her wrist. His clasp was light, but Maxie found that it was impossible to wrench free, even though she was exceptionally strong for her size.

"Don't do it, Maxie," he said, his gaze holding hers. "You're quite right, I am presumptous. But you had better accept that I intend to ensure that you arrive safely at your destination." Robin's soft tenor had undertones of steel. "You are one of the two most formidable women I have ever known, but you are a stranger crossing a country rife with unrest. Besides the usual bandits, there are starving soldiers released from the army and unable to find work, angry radicals who want to bring down the government, and God knows what else. You might be lucky all the way to London, but that is unlikely. While you may think I am ineffectual, I guarantee you will be safer with me than alone."

She could have fought him, but the last few minutes had changed Maxie's views on his ineffectuality. It was clear that her companion was a good deal more forceful than she had guessed. Not just forceful, but a man who could be dangerous. However, she sensed that his desire to protect her was genuine. Doubtless he had other, less honorable motives as well, but she was experienced at resisting seduction and didn't think it likely that he would force her. If his fraudulent lordship wanted a woman, all he had to do was give one of those melting smiles in a village and females would be following him down the street. In the meantime, his escort might prove useful.

Reserving judgment on whether she might choose to escape him in the future, Maxie said, "Very well, Mr. Andreville, I accept the inevitability of your company, at least for the moment. Just remember to keep your hands to yourself, or you will find them taken off at the wrist." As he released her, she found herself asking, "Who is the other of the two most formidable women?"

He grinned. "An old friend of mine. You'd like her."

"I doubt it." Maxie turned and resumed walking along the road. It would be light for at least another hour, so they might as well put some more distance behind them. "I just hope that your aristocratic self can survive sleeping under a hedge when there isn't a barn."

Robin laughed as he fell into step beside her. "There are worse places to sleep than under a hedge. Just about any jail, for example."

"Have you been in many jails?" She suspected that he had, and hoped that it had been for no more than vagrancy, though doubtless he was guilty of much worse.

"A few," he admitted. "The best was a castle in France with very tolerable food and wine, and a duke for company."

From the sparkle in his eye, Maxie guessed that he had just made this particular tale up and that he was aware that she knew it. Well, no reason why she shouldn't enjoy his stories as entertainment. Her lips quirked up in a reluctant smile. "Sounds pleasant. What was the worst prison?"

He pondered. "That would probably be the one in Constantinople. I didn't speak much Turkish, and I didn't even know the local gambling games. A sad situation. But I met the most interesting Greek chap there . . ."

As they walked along in the gathering dusk, Robin's flexible tenor wove an outrageously improbable and amusing tale of subversion and escape. Perhaps he really had been in a Turkish jail, or perhaps he merely had a colorful imagination and a gift for storytelling. In either case, Maxie decided that she might as well enjoy his performance rather than sulk.

Shortly before the sun set, they encountered a tinker's wagon, and Maxie watched in admiration as Robin bargained for a razor, a spoon, a battered tin pot and two mugs, and several ounces of the tinker's personal tea supply. His haggling skills would have done credit to a horse coper.

They were in rolling moorland by now, where there would be no barns or sheds to sleep in. At the top of a hill, Maxie paused to scan for a suitable place to stop for the night.

"Perhaps down there." Robin gestured to a spot in the distance, barely visible even from this vantage point. "The trees indicate that there is water, and it is far enough from the road to be private."

She evaluated for a moment, then nodded. "Very well."
Clearly her companion was experienced at traveling rough.

It took another half-hour of walking to reach the trees. A circle
of stones by the small stream showed that the site had been used
by travelers in the past, though not recently. As darkness fell,
Maxie and Robin gathered wood for a fire, since the night would
be a cool one. Maxie used her flint and steel to start the fire,
then rigged a crossbar to suspend the tin pot to heat water for
tea. Thus engaged, she lost track of Robin for a few minutes,
and was surprised when he returned to the campsite with an
armload of large cut ferns.

"Bracken," he explained as he laid down his load. "It makes
quite a decent bed."

"I assume that what you really mean is that it will make two
quite decent beds?" she asked frostily.

"But of course." Robin's face was serious, but his eyes
laughed at her suspicions. He made three more trips, shaping
the bracken into pallets on opposite sides of the fire. All very
proper.

Maxie had been dubious about how this strange partnership
would work out in practice, but Robin's matter-of-fact attitude
made everything easy. Odd how comfortable she felt around
him, considering that they had known each other for mere hours,
and she had doubts about his motives and his very presence.

By the time the beds were made up, the tea had steeped and
Maxie handed Robin a mugful as he settled cross-legged on the
far side of the fire. They sat and sipped together in companionable silence as the night air cooled.

As she finished her tea, Maxie found herself saying, "You'll
be cold without a blanket."

"I've been cold before." He shrugged. "The bracken will
help."

Maxie had replenished the water in the pot and it was now
boiling, so she brewed more tea, thriftily reusing the leaves.
"You're quite mad, you know. Surely wherever you slept last
night was more comfortable than this."

"Correct but irrelevant." Robin chuckled. "I haven't enjoyed
myself this much in a long time."

"Quite, quite mad." But harmlessly so. At peace with the
world, at least for the moment, Maxie brought out her

harmonica and softly began to play as she often had when she and her father slept beneath the stars.

As the plangent notes wove through the night air, Robin murmured, "Lovely," and subsided back onto the bracken, his arms crossed behind his head.

The flickering light gilded the blond hair, and as he listened to her playing, his profile was as remote as it was flawless. His speech and obvious education marked him as a child of privilege, and Maxie wondered why Robin had been banished to the world of ordinary mortals who must struggle for an existence. Her father's sins had been the obvious ones of youth, gaming, and women, but there was something about Robin that made her doubt that the conventional vices had been his downfall. Perhaps, rather than being cast out for his sins, his family had fallen on hard times. Or perhaps he was illegitimate, raised with some advantages, then abandoned to make his own way.

Maxie first played traditional ballads of the frontier, most of them British in origin, then drifted into themes from famous European composers. Finally, as the fire crumbled to embers, she began to play the music of the Iroquois. The first songs she had ever heard were her mother's lullabies, and later she had learned many of the ceremonial and work tunes of the Mohawks. There were no Indian instruments like the harmonica, but with practice she had learned to approximate the plaintive intervals and strange, ever-changing rhythms.

Maxie had thought Robin was asleep, but as the music changed, his head turned in her direction, his eyes shadowed and unreadable on the far side of the fire.

She played a little longer, than tucked her harmonica away and pulled her cloak from her pack.

"Good night." Robin's voice was scarcely louder than the wind over the moor grasses. "Thank you for the concert."

"You're welcome." Maxie would not have admitted it for the world, but as she curled up in the nest of bracken, she was secretly glad for his company.

The moon had set when a strange sound wakened Maxie. She came instantly alert, her hand reaching for her knife as she listened. At first she thought the soft choking noise had been made by an animal, but when it was repeated, she realized that it came from the other pallet. Wondering if Robin was having some kind of breathing attack, she rose and silently crossed the kneel by his side. His face was a pale blur in the starlight, and his breath came in shallow gasps, the bracken rustling as he shifted uneasily.

She laid a hand on his shoulder. "Robin?"

He tensed instantly, his muscles going hard under her fingers. The choking sounds stopped and she saw his eyes open, though it was too dark to see any expression. Drawing in a ragged breath, he said, "Was I having a nightmare?"

"I think so. Do you remember what it was?"

He drew the back of his hand across his forehead. "Not really. Could be any of a number of things."

"You have nightmares often?"

"Regularly, if not precisely often." She recognized the conscious effort he was making to steady his breathing. "I'm sorry for disturbing your rest."

His right hand lay near her knee, and for a moment she let her fingers rest on his. "No great matter. I'm a light sleeper." In spite of the chill night, his fingers were warm. "Better to be woken by you than by a hungry wolf."

"In these parts, sheep are far more common than wolves." He chuckled and gave her hand a light squeeze. "Not that I don't have faith in your ability to protect my ineffectual self from the perils of the wild."

Maxie smiled and returned to her own pallet to take advantage of what remained of the night, but sleep eluded her at first, though Robin's breathing was soon quiet and regular. The Iroquois took dreams seriously, regarding them as wishes of the soul that must be satisfied. Did that mean nightmares were injuries to the soul that must be healed?

As she drifted back to sleep, Maxie wondered what haunted Robin's nights.

3

Had Desdemona Ross known just how difficult it would be to trace a runaway, she might have been content to leave the task to her brother's experienced agent. Having begun, however, she was not about to admit she wasn't equal to the challenge.

The search had seemed a simple exercise in logic. Knowing her niece's background, Desdemona had calculated how much distance a vigorous walker could travel in the time Maxima had been gone. Then she had targeted the three most likely routes and started making inquiries at taverns and posting houses along the way. She asked for a boy, sure that her niece had too much sense to travel in female garb.

Regrettably, her inquiries produced either too many sightings of young boys, or none at all, but never anything that proved useful. After three days of futile searching, Desdemona was thoroughly tired of the business, and only her stubbornness kept her going.

Then her luck changed, at still another Yorkshire inn, this one named the King Richard. It was early afternoon, and a scattering of locals nursed their ale in the taproom when Desdemona entered. Wasting no time, she marched over to the woman behind the bar. "Excuse me, madam. I am looking for my young nephew. The lad ran away from school and it is likely that he came this way."

"Aye?" the landlady said with profound disinterest.

"Yes. About this tall"—Desdemona gestured with her hand—"dark coloring but probably wearing a hat to hide his face, and dressed so as not to be noticed."

"There was a lad like that in here t'other day." The answer came not from the proprietor, but from a toothless beldame sitting in the group across the room. The old woman clambered to her feet and made her way across to Desdemona. "But he's found hisself a friend." She cackled merrily.

"Oh?" Desdemona asked in an encouraging tone.

Another woman came to join them, a middle-aged female smoking a clay pipe. "Aye, if 'twas your nephew, he's all right." Her gaze evaluated the cost of Desdemona's clothing. "Lord Robert Andreville was with him. Happen you might know him, all the Quality being related like. Must've recognized the lad and taken him home to send him back to you."

The beldame disagreed. "Gent said he wasn't Lord Robert."

"Nothing wrong with my eyes, Granny. That was Lord Robert, no matter what he said," the smoker insisted. "That yaller head couldn't't've belonged to anyone else."

"What exactly happened?" Desdemona asked.

"The lad and his lordship had a bite of supper here," the landlady contributed, showing more interest in the debate. "Sat in a dark corner, which is why no one recognized Lord Robert at first. Then the lad slipped out the back."

"Aye, tried to run away again," the beldame agreed. "That's why I think it must be the lad you're looking for. His lordship caught up with him outside and made your nevvy go with him."

Desdemona frowned. "You mean he forced the boy?"

The smoker nodded. "Took the lad by the arm and marched him out of town. Must have had a carriage waiting. Shouldn't think a lord'd walk very far." She shrugged: clearly no vagary was beyond the Quality.

Desdemona had heard of the Andrevilles, of course, and knew that their principal seat was nearby. But none of that family should know Maxima, who had only been in England for a few months. At least, no one should have recognized the girl as a runaway of good family. "Tell me about this Lord Robert."

That produced an enthusiastic chorus of comments informing Desdemona that Lord Robert was the younger brother of the current Marquess of Wolverton, that he had done dire and dangerous things during the wars, that he was as handsome as a fallen angel and a devil with the ladies. The zeal with which the villagers competed to describe his exploits implied that they were deeply proud of their neighborhood black sheep.

Even if only half of the tales were true, the portrait that

emerged was alarming. It seemed likely that the dissolute Lord
Robert had recognized that Maxima was female and had forced
her to accompany him for no good purpose. The one thing Lord
and Lady Collingwood had agreed on was that the girl was
strikingly attractive, just the sort to draw unwelcome attentions
from a rake. And now it appeared that a rake had found her.

Her mouth grim, Desdemona asked, "How can I get to Wolverhampton?" After receiving directions, she dipped into her
reticule and laid two gold guineas on the bar. "Thank you for
your help, ladies. This afternoon's ale is on me."

Desdemona stalked outside to her waiting coach, ignoring the
gleeful toasts to her continued good health. She was busy
planning just what she would do to a depraved aristocrat who
would ruin an innocent young girl.

The Marquess of Wolverton had set the afternoon aside to
answer his correspondence. His secretary, Charles, would read
a letter, Giles would dictate the gist of a reply, and they would
move on to the next. All perfectly, boringly normal.

Normality was shattered by the entrance of an angry Amazon
who pushed past the footman who was trying to announce her.
"I'm sorry, your lordship, Lady Ross insisted on seeing you,"
the beleagured footman apologized. "She's here about Lord
Robert."

That focused Giles' attention. Robin had vanished three days
ago, the very day he had said not to worry if he wandered off.
However, it was proving difficult not to feel some concern, even
though Giles knew his brother had dealt with far worse dangers
than the Yorkshire countryside offered.

The marquess rose to greet Lady Ross as she swept into the
study, her voluminous cloak and bonnet billowing like a ship
in full sail. The parasol she brandished could stand in for a mast.
Reproving himself for fancifulness, Giles said, "I am
Wolverton. You have news of my brother?"

"So you don't know where he is, either!" Lady Ross was
tall and Junoesque, and would have been quite attractive if her
handsome features had not been drawn into a scowl. "Your man
said he wasn't at home, but that might only have meant that
he is ashamed to show himself."

"He has been away for several days. I am unsure when he will be returning." Giles was taken aback by her obvious hostility. He had heard of a Lady Ross but couldn't recall the context. "What business do you have with him?"

"The question is not my business with him, but what he has done with my niece." Her ladyship glowered at the marquess. "The evidence suggests that your brother has abducted her."

"The devil you say!" said Giles, shocked into unaccustomed profanity. "Who is spreading such preposterous slander?"

"Some of your tenants saw Lord Robert forcing a young person to come away with him." The tip of her parasol quivered like the tail of an angry cat. "From the description, it was my niece, Miss Maxima Collins, a young American girl."

The marquess gave his footman a glance that sent the servant hastening from the room. He considered dismissing his secretary as well, but Charles was discreet, and it might be wise to have a witness, since this female was making wild accusations. He fixed his visitor with a level gaze. "How and when did the girl come to be abducted? I refuse to believe that my brother kidnapped an innocent young girl away from her family."

"I'm not sure exactly what happened." Lady Ross's gray eyes shifted away. "Maxima had been living with my brother, Lord Collingwood. Her father died soon after they arrived in England and the girl has been overset. About a week ago she impulsively left Collingwood's house, leaving a note that she was on her way to me in London. In fact, I was coming to visit her in Durham. I have been looking for her since we realized that she had disappeared." Her gaze snapped back to the marquess. "It was three days ago that the villagers saw Lord Robert with his unwilling companion."

Giles' lips tightened. Robin would not have abducted a girl from her family, but might he have taken off on a lark with a young and willing runaway? That would depend on how young and how willing she was. "How old is your niece?"

Lady Ross hesitated before admitting, "Twenty-five."

"Twenty-five! The way you are carrying on, I assumed she must be fifteen or sixteen. She's hardly a green girl. At your niece's age, most females are wives and mothers. If she went with my brother, it must have been voluntarily."

"Maxima has only been in England for three months and she was orphaned almost immediately." Lady Ross's glower was back in full force. "She is an innocent, alone in a foreign country. A man who would take advantage of that is beneath contempt."

"We have not established what, if anything, has happened," Giles pointed out in his most magisterial manner.

"If Lord Robert hasn't taken her away, then where is he?" she demanded. "What you said when I arrived implies that your brother is away from home unexpectedly. And according to the villagers, he has a reputation as a devil with the ladies."

"That's utter nonsense," Giles scoffed. "Robin has been out of England for years, and in the six months since his return, he has been living here quietly, not cutting a swath through English womanhood."

"Your tenants didn't seem to think so."

"People are fond of telling lurid tales about the local gentry. I don't provide them with much to work with, but Lord Robert is an attractive and romantic figure—if he so much as smiles at a local girl, I'm sure the tenants fancy him an incurable rake." Giles considered a moment. "Even if my brother had a female companion, are you sure that she was your niece? As a runaway, she could be almost anywhere."

"I am sure that Maxima must be in this area, and the description the villagers gave sounded like her." Lady Ross refused to give way. "I fear the worst."

"You have shown me no proof that Robin has behaved badly, or even that he and your niece are acquainted," the marquess said with exasperation. "While I will make allowances for your concern, I would advise you not to make baseless charges against my brother. Good day, Lady Ross." He had never been rude to a female in his life, but a few minutes with Lady Ross was on the verge of changing that. Sitting down at his desk, he delved into the papers he had been working on when his visitor arrived.

By rights, Lady Ross should have accepted her dismissal and left. Instead, the marquess caught a glimpse of swift movement and raised his head just in time to see Lady Ross's parasol smash down on the desk in front of him, missing his face by inches. "Don't think you can dismiss me like one of your servants, Wolverton," she snarled.

If the lunatic woman had wanted to get his attention again, she had succeeded. As papers slid off the desk from the force of the impact, the marquess gaped at Lady Ross, torn between appalled shock and the irrelevant thought that it was a pity she didn't play cricket; she would have made an impressive batsman, if her parasol-wielding was any indication.

The two glared at each other. Through gritted teeth, Giles said, "Even if your absurd accusations about my brother are true, just what do you expect me to do about it? I have no idea where to find him or your niece, either together or singly."

"I don't expect you to do anything," Lady Ross said with disgust. "I realize that men of our order will ruin a girl as casually as they will discard a cravat. I came here hoping against hope that Lord Robert had found my niece in need of protection and behaved as a gentleman by restoring her to her family. Instead, he has apparently taken her away against her will, a fact that does not disturb you anywhere near as much as it should. However, Maxima is not without family, and I swear that if Lord Robert has injured her or her reputation in any way, he will pay for it."

Appalled realization dawned on the marquess. "Suddenly I understand what this is all about. You and your niece are working together to trap my brother into marriage." He stood and leaned forward, his hands braced on the desk and his broad shoulders tense with anger. "She set out to seduce Lord Robert. Then you came here crying that she is an injured innocent and justice must be done, hoping that I will force my brother to marry her. Well, it won't work, madam, not on my brother and not on me. He would not have gone off with her unless she was willing, and he will certainly not marry a short-heeled wench who is trying to entrap him."

If Lady Ross's parasol had been a sword, there would have been murder done. Gray eyes flashing, she said furiously, "Believe me, I have no intention of forcing the girl into marriage with a degenerate wastrel, and I will stand up to the head of my family or anyone else who might try to coerce her. What I do intend is to see your brother in Newgate. Remember, Wolverton, kidnapping is a capital offense. Don't think you can buy his freedom with your influence. I am not without influence of my own, and if a crime has been committed, I intend to see Lord Robert prosecuted to the fullest extent of the law.''

She spun on her heel and began stalking toward the door, her parasol clenched in her hand like a club. ''If your benighted brother returns here, my lord, you would be wise to advise him to leave England, instantly and forever.''

Just as she reached the door, the marquess remembered who Lady Ross was: a bluestocking reformer who had the ear of some of the most prominent politicians of both parties. Giles had heard of her for years and vaguely assumed that she was an older woman. To find that the celebrated reformer was a firebrand some years younger than himself was a surprise. Much worse was the realization that she might indeed have the influence to cause the Andreville family considerable grief even if Robin had done nothing illegal. Swearing under his breath, he got to his feet. ''Lady Ross, please hold a moment.''

''Yes?'' she said ominously, looking back over her shoulder.

''Of course you are concerned for your niece, but truly, I think you are making a mistake. What is important is locating the girl, and I doubt that you will find her with my brother.'' Giles crossed the room to stand by his visitor, doing his best to sound conciliatory. ''While there are men whose behavior toward females is unconscionable, Robin is not one of them.''

Her auburn brows arched. ''Are you absolutely sure of that?''

Giles started to say that he was, but hesitated. ''How much in life can one be absolutely sure of?''

Lady Ross's lip curled. ''That is not an inspiring recommendation for Lord Robert's honor.''

''I have no doubts at all about my brother's honor.'' Incurably honest, Giles found himself adding, ''However, some of his actions might be unconventional.''

''I suggest that you stop trying to defend him,'' she said dryly. ''You are making matters worse, not better.''

''I would trust him as I trust myself.''

For a moment Lady Ross's face softened and Giles thought he might be persuading her. Then the stubborn set came back to her jaw. ''You have the reputation of a just man, and your loyalty to your brother is commendable. Unfortunately, men can be honorable with each other, yet think nothing of mistreating women. If Lord Robert has been away from England for so many years, do you really know what he is capable of?''

The blasted woman was right. On an emotional level Giles felt that he knew Robin well, certainly well enough to trust him. Yet surely his brother could not have survived a dozen years of spying in the heart of Napoleon's empire without a capacity for ruthlessness. ''Robin has been shaped by forces different than the English *beau monde*,'' he said slowly, ''but I am sure he would never injure an innocent.''

Lady Ross shrugged and turned away. ''We shall see. I will not stop searching until I find my niece. And if your brother has harmed her, may God help him.''

Then she was gone. Giles stared at the closed door for a moment, feeling as if he had been thrown by his horse and then had the whole hunt field ride over top of him. ''What did you think of all that, Charles?''

''I think,'' the secretary said, choosing his words with care, ''that I would not like to have Lady Ross angry at me.''

''And that if Robin is dallying with the lady's niece, he may find himself in a rare bumble broth?'' Giles suggested as he returned to his desk.

Charles smiled. ''Exactly, my lord.''

Ignoring both correspondence and secretary, the marquess settled deep in his leather-upholstered chair and applied his excellent analytical abilities to the situation. Preposterous though the idea seemed, the missing Maxima must be traveling to London by foot; otherwise Lady Ross wouldn't be so sure that her niece was in southern Yorkshire a week after leaving Durham. It was hard to imagine a gently bred female undertaking such a journey; the chit must be desperate, depraved, or mad. Or perhaps it was just that she was an American.

Someone walking south from Durham might well take the road that bounded the east side of Wolverhampton. Giles was sure that Robin had not intended to go off, because there would have been no need to conceal such a fact. However, his brother had been ripe for distraction, and if he had encountered an attractive, madcap girl, he could have gone with her on impulse. While Robin was no rake, he was also no saint, and he couldn't know the potential for scandal in taking up with this particular female.

Since he had intended only a ramble across Wolverhampton, Robin would have had little or no money on him. Maxima Collins likewise would not have been in funds, or she would have taken a coach to London. Giles thought that a romantic interlude without a feather to fly with sounded dashed uncomfortable, but of course he was boringly conservative in his habits.

Could Robin have decided to escort the girl to London? Giles seized on the thought with relief; it was exactly the sort of quixotic thing his brother might do. If so, and if the wench was twenty-five, willing, and concealing the fact that she was wellborn, they might soon be on terms far more intimate than the girl's aunt would approve of. Not that the details mattered; the mere fact of traveling together was scandalous enough.

Lady Ross herself was an interesting subject of speculation. Giles thought the lady was more agitated than the situation warranted. The missing niece was no green girl, after all, so there must be more here than met the eye. After a moment, Giles mentally shrugged; he was in no position to guess what Lady Ross's real concerns were. Remembering her rage at the suggestion, he acquitted her ladyship of cooperating with her niece to entrap Robin, but that didn't mean that the girl herself was innocent of such intentions. Between his fortune and his personal attractions, Robin was a very good catch indeed, and possibly the girl had recognized that fact and decided to take advantage of the situation.

Shifting his position and crossing his long legs, the marquess summarized his thinking. The facts were that Robin had gone missing, and so had Miss Collins, and they had tentatively been identified as being together. The assumption was that they were traveling south toward London together.

Another fact was that Lady Ross was heading after the fugitives, breathing fire and brimstone. A scandal would injure the girl far more than Robin, but a vengeful Lady Ross might not care. Giles did not doubt that his brother could handle even as formidable a lady as this one, but a damned unpleasant situation was in the making. Any number of things might happen, and Robin would be handicapped by lack of money and identification. And while his younger brother might be indifferent to scandal, the marquess was not.

The conclusion was inescapable: Giles had best go after the runaways himself. With luck, he would find them before Lady Ross did, in time to head off disaster. And if a furious Lady Ross caught the two, or if the niece insisted that only marriage would save her from ruin, well, the marquess would have something to say about that. Quite apart from Robin's personal happiness, his brother's wife would likely be the mother of a future Marquess of Wolverton, and Giles would rather not see the line tainted with the blood of a vulgar, scheming baggage.

He was going to feel like a damned fool chasing across the countryside after an American doxy, a retired spy, and a firebreathing reformer.

As he thought about the prospect, the Marquess of Wolverton realized that he was smiling.

It took time for Simmons to determine which route his quarry had chosen, but once he found people who remembered seeing her, tracking was dead easy. Since Lord Collingwood's niece had no reason to suspect that she was being followed, she was walking along the one road, just waiting to be caught.

Disguised as she was, at first the wench was easy to overlook and not many people recalled seeing a little lad with a large hat. Simmons' job got easier after she took up with a blond gent; all the females along the route remembered him quick enough. With a touch of malicious amusement, Simmons wondered how Collingwood would react to the news that his niece was no better than she should be. Or maybe his lordship wouldn't care; his main concern had been to prevent the girl from reaching London, where she might find out about her pa. Not that Simmons blamed Collingwood for wanting to conceal that particular information.

Though the chit had had several days' start, by the time Simmons reached Blyth he was on her heels. It was getting late and he was tempted to stop for the night, but he decided to push on; his hunter's instinct said that the girl and her fancy man were likely dossed down in a barn or camp within the next mile or two. She might not want to leave the fellow to return to Durham, but Ned Simmons was more than a match for both of them, and he would do whatever was necessary to accomplish the job.

4

Without a doubt, Maxie decided, it had been the oddest three days of her life. Her self-appointed escort was pleasant and undemanding company, and apparently no more nightmares troubled his sleep. They talked of neutral topics: the passing scene, the agreeable weather, the late regrettable war between their countries. Robin also told entertaining and wholly unbelievable tales of his adventures. In fact, he never said anything about his past that Maxie felt sure she could believe—not surprising, considering that she didn't know what his real name was. Another mystery was that he contrived to look neat and casually elegant even though he was living in his clothes the same as she was.

Perhaps the strangest aspect of the trip was that Robin behaved as a perfect gentleman, so perfect that Maxie was beginning to wonder what was wrong with her that he didn't try anything. Perhaps, she thought acidly, his preference was for English females as blond as he himself. Not that she wanted him to pounce on her, but at least that was behavior she could understand.

Instead, she had a charming companion who was utterly incomprehensible. The fact that he was an enigma increased her wariness, while the fact that he was the most attractive man she had ever met threatened to unbalance her judgment. It was all most unsettling, and far too easy to forget that in spite of his charm, Robin was basically an unreliable rogue.

Maxie herself said as little as possible about her own background, and was grateful that Robin didn't probe further. She was still debating whether to escape from his unwanted escort; if she did try again, she would not repeat the mistake of underestimating his intelligence.

The shadows were lengthening when the charming companion

interrupted her circular thoughts. "I think there may be a gypsy campground down that track to the left. We're not likely to find any barns in this area, so shall we try that for the night? The gypsies wouldn't use it unless there was water and a place to build a fire."

"You're right, we probably won't do better," Maxie agreed. She followed him down the faint trail, and two hundred yards from the road they found themselves in a sizable clearing that showed signs of regular occupation. Gratefully she swung her pack to the ground. They had developed a routine over the last days, starting with gathering wood.

Robin was laying a fire in the circle of stones when Maxie set her load of wood down by him. "I'll go find the water and make some tea."

Robin glanced up at her, his blue eyes teasing. "Will you take it as a mortal insult if I suggest that you sit and rest for a while? I'll fetch some water when I've got the fire going."

The thought of sitting down was enormously tempting. Still . . . "I didn't ask for any special consideration."

"I know you didn't." He chuckled, glancing down as he struck the flint and steel. "However, we've covered quite some distance today, and considering the difference in the length of our strides, you have done about a third more walking than I have. Since you've walked so much farther, it makes sense that I should make the tea. If it will make you feel less indulged, you can be the one to rise early to make the morning tea."

Maxie briefly considered belligerence, but acquiescence was so much easier. "You could sell rope to a man on the gallows," she said wryly, settling on the grass and tugging off her boots. Well-made and comfortable though they were, she was still glad to let her feet free after more than twenty miles of walking. "Or if honest labor wasn't against your philosophy, you could have become a lawyer, arguing either side of any case."

Pulling off her hat, she unpinned her hair, sighing with relief as the thick black coils fell loose about her shoulders. She was getting very tired of boots, pinned hair, and bound breasts, and the aspect of Chanleigh she missed most was the hot baths. "In fact, are you a lawyer? Some of your remarks have implied that lawyering might be in your checkered past."

Robin shot her a horrified look. "Good Lord, no. I may have done a number of reprehensible things in my life, but I do have some standards."

Laughing, Maxie lay back on the grass, her hands tucked under her head. "Are you never serious?"

There was a long pause, and she glanced up to find him watching her, an unreadable expression in his eyes. When he caught her looking, he smiled and said in his usual light tone, "As seldom as possible." He struck the flint and steel again, then bent over to blow on the sparks. After the fire was burning reliably, he stood and retrieved the tin pot from his pack, then followed the sound of running water into the woods.

Maxie closed her eyes, half-dozing. There was no question that having a companion made everything much easier. Enigmatic though Robin might be, she felt safer with him near, and the shillings he had been able to contribute for food and supplies have been most welcome. In fact, he was as adept at the traveling life as she was; Robin really was the most mysterious creature, she thought for the hundredth time as she drifted off.

The stream was farther than Robin had guessed. He also took the time to wash up, so nearly half an hour had passed before he returned to their makeshift camp. If Maxie hadn't been so tired, he would have worried about letting her out of his sight for so long. Though she had provisionally accepted his presence, Robin knew full well that behind that exotically lovely face a razor-sharp brain was at work and that Maxie was by no means convinced his presence was an asset. However, even if she decided that she was better off alone, she would not find him easy to elude. Something serious lay behind Maxie's determination to reach London, and Robin had a feeling that she would need some help before she was done. He was more than willing to help; the trick was convincing her to accept aid from anyone.

Just thinking about her made him smile as he moved through the woods with a quietness that was second nature. Miss Maxima Collins, if that really was her name, was the most extraordinary female he had ever met, not excluding Maggie. When he reached the edge of the clearing, Robin paused behind a protective shield of shrubbery, pleased to take a moment to admire his dozing companion without her knowledge. Maxie lay on her side by the fire, her head pillowed on one arm and her shining ebony hair partially veiling her face.

Certainly her flawless features and petite, curving body were beautiful, but Maxie also had qualities beyond mere beauty: independence, certainly, to a fault; also intelligence, humor, and a directness that was wholly unlike any of the females he had met in the upper reaches of English society. A lifetime would not be too long to admire such a fascinating creature.

A lifetime? Robin halted, astonished by the direction of his own thoughts. He had carefully avoided examining the impulse that had caused him to walk away from Wolverhampton half an hour after meeting Maxie, preferring to think of this as a lark with altruistic overtones. Of course he was fooling himself, but for the moment, he was unwilling to contemplate the consequences of what he was doing.

Fortunately for his peace of mind, interruption came in the form of twigs cracking under heavy footsteps. Robin glanced up, his gaze hardening at the sight of a burly man approaching from the far side of the clearing. The newcomer had the build and physiognomy of a pugilist past his prime, and a broad smile of satisfaction crossed his face at the sight of Maxie. Robin recognized the type, and was instantly alert for possible danger.

"There you are, Miss Collins. Time to go 'ome now." The intruder had a thick London accent, and even his present geniality did not disguise an air of menace.

Maxie had come awake at the sound of the heavy footsteps. Tense and alert, she pushed herself to a sitting position, watching the man with narrowed eyes. "Who are you?" she asked with admirable coolness. "I saw you at my uncle's."

"Right you are. The name's Ned Simmons, and your uncle sent me to bring you back," he said, advancing toward his quarry.

Robin set down the pot of water and silently began to work his way around the edge of the clearing so that he would be behind Simmons if action proved necessary.

Maxie scrambled to her feet and watched Simmons warily, looking like a terrier facing a bull. "You have no right to force me to return to my uncle," she said, backing away across the grass. She was in her stocking feet, very much at a disadvantage if she wanted to run or fight. "He is not my guardian. I am of legal age and have committed no crimes."

Still with that eerie geniality, Simmons said, "Come now, miss, don't be difficult, or I'll have to take you to a magistrate and explain how you stole a map, and some food as well. In England, folks can be 'anged for crimes like that. Not that yer uncle will be difficult if you just come along like a good girl." He reached out to grasp her shoulder. "Where's yer fancy man? 'E run off and leave you already?"

Laying a hand on Maxie proved to be a mistake. She twisted away from the Londoner's grip, at the same time kicking out with wicked intent. Simmons was fortunate that she was not wearing her boots, for her aim and quickness were excellent. The man dodged but could not entirely avoid the blow, and he doubled over with a howl.

"You little . . ." The curse that followed was so filthy that Robin was glad that it was spoken in thief's cant, which Maxie was unlikely to understand. Still swearing, Simmons reached under his coat and pulled out a pistol.

Before he could even aim it, Maxie had dived at him and grabbed the weapon, using her weight to wrest it free. Her momentum carried her into a rolling tumble across the ground. Then she was on her feet while Simmons was still gasping with astonishment. Holding the pistol with both hands, she cocked the hammers, saying in a hard voice, "I would prefer not to use this, Mr. Simmons, but I will do so rather than go with you. Now turn around and leave."

Simmons stared at her in stunned disbelief. "Put that down, you little bitch, or I'll make you sorry you was ever born."

The intruder was making the potentially fatal mistake of underestimating Maxie. Knowing that if he didn't intervene she might kill the man, Robin sprinted across the clearing as Maxie raised her pistol and took aim. Since he was directly behind the large Londoner, Robin didn't know if Maxie saw his approach, nor was he sure that she would hold her fire if she did see him. Launching himself in a long, flat dive, he caught Simmons around the legs and knocked the man down as a shot exploded too close for comfort.

Even with the wind knocked out of him, Simmons was a

formidable opponent, but Robin had the advantage of surprise and was skilled in all forms of rough-and-tumble fighting. After a brief, violent struggle, the Londoner was facedown in the leaf mold with Robin straddling him. Twisting his opponent's right arm behind his back, Robin held it at the excruciating point just short of breaking a joint. "The fancy man is still around," he said between gasps for breath. "You should be more careful."

Simmons had plenty of bullheaded courage and a high tolerance for pain; he began thrashing furiously, and he was so powerful that he threatened to break free. Robin leaned forward and applied intense pressure to a precisely chosen point at the base of the Londoner's neck. The blood supply to his brain cut off, Simmons made a strangled noise and one last convulsive heave before slumping into unconsciousness.

Maxie had been watching with the second barrel of the pistol at the ready, but now she lowered the weapon and uncocked it. "That is an impressive trick. Will you show it to me?"

Robin eased off on his grip and rolled Simmons onto his back. "Definitely not. It's dangerous to use, because it can cause death or permanent damage if held too long. And if I showed you how, you might try it on me the next time I did something to irritate you."

"Probably wise of you not to teach me," she agreed. For all the insouciance of her words, her dark complexion had a gray tinge. "When I lose my temper, anything might happen."

"So I noticed," Robin said dryly. He found a handkerchief in the Londoner's pocket and used it to tie the man's wrists together. "Were you shooting to kill?"

"No, though I was tempted." She retrieved her boots and pulled them on. "I was aiming to graze his arm, hoping that would stop him. I still had another barrel if it didn't." She went to the fire and tossed earth on it. "I'm sure that we are in agreement about leaving as soon as possible."

"We are." Robin was deftly going through Simmons' pockets. "He'll be unconscious for a little longer, but I didn't tie the handkerchief very tightly and it won't take him long to free himself."

Robin removed the ammunition pouch concealed under the Londoner's coat and tucked it in his own pocket. Continuing his search, he found that Simmons had little in the way of identification, but his wallet was well-filled. Robin considered it thoughtfully; there was more than enough to pay for two coach fares to London, but if the truth be known, he was in no hurry to deliver Maxie to her destination.

"Are you going to rob him?" Maxie's voice carried disapproval.

"Only of his pistol." Robin returned the wallet to Simmons' pocket. "He's going to be quite angry enough when he wakes up."

"So your honesty is a result of pragmatism rather than moral scruples?"

"Exactly so. Moral scruples are an expensive luxury," he said blandly as he rose to his feet.

Maxie's snort was an eloquent comment on his dubious logic. Robin grinned. "Theft is a fairly benign response to attempted assault. You are the one who was ready to blow his brains out."

"Only if necessary." Maxie pinned her hair up again, then pulled her hat on. "How was I to know that you would come charging to the rescue?"

Robin stood. "Did you really think I would abandon you to your fate?"

Their gazes caught and held for a moment before Maxie turned away to lift her knapsack. "There wasn't much time for thinking."

And Maxie was not the sort of female to sit and wait to be rescued. Robin retrieved the pot of water he had put down before attacking Simmons. After offering his companion a drink, he poured the rest out and packed the pot away. As they left the clearing, the only trace of their brief occupancy was Simmons, snoring peacefully as he lay on his back with his hands trussed up in front of him.

Near the edge of the road, a depressed-looking horse was tethered. Robin stopped and eyed it speculatively. "I suppose this belongs to your friend back there?"

"He's no friend of mine," was the reply. "But yes, it must be his horse."

"Very well." Robin untied the reins and swung into the saddle.

''You're not going to steal it?'' Maxie exclaimed. ''What happened to pragmatism?''

''I would have turned the horse loose anyhow to slow pursuit, so we might as well ride it and put a few miles between us and Simmons.'' He offered his hand to Maxie. ''The poor beast isn't up to carrying two people very far, but it will give us a start.''

''You are nothing if not practical, Lord Robert.'' Maxie's tone was ironic, but her hand was icy cold when he pulled her up behind him.

Robin guessed that the encounter with Simmons had shaken her more than she was willing to admit, and her arms around his waist were tighter than the sedate pace of the horse required. He wondered what the devil she was mixed up in, but refrained from asking. Better to give her time to recover before probing.

Several miles later, when full dark had fallen, Robin pulled up at a fork in the road. ''Time to send our fiery steed back to his owner.'' They dismounted, then Robin turned the horse around and gave it a slap on the hindquarters to send it ambling back in the direction from which it had come. ''Swinging west here, away from the direct route, might throw friend Simmons off the trail. I hope so. He doesn't seem the sort to give up easily.'' He put his hand out. ''Give me the pistol.''

Without thinking, Maxie pulled it from her pocket and handed it over, then gave a cry of outrage when he took out the remaining ball and pitched the weapon into a heavy patch of shrubbery. A moment later the ammunition pouch followed it. ''Damnation, Robin! Why did you do that? A pistol could be very useful.''

''Guns are a bad idea. When they are around, people get killed unnecessarily.''

''Maybe Simmons will need killing!''

''Have you ever killed anyone?''

''No,'' she admitted.

''I have. It isn't an experience one enjoys repeating.''

Robin's tone was so cool that Maxie felt her face flush in the dark. Most of the stories he had told her were just fairy tales, but she had no doubt whatsoever that he spoke the truth about having killed, and she did not need to hear that note in his voice to know that it was not something he had done lightly. "I didn't really mean that. About killing him, I mean."

"I know you didn't." His voice softened and for a moment he put a comforting arm around her shoulders as they proceeded in silence through the night.

They walked for nearly an hour before finding one of the isolated farm buildings that were so convenient for impoverished travelers. As barns went, it was a comfortable one, with few drafts and a large pile of sweet-smelling hay. They shared bread and cheese by the dim light washing through two high windows. After the simple meal was over, Robin leaned back against the hay, his legs crossed in front of him and his pale hair silvered by moonlight. "It might be a good idea if you explained to me just what is going on. Is the road to London going to be filled with large gentlemen who want to abduct you?"

Though Maxie was not used to confiding in anyone, she owed Robin an explanation. The fact that he had come to her defense, with impressive skill and no questions asked, had strengthened the tenuous bonds between them, and Maxie's wariness was giving way to trust. At least, up to a point. Her companion was all too skilled at lies and casual theft, she didn't know his real name, and he was almost certainly some kind of swindler, but he was proving to be a friend. And she very much needed a friend.

Whatever Robin's reasons for attaching himself to her, she was sure that he would help her reach London. The fact that Lord Collingwood had sent a bullyboy after his niece confirmed Maxie's worst suspicions that there was something horribly wrong about the manner of her father's death. It had also hardened her determination to find out the truth, no matter how long it took. She sighed, reaching up to release her hair for the second time that evening. "I'm not sure exactly what is going on. I don't even know where to begin. What do you want to know?"

Robin's flexible voice was very gentle in the darkness. "Whatever you are willing to tell me."

Suddenly Maxie wanted to tell him everything, about her strange background and how she came to be an alien in England. "My father, Maximus Collins, was a younger son of what is

called a 'good family.' His expectations were not great to begin
with, and he quickly wasted them in gaming and dissipation.''
She smiled wryly. ''My grandfather decided that Max was a
useless, expensive nuisance, which was probably true, and
offered him an allowance if he would remove himself to one
of the colonies. Max didn't have much choice but to agree. I
expect that bailiffs were about to overtake him. So he went to
America.''

Maxie was cold, and she thought longingly of the tea that
hadn't been made at the gypsy campground. Well, there was
no help for it. She pulled out her light cloak and wrapped it
around herself, wishing it was thicker. ''My father wasn't a
bad man. Just''—she searched for a word—''rather casual about
things like money and propriety. Max stayed in Virginia for
a time, then wandered north.

''After a stay in New York, he made the mistake of trying
a winter journey from Albany to Montreal, and almost died in
a blizzard. An Indian, a Mohawk hunter, rescued him. Max
ended up spending the rest of the winter at the hunter's longhouse. That's where he met my mother.''

She paused, wondering what Robin's reaction would be to
the knowledge that she was a half-breed. Such an ugly word,
''Half-breed,'' more American than English. He must have
guessed from her appearance that she was of unusual ancestry,
but she doubted that he had realized quite how unusual.

His voice revealing only interest, with not a trace of distaste,
Robin commented, ''The Mohawks are one of the Six Nations
of the Iroquois confederacy, aren't they?''

''Yes, the Keepers of the Eastern Door, who defended the
Nations from the Algonquian tribes of New England,'' she said,
surprised and pleased at his knowledge. ''Four of the six tribes
live mostly in Canada now, because they were loyal to the
British during the American Revolution. But at least my
mother's people survive and still have some pride left. Not like
the Indians of New England, who were virtually destroyed by
disease and war.''

There was a long pause before Robin said, ''It's not a very
pretty story. From everything I've read, the Indians were a
strong, healthy, generous people when the Europeans first came.

They gave the English corn, medicines, and land, and we gave them smallpox, typhus, measles, cholera, and Lord knows what else. Eventually, bullets." After another silence, he asked, "Do you hate us too much?"

Maxie was startled; no one had ever asked her such a thing, had even guessed at the buried anger she felt on behalf of her mother's people. Oddly, Robin's perception eased some of that anger. "How could I, without hating myself? After all, I am half-English. More than half, since I spent less of my life with my Mohawk kin." Then, with dryness, "They accept me with more warmth than my English relations did." She shivered, her teeth chattering from a cold that was as much internal as external. Even among the Mohawks, she had not truly belonged.

Hearing the sound, Robin moved closer and pulled her into his arms. She tensed, not wanting passion, but what he was offering was simple solace. "It's getting cold. We'll both be more comfortable closer together," he said quietly. He said no more, just held her, one hand stroking her back.

His warmth and nearness slowly dispelled Maxie's chill. Her head relaxed against his shoulder and she felt the steady beat of his heart and the light touch of his breath stirring her hair. With a shock, Maxie realized just how much she felt at home in Robin's arms.

The last thing she needed was a man as charming and heedless as her father had been. She moved, putting a little more distance between them. "My mother was young and restless, interested in the world that lay beyond the longhouse. Strange though it seems, she and my father fell in love with each other."

"Perhaps not so improbable," Robin suggested, "not if they were both rebelling against the life they were born to."

"I suppose you're right," Maxie said. She had never thought about her parents' marriage in those terms; Robin's comment was very perceptive. "It didn't hurt that my mother was very beautiful. At any rate, when winter ended, Max asked her to come away with him, and she did. I was born a year later. We lived most of the time in Massachusetts, but every year we would visit the longhouse. My mother wanted me to know the language and ways of her people."

"Did your father go with you?"

Maxie nodded, forgetting that he could not see her. "Yes. He told me once that he got on better with the Mohawks than with his own family. Now that I've come to England, I understand why. Indians are a poetic people, and they love stories and games and laughter. My father could quote poetry by the yard, in English and French and Greek. He spoke the Mohawk language well, too. I remember when I was little, sitting with him while he held the whole longhouse spellbound with the *Odyssey*." She chuckled. "Thinking back, he translated it rather freely, but it was still a fine tale."

Her smile faded. "There were two other babies that died soon after birth. My mother died herself when I was nine. Her family offered to take me, but my father refused. He had never found a steady job that suited him, so after Mama died he became a book peddler and took me with him on his journeys."

"So you grew up traveling. Did you enjoy the life?"

"Most of the time." Maxie turned around so that her back nested against Robin's chest. "Books and education are revered in America. Since many of the farms and villages are very isolated, we were always welcome wherever we went."

Too welcome in some cases; there were plenty of men interested in testing the virtue of a half-breed female. Maxie had learned early to defend herself when necessary. "We had a regular route through New England and part of northern New York, where we would always stay with my mother's family for a few days. Besides a regular stock of books, we would also bring special orders to people."

"Fascinating," Robin murmured, linking his arms around her waist. "What was your usual stock?"

"Mostly New Testaments, chapbooks of sermons and songs, pirated editions of English books. But there were other kinds as well. A farmer in Vermont ordered one book of philosophy every year. Then on our next visit, he and my father would discuss the previous year's book. We always stayed two days with Mr. Johnson, and I think it was the high point of his year."

She smiled. "Peddlers like my father did a good business, enough so that publishers put out books just for the traveling bookseller trade. Things like *The Prodigal's Daughter*, which piously decried immoral behavior."

"In great detail no doubt," Robin said with amusement.

"Exactly. How could people know how wicked the behavior was unless it was described?" Maxie chuckled. "We sold a lot of copies of that one, and other novels as well."

Her words made it clear to Robin why Maxie was such an interesting mixture of maturity and innocence. What a strange life she had had, being raised between two cultures, not quite belonging to either, living an unrooted existence not unlike his own. Clearly her father had been well-educated and charming and she had adored him; equally clearly, Max had been feckless to a fault. Robin would be willing to lay odds that Maxie had grown up managing the business end of the bookselling and generally taking care of her erratic parent.

And that strange background had produced this independent young lady who fit so perfectly in his embrace. Holding her had certainly dispersed the damp chill of the night, and Robin was warm in a way that had nothing to do with the temperature. It had been a long time since he had felt this kind of desire— too long.

Robin raised one hand and drew a feather-light finger along the line of Maxie's jaw. "It sounds like an interesting life, but an unsettled one."

Maxie shifted slightly, just enough to imply that further advances on his part would not be welcome. With an internal sigh, Robin invoked his formidable self-control. He had been raised as a gentleman, and even his dubious deeds in the intervening years could not make him forget that gentlemen did not seduce innocents, no matter how warm and lovely they were.

"I used to think that it would be nice to have a real home," Maxie said wistfully. "We spent winters near Boston, staying with a widow whose children had grown. I was always glad to return there and know that we would be sleeping under the same roof for the next four months. Still, being a peddler suited my father. He didn't do very well with regular jobs."

Robin was not surprised to hear that. But at least Maximus Collins seemed an affectionate father, more so than the late, upright Marquess of Wolverton. Reading between the lines, Robin suspected that Maxie had been more fortunate in her parents than he had been in his. "What brought you to England?"

"It had been a long time since my father left, and he wanted to see his family. He wanted me to meet them, too."

Robin felt Maxie tense again in his arms; she had implied rather strongly that her Collins relatives had been less than gracious, and knowing the English gentry, he was not surprised. "Your father died here in England?"

He felt her nod. "In London, two months ago. It wasn't a surprise. His health hadn't been good. In fact, I think that is the real reason he came back: to see England once more before he died." Her voice broke before she continued. "Max was buried at the family estate in Durham. Then, right after I had decided that it was time to return to America, I overheard a conversation between my aunt and uncle."

Maxie went on to recount what they had said, as closely as she could remember the exact words, and how she had decided to go to London to investigate. She even included her fears that her father might have decided to try some genteel extortion, her flat voice refusing any possible sympathy. "That brings us to the present," Maxie finished. "I never expected my uncle to send someone after me, and I still have trouble believing there was foul play involved in Max's death. But I can't imagine why else they would try to hide the truth from me. What do you think?"

"Obviously your uncle is concealing something," Robin agreed, considering the possibilities. There was at least one that did not involve criminal behavior on anyone's part, but he preferred not to speculate about it to Maxie. "Sending Simmons confirms that. I think you are right that your best chance of learning what happened lies in London. But there could be danger for you, and nothing you learn will bring your father back. Is it worth the risk?"

"I must know the truth," she said, her voice hard. "Don't try to persuade me otherwise."

"I wouldn't dream of it," Robin replied mildly. "In the meantime, it is late and we are both tired. Morning will be soon enough to decide how to avoid Simmons and reach London."

"You'll help me?" Maxie asked uncertainly.

"Yes, whether you want me to or not. As I said, I have nothing better to do, and this seems a worthy task." The hay made a soft, fragrant bed, and Robin lay back, pulling Maxie with him. She resisted for a moment, then surrendered to comfort and relaxed, her back against his front. "I thought Indians were a tall people?" he asked, wrapping his arms around her.

"There are exceptions in any group. I'm the smallest person on either side of my family." She yawned, then tucked her cloak over them like a blanket. "This is like bundling."

"Bundling?"

"It's a frontier custom for courting couples." Robin's arm encircled her, his hand fortunately staying in neutral territory where she would not feel compelled to protest. And Maxie really did not want to protest. "A young man will call on his sweetheart, and if it's too far to go home that night, they'll share a bed, both of them wearing clothing to keep matters from getting out of hand. The girl might even be in a bag tied around the neck. More often the bed will be divided by a board down the middle, with jagged teeth on top." She yawned. "In the old days, travelers might bundle with a female of the household if there was a shortage of beds, but that's uncommon now."

"Sounds like a custom the English could practice profitably. Over here, being caught in a garden kissing a girl can lead to a fast and unwelcome marriage." Robin laughed quietly. "I'm sure your countrymen realize that neither bundling board nor clothing will stop determined people."

"Jumping the board is not uncommon," Maxie admitted. "There are a number of bundling ballads. I know one that says, 'Bundlers' clothes are no defense, Unruly horses push the fence.' " She gave a husky chuckle. "Sometimes the wedding takes place sooner than expected. But farms need children, so most people don't think it any great sin." Then, warm and secure for the first time in far too long, she drifted into sleep.

The Marquess of Wolverton was half-asleep and thinking that he should have stopped in Blyth when his carriage creaked to a sudden halt. Jarred to wakefulness, he looked out to find his coachman talking to a burly man who had been trudging along in the dark.

"What seems to be the problem?" Giles asked, climbing out of the carriage.

The walker said, in a heavy London accent, "I was robbed and me 'orse stolen." After a glance at the crest on the carriage door, he asked with a fair stab at humility, "Could yer lordship give me a ride to the next town?"

Giles nodded. "Of course." A snort from behind registered the coachman's disapproval, which the marquess ignored. Admittedly the Londoner looked like a ruffian, but if he had been part of a gang, the other highwaymen would have appeared by now.

When they were settled inside and the carriage was moving again, Giles lit two of the interior lamps. In the soft light, the passenger's dishevelment and facial bruises confirmed the story of an assault.

"That's quite a black eye," the marquess said conversationally, taking a flask of brandy out of a door pocket and offering it to the victim.

"Won't be the first." The man took a swig of the brandy.

"I shouldn't think so. You're a boxer, aren't you?"

"Used to be." The Londoner brightened. "Name's Ned Simmons, but I fought as the Cockney Killer. You see any of me mills?"

"Sorry, I don't follow the Fancy, but a friend of mine won a good sum on you once." The marquess cast his memory back. "For defeating the Game Chicken in seventeen rounds, I believe."

"Nineteen rounds. Aye, that was the best mill of me life."

Observing the massive strength of his passenger, Giles said, "It must have taken several men to bring you down tonight."

The comment was a mistake. Simmons erupted with oaths and excuses, the gist of which was that he had been done in from behind. Giles listened with only moderate interest until the words "yaller-headed fancy man" caught his attention.

"You were assaulted by a blond man?" Startled, the marquess wondered if the unknown villain might be his brother. But why would Robin attack Simmons? Probing for information, Giles remarked, "Must have taken a strapping big fellow to defeat you."

Simmons paused, visibly balancing whether to tell a truth that was unflattering to himself. "Kind of a skinny cove, actually, and talked like a swell. Wouldn't have thought 'e could fight the way 'e did," he said grudgingly. "But 'e wouldn't 'a taken me if 'e 'adn't jumped me from behind, and if his mort 'adn't 'ad a pistol on me."

Giles felt a stab of excitement. It sounded like Robin and the sheltered innocent had been along this road very recently. At a guess, Miss Collins and her ferocious Aunt Desdemona had a great deal in common. "Exactly what happened?"

"Can't say more." Suspicious of the marquess's interest, Simmons scowled and gulped more brandy. "Confidential business."

Giles was considering whether offering a bribe to the bruiser would elicit more information when a horse whickered outside and the carriage creaked to another stop.

Simmons' head snapped up and he peered outside. "It's me 'orse! Bloody prigger probably couldn't ride," he said with satisfaction. " 'Ope he cracked 'is head when the nag threw 'im."

The marquess had never heard of a horse that could throw his brother, particularly not a tired hack like this one. Robin must have turned the beast loose; Giles could only be grateful that his brother hadn't added horse theft to abduction and assault.

The mount was tethered to the carriage and they proceeded to the next town, Worksop. Unfortunately, the Londoner refused to impart more information. Giles guessed that Simmons was the man whom Lord Collingwood had sent after Miss Collins. Rather a rough fellow to send after a gently bred female, though the more he heard, the more the marquess doubted the girl's gentility.

At Simmon's request, Giles left the man off at an inn that was little better than a hedge tavern before stopping at a more comfortable hostelry himself. Over a late supper, he speculated about what was going on, but the only conclusion he reached was that Lady Ross had not yet found the fugitives. With luck, Giles would find them first, at which point he was going to have a lot of questions for his younger brother.

As he went to sleep, Giles found himself thinking not of the fugitives and the potential scandal, but of Lady Ross. She really was a rather splendid Amazon.

The Londoner had worked in this part of the country before, and within an hour of reaching Worksop he had purchased another pistol and recruited assistance for his pursuit.

Later, as he held a piece of raw beef to his eye and gulped pints of local ale, he thought about the blond swell who had jumped him from behind. Collingwood wouldn't like it if his precious niece was returned damaged, but there was nothing to prevent Simmons from breaking her fancy man in half. As he drank his ale and brooded, he looked forward to meeting the fellow in a fair fight.

5

With Robin's lean warmth folded around her, Maxie slept well and dreamed pleasant dreams. Her waking, however, was a good deal less enjoyable. The door squeaked and sunshine flooded in, followed immediately by furious barking. Her eyes flew open to find two huge mastiffs looming less than a yard away, all red mouths and white fangs as they barked hysterically. She froze, knowing that any movement might precipitate an attack, and from the tension she felt in Robin's alert body she knew that his reaction was the same. She had stashed her knife in her knapsack for the night, but the dogs would be on them before the two-foot distance could be covered.

A loud voice bellowed over the dogs' racket. "Hold!" The mastiffs stopped barking, but glittering eyes and hot canine breath demonstrated their eagerness to tear the trespassers limb from limb. An angry farmer appeared in the door, silhouetted against the morning light. "Filthy vagrants," he snarled. "I should turn you over to the magistrate."

Robin replied soothingly, "You could, o' course, but we've done no harm.," Maxie felt him sit up behind her. Interestingly, he was speaking with what seemed to her foreigner's ear a perfect Yorkshire accent. "Beg your pardon for the trespass, sir. We meant to leave early so's not to upset anyone, but we walked a long way yesterday and my wife is in a, um, delicate condition."

Maxie sat up also, giving her companion an indignant glare. With her hair down she couldn't pass as a boy, but did she have to become a pregnant wife? Robin returned a suspiciously cherubic glance, then stood and assisted her up with tender care.

Unimpressed, the farmer, a portly middle-aged chap, scowled at them. "That's none o' my concern, but tramps on my

77

property are. Come out here 'fore I turn the dogs loose.''

"If you have some chores, sir, we'd be happy to do them to pay for our night's lodging," Robin offered.

While her companion was acting the earnest innocent, Maxie began talking to the dogs, murmuring in Iroquois that they were fine brave fellows and she was pleased to make their acquaintance. At first they growled, but she had always gotten on well with dogs. One tail began to wag and the ears unflattened. Still speaking softly, Maxie extended one hand, introducing herself by her Mohawk name, Kanawiosta. After a moment, the dog stepped closer and gave a tentative sniff at her hand, followed by a rasping lick. She smiled and began scratching behind the animal's ears and was rewarded by a lolling, imbecilic doggy grin. The other dog gave a jealous whimper and pressed forward, demanding equal attention.

The farmer was in the middle of a tirade about worthless thieving vagrants, but he broke off as his mastiffs began twining around Maxie's legs, almost knocking her from her feet with their affection. "What the devil . . . ?"

"My wife has a way with animals," Robin said, rather unnecessarily.

"Ain't that the bloody truth," the farmer muttered. "Either one of 'em weighs more 'n she does. Your wife, you say? Where's 'er wedding ring?''

Maxie glanced up, and was amazed to see the transformation Robin had undergone. Usually he looked like a wayward aristocrat, but his whole demeanor had changed. Not only did he speak like a Yorkshireman, his casual elegance had vanished, replaced by the shabby air of a man of modest birth and fortune who had fallen on hard times.

For a moment she stared, thinking that she would be a damned fool if she ever believed a word Robin said; with his acting talents, it would be impossible to ever know if he were telling the truth. Her thoughts must have showed, because his dark-blond brows drew together before he turned his attention back to the farmer.

"Had to sell her ring," Robin said with deep regret. "Times are hard now the war is over. We're on our way to London, where I've hopes of a job."

"You were a soldier?" the farmer said, ignoring the last sentence. "My youngest boy was with the 51st Foot."

"One of the army's best regiments," Robin replied, his handsome face respectful. "I was in the Peninsula myself. Was lucky enough to meet Sir John Moore once, before he was killed at La Coruña."

The farmer's thin mouth worked for a moment. "My boy died at Vitoria. He used to say Colonel Moore was the best, bar none." His hostility had disappeared; unlike Maxie, he didn't notice that Robin had not actually said that he had been a soldier. He went on gruffly, "You folks have a long journey ahead. If you're hungry, you can have a bite 'fore you move on."

It was nearly noon before they were on the road again. In the interim they had been fed a massive breakfast of eggs, sausage, hot muffins, strawberry preserves, and tea. In addition, Robin had charmed the farmer's wife, Mrs. Willoughby, into melting adoration, then repaired the woman's cherished mantel clock, which hadn't run in several years.

While Robin fixed the clock, Maxie was fluttered over, told gruesome stories about the trials of childbearing, especially for "a little bit of a thing" like her, and sent off with extra food and an admonition to take care of herself for the baby's sake. Mrs. Willoughby waved good-bye to the travelers, and the two mastiffs trotted in escort to the edge of Willoughby land, halting with obvious reluctance.

As they headed southwest into rolling hills, Maxie asked, "Aren't you ever ashamed of yourself?"

"Should I be?" Robin asked. His accent reverted to normal— or, more precisely, to the well-bred speech Maxie was used to.

"The truth isn't in you, Lord Robert."

Robin had noticed that Maxie used his title, laced with sarcasm, whenever she disapproved of him. Unrepentant, he pointed out cheerfully, "Our hosts have the satisfaction of doing a good deed, we had an excellent meal, the dogs made a friend, and Mrs. Willoughby's clock now works. Where's the harm in that?"

"But so many lies!"

"Only a few. I did spend time on the Peninsula, and I did

meet Sir John Moore once. I never claimed to have been one of his soldiers or to be an intimate friend." He assumed an anxious expression. "I know why you're out of sorts: it's because you're breeding."

"You, you . . . impossible man," she exclaimed, between exasperation and laughter. "How dare you tell him that I am your pregnant wife!"

Even with her hair hidden away again, Maxie looked quite enchanting, her brown eyes flashing, her neat white teeth ready to take a piece out of his unworthy hide. A distracting but delightful thought. "If you object to the falsehood, we could correct it easily enough, or at least part of it."

Maxie gave a disgusted sniff as she drew over to the edge of the road to avoid a passing farm wagon. "I have received many dishonorable offers in my life, but that has to be the least flattering. And even if I were interested, which I am not, it would be most inconvenient to be breeding while being pursued across the English countryside."

"I was thinking of the other part. We would have to head north to Gretna Green," Robin said thoughtfully as the cart passed them, "since I haven't the price of a special license on me and there aren't any archbishops handy even if I did."

American though she was, Maxie knew what that meant. She scowled. "Your jests are getting worse and worse, Lord Robert. It would serve you right if I accepted that idiotic offer and shackled you for life."

"There are worse fates."

Maxie stopped stock-still in the road to stare at him. Robin stopped also, and it was one of those odd moments when he seemed sincere, something serious and unreadable at the back of his blue eyes. She was startled by the realization that if she agreed, he would turn around and escort her north to Gretna Green, exactly as he said.

The last thing Maxie needed was a charming rogue. What shocked her was that the idea was not without appeal. Robin might be temperamentally unsuited for gainful employment and unreliable in word and deed, but he was also kind and amusing. More than that, he accepted her exactly as she was, breeches, Mohawk blood, and all.

But he was still a rogue. If she ever did marry, she would choose a man who could at least keep a roof overhead. She broke away from his unnerving gaze and resumed walking. "I expect you have three or four wives scattered around Europe already, so that acquiring another would be the merest trifle. Unfortunately I detest crowds, so I will decline the honor."

"No other wives. As you observed, I'm not good at making offers. The only time I did . . ." Robin stopped abruptly.

Driven by irresistible curiosity, Maxie asked, "What happened?"

"The lady declined, of course. A woman of great good sense. Not unlike you." He grinned. "I'm not sure I would want to marry a woman who had the bad judgment to accept me."

Robin was back in the realm of impenetrable whimsy again, though Maxie suspected that some painful truth was buried in his words. Returning to practical matters, she said, "Now that we know that Simmons, and perhaps others, are after us, we had better make some efforts to avoid notice."

She surveyed Robin, his pale-gold hair bright in the sunlight, his chiseled features memorable to any woman who had ever seen him. "No one would look twice at me, but you're rather conspicuous. At the least, you need a hat to cover that hair. And perhaps you should let your beard grow."

"That wouldn't help. It grows out red and makes me even more conspicuous, which is why I shave every day, even when traveling like this. But you're right about the hat, though I doubt I could ever find one with quite the"—he paused to consider—"the character that yours has."

"If you mean that it's frightful, you're right. But it does a good job of obscuring my face and hair." Maxie gave the brim a reflexive tug lower over her eyes while she thought. It wasn't just Robin's face and coloring that were distinctive; his clothing was old but conspicuously well-cut, fitting his lean body with damn-your-eyes elegance. Probably Robin had once had a windfall and spent it all in a tailor's shop; Max had done things like that. "You could trade your present clothing in for something more nondescript at one of those village shops where they will buy, sell, or barter anything."

A pained look crossed Robin's face, but he nodded agreement.

"Very well, the next such shop we come to. But I am not going to accept any clothing that domiciles lower orders of animal life."

"Agreed." Maxie smiled briefly before applying herself to the next pressing question. "Do you have a particular route in mind? We're off the roads covered by my map, and my knowledge of the English countryside is nonexistent, apart from the fact that we must head south."

"London is a hard city to miss. Just as all roads led to Rome in ancient times, in England they all lead to London," Robin said absently. After a pause, he continued, "I have an idea. It wouldn't be the fastest route, but we would be very hard to track. Do you know about the drovers?"

"You mean the men who drive livestock to the cities?"

"Correct. All cities need food to be brought in, and London is so large that it draws supplies from the whole of Britain. Most of the cattle eaten in the city are driven in from Wales and Scotland."

"All the way from Scotland?" Maxie said in disbelief. "It must be very tough beef by the time it arrives."

"The beasts are generally fattened in southern pastures before going to market," Robin explained. "And it isn't just cattle, though they are driven the farthest. Drovers herd sheep, geese, turkeys, even pigs, though not over such great distances."

Diverted, Maxie asked, "How does one drive turkeys?"

"With great difficulty," he said, a twinkle in his eye. "It's quite a sight. At the end of the day, the turkeys will roost in trees for the night, as many as a thousand of them."

Maxie spent a delighted moment envisioning branches bowed with sleeping turkeys. "But what has this to do with us?"

"The drovers' routes are separate from the regular roads, for obvious reasons. They follow the high country when possible, and stay away from toll roads," Robin explained. "Travelers often accompany the drovers, for companionship and safety, sometimes just for the adventure of it."

"I see. If we joined a group of drovers, Simmons might have trouble finding us. Are there any drove roads nearby?"

"I don't know many of them, but there is one south of here, near Nottingham. At this season, we've a good chance of finding drovers on it within a day or so."

Curious, she asked, "Have you traveled with drovers before?"

"Yes, that's why I know this particular trail. I traveled on it one of the times I ran away from home."

Maxie glanced askance, trying to decide if this was one of his fairy tales. Running away had the ring of truth. "You must have been a rare handful for your mother."

"Not in the least," Robin said after a moment. "She took one look at me after my birth and promptly expired from shock."

"I'm sorry." This was a statement that she could not doubt.

"Nowhere near as sorry as my father was," he said dryly. "I look just like her, according to the pictures, and he couldn't see me without flinching."

They were walking under trees now, and Robin's profile was as cool and remote as the shadows. "Why are you telling me this?" Maxie asked softly.

They continued a dozen paces before he replied. "I don't know. Perhaps I weary of being obscure."

In a flash of insight, Maxie realized that Robin's prosaic words signaled a willingness to let her see the contradictions that lay beneath his polished, impenetrable exterior. Like a ball of yarn, he was made of tangled strands of humor and evasion, intelligence and guile, kindness and detachment. Now, for some reason, he was handing her the loose end of the skein, to unwind if she chose. And if she did, what would she find at the heart of his mystery, when all the complex strands had been raveled away?

Before she had even formed the question, Maxie suddenly knew the answer: at the heart of all that wit and skill and charm lay loneliness.

Desdemona gave a sigh of weary exasperation as she climbed out of her carriage in the dusty high street of still another village. It seemed as if she had been crisscrossing the north Midlands forever, seeking traces of her niece and the unprincipled rogue who was taking advantage of her. Her opinion of Lord Robert Andreville was not improved by the fact that the pair was still traveling by foot; one would think that any self-respecting rake would at least hire a postchaise.

There had been no more reports of Lord Robert using force on Maxima, though that might only mean that the girl was cowed and intimidated. The reflection revived Lady Ross's flagging determination. It was surely too late to preserve her niece's virtue, but she might still be able to save Maxima from a disastrous future.

At first the travelers had been easy to follow and she had gotten to within a half-day of them. Then, two days before, she had lost the trail. For whatever reason, whimsy or a realization that they were being pursued, the pair had changed their route or gone to ground. Since then Desdemona had had no success in her search, though she was becoming most adept at asking questions.

The tiny villages, where all strangers were noticed, were the best places for hearing news of her quarry, and the best people to ask were the elderly gentlemen who clubbed together at the local public house. Such worthies could generally describe any person or vehicle who had passed in the last month, and were more than willing to do so in return for a pint. Almost equally good were shopkeepers, who habitually kept an eye on the street for possible trade.

For the fourth time that day, Desdemona entered the only shop in a tiny village. She was a few miles south of Chesterfield in a hamlet called Wingerworth, or something like that, not that it mattered. Like most such places, this one was a jumble of oddments such as bolts of plain fabric and cheap ribbons, needles and thread, pottery jugs, staple foods like salt and sugar, and jars of sweets for children. A ginger cat snored softly on a pile of used clothing, its nose covered by its tail.

At Desdemona's entrance, the stout proprietress hurried forward to greet her, eyes sharpening at the sight of the expensively dressed visitor. "How may I serve you, my lady?"

"I wonder if you might have seen my niece and her husband walk along this road within the last week or so," Desdemona said. "She's dark and quite small, only about five feet tall and dressed like a boy. He's about average height, very blond and good-looking."

"Aye, they were in this very shop not two days ago." The woman's eyes held shrewd appraisal. "The gent traded his clothes for some others. Couldn't understand why; even though it was a mite worn, his own gear was better quality than anything I had. I was that curious."

The faint lift at the end of the speech was clearly a question, so Desdemona went into her prepared story. "It is the most errant nonsense. My niece's husband made some silly wager about walking to London, and my niece decided to accompany him. They haven't been married long and she considered such a journey a great lark. I didn't approve, of course, but it wasn't my place to forbid it."

She gave a doleful sigh. "There would have been no harm in it, except that the girl's father has taken seriously ill. Indeed, his life is despaired of, and my niece's place is at his side. It will be weeks before the couple arrive in London, so we are trying to find her in hopes that she can reach her father before it is too late." Desdemona's voice had a slight quaver; if she told this story many more times, she would believe it herself. "Did my niece or her husband mention anything about the route they were taking from here? Time is of the essence."

"Indeed?" The proprietress raised her brows, her expression delicately conveying that she had grave doubts about the story but wouldn't dream of calling a distinguished visitor a liar.

The next move was Desdemona's. She guessed that a respectable woman like this one might be offended by an outright bribe; something subtler was called for. Desdemona glanced around the crowded shop until she found an appropriate object. "Oh, what wonderful ribbon. I have been searching forever for just that shade of blue." She pulled a spindle of ribbon loose from a mound of fabric trimmings. "Would you consider selling the rest of this color to me for, oh, five pounds?"

"Five guineas and it's yours." The ironic gleam in the shopkeeper's eye left no doubt that she knew what the real transaction was.

"Splendid," Desdemona said heartily, as if she didn't know that the true value of the ribbon was less than a pound.

The shopkeeper wrapped the spindle of ribbon in a piece of creased paper. "Happen that when I was in the back of the shop I heard the young couple talking. Something about being sure the new gear was rugged enough for droving."

"Droving?" Desdemona asked, perplexed.

"Aye, there's a big drove road south of here, above Nottingham. Maybe they intend to travel along with the drovers. Wouldn't be the first Quality to try droving as an adventure."

Desdemona pursed her lips. It made sense, while complicating her search still further. "Could you describe the clothing that my niece's husband is now wearing?"

The proprietress's eye drifted to her customer's hand. Desdemona promptly handed the money over and received a detailed description of the practical country attire that Lord Robert had acquired. Just before leaving, she asked one more question. "Did my niece and her husband seem to be getting on well?"

The shopkeeper shrugged. "Seemed to be on easy terms. Leastwise, they laughed a lot."

Desdemona gave a false smile. "So pleased to hear that. I was afraid the rigors of such primitive travel might put them at odds with each other. That would be a pity when they are newly wed."

As Lady Ross's carriage rumbled off in a cloud of dust, the shopkeeper permitted herself a wide, gap-toothed grin of satisfaction. That pair of young rascals were the most profitable customers she had ever had, and not just because of the long price she'd gotten reselling the gent's fancy London clothes.

The real windfall was what she had earned by talking about them. The big Cockney, who claimed he was looking for two thieves, had been good for three pounds, but it was the nobleman with the crest on his carriage who had tipped her off that something strange was afoot. *He* was looking for two young cousins, off on a lark from university. That time was search was on behalf of a dying granny, not a father. His lordship had been good for five quid. And now here was the lady, looking for her niece and nephew-in-law. Should have held out for ten pounds.

As the shopkeeper lifted her skirt to tuck the five guineas into a purse slung around her waist, she wondered if anyone else would be along. More than that, she wondered what would happen to the fugitives when their pursuers caught up with them. Then she gave a cackle of laughter. She'd put her blunt on the blond man; with a tongue as gilded as his hair, that young fellow could talk his way out of anything.

Maxie sank into the tub of steaming water with a shiver of pleasure so intense that a Puritan minister would have sent her straight to hell. After ten days of hasty, partial washups in cold streams, a real bath was bliss unbounded. This high country inn called the Drover was primitive by most standards, but it was luxury compared to the hedges and barns she and Robin had been sharing.

An occasional lowing sounded outside the inn, where a vast herd of black cattle was at pasture. She and Robin had been lucky to find a band of Welsh drovers so quickly. Men and beasts had been taking a day of rest and forage since they didn't travel on Sundays, but first thing in the morning they would be on their way, Maxie and Robin with them.

When they reached the inn, Maxie had asked, with an embarrassing amount of wistfulness, whether Robin thought their exchequer could stretch to a bath and a real bed for one night. He had given her a mischievous grin, then sought out the innkeeper and put on an impromptu sleight-of-hand show, pulling shillings out of the landlady's ear, causing coins and handkerchiefs to appear and disappear, juggling three empty tankards, and generally dazzling and delighting the staff of the inn. The upshot was that the innkeeper let them have a double room for four pence, dinner and hot bath included. In exchange, Robin would perform again in the taproom later in the evening. Judging by the roars of laughter from below, he was having as much success with the drovers as he had had with the staff.

When the water cooled, Maxie rinsed the soap from her hair and emerged. Even though the tin tub was behind a screen, she preferred to be dry and dressed before Robin returned from his impromptu performance. Earlier in the evening she had washed her linen, as well as the spare set Robin had acquired in Wingerworth, and draped the garments over a chair in front of the tiny coal fire. They had paid two pence extra for the coal, but it was worth it to know there would be clean, dry clothing in the morning. It was all very domestic.

Maxie had dug out her one shift to use as a nightgown, and

it was delightful to feel the whisper of soft muslin against her skin, to have her body unbound by tight clothing. For just this one night, she was going to sleep like a proper female, even though in the morning it would be back to boots and breeches.

After roughly toweling her hair, she sat cross-legged in front of the fire and began the time-consuming business of combing and drying the thick tresses. It was the first time she had been alone since she had met Robin, and her mind turned to London, speculating about what she would find there.

The deceit about her father's death had left her in a cold rage, impatient to know the truth and determined to see justice done if Max had really been murdered. Yet part of her feared learning what had happened. She had loved her father in spite of his failings, but she would not enjoy confronting new evidence of his weaknesses. Beyond that, if Lord Collingwood was the villain, justice would be tempered with regret, though not enough to swerve her from her duty.

It was easier to live in the moment, in this journey that had taken on a curious, suspended-in-time quality. In the past lay grief; in the future lay hard decisions, not just about her father's death, but about what she would do after she learned the truth. At the moment, however, she was content to be journeying with a man who in most ways was a complete stranger to her.

Maxie stopped combing, her hands relaxing on her lap as she reconsidered her last thought. She still knew very few mundane details about Robin, not his name or birthplace or his doubtless dubious ways of earning a living. But she was coming to feel that she understood him, at least a little, in an emotional sense. He had traveled hard roads before he had met her, and under his light words lay old sorrows. He might be too restless and unconventional to find a niche in normal life, but he had his code of honor and she believed that he had indeed decided to accompany her out of concern for her safety, though boredom might have been a stronger motive.

Certainly Robin wasn't escorting her because he desired her, in spite of his bizarre suggestion that they go to Gretna Green. He was so much the perfect gentleman that he must not be interested. Of course she was grateful. Yet, after years of resenting the heavy-handed persuasions of lust-driven males, it was a little disconcerting to be with a man who treated her like a little sister, particularly when the man was so attractive.

Maxie chuckled ruefully and resumed her combing, fluffing the glossy black strands in the fire-warmed air. She was like the cat who was always on the wrong side of the door. She had never liked being an object of lust; now she found that she didn't like being the object of unlustful friendliness either.

Balancing a copper of hot water, Robin rapped discreetly on the bedchamber door to warn Maxie that he was coming, then entered. She looked up from where she sat cross-legged by the fire and he stopped, momentarily stunned by her exotic beauty. While Maxie was always lovely, for the first time since they had met she was also perfectly and exquisitely feminine, and the sight almost overwhelmed him. Her shining black hair tumbled over her shoulders to fall thick and straight almost to her slim waist, and the fire limned her in light, turning the thin fabric of her white shift translucent.

Robin had known that under her shapeless boy's apparel was a trim feminine figure, but the actuality far surpassed his imagination. It also came perilously near wrecking the self-control he had been exercising since they met. Her nearness had kept him in a slow simmer of desire, and he had become accustomed to the sensation, had even enjoyed it. But now the temperature shot up to melting point. It was difficult not to stare at the low neckline of her shift, where a glinting silver chain complemented the smooth dark ivory of her skin, and even more difficult not to cross the room and lift her in his arms and find if his passion might ignite hers.

Blithe and oblivious to his reaction, Maxie remarked, "Judging by the laughter, the drovers liked your performance."

"They were a good audience, ready to be amused. Not like some." Released from his temporary paralysis, Robin crossed to the screened tub and poured in more hot water. This was not the sort of dandified establishment that believed perfectly good water should be thrown out just because it had been used once. Warming it was good enough for guests at the Drover.

"What time will we be leaving in the morning?"

"About seven." Standing behind the screen, Robin removed

his loose brown coat and laid it over the upper edge of the partition. "Drovers move slowly, but they travel for twelve hours or so a day."

Maxie gracefully rose to her feet and began plaiting her hair into a heavy ebony braid. "Since we must rise early, I think I'll go to bed now."

Robin would not have said that she was nervous—that was not a concept that went with Maxie's blade-bright directness—but she avoided his eyes as she walked over to the bed. As he unbuttoned his shirt, he said casually, "Strange, how different it is to be in a bedroom."

She gave him a grateful glance. "You're right. We've slept together in perfect comfort and innocence the last several nights, but for some reason sharing a bed feels different. Not quite right, in a way that I didn't feel before."

It didn't sound as if Maxie was trembling on the brink of uncontrollable passion. Robin knew that he probably had the skill and charm to seduce her if he tried, but seduction was not what he wanted. He had traveled through many nations and levels of society, seen vastly different customs of sexual behavior, and the philosophy he had developed was to wait for a female to give an unmistakable sign that she would welcome an advance from him.

Maxie had shown no such sign. Even if she had, his conscience would have a few things to say about the ethics of making love to a vulnerable young woman who was essentially alone in the world. Under his companion's tough, worldly pragmatism there was a fragile innocence too precious to risk damaging, no matter how great Robin's desire.

He sighed. Usually passion responded to mental strictures rather well, but not where Maxie was concerned. "I'll sleep on the floor," he offered as he removed his shirt and laid it over his coat.

Her glance flickered to his bare shoulders and the portion of his chest visible above the screen, then quickly away. "Nonsense. We have this room because of your performing skills, and I would be a poor sort of person to condemn you to a hard floor because of missishness. I trust you. Besides," she added practically, "it's a large bed."

She would be less trusting if she knew just what thoughts were running through his mind! Robin almost laughed out loud at himself. It was an extremely mixed blessing that women did trust him, because that trust bound him as securely as fetters of steel. "I can't really imagine you as missish."

"You're right." She yawned, then slid under the worn counterpane and closed her eyes. "I think missishness is a luxury for those females who have the money and leisure to indulge in it. A woman who has to make her way in the world hasn't the time for such things."

As he unbuttoned his buckskins, Robin considered Maxie's words and decided that she was right. It was missishness that made girls of his own background so tedious; they would never have the opportunity to develop the trait if they had to worry about day-to-day survival. Not that well-bred girls had to be missish, but they were regrettably encouraged in that direction.

Robin took his time bathing, knowing that it might be a while before the next opportunity. The older he got, the more he appreciated simple creature comforts. When he thought about some of the conditions he had endured in his adventuresome days, he was amazed. Youth had the damnedest ideas of what was amusing.

By the time he had finished, dried himself, and put on the drawers that Maxie had washed and dried for him, his companion was asleep, her breathing soft and even. She looked very young in the flickering firelight, her face unlined and innocent. Young and lovely, but even asleep she had the quality of fierce independence that was so much a part of her.

He climbed in the bed, carefully keeping to his side. Hard to imagine how the Americans managed bundling; even wearing as many layers as an Eskimo wouldn't have been enough to protect Maxie's virtue. What protected her was a fragile thing called trust . . .

Robin would have liked to roll over and put his arms around Maxie as he had other nights, but she was right: being in a bed was different from sleeping in a hedgerow, and much more dangerous. Beds were for making love in a way that barns weren't, not that a pile of hay couldn't be a delightful spot to dally on occasion.

He forced himself to relax, to ignore the knowledge that an alluring female body was just inches away.

On the whole, it would have been easier to sleep with a scorpion.

6

Maxie was not surprised to wake and find herself snuggled against Robin. The room had cooled as the fire died, and her companion's warmth had attracted her like a lodestone. In truth, she admitted to herself, the attraction was more than just warmth. In her travels to isolated New England farmsteads, Maxie had sometimes shared a bed with children or spinsters of the household. Having spent many a night contending with elbows, knees, and semiconscious struggles for the bedcovers, she had learned that most people were not easy to sleep with.

Interestingly, she and Robin appeared to be natural bed-partners in the strictest sense of the term. Through the night they easily shifted and adjusted to each other's movement, always close, always comfortable. More than that, Maxie at least always woke happy and well-refreshed, even when they had slept on the hard cold earth.

It was first light, the sun still below the horizon. They would have to rise soon, but for the moment she was content to drowse with her head on Robin's shoulder and her arm across his bare midriff. Under the counterpane he was wearing drawers, which was the absolute minimum permissible for bundling. In fact, she thought sleepily, it was undoubtedly less than the minimum.

Her braid had loosened and she pushed her hair back over her shoulder, then stroked an idle hand down his chest. Though Robin gave the impression of being lightly built, his shoulders were wide and he was surprisingly well-muscled. Or perhaps not surprising when she recalled how efficiently he had dealt with the much larger Simmons.

Her fingertips found the ridge of an old scar under the fine golden hair. She considered it thoughtfully: from the rough-ness, perhaps a bullet wound. What had Robin been doing to get himself shot? Something nefarious, she feared—he was

fortunate to have survived. Like a cat, he must have multiple
lives. Thank God.

Under her palm, his heart beat with a strong steady rhythm.
The room was now light enough to see his perfectly carved
profile, relaxed and almost boyish in the pearly dawn. He really
was the handsomest man she had ever met, and one of the
kindest, even if he was a rogue. On an impulse of pure affection,
she raised her head to brush his lips with hers. A pity men and
women so seldom managed to be friends. Why couldn't it always
be this simple?

Robin stirred at her light touch and turned toward Maxie,
finding her lips to return the caress. He was even more asleep
than she, and at first the kiss was gentle and undemanding and
thoroughly pleasing. Then it deepened and became more enjoyable yet. Maxie had enough experience to know that kissing
could be a most agreeable pastime, but she had never met anyone
who kissed as well as Robin did. Still another skill he excelled in.

Even as her arm went around his neck, Maxie knew that this
was not a wise idea. The simple enjoyment of closeness was
changing to a languorous desire to continue what they were
beginning. She was half-asleep, Robin even more so, but he
was bound to wake soon at this rate, and it would hardly be
fair to turn suddenly prudish when she had been cooperating
wholeheartedly. Besides, prudishness would be ludicrously out
of place when they had been sleeping together for days.

They were lying on their sides face to face, and Robin's hand
drifted down her back and hip, the thin muslin of her shift an
insubstantial barrier. Then he lifted his hand to cup her breast,
and his expert caress produced a fiery reaction far beyond the
languid sweetness that had carried her this far.

Maxie gasped, needing more breath even as she continued
the endless, intoxicating kiss. Her experience of passion in the
past had not convinced her that it was an activity worth the effort
and potential complications, but she was not unwilling to be
persuaded otherwise. It was said that physical intimacy could
be an exquisite sharing, and she knew beyond doubt that such
would be the case with Robin.

His hand stroked downward, leaving aching desire in its wake,
and she moaned and pressed full-length against him, loving the

way her sensitive breasts crushed against his hard muscular body, feeling the quickening beat of his heart.

Her response fired Robin and he rolled above her, enfolding her with touch as she yearned to melt with welcome. "Ah, Maggie love, it's been so long," he whispered, his lips near her ear, his hand sliding into the thick masses of her hair.

Maxie froze, her amorous mood shattered. "Not Maggie," she said with ice-edged precision. "Maxie."

Her words and changed response jarred Robin to full awareness. His eyes snapped open, so close that she could see shock and something darker in the azure depths. After a paralyzed moment of locked gazes, he flung away from her.

Sitting up on the edge of the bed with his elbows on his knees, Robin buried his head in his hands. His breathing was ragged and his reaction so strong that Maxie knew it was not solely frustrated desire.

"I'm sorry," he said, his voice unsteady. "I did not intend such a thing to happen."

Cold and bereft, Maxie sat up herself, struggling to maintain her composure amid confusion and thwarted passion. "It wasn't your fault. If there is any blame, half belongs to me and half to the bed." She took a deep breath. "Being so cozily bundled up must have taken you back to when this Maggie was your mistress." Then, hating herself for her jealousy, she added caustically, "You wish I were she?"

Robin's wide shoulders were tense, the strained muscles of his back clearly defined under his fair skin. After a long, awkward silence, he spoke from behind his hands. "Some questions shouldn't be asked. And if they are, they shouldn't be answered."

"Shouldn't be, or can't be?" Maxie asked softly. Compassion was winning over frustration and jealousy; she did not know what thoughts were in Robin's mind, but they could not be pleasant.

His hands dropped away from his face. "Can't be, I suppose." He stood and walked to the window to stare out at the misty hills, crossing his arms over his bare chest, his blond hair more silver than gold in the half-light.

"Who is Maggie?" Maxie was curious on her own behalf, but also sensed that he might be better off for speaking.

Without looking at her, Robin said quietly, "We were friends, lovers, partners in crime for many years. But most of all, friends."

Partners in crime? Maxie put the thought away for later consideration. "She died?"

He shook his head. "On the contrary. She is happily married to a man who can give her a great deal more than I."

Maxie felt a spasm of rage at the absent Maggie. A woman who could abandon a man like Robin for another of greater fortune was not worth such bleak longing. She would have said as much if words would have cured Robin of his grief, but even angry, she knew that logic held no sway in matters of the heart. Besides, perhaps Maggie's choice had been made for security more than wealth; as a woman, Maxie could understand that. Life with Robin would have been stimulating and rewarding in a multitude of ways, but doubtless it had lacked stability.

The room was cold. As a gesture of silent comfort, Maxie rose and took Robin's clean shirt over to him, draping it around his shoulders. "Your Maggie was a fool."

Robin finally looked at her, a faint smile on his face. He pulled the shirt on, then wrapped his arm around Maxie's shoulders and tucked her close against his side. "She wasn't, but I appreciate your partisanship."

Maxie's shift provided little warmth in the chilly dawn air, and she slipped her arm around Robin's waist and leaned against him. There was an odd kind of closeness between them, even though the accidental passion of the bed was gone. But as they silently watched the sun inch over the horizon, she realized that something important had changed. Until now, she had appreciated Robin as a friend and had been grateful that he wanted no more.

But now, *she* wanted more. Maxie was no sheltered English miss, raised to bestow her body only on a man who would pay the price of marriage for the privilege of having her. Among her mother's people, an unmarried woman could take a lover without censure; on the frontier farms of America, there was an earthy acceptance of one's physical nature.

Coming from such roots, Maxie recognized and admitted to

herself that she desired Robin. The conflict lay in deciding what to do about it. If she had been a woman of the Six Nations, living in her own home among her own kin, she would have been proud to take a lover, but among the English there was no such simplicity. An unmarried mother would bring disgrace on both herself and her innocent babe, and Maxie had no family to help her raise a child.

Worse, white men had their own strange views of women: they might desire a female and do their utmost to seduce her, then despise her for succumbing to their lures. The outrageous injustice of such thinking had kept Maxie on the boring path of virtue; she had early decided that she would be no man's half-breed conquest.

Now she wanted to throw virtue to the winds, yet caution fettered her desire. It would be impossible to coax a restless man of the road into marriage, a mistake even to try; their backgrounds were too different to imagine a permanent union. Robin was English, surely of good birth, a product of a class-ridden society, while she was a mixed-blood American nurtured on democracy and prickly independence.

More than that, under Robin's insouciant exterior a wall of reserve concealed all but occasional flashes of the real man, while Maxie was direct to a fault. And she wanted a stable home, a goal unlikely to appeal to Robin. That did not mean there could be nothing honest and true between them, but to give in to passion might have disastrous consequences for her future. Maxie would be a fool to hope for promises of love eternal, and a fool to settle for less. More than that, she had no idea if Robin wanted her, even as a dim surrogate for his lost love.

She leaned her head against Robin's shoulder and felt his arm tighten around her as she surrendered to logic. Between now and when they parted in London, she would accept and enjoy what friendship and closeness were between them, and she would be sure to allow no greater intimacy than had occurred so far.

Bleakly she acknowledged that logic would make for cold memories in the future when Robin was gone.

* * *

The carriage pitched and swayed in the rutted track. Desdemona Ross braced herself wearily, avoiding the long-suffering expression of her maid and hoping the vehicle wouldn't break an axle before they reached their destination, an isolated inn called the Drover. It was a regular stop for traveling herds, and doubtless it was more easily reached on four legs than on four wheels.

With a final lurch, the carriage halted and Desdemona let herself out without waiting for her coachman to open the door. For a moment she stood still in the midafternoon sunshine and savored the absence of rocking motion.

The wind blew restlessly over the barren hilltop, rippling the grasses and shaping the clouds overhead. From the general aroma of the area, a herd had stopped recently, and Desdemona wondered if Maxima and Lord Robert had been there. Well, she should soon know.

It had taken time to find exactly where the drovers' route ran, and more time to locate this outpost, which was one of the more accessible spots along the old ridgeway. The inn was built of wind-eroded stone and had served drovers for centuries. Between cattle drives, it survived by acting as tavern to the farmers and laborers scattered through the nearby hills.

Because her own carriage blocked her view, she didn't see the other vehicle until she was halfway to the inn. Desdemona stopped and stared. What the blazes was a rich man's carriage doing in the middle of nowhere? Then she saw the crest on the door and knew the answer. Her jaw tightened. How *dare* he?

She was mentally composing imprecations when the Marquess of Wolverton himself emerged from the inn. The tall powerful figure paused in the doorway for a moment. Then he gave her such a pleasant smile that Desdemona was temporarily nonplussed. The marquess really was a fine figure of a man; pity he had such an unscrupulous younger brother.

The thought firmed her resolve and her jaw. "What brings you here, Lord Wolverton?"

"The same mission you are on, I imagine," he said with undiminished good nature. "Looking for the runaways. Shall I share with you what I have learned?"

Desdemona hesitated, glancing at the inn, then back at the

marquess. Reading her unspoken objection, he said helpfully, "You can always interrogate the innkeeper later to discover if I have been withholding information, but I think it would not be a bad thing if we talked."

Good Lord, was she that transparent? Desdemona sighed; yes, she was. No one ever had any trouble knowing what she thought, which was a drawback for a woman of her political proclivities. "Very well," she said, knowing she sounded ungracious.

The marquess offered his arm as if they were in St. James's Park, then led her away from the inn. The sun felt good on her shoulders, the grass was soft underfoot, her companion's arm a steady support as they picked their way along the spine of the hill. Desdemona could not help thinking that this would have been a pleasant walk under other circumstances.

When they were well out of earshot of servants, Wolverton said, "A group of Welsh drovers went through two days ago, and apparently your niece and my brother joined them here. They will be near Leicester by now." He chuckled. "I'm not positive about the identification of Miss Collins—she has a talent for remaining unnoticed—but someone entertained the drovers with juggling and sleight-of-hand tricks in return for food and lodging, and I'm sure that was Robin. As a boy he was fascinated by legerdemain, and he practiced until he became very good at it."

It made the rogue sound rather likable. Fighting an inclination to soften, Desdemona asked, "Where was my niece while Lord Robert was playing the mountebank?"

"Upstairs taking a bath." The marquess gave her a measuring look. "I hope you won't take offense at the observation, but she had ample opportunity to escape and didn't take it, which supports the conclusion that she is traveling with Robin of her own free will."

Desdemona made a growling noise in her throat.

After a startled moment, Wolverton's lips twitched, as if he was suppressing a smile. "After you called at Wolverhampton, it occurred to me that perhaps my brother had offered Miss Collins his escort to London. It seems the kind of eccentric, honorable thing he would do, and it would mean that she was in no danger. Quite the contrary. It also explains why the young lady has no wish to run away from him."

"Your imagination does you credit, my lord, but I am not convinced." They had come to a boulder on the brink of the hilltop, and she sat down, examining the marquess's face as she did. His firm jaw and open face invited confidence, but she knew better than to succumb to impulse. "Maxima may be too intimidated to try to run away. For all you know, she may have been imprisoned upstairs rather than bathing. I will not be satisfied until I find her myself."

"Somehow, I am not surprised to hear that," her companion murmured, sitting next to her and crossing his long, booted legs.

Desdemona gave him a frigid glance. "What are your intentions if you find the pair of them before I do: to buy your family name free of scandal, whatever the cost?"

She was a tall woman, but he towered over her. "That's one possibility." His slate eyes were steady. "I won't know until the time comes."

"If you are forced to choose between justice and your brother, what will you do?"

The marquess sighed and looked out over the rolling hills. "I sincerely hope it does not come to that." His expression was rueful. "Tell me, Lady Ross, you know your niece. Is she so virtuous that it is unthinkable she could behave with less-than-perfect propriety? She is no green girl, and I've heard that Americans are less rigid in their ways than we are."

Fairly caught by the question, Desdemona could feel color rising in her face. Wolverton watched her quizzically, and she could see the moment when he made an intuitive leap.

"Just how well do you know her?" he asked, his gaze sharpening. "Miss Collins has only been in this country a few months, and you said that you were going to Durham to visit her."

Her color deepened, and Desdemona looked down at her parasol, toying with the carved ivory handle. "We've never met in person," she admitted. "However, we have corresponded extensively."

"Good Lord," Giles exclaimed, "you don't even know the girl?" Exercising heroic restraint, he suggested, "Possibly your concern for her is excessive. From what I've learned in my inquiries, she seems to be an independent and forceful young lady." Quite capable of holding a pistol on that rough fellow named Simmons, for example. "Perhaps you should await your niece in London. I'm sure she will arrive there soon, and you would be spared this tedious searching."

Lady Ross stood and glared down at him. "You will not get rid of me so easily. Perhaps you are right and Maxima will reach London safe and sound. However, I lack your touching faith in your brother's integrity, and I will not be satisfied until I have personally assured myself of my niece's safety."

Giles would have been disappointed if she had been so easily dissuaded from her quest. Looking at her arched, dark-red brows, he found himself asking, "What color hair are you concealing under that very decorous bonnet?"

His words startled her and she stared, her gray eyes wide and disconcerted. The marquess was usually a pattern card of propriety, but now he gave into an irresistible urge to behave improperly. He stood, and very slowly, so that she could stop him if she chose, he untied the ribbons of her deep-brimmed straw bonnet and lifted the hat from her head, exposing a blaze of fiery red hair that coiled around her head in thick braids. Bareheaded she did not seem like a high-minded reformer; if she loosed that hair, she would be a pagan goddess of the hills.

"You see why I cover it up." Lady Ross drew in her breath, her expression vulnerable. "It is not respectable hair. My sister-in-law, Lady Collingwood, was in despair when she brought me out. She said my appearance was better suited to a courtesan than a lady."

Giles smiled and lightly touched one of the shining braids. "I won't comment on that, but your hair is very beautiful." He decided to take another risk and ask a dangerous question. "I have thought from the beginning that your anxieties about your niece seem greater than the situation warrants. Why do you mistrust men so?"

She looked away. Her skin had the milky translucence of the true redhead, and bright tendrils escaped to curl around her long neck. "I don't mistrust all men," she said stiffly. "Fathers and brothers are well enough, and some others."

Husbands were not on the list. Giles said softly, "I recall hearing that your late husband, Sir Gilbert, was an unsteady sort of man."

Her head whipped around, her expression hardening and her

glare reappearing. "You are presumptuous, my lord. If a man with your reputation for rectitude can be so impertinent, it is hardly surprising your younger brother is a thoroughgoing rogue." She snatched her bonnet from his hands and jammed it on her head, covering the bright-red hair . . . and with it her moment of vulnerability.

As she stalked away, her back was very erect in the concealing folds of her cloak. It occurred to Giles that she was a well-armored female, and as he followed, he wondered what she would look like in less-enveloping clothing.

The speed of Lady Ross's retreat to the inn was inhibited by her light slippers and the necessity of picking her way carefully through the grass, and Giles kept up with her easily.

"In two days, the drovers will be going right through the town of Market Harborough," he said, ignoring her irritation. "You can easily get there in time to intercept them."

"Will you be there also, Lord Wolverton?" Her voice was chilly, her face now safely hidden behind the rim of her bonnet.

"Of course. I think it the best possible place to find our fugitives." In spite of his optimistic words, Giles doubted whether Robin could be intercepted unless he wanted to be; elusiveness was surely an important skill for a spy, and his brother could not have survived years in the heart of Napoleon's empire if he wasn't expert at avoiding detection and pursuit.

The marquess chose not to reveal one important fact: Robin's path would take him near the estate of Ruxton, and it was quite possible that he and his companion would go to ground there for a time, particularly if they suspected they were being pursued. If so, Giles might be able to find them there. Given Lady Ross's suspicious nature, it would be a good deal better for all concerned if the marquess was the one to locate the fugitives.

7

Her supper finished, Maxie leaned back against the sun-warmed stone wall in contentment. "Traveling with drovers has only one drawback."

"What's that?" Robin took a bite of his sandwich, which consisted of a slab of ham between two thick pieces of fresh bread, then washed it down with a draft of ale.

"The aroma that is inevitable with several thousand cattle."

Robin grinned. "In another day or two, you'll scarcely notice."

"Probably not." It had been an enjoyable interlude. As Robin had foretold, the drovers traveled steadily, but at an easy pace that would not bring the beasts to market in poor condition. "I like the drovers," she said. "They remind me of the farmers in New England. Not surprising, I suppose. Farmers everywhere must have certain things in common."

"Drovers are usually good steady fellows," Robin agreed. "Because they are entrusted with their neighbors' money, they have to be over thirty, married, and householders to be granted a license."

With more than a hint of disapproval, Maxie commented, "Too many things in England seem to require licenses and regulations."

"The price of civilization." Robin's blue eyes twinkled mischievously. "An Englishman who finds it burdensome can always go to America to find life, liberty, and happiness."

Maxie started to answer in all seriousness before she realized she was being teased. "Individuals have more liberty in America," she said slowly, "but one can pursue happiness anywhere. Unfortunately, no law can assure that one finds it."

Robin gave her a wry glance of acknowledgment, then returned to his sandwich. The herd was settling for the night

103

and most of the drovers were inside the tiny inn having their evening meal. She and Robin had elected to stay outdoors, partly because of the fine weather and partly because Maxie's masquerade as a young lad depended on not being studied too closely, which meant keeping her infernal hat on.

She caught movement from the corner of her eye and turned her head to investigate. "What is going on over there, Robin?"

He glanced up. "That's a portable forge. You may not have noticed, but the cattle are shod so they won't go lame on the long journey. The drovers will either bring a forge of their own or use local blacksmiths to replace cast shoes."

Maxie had indeed not noticed that the cattle were shod; perhaps too much of her attention was on Robin and regretful memories about what hadn't happened at the Drover. Hastily she asked, "How does one shoe a beast with cloven hooves?"

"Two separate pieces are used for each hoof. They're called cues, I believe," he explained. "Most likely the smith has brought along preformed cues and will use them rather than forging new ones. Very little hot iron work is needed that way."

Intrigued, Maxie rose to her feet. "I think I'll go watch."

The massively built drover at the forge was a ruddy-faced fellow with the prototypical Welsh name of Dafydd Jones. He was one of the few drovers who was fluent in English, and Maxie had talked with him occasionally as they followed the herd. Dafydd's Welsh accent was so strong that she could not always understand what he said, but she loved the sound of his mellifluous baritone.

"Care to help me, lad?" he asked cheerfully.

Maxie looked dubiously at the dozen black Welsh cattle grazing placidly nearby, unaware of the indignity about to be visited on them. "I'd be happy to, sir, but I don't know if I'd be much use. I've never worked a forge, nor cued an ox, and I'd think you would be needing someone larger than me."

"All ye need do is hand me the cues and the tools as I ask for them." Dafydd indicated the waiting supplies, then lifted a coil of rope and deftly threw it over a beast that had been separated out by one of the short-legged herd dogs. When the loop had settled nearly to the ground, Dafydd pulled it tight around the bullock's legs and jerked. The heavy animal fell to the ground with a bellow, more surprised than angry.

Maxie handed a preformed metal piece to the drover, then passed the nails one at a time. The bullock thrashed, but Dafydd's skill and great strength made controlling the animal's struggles look effortless. Quickly the Welshman nailed the cue in place, bending the ends of the nails over and pounding them into the edge of the hoof. Only one shoe needed replacement on this particular animal, so it was now released to scramble up and make its way to quieter pasture, its tasseled black tail twitching indignantly.

The rest of the waiting cattle were shoed with equal ease, and Maxie found it a rare treat to watch such an expert at work. Behind them in the inn, male voices were raised in Welsh song, a musical accompaniment to the setting sun. Maxie continued to pass cues and nails and hammer as needed, thinking how long the daylight lasted here. Strange to think how much farther north she was than in her native land, even though the English winters were so much milder.

His supper finished, Robin ambled over to watch, careful to keep out of the way of the workers. Even though her back was to him, Maxie had a prickly awareness of his presence. She was going to miss him when they parted, she surely was.

The cuing was going swiftly and there would be just enough light left to finish the task. Then the thirteenth and last animal proved as unlucky as its number. It was a nervous beast, white rims showing around the dark eyes and only the attentions of the dogs keeping it from bolting. Dafydd tossed the rope and drew the bullock's legs together so that it fell with a heavy thud and a more than usually angry bellow.

Disaster struck when the Welshman moved in to begin the shoeing. Almost too quickly for the eye to follow, the bullock broke free of its bonds and exploded to its feet, swinging its massive head and bellowing furiously. One of the sharp horns gored Dafydd in the ribs, ripping through his smock and knocking him to the ground beneath the raging ironclad hooves. The black Welsh are small as cattle go, but they are large and heavy enough to pound a man to a bloody rag in seconds.

Appalled, Maxie froze as she considered what to do. All the other drovers were in the inn, and a scream would never be heard over the ale-fueled singing, taking place there. If she tried

to get Dafydd away by herself, the bullock could easily gore
and trample her too.

She had forgotten Robin. Even while the alternatives were
flashing through her mind, he bolted past her and grabbed the
beast's horns from behind its head. Using all his wiry strength,
he began twisting the bullock's head sideways, trying to wrestle
it to the ground. As the strain on its neck forced the animal off-
balance, Robin called urgently, "Maxie, get him out of the
way!"

A flailing hoof knocked her hat off and grazed her shoulder
as she stooped to grab the Welshman under his shoulders. Maxie
was very strong for a woman of her petite size, and fear also
lent power as she dragged Dafydd across the rough ground. His
limp weight strained her arms, but she didn't stop until the forge
was between them and the thrashing bullock.

When she was behind that slight barrier, she looked up to
see a perilous tableau. Robin's hands gripped the bullock's
straight horns and his arms were rigid with effort as he kept
the furious bullock pinned to the ground. It bellowed con-
tinuously and heaved against the human, but was unable to use
its brute strength effectively.

Maxie was awed by the sheer power and mastery visible in
Robin's straining body. Yet, though he was temporarily in
control, the situation was very much like having a tiger by the
tail. She feared that he would be unable to escape without injury.

She was about to run to the inn for help when Robin found
enough breath to give a series of piercing whistles that
summoned several of the dogs. Then he released the bullock.
As both man and beast scrambled to their feet, the enraged
animal tried to gore him, but Robin skillfully danced out of
range.

Before the bullock could try again, the short-legged herd dogs
closed in, so low to the ground that they dodged under the
bullock's kicks. Harrying the animal's fetlocks, they drove it
back to the main herd, where it abruptly forgot its rage and
began to graze again.

Breathing hard and more than a little disheveled, Robin joined
Maxie. "How is Mr. Jones?"

The drover had been stirring and he sat up as Robin knelt

beside him, shaking his head. After what sounded like Welsh oaths, Dafydd muttered in English, "I'll not be sorry to see that beast turned into roast beef." Muddy hoofprints showed on his trouser leg where the bullock had trampled him. "Mayhap in the future I'll only shoe geese."

With Robin and Maxie's help the Welshman was able to get to his feet with no more than a few winces. "There's nought broken, thanks to you two."

While Dafydd gingerly felt his ribs, Robin retrieved the rope that the drover had been using. After investigation, he held up a ragged end. "It looks like the rope was already frayed and it broke when the bullock began kicking."

Dafydd examined the rope end. "Aye. Easy to be careless, but one such mistake can kill a man. I owe you two a draft of ale and then some." His gaze fell on Maxie and a smile quirked. "You'd best put your hat back on, lass."

Maxie flushed, suddenly remembering, and recovered her hat. Her hand was trembling with the aftereffects of danger as she pulled the brim down over her face.

"Whatever your reason for pretending you're a lad, your secret is safe with me," Dafydd assured her. "May I buy you some ale now?"

"Perhaps for Robin." She glanced at her companion. "I wouldn't mind a cup of tea."

"I wouldn't object to the ale," Robin said, "but I think both of us would prefer that no one else learn of this. It was a minor accident, after all."

"I wouldn't have thought it minor if the beast had killed me," Dafydd said dryly. "But if you have reason not to draw attention to yourselves, I'll not mention it to the others." Then he dug into a pocket and handed two coins to Maxie.

When she tried to give the money back, the Welshman laughed. "That's not for saving me. Such things can't be paid for, and if they could, I'd put a higher value on my life than two shillings. This is what I was going to give you for helping me with the cuing."

Doubtless the amount was greater than if there had been no accident, but Maxie smiled acceptance. "Thank you."

Dafydd disappeared into the noisy inn, sending out a maid

with a tankard of ale and a steaming mug of tea. Maxie and Robin made their way to the spot by a hedgerow where they had left their packs and blankets. A dozen or so other travelers were also bedding down outside, but their hedgerow was separate enough for privacy. Though it was almost full dark now, there was enough moonlight to see the pale shine of Robin's hair.

"Have you wrestled bullocks often?" Maxie asked as she sat on her blanket and drank a mouthful of tea.

"This was the first time, but I've seen others do it," Robin replied. "I also learned at a tender age that I would never be large enough to overpower others by sheer size, so I had best learn how to fight intelligently. The trick is not to let your opponent use his strength against you. Keep him off-balance. If possible, turn his own strength against him."

"I see." Maxie considered. "You used the same principles with the bullock that you did with Simmons."

"There was more than a passing resemblance between them," her companion said with amusement.

Remembering Simmons' massive neck and shoulders, Maxie had to agree. As she rubbed absently at the bruise the bullock's hoof had left on her shoulder, another question occurred to her. "When Mr. Jones mentioned shoeing geese, did he mean that literally or metaphorically?"

"Believe it or not, that was literal." With a rustle of fabric Robin stretched out on his simple bed. "When geese are going to be herded long distances, they are first driven through tar, then through something like sawdust or crushed oyster shells so that pads form and their feet won't wear out before they reach their destination."

"It certainly sounds safer than shoeing oxen." Maxie took a deep draft of her tea, which had been liberally laced with milk and sugar. "Robin, you are an absolute gold mine of irrelevant information. How do you keep it all straight?"

"But it's not irrelevant," he protested. "One can never tell when one will need to shoe a goose."

"Or summon a herd dog," Maxie murmured. "I gather that you learned the signals on the off chance you might someday need them." If Robin was engaged in a criminal life, such constant observation must be what kept him alive and free, but that was a remark she kept to herself.

They drank in companionable silence for a while. Then Robin asked, "Do you never drink anything with alcohol in it?"

"Never." That sounded too terse, so she added, "I decided when I was twelve that alcohol was a habit I was better off without."

"You were unusually clear-sighted for your age, or for any age," he said quietly. "It's a rare person who knows what is good for him. Or her."

Maxie had sometimes been ridiculed for her abstinence, but she should have guessed Robin would understand, or at least accept. "My mother's people often have trouble with alcohol," she explained. "In fact, alcohol helped inspire a new religious movement among the Iroquois."

After a thoughtful silence, Robin asked, "Is that good or bad?"

"Good. Ganeodiyo of the Seneca, called Handsome Lake in English, was an old man, dying of drink, among other things. Then he had a vision, saying that firewater was for the white man and that the Great Spirit forbade his people to drink it.

"The next day Ganeodiyo was healed of his illness and he began preaching of his revelations, of faithfulness in marriage, of love among families, of children's obedience to their elders." Maxie spoke slowly, less aware of the present than of what she had been told by her mother and her mother's kin. "He said, 'Life is uncertain, therefore, while we live, let us love one another. Let us sympathize always with the suffering and the needy. Let us always rejoice with those who are glad.' He died just last year, at a great age."

Maxie's throat tightened and she stopped abruptly. She had never spoken of such things to a white man, had never dreamed that she would. For the moment she was not Maxima Collins but Kanawiosta, and if Robin denigrated her words, she would never forgive him.

Instead, he said softly, "Truly Ganeodiyo was a great teacher, for that is a message that all of the world's great teachers have given." He pronounced the Seneca name exactly as Maxie had.

Then, with his uncanny perception, he added, "I am honored that you speak of him to me."

"I am amazed that I did," Maxie admitted with more candor than tact. "You are diabolically easy to talk to."

"I hope that is a compliment." After a pause, he continued with a questioning lift to his voice, "I notice that you wear a silver cross."

"It was my mother's. She was a Christian, but did not believe that invalidated the beliefs of her own people." Maxie sighed, instinctively touching the cross beneath her worn shirt. "My mother believed that survival lay in blending the best of her own people's traditions with the best of the white man's culture. Perhaps that is one reason she married an Englishman."

"I see where you inherited your wisdom." After a stretch of peaceable silence, Robin continued, "I imagine that you have a Mohawk name as well as the English one."

After only a moment's hesitation, Maxie replied, "To my mother's kin, I am Kanawiosta."

"Kanawiosta." The name rippled from his tongue. Except for her father, Robin was the only white man ever to speak it. "Does it have a particular meaning?"

She shook her head in the darkness. "Nothing that is easily defined. It implies flowing water, and also improvement, making something better."

"Flowing water," he said thoughtfully. "It suits you."

Maxie laughed. "Don't romanticize my name. It could just as easily be translated as Swamp Beautifier. How many English folk know the original meanings of their names?"

He chuckled. "Robert means 'of shining fame.' "

"But you prefer Robin, as in Robin Hood." Maxie set the empty mug several feet away from her, to be returned to the inn in the morning. Did the fact that he knew what Robert meant imply that it really was his name? Given his magpie assortment of knowledge, it proved nothing. She yawned, then rolled herself in her blankets. "If I'm going to keep losing my blasted hat, perhaps I should cut my hair."

"Don't do that," Robin said swiftly. "We'll be in London soon. It would be a great pity to cut your hair when it took so long to grow it."

Maxie was not displeased that he seemed to like her hair. Less pleasing was the space between their blankets. The inns the drovers stopped at were tiny, and the few rooms available were reserved for the chief drovers. Since the others who accompanied the drive slept scattered about outside, discretion kept Maxie and Robin a respectable distance apart.

"I'll just have to hang on to my hat better." After another yawn, she whispered, "Good night."

Maxie was acutely aware that Robin was both too near for safety and too far for comfort. Doubtless it was fortunate that there was no room at the inn, since sharing a real bed had proved hazardous. The real danger lay in the fact that this was one hazard she wasn't sure she wanted to avoid . . . Half asleep, she laid a tentative hand on the grass between her and Robin.

To her great pleasure, he reached out to cover her hand with his, his warm fingers interlacing with hers. She relaxed, knowing she would sleep better because they were touching.

Robin woke at first light. The predawn air was damply chill, and to his unsurprised amusement, he found that he and Maxie had gravitated together during the night and she was tucked under his arm. She had an innocent sensuality, a quality of being comfortable with her body, that he had never seen in a European woman. She also had intelligence and courage.

What Maxie did not have was any obvious interest in acquiring a mate. Her initial distrust of Robin seemed to have turned to liking, perhaps even occasional approval, but he was afraid that after she had investigated her father's death, she would walk away from him like a cat, without looking back.

His arm tightened around her as he realized how reluctant he would be to see her go. Maxie had revitalized him; he felt as if he had shed several decades of weariness in the last week. For the first time he squarely faced the thought of marriage. He was not interested in a flirtation or an affair, and certainly not in a platonic friendship. What he wanted was a companion with whom he could laugh and play and make love. Once he had had that with Maggie, until, because of whatever mysterious lack in him, she had stepped back from intimacy.

It was more than unfair to compare Maggie and the young

woman in his arms; it was impossible. Yet both had generous
and valiant spirits, and perhaps in time he might find the sort
of closeness with Maxie that he had known with Maggie. It
would take time for trust and openness to grow, but he believed
there were deep similarities between him and Maxie, in spite
of the many superficial differences.

One way they resembled each other was in their practiced
defenses. But day by day, each was revealing more to the other.
It was promising that Maxie had spoken of matters sacred to
her mother's people. As for Robin himself, more than once he
had found himself saying things he had not intended, things that
made him vulnerable in uncomfortable ways.

He smiled ruefully. He was willing to put up with the discomfort in the hope that something lasting would come of it,
but he had no idea if Maxie had any interest in that outcome.

Her exotically lovely face lay close to his, and Robin
succumbed to temptation and lightly kissed her on the end of
her elegant little nose. At his touch, her eyes opened and she
regarded him with an unblinking brown gaze. "Which of us
moved during the night?" she asked softly.

Robin grinned. "We both did, I think."

"People will be waking soon. We should get up, or at least
retreat a few feet."

"Quite right," Robin agreed, but he didn't release her, and
she made no attempt to move away.

They lay together for a few more minutes, until the sound
of other voices was heard as some of the drovers began stirring.
Regretfully Robin removed his arm from Maxie. "If anyone
notices that you are a female, it will do your reputation no
good."

She smiled mischievously and sat up. "And if they think I
am male, it will do both our reputations even less good."

Robin laughed out loud as he stood and stretched the kinks
from his muscles. The days ahead seemed full of promise, and
he looked forward to them as he hadn't look forward to anything
in many years.

Simmons scrutinized the wide square, then nodded with
satisfaction. His inquiries had established that the habits of the

drovers were invariable, and at this time tomorrow the whole herd of Welsh blacks and their attendants and followers would come pouring through this square on their way to the cattle market where some of the beasts would be sold. In theory his quarry might slip away during the herd's passage through the town, but Simmons would wager a pretty penny that the fugitives would be staying close in the hopes of passing undetected in the press of cattle and drovers.

He would also wager that the blond popinjay wouldn't be expecting to find Simmons waiting here at Market Harborough. The Londoner smiled evilly. Ned Simmons was the best at what he did, and no chit of a girl and her fancy man would get by him. Just in case, his men would be posted elsewhere in the town, but he himself was taking the most likely position. He couldn't wait to see the expression on the blond man's face when the fellow realized there would be no tricks or attacks from behind this time.

8

Without removing her gaze from the spectacle beneath her, Desdemona Ross finished her fourth cup of tea. This chamber at the front of the Three Swans had already been bespoken the night before, but she had used a combination of gold and bullying to secure it for herself. When the cattle first began flowing by in early morning, she had been tense with anticipation as she watched from her vantage spot.

Now, an interminable length of time later, she was weary, bored, and fearful that her vigil was doomed to failure. She had seen more black oxen than she had dreamed existed, a goodly number of Welsh drovers in smocks and trousers and long wool stockings, and a handful of people traveling with the drive. She had not, however, seen anyone who might be Maxima Collins.

Setting her cup down, she wondered where the Marquess of Wolverton was. She had no doubt that he was near and watching as carefully as she. It was even possible that he had already intercepted their quarry, which would explain why Desdemona herself had had no success. If so, she thought Maxima would be in good hands; the marquess's first priority might be the protection of the Andreville name, but he was an honorable man.

The end of the cattle drive was in sight, and bringing up the rear were three people. With a gasp, Desdemona leaned forward, squinting to confirm what she had glimpsed. One of the three was a drover, one a light-footed man of middle height, and the third was a very small figure dressed like a boy and wearing a disreputable hat that had been described time and time again.

With a flare of excitement, Desdemona raced for the stairs of the inn.

A cattle drive was not quiet in a country lane, but it was far noisier when the clattering hooves and aggrieved lowing were confined between buildings. As the unruly river of black oxen poured through Market Harborough, Maxie and Robin walked at the tail of the drive, along with Dafydd Jones and a cluster of beasts with missing shoes or other problems that slowed their pace. Dafydd was in charge of the laggards, with two dogs to prevent the oxen from wandering down side lanes. Most of the citizens of Market Harborough had prudently withdrawn behind doors to wait for the drive to pass, a progress that had taken much of the morning and was leaving the high street in dire need of a cleaning.

This was the first town they had gone through since joining the drive, and Maxie had a prickly feeling of vulnerability after the openness of the ridgeways. Still, there had been no sign of Simmons, and it was hard to believe that he still pursued her.

She should have trusted intuition over logic. They were nearing the town's central square when a familiar voice triumphantly roared, "There they are!"

Not thirty feet away, Simmons emerged from the shelter of a doorway with a look of savage delight on his battered face, another bruiser at his side. As Robin swore under his breath, Maxie whirled, only to see two more men coming from behind them. They were trapped along a stretch of road with no turnoffs, only sheer, blank-faced buildings. With a sick feeling in her stomach, Maxie knew that there was small chance of fighting free against such odds.

Then an ear-shattering whistle split the air. Dafydd Jones had summed the situation up with a speed of thought at odds with his slow-moving exterior, and his whistle commanded the dogs to turn the group of bullocks and bring them back along the high street at speed. A well-trained herd dog does not question a command, no matter how contrary to custom, and within seconds the street was blocked by churning, confused bullocks. Harried by the sharp nips of the dogs, some beasts turned quickly and were persuaded to move faster while others milled and bellowed. The overall effect was pandemonium.

A mass of turbulent, blaring oxen now separated Maxie and Robin from the approaching ruffians. Robin called to the drover,

"Many thanks!" Then he grabbed Maxie's arm and turned her back in the direction from which they had come.

Dafydd waved a hand and yelled, "Luck to you!"

Maxie caught a last glimpse of Simmons' furious face as the man tried to fight his way through the turmoil. Then she concentrated on escape. The cattle kept a small distance away from the faces of the buildings, so it was possible to force a passage along the edge of the street. The bullocks' bulk made them a danger, and Maxie felt small and fragile as they jostled by, but the beasts were not usually aggressive, and as long as she and Robin kept on their feet and stayed by the walls, they were safe enough.

After a chaotic interval of battling along the street, they came to the mouth of an alley and darted inside. Robin paused, touching her shoulder lightly. "How are you faring?"

"Bruised but unbowed." Maxie dragged a dusty hand across her forehead. "Do you know your way around Market Harborough?"

"No, but we're about to learn." Robin accompanied his words with a flashing smile of approval and encouragement.

Maxie felt a burst of irrational exuberance. Robin might be a rogue, but under these circumstances, she couldn't imagine a better companion. To be honest, she couldn't imagine a better companion for any circumstances.

Desdemona reached street level just as the steady stream of oxen disintegrated into chaos. Aghast, she stared into the milling, bellowing mass. Oxen were much larger close up than they appeared from above, and their horns a great deal sharper.

Shouting sounded over the general clamor and she glanced down the street to see the backs of two rough-looking men who were forcing their way through the cattle. Grimly Desdemona decided that if they could do it, so could she, and she stepped out onto the street. From behind her came a horrified cry from the owner of the Three Swans, doubtless thinking that having a guest overrun by oxen would be bad for business. She ignored him and flattened herself against the front wall of the inn and began edging her way up the high street, thinking that she should have brought a groom and that she really had not dressed properly for a cattle riot.

Tenaciously she worked her way back to where she judged
Maxima had been. In the distance she saw the two ruffians
disappear down an alley, but there was no sign of her niece.
Furious with exasperation, she rose on her toes and shaded her
eyes, trying to see what was going on.

Her movement was a serious mistake. A horn from one of
the crowding bullocks caught the sleeve of her pelisse and
dragged her sideways, and when Desdemona tried to regain her
balance, she became tangled in her skirts. Then the fabric of
her pelisse ripped away entirely and she fell, sprawling across
the hard cobblestones. Horrified, she looked up to see the iron
shod hooves of a bullock descending on her.

Maxie and Robin followed the alley until it emptied into
another street that paralleled the high. Just as they turned into
it, a shout echoed behind them, proof that Simmons and his
companions had caught up in time to see which way they fled.

The new thoroughfare was busy with traffic displaced from
the high street, and they zigzagged their way around incurious
citizens. The narrow way was blocked by a massive dray
unloading goods at the rear of a shop, and without pause Maxie
dropped to the ground to scramble under it, Robin right behind
her.

They regained their feet on the other side of the dray to find
a draper's shop directly in front of them. After dusting his knees,
Robin led the way inside and gave the woman behind the counter
a smile of paralyzing charm. "Sorry to disturb you, but we have
urgent need of your back door."

As the dazzled female made confused sounds, Robin crossed
the sales room and opened the only other door. Half-expecting
to have a bolt of fabric hurled into her back, Maxie hastened
after him into a corridor that led to a kitchen at the back of the
building. Robin gave the startled cook another disabling smile
and they walked through into the garden. The iron gate at the
bottom was unlatched and opened into another alley.

Like many old towns, this one had grown up on a twisted
medieval street plan, and the internal compass in Maxie's brain
was uneasily aware that their route was starting to double back.
Nonetheless, they were almost clear and away when bad luck
gave one of Simmons' men a glimpse of them.

The man shouted, and even with the length of an alley between them, they could hear the sounds of other feet coming to join in the pursuit. Maxie and Robin began to run through the tangle of alleys, more agile than their pursuers, but the choice of routes was limited.

The next turn took them up a steeply angled lane where empty wooden casks were piled behind a tavern, redolent with the tang of hops. Struck by inspiration, Maxie stopped to tip one onto its side, then push it down the sloping ground. With a breathless gust of laughter, Robin joined her, and within a minute six casks were crashing down on their pursuers, making hollow booming noises as they collided with the walls and one another. From the abruptly curtailed yelp of protest, at least one cask hit a ruffian, and Maxie and Robin gained a precious few yards.

If it had been dark, they would have lost the hunters by now, but in daylight the advantage was to Simmons. Maxie's lungs burned with strain, but she continued running, grateful for the active life that gave her stamina. Robin was paying her the compliment of assuming she was equal to what was necessary, and she was determined not to falter.

The alley they were in now made a sharp turn to the right, and when they swung around the corner, Maxie gasped with dismay. The lane ended in a brick wall, well over the height of a man's head, and there was no other way out.

Desdemona was rolled onto her side by the grazing hooves of the first bullock, and her breath knocked from her lungs. Even as she struggled to rise, she knew that her attempt would fail and that in another few moments she would be past caring.

Then strong arms seized her and lifted her clear of the street to the relative safety of a shallow doorway. She was shaking violently and she came to rest with her face pressed into the shoulder of a wool coat, but even so she knew that it was Wolverton who had rescued her and that it was his protective embrace that surrounded and guarded her from the buffeting of the oxen. Fingers gripping his lapels, she went into a paroxysm of coughing from the dust she had inhaled when lying on the ground. With resigned self-mockery she realized that a female could hardly appear at worse advantage than she did at the moment.

With a small shock, Desdemona realized that it was the first time she had wanted a man to admire her since she was eighteen. It was an outrageous and unwelcome thought, but even so, she did not push away from Wolverton; his arms were too welcome.

The marquess's amused baritone sounded in her ear. "Did anyone ever tell you that your courage greatly exceeds your common sense?"

A bubble of laughter escaped her. "Yes. Frequently."

Behind them the noise and turbulence of the cattle was diminishing, and with regret Desdemona stepped away from Lord Wolverton. "I'm quaking like a blancmange," she said unsteadily.

"A perfectly normal reaction. You had a narrow escape."

"I'm in your debt, my lord. You might have been trampled yourself." Desdemona's bonnet lay smashed in the street, and with a trembling hand she pushed at her hair, which was falling around her shoulders.

He gave a deprecating shrug. "I spend a fair amount of time with cattle and am used to their ways."

Even though most of the British aristocracy derived their fortunes from the land, few of the men Desdemona knew in London would so casually confess to being farmers. Perhaps she spent too much time in London.

Behind them, the now-orderly oxen had settled down and resumed their progress to market. The Welsh drover whom Desdemona had seen earlier came up, concern on his weathered face. "I hope you took no harm, ma'am. I'd not forgive myself if you'd been injured."

"I'm fine," she reassured him. "It was foolish of me to come into the street when the drive was going through."

As the drover started to move away, Wolverton asked, "Why did you turn the cattle like that? It was dangerous."

The drover stopped, an opaque expression in his eyes. " 'Twas a mistake. The dogs misunderstood the command."

Still pleasantly but with a hint of steel, the marquess said, "They say that when a drive is over, the herd dogs make their own way home all the way from southern England to Wales or Scotland while their masters return by coach. Hard to believe that dogs so intelligent would misunderstand the whistle."

"You've caught me out." The Welshman's voice was

properly abashed, but there was a gleam in his eyes. "The problem was not the dogs' lack of wit, but mine. I whistled the wrong command, and the dogs obeyed. Lucky no damage was done."

"I'm sure you will tell me that turning the cattle had nothing to do with the two people who were with you, and the men who were after them," Wolverton said dryly.

"Aye, nought to do with them." The Welshman touched the brim of his hat with two fingers. "I must look to my beasts now. Good day to you and the lady." Then he followed his oxen down the high street.

Desdemona stared after the drover. "You mean he did that deliberately to help your brother and my niece escape?"

"Undoubtedly. That was definitely Robin, though I didn't see much of his companion under that dreadful hat."

"Who were the ruffians you mentioned?" Desdemona frowned, trying to understand what had happened.

Wolverton tucked her hand under his arm and headed toward the Three Swans. "I'll explain over lunch."

Desdemona opened her mouth to disagree on general principles, then closed it again. She found that she didn't really want to protest.

Robin was undaunted by the sight of the dead-end alley. "We're not at a standstill yet."

He sprinted down the alley, his pace lengthening, and a stride from the brick wall he used his momentum to hurl himself upward, his hands just barely catching and holding on the upper edge. After swinging lithely onto the top of the wall, he unslung his knapsack and lowered it strap-first.

Maxie grabbed the strap, which strained under her weight but held. As Robin lifted, she walked up the wall and in a moment she was next to him. He grinned, one hand steadying her elbow as she caught her balance. "It's clear you didn't spend your childhood on anything as useless as embroidery."

Maxie grinned back. "It was a point of pride for me to outrun, outswim, and outclimb all of my Mohawk cousins."

Their pursuers were almost to the foot of the brick wall. Robin gave them a jaunty wave, then without further ado he and Maxie lowered themselves down the far side.

The high brick wall had concealed a well-tended garden behind a town house. Robin dropped to the ground, then caught Maxie's waist with strong hands to bring her gently down. To her surprise, the first thing she saw was an archery target with bow and arrows lying beside it in the grass, as if someone had gone inside for a cup of tea and would be back momentarily.

Robin was starting to cross the garden when she said, "Just a moment." Picking up the bow, she nocked an arrow and waited.

After angry muttering and scuffling sounds on the other side of the wall, one of their pursuers heaved gracelessly into view on the shoulders of one of his mates. Taking her time, Maxie drew the bow, then sent her arrow through the man's hat. Howling, he disappeared from view.

"Well done!" Robin's voice was full of laughing admiration.

Maxie lay the bow down, not without a certain smugness. Being a savage definitely had its uses.

"Gawd a'mighty, did you see what this little mort did?" Simmons' cohort retrieved his arrow-struck hat, his face ashen under its habitual grime. "I coulda been killed!"

"If she wanted to kill you, she'd've done it," Simmons said brusquely. Even as he let loose a string of oaths that should have scorched the whitewash on the alley walls, the Londoner had to admit to himself that the two fugitives were worthy game.

Ignoring the profanity, one of his men said, "I'm not goin' over that wall after 'em."

Simmons broke off. He knew Market Harborough well, and he should be using that knowledge instead of wasting time. "No need, there's a way around. If we hurry, we should be able to catch them. Now move your bloody backsides!"

As Maxie and Robin crossed the garden, an angry complaint at the trespass came from a window of the house.

"Try not to step on any flowers," Robin warned. "Hell hath no fury like an English gardener whose roses have been profaned."

Maxie felt like giggling but lacked the breath. The far wall of the garden had espaliered fruit trees growing against it, the branches trained into improbable lattices, tiny green peaches visible among the leaves. The fruit trees made an excellent ladder, and before anyone could come outside to give chase, they were over the wall and down the other side on a quiet street.

"We're allowed to profane fruit trees?"

"A grievous crime, but not so bad as injuring roses," Robin assured her. His face grew serious. "The pursuit is amazingly tenacious. Your uncle must want you back a great deal."

"So it seems," Maxie agreed. Her voice faltered. "I'm sorry to have involved you in this. It is more than you bargained for when you offered your escort."

He smiled, his blue eyes warm and intimate. "I didn't offer my escort, I forced it on you. And I'm not sorry at all." Then, more briskly, "A canal runs north from Market Harborough to Leicester, and I think we should follow the towpath. It's less likely to be watched than one of the roads."

"Do you really think all of the roads are watched?" Maxie exclaimed. "Simmons would have to have a small army."

Robin shrugged, then headed left. "Perhaps the roads are safe, but when in doubt, assume the worst."

That made sense; Maxie did not doubt that Robin's experience of being pursued greatly exceeded her own. She fell into step beside him. In the middle distance were several large buildings that looked like warehouses, and probably the canal was on the other side. This part of town was empty of traffic, and she quickened her pace, wanting to be away.

They had gone no more than two hundred yards when Simmons came pounding out of a lane in front of them, a smile of wicked satisfaction on his face and one of his cohorts at his heels. With sickening anxiety, Maxie glanced behind and saw two more men emerging from another alley. She and Robin were trapped, and this time there was no helpful Dafydd Jones with a herd of oxen.

Genially Simmons said, "You're not getting away this time. The wench is going back to her uncle, and you, my pretty lad, are going to be taught a lesson for attacking me from behind."

"You should be grateful I did come from behind. At least that gave you an excuse for losing." His voice calm, Robin peeled off his coat and handed it and his knapsack to Maxie. "But if you insist on attempting revenge, I suppose I must oblige you."

"You're damned right you'll oblige," Simmons said explosively. "And no matter how good you are, remember that a good big man will beat a good little man every time."

"That depends on just how good the little man is, doesn't it?" Robin said pleasantly. He gave Maxie a sunny smile. "Don't worry. I don't think friend Simmons intends to kill me, and I certainly don't intend to kill him."

His words goaded the Londoner into action, but Robin was prepared when Simmons charged, fists swinging. Neatly Robin stepped aside, catching his opponent's arm and twisting it as he shifted his own weight. The larger man spun and crashed to the dirt road with numbing force. For a moment Simmons lay stunned. Then he regained his feet, eyes narrowed, his anger now tempered by caution. "You didn't learn that in Jackson's salon."

"No, I didn't," Robin agreed. He looked slight and elegant, a David to Simmons' Goliath. But his stance was that of a fighter as he balanced on the balls of his feet, knees bent, arms relaxed and ready. "I never claimed to be a student of Jackson's. I learned in a harder school, where the stakes were higher."

"So did I, laddie boy," Simmons growled, falling into the same stance. "If that's the way you want it, you've got it."

While Maxie watched, half-suffocated with tension, the two men engaged in a series of brief, violent clashes punctuated by taut wariness as they slowly circled each other. Robin kept his distance as much as possible, moving in for lightning attacks, then darting out of range again. He clearly had the edge in speed, but the Londoner had the advantage of reach and weight.

To Maxie's intense disgust, she realized that Simmons was enjoying himself. After a particularly clever sally on his opponent's part, the big man said with open approval, "You really are good, 'specially for a gentry cove."

He accompanied his words with a series of murderous punches to the head and shoulders. Robin skipped back, but was unable to block the barrage entirely and was left gasping and off-balance.

Simmons followed up his advantage with a massive fist in Robin's midriff that sent the smaller man to the ground. Crowing with triumph, the Londoner moved in to finish the fight.

But Robin was a good deal less defeated than he looked, and

with a scythelike sweep of his leg he knocked Simmons from his feet. Even as the larger man was falling, Robin exploded into a blur of movement too swift for Maxie to follow, but it ended with the Londoner immobilized facedown on the ground. Robin's knee was in his back and he was applying a wrestling hold that could break the neck of a man too foolish to surrender.

No fool, Simmons reluctantly raised one hand in submission, but defeat was not a result his colleagues were willing to accept. With snarls and no thoughts of sportsmanship, two of them went after the man who had beaten their employer.

Maxie screamed, "Robin!" She scooped a handful of dust and gravel from the road and tossed it in the faces of the bruisers.

The two men howled, and Robin used the moment's warning to leap to his feet. Though his lightning-quick moves had a dancer's grace, within seconds both opponents were lying on the ground, one with his arm bent at an unnatural angle.

As he saw how efficiently his cohorts were disposed of, the third man grabbed a rock and swung it at Robin's skull with lethal force. Maxie dived at the man and clutched his arm, using her whole weight in an attempt to deflect the blow. She was only partially successful, and the stone connected above Robin's ear with a sickening dull thud that sent him crumpling to the ground.

For an instant Maxie was paralyzed with terror as she prayed that the blow was not a fatal one. Then fury took over. Even before Robin's body hit the ground, she was raking at the third man's eyes with clawed fingers. As he tried to protect his face, she kneed him viciously in the groin and had the satisfaction of seeing him fold over on himself like a suit of empty clothes.

The least damaged man present, Simmons lunged to his feet and grabbed Maxie in a bear hug, trapping her arms and legs. Twist as she might, Maxie couldn't get free, though she managed a few good butts and bites.

"Stop that, you little hellion," Simmons gasped, securing her hands behind her back in one meaty fist. "Your fancy man is damned good. My lads shouldn't've interfered in a fair fight, but if you don't behave, I'll make you very sorry."

Recognizing that it was time for a strategic truce, Maxie ceased struggling. Keeping a firm grip on her, Simmons scowled at the two of his men who were slowly getting to their feet.

"You fought like a bunch of girls," he said contemptuously. "Worse—this wench here has more skill and spirit than the three of you put together."

His expression vicious, one of the bruisers drew back his foot to kick Robin, who lay senseless in the dust, his blond hair stained by the slow seep of blood. Simmons snapped, "Touch 'im and I'll break your arm myself. You two get over to the livery stable and bring the chaise 'round."

In a cloud of surly muttering, the two men left. The third man still lay in the road, sublimely unaware.

Maxie wondered angrily where the citizens of Market Harborough were, but this was a drab back street, more warehouses than homes, and no one came. "Let me go so I can look at Robin," she said tightly. "He may be badly hurt."

"He'll survive, though it might 'a gone hard with him if you hadn't grabbed Wilby's arm." Simmons shook his head. "Wilby really shouldn't 'a done that. It's hard to get reliable help."

Maxie's sympathy with the Londoner's complaint was nil, but for the moment discretion was the better part of valor. Trying to sound resigned, she asked, "What are you going to do with us?"

"You're going to Durham, trussed like a Christmas goose if necessary. Now, as for your friend, that's a question, and no mistake." Simmons frowned. "I could just leave 'im here, but 'e might come after me. 'E seems the stubborn sort. Mebbe I'll give 'im to the local constable, say 'e stole my horse." After a moment's thought, he chuckled, "Aye, that's the ticket. By the time 'e's brought up to the magistrate, you'll be in Durham, and then you're Collingwood's problem. Better 'im than me." Simmons watched his men disappear, rubbing absently at a wide bruise forming on his cheek.

As he talked, his grip on her hands had loosened, and Maxie decided that there was no time like the present to try to break free. She jerked away from the Londoner, but he managed to catch one of her wrists before she could get clear, and another skirmish followed. Even knowing it was hopeless, Maxie continued to struggle, getting a good swipe at Simmons' face with her fingernails, gouging his bruised cheek until it bled.

Swearing, Simmons said furiously, "I warned you, you little vixen." He pulled Maxie over to a large rock by the road, then sat down and turned her over his knee and began to spank her with a large, heavy hand.

For a moment, Maxie was stunned with disbelief and the sheer indignity of what he was doing. Indians did not believe in being violent with children, and her father had also preferred reason to force, so she had never been spanked in her life.

The fighting that had gone before had been fierce but without deadly intent. Now the last traces of her English restraint dissolved. Maxie inhaled a deep lungful of air, then gave a Mohawk war whoop that vibrated the panes of glass in nearby windows, a savage explosion of sound unlike anything practiced in England even when the natives wore blue paint.

Simmons gasped, his hand suspended in midair. "Gawd a'mighty, what was that?"

And in that moment while he was distracted, Maxie twisted, pulled the knife from her boot, and came up slashing.

9

Robin never wholly lost consciousness, but for a time he was very detached from what was happening around him. As his body and mind reacquainted themselves, he realized that Simmons was the only opponent still left and upright, and that his attention was occupied with Maxie. If Robin had been more capable of speech, he would have warned the Londoner that trying to spank his captive was not a wise idea.

Instead, with dizziness and near blackout, Robin slowly pushed to his knees. Then Maxie's war whoop gave an electrifying jolt to his system and he looked up to see her swinging her knife at Simmons' throat. Swearing, the Londoner dodged back and the blade skimmed his shoulder.

Before his bloodthirsty comrade could try again, Robin croaked, "Stop it, Maxie."

Her wild brown eyes shifted to him, and she hesitated as rage and reason debated. In the moment before something worse could happen, Robin managed to get behind Simmons and render the man unconscious with the blood-stopping neck hold he had used the first time they had fought. Robin had lacked both opportunity and will to use the hold earlier, but dangerous though it was, Simmons' chances of survival were greater if he was knocked out this way than if Maxie was the one to end the fight.

Simmons made a choking noise, then keeled off the rock, almost taking Robin along. Before Robin could fall, Maxie caught him, her arms supplying much-needed support. Her words, however, were tart. "You should have let me take care of him."

As Robin's eyesight darkened around the edges, he clung to Maxie, for once not appreciating the delicious feel of her. "Sorry," he said unsteadily, "but I really don't like seeing people killed."

Maxie made a sound that suggested both disdain and that the conversation would be continued at a more suitable time, but with an admirable focus on the immediate she asked, "Can you walk? The others will be back soon."

Robin folded down on the rock and buried his face in his hands, trying to think his way through the shattering pain in his head. "I'll need help."

Moving briskly, Maxie returned her knife to her boot, helped him into his coat, slung both knapsacks on her own back, then pulled Robin to his feet and draped his arm over her shoulders.

As they wove their way down the street, Robin reflected with dizzy appreciation on how much strength Maxie had in such a small frame, but it was still fortunate that the canal was only a few hundred yards away, on the far side of the warehouses. The question was, what would they do when they got there?

As soon as they entered the Three Swans, Giles ordered a private parlor, with brandy immediately and food to follow. The landlord was delighted to see his distinguished lady guest more or less intact, and obliged with alacrity. Lady Ross was still shaken by her narrow escape, and she let herself be escorted to the parlor with a docility that Giles did not expect to last long. Her face was ash pale beneath the flamboyant red hair.

In the parlor he pressed her into a Windsor chair, then inspected her upper arm where the ox horn had gored. Both pelisse and dress were ruined and the white skin beneath was scraped, but the wound was superficial, with only traces of blood. "No serious damage done, though you'll have heavy bruising."

A maid brought in the brandy and Giles poured some, then handed it to Lady Ross. She choked on the first mouthful, but color began to return to her face. "There will be bruising in a number of less mentionable spots as well," she said with a crooked smile.

He grinned. "You would know that better than I."

She pushed her loose hair off her brow with fingers that were almost steady again. "Give me a few minutes to go to my room and make myself presentable. Then I want to hear about the men who were after Lord Robert and Maxima."

Lady Ross restored herself to thunderous respectability very quickly. When she returned, her hair had been rebraided and pinned up under a cap, she had changed into another dress as drab as the previous one, and her full figure was swaddled in a shawl. On the whole, Giles preferred her disheveled.

Food had just been brought on a tray, and by common consent they ate before addressing the serious issues. When they had reached the stage of coffee, Desdemona cocked a brow at the marquess. "About those men?"

"One of them I recognized, and I suspect that he is the agent Lord Collingwood sent after Miss Collins." Wolverton explained how he had aided the man called Simmons several days earlier. "So not only are you and I hot on the trail in our separate ways, but apparently Simmons and his helpers as well."

"There is an element of farce to this." Desdemona's mouth quirked in an unwilling smile, but she sobered quickly. "From what little I could see, I didn't like the looks of Simmons and his accomplices."

"Men who do such work aren't drawn from the most genteel ranks," the marquess said dryly. "If they have been hired to take Miss Collins back to Durham, I don't imagine they will hurt her, but they might not be so careful of my brother's welfare."

"From what you've told me, Lord Robert seems to have won every round so far." Desdemona took a deep swallow of scalding black coffee, welcoming the stimulation of it. "You said that he had been out of England for a number of years. What was he doing—diplomatic work, the army, or what?"

Wolverton sighed and toyed with his own cup, visibly wondering how to answer. Finally he said, "I'll tell you, but on the condition that you speak of it to no one."

"His behavior was that disgraceful?"

The marquess lifted his head, his slate eyes colder than she had ever seen them. "Quite the contrary. But what he did was highly confidential and there may be ramifications for years, even decades, to come. Nor is the story mine to tell."

"Your brother was a spy?" The deduction was not difficult. She added with heavy sarcasm, "One can see how he developed his notions of honorable behavior."

Wolverton's eyes narrowed at her tone. "Yes, he was a spy. A practioner of the most dangerous and unrespected kind of warfare, utterly essential and utterly secret. Robin was hardly more than a boy, traveling on the Continent during the Peace of Amiens, when he stumbled over something he thought the Foreign Office should know. He was encouraged to stay on, and for the next dozen years he risked his life and sanity a thousand times over so that fewer people would die."

He stopped, his silence gathering menacing weight, then finished in a soft, hard voice, "And so that people like you could sit safe and smug in England and judge him."

Blushing is the curse of the redhead, and Desdemona could feel waves of hot, humiliated color spread from her hairline to her neck and below. "I'm sorry," she said with painful apology. "No matter how angry I am about what your brother has done to my niece, I should not have spoken as I did." She was more than just ashamed of herself; she also felt bereft at the withdrawal of Wolverton's usual warmth.

His expression eased. "Your reaction is not that uncommon. Spying requires nerves of steel and a number of skills a gentleman shouldn't have. Robin was very, very good at it, or he would never have survived. He has been tested in ways that would break most men and that very nearly broke him.

"I know very little beyond what he has chosen to tell me since he returned to England, and I am devoutly grateful that I was not better informed during the years he was abroad. God knows it was bad enough wondering if I would ever see him again, or if he would just disappear, one of the nameless unmourned dead, and I would never know how or when."

The marquess broke off abruptly, his face tight, and it was a moment before he could continue. "To give you an idea of one of the things he accomplished in his 'disgraceful' career, last year he helped frustrate a plot aimed at blowing up the British embassy during the Paris peace conference."

Desdemona gasped, thinking just who might have been killed in such an explosion. Likely the Foreign Minister, Castlereagh, perhaps even Wellington. The political ramifications were staggering, not just for Britain but for the whole of Europe.

Wolverton smiled wryly. "You see why I said this must be

confidential? I'm told the powers at Whitehall are considering making Robin a baron for services rendered, only they aren't quite sure what to say that could be made public knowledge."

It was another startling statement and it took a moment to absorb it. "Being created a lord for espionage might be a first," she ventured.

"Robin has been breaking new ground his whole life. As a boy there was no harm in him, but he could be mischievous in amazingly inventive ways." The marquess's expression lightened. "For example, I believe he was the only boy ever expelled from Eton on his very first day of school."

Desdemona had to chuckle. "A dubious honor. How did he do that?"

"He introduced six sheep into the headmaster's drawing room. I never did learn how he managed it. It was a calculated act, performed because he wanted to go to Winchester, not Eton." Wolverton smiled reminiscently before returning to seriousness. "Even if a title is offered, I'm not sure he would take it. My brother never set much store by such things. At heart, I'm not sure he even approves of the idea of nobility. Once when we were boys, we were swimming in the lake at Wolverhampton and I got a vicious cramp and almost drowned. Robin pulled me out, an impressive feat considering that I was twice his size and thrashing like a reaper.

"When I had recovered somewhat, I pointed out that he could have left me in the water and been the next Marquess of Wolverton."

"And . . . ?" Desdemona prompted.

His eyes twinkled. "Robin said that that was the best possible argument for fishing me out of the lake."

Desdemona bit her lip. "The more I hear about your brother, the more dreadfully likable he sounds."

"He's extremely likable. Robin inherited all the charm and dash in the family, and in spite of what you think, he is honorable as well."

Desdemona surveyed the marquess's substantial frame, a faint smile on her face. "You seem to have inherited an adequate share of all three traits."

Wolverton stared for a moment, color rising in his face. Then he got to his feet and wandered to the window to avoid her eyes. It was the first time she had seen him disconcerted.

Served him right, Desdemona thought with satisfaction; he had been disconcerting her from the first time they met. Deciding that it was time to leave the personal, she asked, "Do you suppose Simmons caught up with our fugitives?"

The marquess's glance outside had been idle, but his gaze sharpened. "I doubt it. There are two very battered-looking fellows walking down the high street. I saw one of them with Simmons earlier, and the other probably was as well. My guess is that Collingwood's agent has been unsuccessful."

She joined him at the window and surveyed the two large but mauled bruisers. "Your brother did that?"

"Probably." Wolverton smiled ruefully. "Robin was small and almost girlishly attractive as a boy. Such are the horrors of the English public schools that he had to choose between fighting or groveling. If he'd stayed at Eton, I could have helped him, but as it was . . ." His voice trailed off.

"It looks like your brother had no taste for groveling." Desdemona realized abruptly how close she was to the marquess's very large, very masculine frame, and she edged away. "What, now, my lord? I doubt they will return to the drovers."

"I agree." Wolverton hesitated. She thought that he was on the verge of saying more, then changed his mind. "Now that they are alerted, it will be almost impossible to find them on the road. There are too many routes, too many ways to be disguised. It might be best to go direct to London and wait there, particularly since you think your niece may call on you."

Desdemona eyed him suspiciously. "You've something else in mind." The sense of alliance that had been between them was eroding rapidly.

"A possibility has occurred to me," he admitted, then forestalled her question with one hand. "I won't tell you what it is, but I promise that if I guess correctly, I will bring both of our runaways to you in London."

"What if they don't wish to come?"

"I will use sweet reason to persuade them." The marquess gave a half-smile. "Using force on Robin would not be advisable."

Remembering the battered ruffians who had just passed, she had to agree.

Wolverton picked up his hat and prepared to leave, then asked suddenly, "Why were you named Desdemona?"

She blinked at the change of subject. "It's family tradition to give the boys Latin names and the girls Shakespearean ones."

"But your niece's name is Latin."

"There are occasional exceptions," Desdemona explained. "My brother Maximus was named after Great-aunt Maxima, and passed the name on to his daughter. Aunt Maxima died a few months back, ripe in years and wickedness. I'm going to miss her."

Wolverton thought a moment. "Do you mean Lady Clendennon? She was the only Maxima I ever met." When Desdemona nodded, he chuckled. "Forceful females seem to be another Collins family tradition. Less and less do I think your niece could have been persuaded against her principles."

"That remains to be seen," Desdemona said dryly. Recalled to a sense of her mission, she gave her shawl a minatory tug, collected her reticule, and prepared to leave.

The marquess stood aside, but before opening the door, he halted and looked down at her, his gaze intense. Then, as if mesmerized, he raised a hand to her face, tracing the lines of temple and ear, brushing across her smooth cheek, caressing the curve of her throat. His touch was very delicate, as if he were trying to memorize the tones and texture of her skin with his fingertips.

Desdemona stood stock-still, fighting to maintain her composure. Wherever he touched blazed with sensation, and her breath caught unsteadily. She had never known gentleness in her marriage, and it was shocking to realize how vulnerable she was to it. She raised her eyes to Wolverton's and was immediately sorry. The warmth she saw there was far more dangerous than a blow. He was so large, powerful not just physically but in his aura of authority. In another moment he would bend over to kiss her, and if that happened . . .

She jerked away and opened the door herself. "I shall hope to see you and our runaways in London, my lord." Then she vanished.

Giles gazed absently at the door that had slammed in his face, considering Lady Ross's reaction. Why would a strong-minded woman of the world become as skittish as a convent-bred virgin when he showed interest in her? The simple explanation was that she had taken him in aversion; he had no doubt that in this case the simple explanation was wrong. It was not distaste he had seen in her eyes, but fear.

The Marquess of Wolverton had a well-deserved reputation as an easygoing man, but when he decided on something, he was immovable. At this moment, he decided that he was going to learn what lay at the root of her distress. Then, perhaps, something could be done about it.

Even though Robin was contributing as much as he could, Maxie was half-carrying him and the canal seemed endlessly distant. The back of her neck prickled in anticipation of Simmons' waking or his men returning to come after the fugitives. Given a choice, she would prefer Simmons himself; he had shown signs of a conscience, but she would trust his men no further than hungry wolves in a butcher shop. As they entered the shadowed alley between two of the warehouses, she prayed for a miracle with what energy she could spare, because they could not go much farther like this and there was very little time left.

Maxie was surprised how quiet the area was until she remembered that it was time for the midday meal. They emerged onto the sun-drenched wharf to find a loaded barge sitting at the mooring, the only people visible a man and boy who appeared to be the crew. The captain was a short fellow with a broad muscular figure and grizzled hair. He eyed them curiously, interrupted in the act of casting off. No doubt his curiosity was because Robin was draped over her like a shawl.

A straightforward plea for aid seemed like the best choice, so Maxie said in as heartrending a voice as she could manage, "Please, can you help us? We were attacked and my husband has been injured."

The captain looked surprised, which reminded Maxie how she was dressed. With her free hand she pulled off her appalling hat and the man blinked at the sight of her face, his interest thoroughly engaged.

Maxie had thought Robin beyond awareness, but he straightened up, taking most of his weight from her, at the same time murmuring in a voice laced with irrepressible amusement, "Brought out the heavy guns, I see. Poor devil hasn't a chance."

"Hush," she hissed, keeping a steadying arm around his waist as the captain jumped from the barge to the wharf and walked over to the newcomers.

"You were attacked by thieves in town in broad daylight?" he asked, visible skepticism on his weathered face.

What story would be likely to appeal to a canal man? When in doubt, tell some variation of the truth. "It wasn't thieves but my cousin and some of his friends. They are trying to stop us from reaching London." She glanced over her shoulder, having no trouble looking apprehensive. "Please, can we go with you for a little way? I can explain everything, but they will be here at any moment."

Maxie returned her pleading gaze to the captain, trying to look like the sort of female a man would feel protective about. She should have paid more attention to her cousin Portia, who had spent years cultivating helplessness.

The freckled-faced boy ventured, "Mebbe they're lookin' for a free ride."

The captain glanced at Robin, who was wavering on his feet. "That blood looks real enough." Coming to a decision, he said, "All right, lass, I'll take you on faith for a mile or two." He stepped forward, stooped, then lifted Robin and slung him over a broad shoulder as if he was a schoolboy. "Come along."

He stepped across the narrow span of water between wharf and barge, and Maxie followed. Now that she had attention to spare, she saw that the barge was simply constructed with two blunt ends and a crude cabin in the middle. Tarpaulin-covered mounds were secured to the deck, and from the shape of them she guessed that the cargo was carpets; Dafydd Jones had mentioned that they were made in Market Harborough.

The captain said, "I expect you would rather be out of sight if your cousin comes after us." Without waiting for a comment, he said, "Take the aft hatch cover off, Jamie."

Seeing the two together, Maxie could see clearly they were father and son. The boy scrambled to obey the order, excitement on his round face. Doubtless desperate passengers were a welcome diversion from the daily routine.

The hatch cover was lifted to reveal a hold packed with more carpets, and the boy climbed in and rearranged the rolls to create space. The captain deposited Robin's limp body with reasonable care, cautioning, "Don't let 'im bleed on my cargo."

Maxie nodded, then climbed into the hold and knelt beside Robin. Parting the golden hair, she found that a lump was already forming but that the skin was not badly broken, and the bleeding had been light. Young Jamie had skipped off, returning with a bottle of water and clean rags. Hoping that the water was not from the canal, she blotted the blood away, then folded a rag into a pad. She was as gentle as possible, but Robin flinched when she tied the bandage around his head.

The captain had been watching her ministrations. "Time we were on our way. Might be best to put the hatch back on."

"You're right," Maxie agreed. "I'm sure my cousin will follow. It's . . . it's a complicated tale."

The weathered face looked satiric. "I don't doubt it." Then he lowered the hatch cover into place.

The darkness was absolute. They were in a space about six feet long, four feet wide, and three feet deep. The yielding carpets beneath them were comfortable and the air redolent with the strong, not unpleasant scent of wool. The overall sensation was rather like that of a cozy coffin. Maxie rigidly clamped down on her unease. What mattered was that they were heading away from Simmons, and she felt instinctively that the captain was a reliable ally.

Overhead she heard dragging sounds and deduced that the captain was shifting carpets onto the hatch cover; even if Simmons followed the barge, he was unlikely to find their hiding place. After silently blessing the captain's foresight, Maxie yielded to her tired muscles and stretched out next to Robin. "Are you there?" she asked softly.

His light tenor voice was scarcely audible. "I have been more or less present through the last act, even though I had to be carted about like a wheel of cheese."

She chuckled, relieved. "Sounds like your wits weren't scrambled by that rock."

"Of course not," Robin murmured. "My head is the most unbreakable part of me." There was a rustling sound as he shifted. "Is there any more water?"

Maxie lifted his head and shoulders so that he could drink from the bottle. Corking what was left, she asked, "Did you sustain any damage apart from the head wound?"

There was a pause while Robin took inventory. Outside the barge Maxie heard Jamie tell the tow horse to get along, and the barge began to move.

"Nothing to signify," he said eventually.

"Good. Then you can think up a convincing reason why my cousin Simmons and his merry men are after us."

"But you're doing such a good job of invention that it would be a pity to interfere," he protested.

"Next to you, I am the veriest amateur at tale-spinning."

"Perhaps at tale-spinning, but that was a splendid bit of acting. If I hadn't known better, I would have sworn that you were frightened and helpless."

"What makes you so sure that I wasn't?" she asked, not sure whether to be flattered at his faith in her or offended by his lack of concern.

"Because, Kanawiosta," he said, amusement and approval in his voice, "a female who will attack a professional fighter three times her size is brave to the point of being suicidal." He rolled over and put one arm around her, drawing her close then added in a drowsy whisper, "You are a woman without equal."

Glowing with Robin's words, Maxie relaxed against him, her cheek against his chest as his breathing slowed and he slipped into a doze. Though she knew it was irrational, she felt safe in his arms, as if the outside world could never harm her.

It would have been easy to sleep after the energetic morning, but Maxie resisted the temptation. Instead, she listened to the soft splash of water against the hull and worked on devising a convincing story to tell the barge captain.

The canal between Market Harborough and Foxton was easy going, and John Blaine had time to muse about the passengers he had taken on the barge *Penelope*. He looked forward to hearing the tale the odd pair would tell him later; with a chuckle, he decided that he was willing to wager it would be entertaining, though he wouldn't put money on whether it was truthful.

The barge had just entered the first of the famous Foxton locks when two men trotted into sight on the towpath. " 'Ey, you there,'' the larger one yelled in a cockney accent. " 'Old a minute, I want to ask you some questions.''

Blaine pulled his pipe from his mouth and surveyed the newcomer. The fellow looked like he'd been in a fight, and no mistake. "A canal boat doesn't stop when it's in a lock,'' he said tersely, then called to his son, "Open the ground paddle.''

Jamie turned the windlass and water began flowing into the lower lock.

"Dammit, I'm speaking to you,'' the cockney snarled.

Blaine did not find the stranger's attitude endearing. The little lady, on the other hand, had been quite charming. "And I've a job to do,'' he said, unperturbed. "Make yourself useful and help with the gates. At the bottom I'll have time to talk.''

The water level between the first and second locks equalized and Jamie opened the gate between them. The horse pulled the barge forward, the gate closed behind, and the paddles on the next gate were opened so water could flow into the lower pound.

As he watched the *Penelope* drop rapidly below ground level, the cockney balanced uncertainly, as if debating jumping on the barge and putting his questions forcefully. Instead, with a scowl, he gestured to his henchman and the two added their considerable weight to working the gates and the paddles.

The Foxton locks consist of two flights of five locks each, joined by a central meeting pool where two boats could pass. Passage through ten locks is a slow business and Blaine could have found the time to answer a few polite questions on the way, but as it was, he kept himself conspiciously busy.

Eventually the barge reached the bottom of the locks, seventy-five feet below where it had begun. With exaggerated courtesy, the cockney jumped on the vessel's deck and asked, "Now will you answer a few questions?''

Blaine tamped fresh tobacco into his clay pipe, struck a spark, and drew on the stem until he was sure it was burning well. Finally he replied, "Aye. What do you want to know?''

"I'm looking for two criminals, a blond man and a young lad. They're very dangerous."

"Aye?" Blaine's expression was bored.

The cockney began to stalk the length of the barge, his suspicious gaze searching for signs of his quarry as he began to describe the fugitives and enumerate their misdeeds.

Lying in the thick warm blackness, Maxie felt vibrations on the deck above and heard a rumble of voices over the softer sounds of rushing water. It seemed that they had been trapped down here forever, though it couldn't have been for much more than an hour or two. Two men were talking, one in the harsh accents of Simmons, but maddeningly she could not hear the actual words.

Robin was still sleeping off the effects of the head injury, but Maxie sat up, too tense to lie still. She scarcely breathed as heavy footsteps approached, the planks creaking under the weight of a large man. Simmons must be almost near enough to push the shield of carpets from the hatch cover, or to hear the hammering of her heart. This was infinitely worse than meeting an enemy in the open, and Maxie's nerves were so tightly strung that she felt a hysterical desire to scream, or to pound the hatch with balled fists—anything to end the suspense.

The footsteps halted no more than two or three feet from her head. At the same time Robin stirred and drew in his breath, as if preparing to speak. Instantly Maxie clamped one hand over his mouth. Above, very clearly, she heard Simmons say, "Anyone who helps criminals is flouting the king's justice, and it will go hard with 'im."

Maxie spared a moment for indignation at the pious way the scoundrel was invoking the law. The devil could cite Scripture for his purposes, indeed!

Robin had tensed when she first touched him, then relaxed. Now he nodded, and Maxie guessed that he was awake and aware of their danger. She lifted her hand, and as she did, he pressed his lips to her palm in a kiss.

Remarkable how differently one could react to different kinds of touch. Why did that deliberate butterfly caress affect her when muting his speech had not? Maxie inhaled, shaken. The darkness around them was no longer charged with danger, but with intimacy, and her fingers curved to stroke Robin's cheek. The faint masculine prickle of whiskers contrasted with smooth skin. His lips were warm, his breath a gossamer touch on her palm. He lifted his hand to cup hers, and for a moment she was sure that he was going to pull her down and kiss her in earnest. She was willing. More than willing. Her lips parted in anticipation.

Instead, after a breathless suspended moment, the energy between them changed, the sense of lambent passion dissipating. Perhaps Robin had decided the present circumstances were inappropriate for making love. Or perhaps the proximity of danger had been erotic, and desire faded as the footsteps above moved away.

Before she reached a conclusion, he did pull her down to the rolled carpets, but into the sort of affectionate embrace that was normal between them. Exasperated, Maxie considered biting his shoulder from sheer frustration. Why couldn't the blasted man be the normal encroaching kind, with only one thing on his mind? Soon it would reach the point where there was only one thing on *her* mind, and then Robin had better look to his virtue.

She had to choke off the gurgle of laughter that threatened to spill out. Far better to concentrate on present dangers and be grateful that the barge captain hadn't given them away. At least, not yet.

After an endless time of waiting, the barge began to move forward again, and Maxie gave a sigh of relief. Quietly Robin said, "It looks like we have made it over this jump. Are we ready for the captain's questions when he lets us out of here?"

"Yes." Maxie did not elaborate.

"Is there anything I should know in support of your story?"

"No. This will come as a shock to you, but I decided it will be best to tell him the truth."

"The truth," Robin said in a tone of wonderment. "That would never have occurred to me."

Maxie snorted. "That is one of the few things you've ever said that I believe unequivocally."

He chuckled. "Believe me, I tell the truth much more often than not. Keeping one's lies straight can be quite exhausting."

"I wouldn't know," she replied, trying to sound blighting.

She could feel Robin's chest shake with silent laughter, and he linked his arms around her waist. "Are we still married?" he asked. "Or did you retract what you said earlier about me being your husband?"

Maxie thought a moment. "I suppose we're still married," she said reluctantly. "I would rather not explain what we are. I don't think there is any proper definition."

She felt his amusement again, but he didn't reply.

Now that Robin was awake and on guard, Maxie felt free to relax and get some rest herself. She settled her head on his shoulder. Soon enough it would be time to face the world again.

Maxie didn't wake until the removal of the hatch cover let in the long rays of the setting sun. She looked up warily, but it was the barge captain's face above, not Simmons.

"You two all right down there?" he asked cheerfully.

"We are indeed, and very grateful to you," Robin replied. He got to his feet and swung up to the deck, then extended his hand to help Maxie out. "My name is Robert Anderson, by the way, and this is my wife, Maxima."

Maxie noted that he was now Anderson, not Andreville, and was grateful that he didn't call himself Lord Robert. At least he had the sense to realize that this was not the best moment to use a fraudulent title. The pair of them looked disrespectable enough without that.

She glanced around, seeing that the barge was moored at the bottom of a large lock, with a stone stable and a small lock-keeper's cottage nearby. It was a lovely pastoral scene, as beautiful in its way as the untamed mountains of New England.

The captain took his pipe from his mouth. "I'm John Blaine. My boy Jamie is stabling the horse."

The two men shook hands. "I hope Simmons wasn't too rude to you," Robin said.

"Happen he was." A smile hovered behind the cloud of pipe smoke. " 'Fraid there was a bit of an accident. The fellow tripped on the towrope and fell into the canal."

Maxie laughed and wondered how Blaine had managed that as Robin said with mock gravity, "Such things do happen."

"Care to join Jamie and me for a bite of supper?"

His words reminded Maxie that they had not eaten since a very early breakfast with the drovers. Was it really only that morning that they had shared a pot of tea and a loaf of bread with Dafydd Jones? "That would be very welcome, Mr. Blaine." She stopped. "Or would it be Captain Blaine?"

"Mister will do. This isn't exactly a ship of the line." Blaine chuckled. "Someday I'll own my own boat rather than running one for the company. Then you can call me captain."

He disappeared into the barge's cabin, and in a few minutes the table inside was covered with cold food that had been prepared by Blaine's wife in Market Harborough. Fortunately, the captain's wife had expansive ideas about what it took to keep her menfolk from starving, and there was more than enough roast chicken, bread, cheese, and pickled onions. The four of them ate in the cabin with the door open to admit the evening breeze.

Maxie and Robin deferred to the canal-boat man's tacit desire to eat first and talk later, and Blaine waited until he had finished and stoked up another pipe before asking, "Now, Mrs. Anderson, you said you could explain everything? Your cousin"—there was a faint, sardonic emphasis on the word— "said that you and your husband were guilty of theft and assault."

Maxie colored, glad the light was dim. "Simmons isn't really my cousin. I said that because it was simpler than the real explanation."

"I didn't see much family resemblance," he agreed. "So what is the real explanation?"

Maxie sketched in the bare bones of the story: that her father had died in London, that she had reason to suspect foul play, and that her uncle was making every attempt to stop her from investigating. She told the truth, though with as few elaborations as possible, particularly where Robin was concerned.

She ended earnestly, "I swear, Mr. Blaine, Robin and I are not criminals." At least, she wasn't; it was probably stretching a point to include Robin among the innocent. Stifling her conscience, she continued, "I have stolen nothing except an old map of my uncle's, and we have committed no assault beyond self-defense to escape Simmons and his men." After all, Simmons' horse had been borrowed merely.

There was silence in the cabin. Outside, the small splashing sounds of water life could be heard.

The captain asked, "Is your uncle your legal guardian?"

"No." Maxie guessed what he was thinking. "I just turned twenty-five. He would have no legal right to interfere with me, even if I wasn't married."

Not just Blaine, but Robin, looked at her. She guessed they were surprised, though it was too dark to read expressions. Because of her small size, people tended to assume she was younger than she really was.

Blaine drew at his pipe, the burning tobacco glowing in the dark. "Sounds like the truth, if not precisely the whole truth." A note of amusement entered his voice. "I'd like to have seen that self-defense between you two and Simmons' gang." Another pause. "I imagine that tomorrow you'll want to be on your way to London, but if you want to spend tonight in the hold, you're welcome to."

On impulse, Maxie leaned across the table and pressed a quick kiss to his leathery cheek. "Bless you, Mr. Blaine. You and Jamie have been wonderful."

She could almost feel him blush. "If you tell your mother about this, Jamie," he warned his son, "mind you mention that kiss wasn't my idea."

They all laughed, and after that, the evening turned social. Tea was brewed, Maxie brought out her harmonica and played, and Robin gave a juggling and magic performance, to Jamie's delight. During the show, the lock-keeper and his family came out to join them, bringing warm spiced buns as a contribution. It was like an informal gathering of New England neighbors, and Maxie felt a kind of contentment she would never have expected to find on this side of the Atlantic.

By the time the evening ended and they returned to the hold to sleep under a borrowed blanket, Maxie felt that she and Robin had earned their supper. As she relaxed within his familiar embrace, she realized how grateful she was to have embarked on this strange journey. She was discovering a different England than that of her aristocratic relations, and it was a warmer, kinder country by far. And most of all, she had met Robin.

Simmons cast about furiously for traces of his quarry, but they appeared to have vanished without a trace. The thick-witted canal-boat captain had had a vague memory of seeing two people beg a ride with a wagon, and there had been several other possible sightings, but all came to naught.

Furious with himself for his failure, he reluctantly sent a message to Lord Collingwood saying that he had lost the trail and could not guarantee that the girl would not reach London. He finished by suggesting that his lordship might wish to make other arrangements to prevent his niece from learning the truth about her father's death.

As for himself, Simmons would continue the hunt.

10

Robin eyed the dark roiling sky without enthusiasm. It was early evening, and it appeared that the day was going to end with a thunderstorm of major proportions. They had had good weather for most of the journey, with only occasional drizzle, but that was about to change, and the oncoming storm helped him decide on a course of action he had been weighing. He asked his companion, "Would you care to spend tonight in style?"

"If that means a bath, yes!"

Maxie accompanied her remark with one of the vivid smiles that made his heart behave in odd ways, as if it couldn't remember how to beat. She was the gamest female he had ever met, cheerfully accepting everything that came their way. Sometimes she found Robin exasperating—and who could blame her?—but never once had she whined or sulked. Maggie was the same way.

With a start, Robin realized that he had not thought of Maggie in days; his present companion's enchanting presence was making the past feel very distant. Which, after all, was as it should be, and about time.

They had made good speed since leaving the canal boat. By pure luck, they had fallen in with a small caravan of gypsies. Robin spoke some of the Romany tongue, and it transpired that he had met the leader's cousin's uncle in Italy once. That and his knowledge of the language had made them welcome guests, and for two and a half days they had traveled south and west with the caravan, which was going to Bristol. The wagons were faster than walking; better yet, by staying inside, Robin and Maxie were invisible to possible watchers.

The previous night they had set out to entertain their hosts as a return for hospitality, though this time it wasn't Robin who was the biggest success; that honor went to Maxie. She had

borrowed a brightly embroidered blouse and skirt from one of
the girls and looked quite devastatingly lovely, but that was just
the beginning. After the evening meal she had played Iroquois
music on her harmonica until the old fiddler had caught the
flavor of it.

Then she had danced. With long skeins of straight ebony hair
swirling about her, concealing and revealing her exotic face,
she looked like a gypsy herself, but her passionate dancing was
from her mother's people, and the gypsies had been as awed
as Robin himself. She was Kanawiosta, and as she danced, she
seemed too distant and mysterious for mortal man to know or
possess. It was an aching thought, one Robin refused to dwell
on.

Later they had all danced, this time in the gypsy style, at which
Maxie was soon as adept as her teachers. Whatever happened
in the future, the sight of her whirling through the light and
shadows of the campfire was one Robin would never forget.

When they had parted company with the caravan a few hours
earlier, it had been with mutual regret and invitations to visit
again. Now they were on a southbound road near Northampton,
only a few days from London.

A flash of lightning, followed almost instantly by a horrendous
thunderclap, interrupted Robin's daydreaming. The rain began,
not a gentle English shower but blasts of water that drenched
them both to the skin in seconds.

Pitching her voice above the torrent, Maxie said, "We might
dissolve if we stay out in this very long. How far is this place
you want to stop?"

"Not far." Robin grinned and put his arm around her
shoulders, increasing their pace so that they were moving along
at a trot. "But this rain is nothing. For vile weather, you should
have seen Napoleon's retreat from Moscow."

She laughed, as always amazed at his powers of invention.
"Are you going to tell me you were with the Grande Armée
then?"

Another thunderclap slit the air. "For a while," he said airily,
"but it wasn't very amusing, so I stole a horse and made my
own way back to Prussia."

She asked teasing questions, which he answered with speed

and improbability, and the last saturated mile passed a good deal more quickly than it might have. The rain was so heavy that they were within fifty feet of the stone wall before they saw it.

"We've reached our destination," Robin announced.

She looked at the wall dubiously. "Doesn't look very comfortable to me."

Robin jumped and caught the top edge of the wall, then swung up to stand on it. He lowered his knapsack for Maxie, but she refused to take it.

"Good Lord, Robin, what are you doing?" she said, aghast. "Isn't this wall around a private estate?"

"Yes, but the owner is away and the house is empty," he explained. When Maxie still hesitated, he said reassuringly, "Truly, it is all right. There will be no trouble."

For a long moment she weighed his confidence against her doubts. As always, he looked angelically sincere, and she was reminded of what she had thought when they first met: the face of a man who could sell you a dozen things you didn't want. But his judgment had been reliable so far, although her judgment might be deficient for trusting him. She grasped the knapsack and scrambled up the wall.

On the other side they dropped down into a stand of large trees, which blunted the force of the rain. Robin led the way along a faint trail, the earth sodden and spongelike beneath their feet. Eventually they emerged at the edge of the woods and Maxie halted, startled and unhappy at the sight of the stately dwelling outlined against the storm-darkened sky.

A flash of lightning illuminated the scene for a moment. Some buildings would have seemed gothic and threatening under these conditions, but that was not the case here. The Jacobean manor house stood on a slight rise, surrounded by well-tended lawns and gardens, serene even in the midst of nature's turbulence. It was neither unusually large nor in any way ostentatious; what made it striking were the graceful proportions and the way it suited its setting like a gemstone.

"Robin, we shouldn't be here," she said with conviction.

He touched her shoulder. "I promise you, it will be all right. There are stewards and gatekeepers and such, but all have their own residences. The house itself is quite empty, and if we are unobtrusive, we can stay with no harm to anyone."

She still balked. "How can you be sure it's still empty?"

"It's useful to know such things," Robin said vaguely. "Come along. I don't know about you, but I'm freezing."

After glancing about to be sure they were unobserved, Maxie started forward. "What is the estate's name and who owns it?"

"Ruxton." He circled the house toward the back. "For many years it has been a minor property of a great aristocratic family. Perfectly maintained, but scarcely ever occupied."

"What a pity," Maxie said, her gaze scanning the mellow stone facade. "It deserves to be lived in. Your English nobility are a criminally wasteful lot."

"I wouldn't disagree." They stopped at a door leading into the kitchen. Robin turned the knob and found, not surprisingly, that it was locked. Without missing a beat, he pulled a stiff piece of wire from his pocket and in less than a minute had picked the lock.

The glare on Maxie's face should have produced steam in the cold rain. "You have the most appalling skills," she said through gritted teeth.

"But useful. I'm a dab hand at pickpocketing as well." He gave a beatific smile. "Wouldn't you rather be inside by a fire rather than out in the rain?"

"It's a near-run thing," Maxie muttered as she entered.

The shuttered windows admitted enough light to reveal that the kitchen was both neat and empty. Dully gleaming pans hung in silent array on the opposite wall, worktables stood scrubbed and ready, but of active human occupation there was none. Maxie was relieved at this evidence that Robin's information was accurate, though she still felt ill-at-ease as she set her knapsack on the flagged floor and peeled off her soaking coat and hat.

"With the storm, I doubt anyone will notice a small amount of smoke from a chimney." Clearly Robin had been here at some time in the past; perhaps he had begged a meal from an indulgent cook in the days when the house was lived in? Or had been a guest in his respectable youth? Whatever the reason, it took him only a few minutes to locate and light a lantern, then build a coal fire and start water heating.

Saturated to the skin and shivering, Maxie was grateful to stand by the hearth and absorb the fire's warmth. After a few minutes Robin came and draped a shawl around her shoulders.

"There is a cloakroom with a variety of old boots and garments," he explained. "While the bathwater is heating, shall we choose rooms for the night?"

Rooms, plural? Maxie didn't like the sound of that. Besides . . . "I'd rather stay here, to be honest. It seems dreadfully intrusive to invade someone's home, even if it isn't regularly occupied."

"But this isn't anyone's home, and hasn't been for a very long time."

Maxie let herself be persuaded to explore in spite of her misgivings. Robin carried a small branch of candles, and the flickering light showed Ruxton to be both handsome and appealing, with a human scale that Chanleigh lacked. The upholstered furniture was under holland covers, but the shapes revealed a timeless elegance dating from the middle of the previous century. The satinwood tables needed only the brush of a hand on their waxed surfaces to bring them alive, deep Oriental carpets hushed the sound of footsteps, the harpsichord sang bright and true under her questing fingers.

"Sad to think there is no one to appreciate this," she said as the notes faded.

"A manor house has a life span of centuries," Robin said quietly. "A few decades of stillness are a minor aberration. It has been a home in the past, it will be again in the future."

A small round window at the head of the main stairs was unshuttered, and Maxie paused to admire the rolling hills, then shook her head and followed her companion into the west wing.

He opened a door and glanced in. "Will this suit you for the night?"

It was twice the size of the room she had occupied at Chanleigh, with a wide four-poster bed and a rose-hued carpet underfoot. "I believe this is the mistress's bedchamber," he continued. "The master's room would be through that door."

She glanced at him, his words confirming what she had guessed earlier. "In other words, a bed is more dangerous to share than a hedgerow or haystack?"

His blue eyes met hers, serious for once. "So it proved before. I think it best that I sleep in the next room."

Of course he was right. Damn him.

By the time they had each bathed and sat down to a belated meal, Maxie's mood had improved. With a blithe unconcern for property rights, Robin had found two velvet robes for them to wear while their own clothing dried. He also pillaged the house's treasures to set a formal table in the breakfast room, the dining room being too large for two people. They ate by candlelight with silver utensils, drank from crystal goblets, and delicate china bowls held relishes and candied fruits from the stillroom. The food they had brought with them looked plebeian on the gold-edged plates, but tasted better for its elegant presentation.

Having finished her meal, Maxie leaned back in her chair with a contented sigh and pushed her red velvet sleeves up her arms once again. The robe was much too large and its hem dragged on the floor, but it was the perfect garment for this lunatic occasion, when her fresh-washed hair fell around her shoulders and wool stockings warmed her feet.

Fatalistically she had decided there was no advantage in brooding about their trespass, so she might as well enjoy this eccentric luxury. While still conscious of the unlawfulness of their presence, she was no longer uncomfortable about it. She would have hesitated to put the thought into words, but she felt as if the house welcomed them. Perhaps it was glad to have inhabitants, even transitory, illicit ones.

Maxie brushed at her hair, glad to feel that it was nearly dry. "Times like this, it would be nice to loll in the chair with a glass of brandy in my hand."

"You can still do that," Robin pointed out. He took a sip of wine, having raided the cellar on his own behalf. "Nothing in that picture says that you actually have to drink the brandy."

She laughed and poured herself tea from a porcelain pot, glad that Robin respected her determination not to drink any kind of alcohol. More often people urged her to try just a little, to see what she was missing.

Through the meal they had chatted amiably on a shifting variety of topics, but as she selected a piece of candied ginger,

Maxie said, "Sometime in your checkered past you must have been a butler." She waved at the table. "You do this so well."

Robin smiled. His robe was blue and was quite a good fit, setting off his wide shoulders and gilt hair and making him unreasonably, dangerously, handsome. "As a matter of fact, you're right. I have had a stint or two of butling, as well as being footman and groom on occasion."

She was taken aback, not having meant the comment seriously. "Is that true, or are you teasing again?"

"Quite true."

Maxie rested an elbow on the table, propping her chin on her palm as she studied his cool patrician countenance. She really shouldn't be surprised; even superior gentlemen with a rooted distaste for gainful employment must sometimes have to work to keep food in their bellies.

"I really shouldn't have trouble imagining you doing such a thing," she said slowly. "You have the chameleon's ability to blend into any setting. Yet . . ." She tried to define the subtle impressions she had acquired in their travels. "Though you talk easily with anyone of any station, you always seem apart, with the group but not of it."

His hand stilled around the wine goblet. "That, Kanawiosta, is entirely too perceptive a comment," he said wryly. Before she could ask what he meant, he continued, "We'll be in London soon. Where do you plan to begin investigating your father's death?"

"The obvious place is the hotel where he died. It is a public place, and surely someone there must know something. I also have the names of some of the old friends he visited."

"And after you have learned what you can, and acted on it, what, then?" His blue gaze was intense.

Maxie shook her head and toyed with a silver spoon, trying unsuccessfully to decipher the intricate engraved initial. "Go back to America, I suppose. I haven't really thought about it. The future seems too far away." She poured more tea for herself, using the moment to think. "No, that isn't quite right. Usually I have a vague idea of what the future holds. Nothing so grand as prophecy, just a sense that actions will be completed. For example, when we traveled I always knew when we would reach our destination and when we would not. When we sailed for England, I didn't doubt that we would arrive safely, and I knew that I would meet my father's family. For that matter, I knew when I left my uncle's that I would reach London, though I certainly didn't imagine meeting you or any of the adventures along the way.''

She gave him a fleeting smile. "But now, when I look ahead, I can't project what will happen. It's like one summer when we planned to visit Albany, but I couldn't quite visualize us there. As it turned out, my father fell ill and we spent several weeks in a village in Vermont and ended up missing Albany that year. It's rather like that now; I have no sense of what will happen after reaching London.''

His brows drew together. "Do you feel that some disaster lies ahead?"

She considered. "No, rather that the future will take a turn I can't envision because it is too different from the past. I never believed I would spend the whole of my life traveling through New England selling books, but I didn't know how it would end, and it was a complete surprise when my father announced that it was time to visit his family in England. Now, even though I can't imagine not seeing America again, I am sure my days as a book peddler are done, but I can't imagine what the future does hold. Do you understand what I mean?"

His face still intent, he nodded. "I think so." Lifting the glass to her, he smiled. "Here's to unpredictable fate and the strange and wonderful things it sends us.''

Maxie raised her cup. "Is a toast drunk in tea binding?"

"With symbolism, intent is everything, the details unimportant," he assured her.

She hesitated a moment, feeling a strange, deep longing. It was getting harder and harder to imagine parting from Robin, with his careless charm and quixotic humor and tranquil acceptance of her mongrel background. But a future with him came under the heading of dreams rather than of possible outcomes; trying to hold him would be like trying to capture the wind in her hands.

Then she smiled wistfully, raising the cup and emptying it in one quick swallow. She was an American, which meant that she should not accept that anything was impossible.

* * *

The Marquess of Wolverton had estimated that it would take the fugitives three or four days to reach Ruxton, always assuming that Robin decided to stop there. That being the case, Giles busied himself with more inquiries but with a signal lack of success; the pair had evaporated from Market Harborough like summer mist.

He had intended to spend the third night at Ruxton, but a violent storm turned the roads to mire and slowed his carriage to the pace of a walking man. Irritated, he chided himself for spending too much time on futile investigation; if he had given up a few hours earlier, he could have reached Ruxton. Now he must stop at the next inn.

As his carriage lurched through the mud, he found himself thinking about Desdemona Ross, who had developed an alarming tendency to invade his mind, both waking and sleeping. He wasn't sure what he wanted to do about her, but he definitely wanted to do something.

Reverie was interrupted when the carriage shuddered to a halt. A moment later his footman opened the door. "There's a private carriage on the road ahead, my lord. A broken axle most likely. We thought you might wish to offer a ride to the passengers."

His servants knew him well. The marquess had been helped by a passing Samaritan himself once under difficult circumstances, and he made a point of extending the same courtesy to others. Shrugging into his greatcoat, he stepped into the torrent and made his way toward the people standing by the stranded carriage.

He was almost on them when he recognized the tall female discussing the situation with her coachman. Whoever had said that it was an ill wind that blew no good was right; this storm was definitely blowing well. "Good evening, Lady Ross. May I offer you a ride to the next town?"

She swung around in surprise. Rain was cascading over the brim of the bonnet, but he saw that her first reaction was a pleased smile, though she quickly erased it with a scowl. "I'm not sure I can bear to be rescued by you twice in the same week, Wolverton."

He laughed. Though the lady was soaked to the skin with water and mud, her spirit was undiminished. "I'm not sure this qualifies as a rescue, but if you prefer, you can stay with the carriage until it's repaired.''

She smiled in reluctant response. ''Even I am not that stubborn, my lord.''

''Shall we take your maid?''

She shook her head. ''Silly wench came down with a streaming cold, so I sent her back to London rather than have to watch her play the martyr.''

The marquess escorted her to his own carriage while Lady Ross's servants retreated to wait for help in the relative comfort of the broken-down vehicle. It wasn't far to the next town, Daventry, and during the short journey Giles told his guest about his futile inquiries, and about Robin's estate, Ruxton, which was only a few miles down the road.

In Daventry they stopped at a blacksmith's and dispatched aid to Lady Ross's damaged carriage, then went to the town's main inn, the Wheatsheaf. There was only one private parlor, and as they entered, quickly followed by a little maid with a tea tray, Lady Ross said, ''This seems very familiar. We always seem to be meeting at inns.''

A small fire had been laid because of the storm chill, and she stood by the hearth as she removed her sodden cloak and bonnet. Curling wildly from the moisture, her red hair fell in a vivid mass about her shoulders and she absently combed her fingers through it in a vain attempt at straightening.

Giles considered making a light comment about the effect that meeting at inns could have on a reputation, then thought better of it. Besides, the sight of Desdemona was having a paralyzing effect on his brain and vocal chords. He had wondered what her appearance would be if she wasn't swaddled in layers of shapeless clothing. Now he learned the answer, and the knowledge was like lightning in his veins.

The first time her ladyship had stormed into his study, parasol in hand, he had thought her rather stout, in a not unattractive way. Stout, however, implied being large all over, while Desdemona was large only in certain places. Her saturated muslin dress clung more closely than any damped petticoats, revealing a spectacular figure with loving detail. Her legs were gloriously long and shapely, and the slimness of her waist made her dramatic curves seem downright flamboyant. In particular, she had a remarkable pair of . . .

Giles hastily straightened his expression. A gentleman would say she had a lovely neck, since what she did have was not a subject for polite comment. Yes, indeed, Lady Ross had a very fine neck, and the rest of her was very fine as well, in a lush Junoesque style.

Sensing his regard, she turned and said accusingly, "You are staring at me."

So he was. Giles raised his bemused eyes to her face and said with regrettable candor, "Lady Collingwood was right."

Her face flared as red as her hair and he realized too late how tactless the comment was. "That was not an insult," he said hastily. "You are a strikingly attractive woman, but not in the common way. Certainly not a typical debutante."

"You mean that you agree with my sister-in-law that I look like a light-skirt," she snapped. "No doubt you are both right, because that is how too many men have tried to treat me." She reached for her wet cloak to cover herself.

Her bitter words gave the marquess an insight into why she was so uneasy about male attention. He stood and took off his wool coat. "Why not put this on? Unlike your cloak, it's dry."

As she hesitated, he said in his gentlest tone, "I'm sorry for what I said. I meant no disrespect. It is just that I was surprised. You've done an excellent job of concealing yourself."

Warily she crossed the room and accepted the coat, as if expecting him to attack her, then she wrapped it around herself and withdrew. The coat returned her to perfect decency, to Giles' regret. He busied himself pouring tea, then handed her a cup along with a small plate of the cakes and tiny sandwiches the inn had provided. At first she perched nervously on the edge of a chair, but she began to relax as the tea warmed her and Giles maintained both polite conversation and distance.

Deciding that it was time to learn why her ladyship was so skittish, the marquess remarked, "It must have been a difficult come-out. Innocence usually arouses protective instincts, but you have the kind of beauty that can make men forget themselves, especially young men with more passion than patience."

Desdemona's eyes flashed up, surprise in the clear depths

when he referred to her as beautiful in such a matter-of-fact way, as if it was an obvious, inarguable fact. Then she looked down at her plate again and crumbled a cake. "It was not pleasant. The first time a young man caught me away from the chaperons I was horrified and guilty, wondering what I had done to encourage him. Eventually I realized that the fault was not in my behavior." She grimaced. "I took to wearing a long pin in my hair."

"I can see why that would contribute to a low opinion of the male half of the race," he said thoughtfully. "But that was just the beginning, wasn't it?"

"Why do you ask, Wolverton?" Desdemona raised her head, her gaze challenging. "If you are just expressing dishonorable intentions in a more genteel than usual way, I can't see that my past is any of your business."

He drew in a deep breath. "My intentions are not dishonorable, so"—the words came with some difficulty—"that means they must be honorable."

She was so surprised that her jaw dropped and she put her teacup down with a clink. Their gazes held in one of those kaleidoscopic moments when everything changes forever. For better or worse, there would be no going back.

When she spoke, her words seemed irrelevant, but he knew they were not. "I met your wife once when she was making her come-out. She was exquisite, like a delicate creature from fairyland."

He felt the old knot deep in his chest and set his own cup down, making sure to do so soundlessly. Turnabout was fair play; if he was going to probe Desdemona, she had the right to do the same. "Yes, Dianthe was very beautiful."

"She and I could not be more unlike."

"I hope to God that is true," he said, unable to keep bitterness out of his voice. "If it isn't, talking to you like this could prove to be the second great mistake of my life."

Desdemona had felt off-balance throughout this conversation, but the marquess's words steadied her. For the first time she began to see the man behind the calm control. "What went wrong?" she asked softly.

Unable to sit still, he got to his feet and began to pace

restlessly, with the long strides of someone who spent much of his time under the open sky. "It isn't much of a story. I was quite besotted when I married her. I couldn't believe that she had chosen me over so many others." He shrugged his broad shoulders. "Pure idiocy that I didn't realize why: I was heir to the best title and fortune available on the marriage mart just then. But she was very skilled at pretending sweet, loving innocence. It was easy to be a fool."

"Yet surely she must have cared for you. No woman would accept a man she didn't like when she had so many choices."

His expression was sardonic. "She didn't precisely dislike me, but during one of our charming discussions later, she said that she was bored with me before the honeymoon was over. She had expected to be bored, but not quite so much, and so quickly."

Desdemona winced; the cruelty of it was far too reminiscent of her own marriage.

He continued, "Dianthe was quite the little philosopher, however. Boring I might be, but she was prepared to tolerate me in return for fortune and position. She had an amazing talent for spending money."

"She died in childbirth, didn't she, along with the baby?" Desdemona had a vague memory of reading about the deaths; she had spared a moment of regret for the beauty's untimely end.

He braced a hand on the mantel and stared into the fire. "Yes." There was a very long silence. "As she was dying, when it looked like the baby might survive, she told me that it was almost certainly not mine. She was rather apologetic. Women in her position usually try to provide a legitimate heir or two before going their own way. She had intended to do that as her part of the bargain, but mistakes do happen."

Desdemona ached for him, and for the first time in her life she went to a man and made a physical gesture of comfort, not worrying whether he would react the wrong way. Laying a hand on his shirt-sleeved arm, she said, "I'm very sorry. She didn't deserve you."

With visible effort he kept his voice steady, but his arm was as tight as strung wire under her fingers. "I don't know about that, but it is certainly true that we had very different ideas about what we wanted of our marriage. My judgment was disastrously bad.'' His voice was almost inaudible as he added, ''And the worst of it was not knowing how to mourn.''

''I understand,'' she said quietly. ''When my husband was killed, I felt relief and guilt along with some impersonal sadness for such a pointless death. It was . . . complicated.''

He raised his hand to rest it briefly on hers. ''I never met Sir Gilbert Ross, but he had the reputation of a gamester.''

''Among many other things, most of them bad.'' It was Desdemona's turn to stare into the fire. She had never spoken about her marriage to anyone, but the marquess's honesty and vulnerability deserved a like response. ''He drowned in a ditch one night when he was drunk. Virtually the only considerate act of his life was to die when he was at high tide with his gaming, so there was enough to pay off his debts with a bit left over.'' She sighed. ''A fashionable courtship is such an artificial thing that it is not surprising that you and I ended up choosing partners who were different than we thought. Though in point of fact, I did not choose my husband.''

''It was a match arranged by your family?''

''No, my family would surely have chosen better. I made my come-out in the usual way, and Sir Gilbert was one of several suitors.'' She gave an acid smile. ''My fortune was not on the order of yours, but I had quite a substantial dowry, and men liked my looks, even if they didn't respect them.

''Gilbert courted me most assiduously, but knew my brother would refuse permission if he made an offer. So he took me for a drive in the park one day and kept on going, not bringing me home until the next day.''

The marquess looked up quickly. ''Did he . . . ?''

She shook her head. ''No, he was most respectful. Took me to the unoccupied house of a friend, swearing undying love and saying that he couldn't live without me. I was furious, of course, but also rather flattered. He was very handsome.''

Desdemona looked down again. ''He didn't lay a hand on me, and didn't have to. The mere fact of having spent an unchaperoned night in his company meant that I was thoroughly compromised. Everyone agreed that I had no choice but to marry him.'' Her full lips thinned. ''I was too young to realize that there is always a choice, so I accepted my fate.''

"And that is why you are so determined that your niece will have a choice, no matter what has happened?"

"Exactly. I will allow no one—*no one*—to coerce her into a miserable marriage." Desdemona lifted the poker and jabbed the glowing coals. "I should have resisted, but as I said, there was a part of me that was flattered that Sir Gilbert wanted me enough to take desperate measures. I liked him well enough. He was very amusing, and I took the fact that he didn't use physical force as proof that he really did care about me. Unfortunately, it was no more love than what your Dianthe felt."

"He was interested only in your dowry?"

"That was the main reason. But apart from the money . . ." She swallowed, not sure she could continue. The marquess put a comforting, unthreatening arm around her shoulders, and she relaxed a little.

"Sir Gilbert told me once when he was drunk that he had made a list of girls who had decent fortunes but who were not such great heiresses that he would not be allowed near them. Then, after he had met us all, he chose me because of . . . because of my breasts." She spoke baldly, amazed that she could say aloud the words that had seared her to her soul.

Wordlessly he pulled her closer to his side. Strangely enough, she thought that he could understand how humiliating she had found her husband's declaration; Wolverton's own experiences had been equally humiliating.

"The basic, underlying transaction in marriage is sex for money: the male supports and protects the female in return for sexual access," he said, his voice reflective. "It's not very flattering for either party. Certainly I didn't enjoy learning that the hard way." His arm tightened. "You had the misfortune to be forced into marriage because of both lust and money. It seems particularly unfair that you were doubly victimized."

For some reason, that struck Desdemona as amusing, and she began to laugh. "Lord, what fools these mortals be," she gasped when she was able, leaning her head back against Wolverton's shoulder. "Is that what all the fine romantic phrases come down to: the man choosing the female who most arouses him, the woman accepting the man who can best provide for her?"

"Not at all. That may be the basic transaction, but it is just the beginning. Humans are complicated creatures, and a good marriage must satisfy many needs and desires.'' He looked down, his slate-blue eyes touched with amusement. ''But in addition to affection, companionship, and trust, it is not inherently a bad thing to find one's partner physically attractive.''

She looked away, shy again but content to stay within the circle of his arm. ''Are we back again to the fact that I look like a light-skirt?''

''Not really. To be blunt, if I wanted a light-skirt I could afford whatever kind I wanted. However, that particular vice hasn't appealed to me since my salad days. What I find most attractive about you is your character. I admire the efforts you have gone to on behalf of a niece you have never even met, and I like your directness.'' He chuckled. ''I also like the fact that you blush so easily that it isn't hard to guess what you are thinking.''

The wave of color that went over Desdemona confirmed his last words, and she found herself on the verge of scuffing her toe in the carpet like a child.

He finished his recitation of her virtues by saying, ''The fact that I like and respect you as a person is the foundation, but given that, I am absolutely delighted that you also look like the most delicious kind of opera dancer.''

She began to laugh again at his absurd and marvelous chain of logic, and the way that it dissolved her self-consciousness about her unladylike appearance. For perhaps the first time in her life, a man's admiration was pleasing rather than threatening.

Then she raised her eyes, and laughter ceased as her breath caught at what she saw in his eyes. Certainly there was desire, but also affection and kindness. When he bent over, she did not attempt to avoid his kiss.

It began as a light, undemanding caress, quite unlike the slavering assaults of the young men who had sometimes cornered her when she was a girl. As Desdemona first accepted, then began to enjoy, she decided that perhaps there was more to kissing than she had realized. Her husband, once he had gained possession, had scarcely bothered to kiss her at all, preferring to go direct to his satisfaction.

As she went beyond acceptance to response, the marquess turned her so that they stood face to face, their bodies fitting together as if they had been designed for each other. As her arms circled his broad chest, his embrace tightened and she stiffened, feeling some of the old fear of being overpowered.

Immediately the marquess ended the kiss and released her. His breath unsteady, he stroked back her tangled red curls. "I'm sorry. It is perilously easy to forget myself. I didn't mean to alarm you."

"You didn't. At least, not quite." Desdemona was more than a little unsteady herself. "Where do we go from here, my lord?"

He grinned. "To begin with, you could call me Giles." His smile turned crooked. "Dianthe always called me by my title, which was appropriate, since the lord is whom she married."

"Fool woman. Very well, Giles." She surveyed him thoughtfully. "Do you think you can manage to call me Desdemona with a straight face?"

"Probably not." His eyes sparkled with mischief. "When you first came blazing into Wolverhampton, it occurred to me that Othello may have had a point when he strangled his Desdemona. The thought has passed through my mind once or twice since then as well."

"That is a ridiculous and unworthy comment." She tried, without success, to look severe but found herself succumbing to undignified hilarity. What a silly chit Dianthe must have been, to find Giles boring. Desdemona had not spent a moment in his company when there was not something interesting, infuriating, or amusing happening. Or all three at once.

"True," he agreed cheerfully. "Is that why you are giggling?"

"I am a widow of mature years and serious pursuits," she stated. "I do not giggle." And then she buried her head against his shoulder in a vain attempt to disguise the fact that her statement was utterly false.

11

In spite of the comfort of the bed, sleep eluded Maxie. The four-poster was too wide, too cold, too empty. Of course Robin was right; a bed was conducive to the sort of behavior that a wise young woman avoided. Unfortunately, Maxie had always found that impetuosity came more naturally than wisdom.

She rolled onto her stomach and pummeled the pillow irritably, using the excuse of making it more comfortable. Maintaining the status quo was the safest course, though she knew that if Robin made a serious attempt to persuade her to impropriety, she would agree with alacrity. But though she might be shameless by proper British standards, Maxie did not quite have the temerity to attempt seduction herself, not when there was a distinct chance that she would be turned down.

Scowling, she sat up and pondered. Perhaps if she opened the connecting door between the bedchambers it would make Robin seem closer and help her to relax enough to sleep. She slipped off the high bed and padded over to the connecting door. Even though it was summer, the room was damply cold, and she shivered in her muslin shift as she quietly opened the door and listened, hoping to hear the comforting sound of Robin's breathing over the steady drum of rain on the windowpanes.

She heard him, but the sound was not comforting. His breath came in the same shallow, choked gasps as the first night they had traveled together, sleeping on bracken pallets on the north country moors. He had had no such spells since; perhaps Maxie's proximity had staved off the nightmares.

The mattress creaked as he shifted weight. Then Robin began to talk, his flexible tenor low but laced with anguish as he spoke in a language that was not English. As Maxie swiftly crossed the room, she identified his speech as a German dialect. One of her father's regular customers had been a Hessian farmer whose household spoke a similar tongue among themselves. She heard the words *das Blut* and *der Mord*. Blood and murder.

Then, with a harshness that would have woken her even through a closed door, Robin cried, "*Nein! Nein!*" and thrashed out frantically at some unseen threat. Concerned, Maxie scrambled onto the wide bed and laid a hand on his shoulder to wake him from the nightmare.

Before she could even speak his name, he exploded under her touch, rolling over with blinding speed and seizing Maxie to force her down into the mattress. Robin's torso was bare and damp with perspiration, and his breath came in wrenching gasps as he sprawled full-length on top of her, his forearm pressed across her throat so hard that she could scarcely breathe. There must be deadly danger in whatever nightmare landscape he wandered, and he was reacting with the lethal fighting skill she had seen twice before.

Maxie was terrifyingly aware of the dangerous strength in his taut, wiry body, and she forced herself to lie absolutely still, knowing that if she struggled he might throttle her or break her neck. Drawing as much air as she could through her constricted throat, she said sharply, "Robin, wake up! You're dreaming."

For a terrifying moment the pressure on her throat increased, cutting off further speech. Then her words penetrated through his nightmare. As he returned to consciousness, she felt his rigid body soften.

"Maxie?"

Too short of breath to speak, she nodded.

"God help me, Maxie. Are you all right?" Violently he flung away from her to lie on his back, his fair skin ghost-pale in the darkness. His voice was trembling and he raised a hand to knead at his temple. "I didn't hurt you?"

She drew a deep breath, grateful to be able to fill her lungs. "No damage done. But what about you?"

"Just . . . just a nightmare."

She raised herself and rolled to lie on her side next to him. To her horror, she realized that Robin was shaking so hard that the mattress vibrated. She wrapped her arms around him in an instinctive gesture of comfort, drawing his head against her breasts as if he were a child. He responded convulsively, embracing her with a desperation that threatened to bruise her ribs and cut off her breath again.

"Are you having an attack of fever?" she asked, wondering if he might have fallen victim to malaria on his travels.

"No." His voice shook with the effort of trying to sound composed in the midst of turmoil. "It's just an attack of nerves. It will pass."

Maxie's mouth twisted. It was very gallant of him to pretend, but she was sure that his reaction went far beyond nerves to a state of blind, soul-destroying panic. She had once shared a bed with a Vermont girl who had been orphaned and nearly killed by a fire. The girl had woken screaming from nightmare in a state very like Robin's, until her aunt had come and coaxed her into describing her nightmares. Talking had relieved the girl's hysteria and Maxie decided to try the same tactic here.

"What happened, Robin? What were you dreaming?"

After a silence so long that she wondered if he had heard her, he replied, "The usual—violence, betrayal, killing men who might have been my friends in other times." His voice was so unsteady it was nearly inaudible and his shaking worsened.

"You were a soldier?"

"Not a soldier," Robin said with bitter humor. "Nothing so clean as that." He had suffered similar spells in the last months, each worse than the last, and he feared that it was only a matter of time before he fell over the edge of sanity. He wished that Maxie was not here to see him in his weakness, but since she was, he was unable to stop himself from clinging to her as a lifeline in a sea of shattering emotional turbulence.

"If you weren't a soldier, what were you?"

"I was a spy." The bald declaration was not enough. He drew in an unsteady breath. "For a dozen years, from the time I was twenty. I lied, I stole, even sometimes acted the assassin. I was very good at it."

"And here I thought you were a thief or a swindler. You have all the skills." There was amusement in Maxie's husky voice, and she was as matter-of-fact as if they were discussing the weather. "Your acting ability and talent for language must have been invaluable."

"It would have been better if I had been a common thief.

I would have caused less harm." Distorted faces began to crowd around him, images of those he knew and a legion of unknown others who had died because of information he had passed on. His shaking worsened, and he wondered with despair if it was possible for a body to shatter into pieces.

Once more Maxie's voice touched him, her words pulling him from the drowning pool of pain. "A thief works for only his own gain. I can't believe that you became a spy for simple greed."

"No, I worked for England. Besides, spying is not that lucrative a trade." At least, not for honest practitioners of an inherently dishonest art. "I thought the cause was good. It was only toward the end that the blood on my hands . . ." His words trailed off.

"Tell me how you began. Surely you didn't study spying at Oxford." In spite of his sordid revelations, Maxie's voice held curiosity, not revulsion.

"Cambridge, actually, not Oxford." His tension eased some as he found amusement in how aptly she had gauged him. "After my second year at university there was a truce on the Continent for the first time in ten years, so I went on holiday to France. It was obvious that war would resume again soon. I happened to learn something useful and, like a good patriot, sent the information to London. Whitehall was delighted and suggested I stay on when the truce ended."

The suggestion had come from Edward Lattimer, in the days when he was a junior member of the Foreign Office. Lattimer's approval had been gratifying; Robin received very little approval in other quarters. It had been seductively easy to convince himself that he was doing something valuable.

"At the beginning it was almost a game. I was too young and heedless to realize that I was selling my soul, a piece at a time." The suffocating panic began to rise again. "By the time I did realize, there was nothing left."

Maxie shook her head, and her silky hair brushed his cheek with the sweet tang of lavender. "An interesting metaphor," she said softly, "but false. You may have forgotten how to find your soul, but you can't lose, sell, or give it away."

Sweetness and sanity—her words helped focus his splintered

mind. "Is that humor or wisdom?" he asked with a choke of near-hysterical laughter.

"Both." She considered a moment. "If you had no soul, you could not suffer the kind of guilt you feel now. In my experience, dedicated villains sleep peacefully at night."

"By that standard, I must be a saint," Robin said wearily.

After another pause, she said, "You said once that your friend Maggie was your partner in crime. I wondered then what you meant. She was also a spy?"

"Yes. Her father was killed by a French mob. I helped her escape. She had no reason to return to England, so we became comrades. I spent much of my time traveling about the Continent, but home was wherever Maggie was. Most often, Paris."

"Comrades and lovers," Maxie murmured. "She was the linchpin, and when she left you, things fell apart?"

Robin was so startled that his panic receded. "How did you reach that conclusion?" He had never thought of the situation in those terms, but Maxie's analysis was dead-accurate once again.

"Feminine intuition," she said rather dryly, then changed the subject. "I suppose that your stints in service were in pursuit of information?"

"Exactly. People tend not to notice servants."

"And I imagine that you can appear extraordinarily nondescript when you choose to."

She reached out and pulled the blanket over them. Its weight was welcome; he hadn't realized how cold he was. But the vital warmth came from Maxie. Her breasts were soft beneath her thin shift, her gentle hands soothing.

"It has just occurred to me that many of your absurd tales might be true. Were you truly in jail in Constantinople?"

He smiled faintly. "God's own truth."

"And Napoleon's retreat from Moscow?"

Robin's temporary feeling of well-being shattered, and he began to shake again.

Maxie tightened her embrace. "Tell me the worst thing that haunts you."

"No!" Willi's eager young face in front of him, as clear as

the day the boy died, and Robin twisted away, trying to break free.

She held tight, refusing to let him escape. "Tell me, Robin," she urged, her breath light against his forehead. When he shook his head, denying, Maxie continued, "Do you think I am too fragile to hear the truth? I am not a sheltered English innocent from the schoolroom. I have seen life and death in many forms."

He found himself torn by contradictory emotions as the desire to unburden his soul warred with the knowledge that surely Maxie, who was so bright and true, would despise him for the disasters he had wrought.

"Tell me what you've done, Robin," she repeated with implacable compassion. "Burdens are lighter for being shared."

Defeated by her caring, he struggled against tears; what he felt was too deep for tears. "There were so many things," he whispered. "Endless lies. Informants I worked with who were captured and died most horribly." Under cover of darkness it was possible, just barely, to speak. "The French colonel I assassinated because he had the ability to withstand a siege."

"Surely your informants knew the risks as well as you did. As for assassination," she hesitated, choosing her words carefully, "no man of honor could rejoice at doing such a thing, but preventing a siege was a worthy goal. Was your action successful?"

"Without the colonel to lead them, his troops withdrew from the city without fighting." After a long silence, he admitted, "Certainly many lives were saved."

"That can't be wrong."

"Perhaps not. But nothing can make it right to murder an honorable man who was doing his duty." Though her words made sense, logic was not enough to mitigate the crushing weight of self-condemnation.

"I see why you said that war would have been cleaner," she said. "For most soldiers the issues are more clearly drawn, the responsibility left in higher hands. Your work was far more difficult. Often you must have been forced to choose between different evils, trapped in a world of grays without easy blacks and whites, never sure that you had made the right decision. A dozen years of that would be too much for anyone."

"Certainly it was too much for me."

He sounded exhausted, but Maxie guessed there was more, and she pressed on. The more light that was let into Robin's inner darkness, the better the chance of healing. "Is that assassination the worst thing, the very worst, for which you hold yourself responsible?"

His shaking, which had subsided, began again, and she wondered if he would, or could, tell her the rest. Finally he choked out, in short, staccato sentences, "It was in Prussia. I obtained a copy of a secret treaty with grave implications for Britain. The French discovered what had happened. They traced and killed the man who had actually copied the documents and passed them to me. Then they came in pursuit."

In the stillness thunder sounded and cold rain beat harder on the glass.

"I rode west for days, using every trick I knew to elude them. Finally I was sure I had escaped. I needed to stop and rest. My horse was half-dead, and I no better. There was a family near, prosperous farmers. They hated the French, for good reason. They had helped me in the past."

His voice cracked. "They greeted me like a long-lost son. I told them a little of what happened, about being pursued. But I assured them there was no danger. I was so sure." He pulled one hand away from Maxie and balled a fist to pound the mattress, saying with anguish, "God help me, I was wrong."

"And then?"

"I slept for over twelve hours and woke the next morning. The Werners were worried. French troops were searching the neighborhood. I said I would leave immediately and went to the barn, but my horse was gone.

"Then I realized I hadn't seen Willi, their youngest. He was sixteen, my height and build, my coloring. He had conceived something of a hero worship for me. When I saw that my horse and saddle were gone, I knew, somehow I knew, that disaster was at hand. I ran into the forest toward the main road, trying to stop what was going to happen, but I was too late."

There was a film of cold sweat over his trembling body. Maxie felt resonances of his pain deep inside her, but knew she must force him to the end of the tale. "What happened?"

"Willi had decided to lead them away from the farm. I was above and could see how he deliberately let himself be seen by a French cavalry squad. He had my horse, a coat the color of mine, and he was bareheaded, showing that damnable, identifiable blond hair. They spotted him and gave chase. He tried to outrun them. My horse was very good and Willi might have escaped, but another squad came along the road from the other direction. He was trapped. From my vantage point on the hill, I saw it all.

"He bolted off the road into the forest, but he hadn't enough of a lead. The two squads caught him quickly. They gave him no chance to surrender, just shot him down. At least a dozen musket balls hit him." He shuddered, and Maxie felt his heart pounding as if trying to break free of his ribs.

"Willi was a bright lad, and at the end he outwitted them. There was a small river that had cut a deep gorge. He was able to survive long enough to reach it. The horse screamed as it plunged over the cliff into the water."

Robin buried his head against Maxie, shuddering with the broken, agonized sobs of a man at the limits of his endurance. She asked no more questions, just caressed him, whispering soft words in her mother's tongue, saying that everything would be all right, that he was a valiant and honorable warrior, and that she loved him no matter what he had done. For better and for worse, she knew the words were achingly true, though she would not have dared speak them in English.

For a long time there was no sound but rain and distant thunder and grief. In time the echoes of anguish faded, though Robin still held Maxie as if she was his one hope of heaven. At length he said, "Doubtless the French would have liked to retrieve the documents, but the river was high. They decided the water would destroy what the bullets hadn't, and they left.

"I stayed for the next two days and helped the Werners search until we recovered Willi's body. The whole time . . ." His voice broke. "His parents said not one word of reproach. In some ways, that was the hardest thing of all. God help me, but they even apologized that Willi had destroyed my horse and insisted I take their best mount as a replacement."

"From what you say, it sounds as if Willi brought disaster

on himself," Maxie said quietly. Based on what she knew of
the wars, it seemed likely that the disaster had taken place after
the treaty of Tilsit. Robin would not have been so very much
older than the boy whose death he blamed himself for, and for
nine years he had lived with his guilt. "If he hadn't intervened
with his misplaced gallantry, you might have escaped cleanly
with no one suffering."

"Perhaps, perhaps not." He drew an unsteady breath. "But
the fact remains that if I hadn't stopped at the Werners', Willi
would not have died."

"Only God can know that, Robin. Perhaps it was Willi's time
to die, and he would have slipped on the stairs and broken his
neck at that same moment if you had not come. Perhaps he
would have gone for a soldier when he was a year older and
died fighting the French. Only a shallow man would not feel
grief and regret, but crucifying yourself serves no good
purpose." She stroked his head, wishing she could soothe away
the pain inside. "Willi has gone to his rest. Can't you do the
same?"

He sighed and lay back against the pillows. A flash of
lightning illuminated his desolate, exhausted features. "Is that
fatalism the Mohawk in you, Kanawiosta?"

She shrugged and waited for the rolling thunder to fade.
"Perhaps. Or maybe it is the result of a father who taught me
Greek and Latin so we could argue about ancient philosophers
and theology in their own tongues. Or perhaps it is just me."

After a long silence, he said bleakly, "I always tried to do
the right thing. It was just that too often I didn't know what
the right thing was."

"I think most of us do the best we know how, even if our
best isn't always very good." His arm was around her, so Maxie
settled her head on his shoulder, so tired from the emotional
storms she could scarcely stay awake. "There really isn't any
more we can do."

"You're so wise." Robin's hand lightly brushed her cheek,
as if in the darkness he sought to remind himself of her features.
"Too wise to consider marrying me."

His statement acted on her fatigue like a spray of ice water,
shocking her to full wakefulness. For a stunned moment Maxie

replayed his words to ensure that she had heard properly. Then she sat up and fumbled on the bedside table for the flint. After lighting the candle, she turned to her companion.

Robin lay on the bed and watched her with the patient stillness of exhaustion. He was bare from the waist up, and the candle-light glinted from the golden hair of his chest and head, but there was not enough light to read the color or expression of his shadowed eyes.

Maxie stared at him, torn between shock, amusement, and desperate longing. "Is that an offer, or merely a product of your warped sense of humor?"

He sighed, turning his gaze from her to stare up at the ceiling. "It wasn't intended as humor. I guess I can't quite bring myself to make a direct offer. If we did marry, the advantages would all be to me. You would be a fool to accept, and as a woman of intelligence, you know that already."

Maxie didn't know whether to laugh, cry, or shriek. The scalding emotions of the night had forced her to admit that she loved Robin, though she wasn't sure that she understood or even wholly trusted him. Which was not the same as saying that she distrusted him; she had no doubt that he would be true to any commitment he made. And she understood him a good deal better now than she had an hour before. Still . . . "Marrying you is not without appeal, but I can't imagine what sort of life we would have together. Even though we have both been wanderers in the past, that isn't what I want for the future."

"No more do I. I promise you that I can keep a roof over your head." His mouth quirked in a wry smile. "I am not quite so improvident as I look."

"Robin, look at me." When his gaze turned to her again, she asked, "Why do you want to marry me? You have said nothing of love."

His eyes closed in a quick spasm of sorrow. "I can promise many things, Kanawiosta. Security, fidelity, my best efforts to make you happy. But love? I don't think I am very good at love. It is one thing I would be wiser not to promise."

Even when her father had died, Maxie had not ached like this. Robin's painful, despairing honesty made her want to weep. Instead, she lifted his head and kissed it, then pressed it against her cheek. "Do you want me because I am here and Maggie is not?"

"No." His eyes opened and his fingers tightened around hers. "What I feel for you has nothing to do with Maggie. I did, and do, care for her deeply, and I always will, but I don't want you as a substitute for her." Amusement flickered across his handsome, fallen-angel face. "You are far too much yourself to ever be mistaken for anyone else."

"Caring and loyalty are valuable, even vital." Maxie felt adrift, uncertain how to react. "But what of passion?"

"You are concerned about passion?" he asked softly, tugging her hand to bring her down next to him. "Passion is easy."

He rolled over and embraced her, and as their lips met, Maxie thought she would dissolve in liquid fire. There had been lazy desire that night they had shared a bed and woken to kisses, but this was utterly different. Robin's formidable skill and concentration were for her, and her alone, and she responded with all the intensity she had possessed. The drama of the night had scoured away normal defenses and their emotions twined as intimately as their bodies.

For a wild, sweet interval, there were no questions, only taste and touch and discovery. If Maxie had had any doubts that she loved him, they were now resolved as every aspect of body and soul responded and as Robin in turn responded to her. No matter how twisted his past, despairing his present, and uncertain his future, she loved him.

Abruptly, just before they reached the point of no return, Robin pulled away and buried his face in the pillow, his shoulders heaving, his hands clenching the counterpane. "Passion is too easy." His voice was raw. "Neither of us, I think, is in the right state to make an irrevocable decision."

Her own breathing ragged, Maxie stared at the ceiling and tried to collect her scattered wits as her limbs trembled with reaction. "I gather this means you are undergoing another crisis of conscience."

He emerged from the pillow with a wry, self-mocking chuckle. "Exactly so." Gently he tugged her shift over her bare breasts, cupping one with his palm for a moment before regretfully removing his hand. "You are a remarkable woman, as well as lovely enough to make a monk forget his vows. After all I've put you through tonight, you should be having shrieking hysterics.''

"Don't give me tempting ideas," Maxie replied, trying to sound stern but with a smile tugging at her lips for the absurd situation. If they could laugh at themselves, the worst of the night was past. Best of all, there was an intimacy between them that more than compensated for the frustration of interrupted lovemaking. For the first time, she had a real sense of who Robin was; perhaps there might even be a future in loving him. She rolled over and propped her head on one hand, her smile fading. "Just how serious are you about marriage?"

His gravity matched her own, his blue eyes dark with passion and affection and honesty. "Completely."

Maxie closed her own eyes for a moment to marshal her thoughts before speaking. She wanted to say that she loved him, but didn't dare, not after his painful doubts about his ability to love. Nor, if he changed his mind about marrying her, did she want to bind him with guilt. "You are right that now is not the time to make a decision. I need to learn what happened to my father, and you . . ." She paused, not having the words. "You need to learn something, too."

"What?"

She opened her eyes and studied him. The detachment that he had worn like a cloak was gone, and she savored the feeling of closeness. But he was so unreasonably handsome that it was difficult for her to think clearly, especially when her body still throbbed with desire. "I don't know, precisely. Only that there is something, and you must learn it on your own."

"Riddles." He leaned forward and pressed a light kiss on her forehead. "Doubtless you are right. I only hope I am capable of learning. At least you are not saying no."

"Are you sure you want me to say yes?"

"Quite positive." Robin stroked a hand through her thick black hair, twining it around his fingers. "I don't think that I have ever felt more whole or happy in my life than these last days with you. I've been wishing this journey would never end. Now, since there will be no final answers until it does, I want to get to London as soon as possible. It's just that . . ."

She waited patiently for him to continue. Robin might not think he was very good at love, but what he had offered so far was not a bad approximation.

His eyes slid away and his hand stilled. "I don't know if it is wise to marry a woman because I need her so much. I think it might not be good for either of us."

Maxie gave a snort of exasperation and rolled over to tuck her back against his front, in the spoon fashion that was the most comfortable for sleeping. "Your problem, Lord Robert, is that you think too much."

He chuckled and pinched the candle out, then wrapped his arm around her. Maxie felt the tension leaving his body. "Once more you are absolutely right. Sweet dreams, Kanawiosta."

She relaxed into his embrace, enjoying the warmth between them, the comforting sound and rhythm of his breathing. As she slid into sleep, she thought that even if love was never mentioned, marrying for this feeling of rightness might well be enough.

12

Washed clean by the storm, the dawn sky was pale and clear when Maxie woke. Robin still slept, his spun-gold head resting on her breast, his peaceful face very young. Hard to remember his desperate misery of the night before, or to believe that he had done the things he had; he looked scarcely more than a schoolboy.

Maxie shifted, and the motion roused her companion. At close range, his azure eyes had the impact of a cannonball; if she hadn't already been in love with him, she would be after that lazy, intimate smile.

He ran a caressing hand down her body and kissed her. As her blood stirred to full wakefulness, Maxie was aware that each of them was holding passion in check, going so far and no further. A wise precaution, considering their unsettled situation. But there was just a hint that passion might overcome wisdom, and the risk added spice to the embrace.

Wisdom won, alas. With a flattering regretful sigh, Robin ended the kiss and sat up. "Enough of playing with fire and of letting chance control our journey. Today we go to London."

Maxie's sense of well-being started to erode. "What do you have in mind? We haven't enough money left for coach fare, even from this distance."

He gave her a bright smile, the one she automatically distrusted. "I'll explain later. But now we must set off before the estate workers are up and about."

They left a quarter-hour later, leaving a superficially undisturbed house behind them. It was nearing the summer solstice and the days were very long, and there was no sign of other human activity even though the sun was fully above the horizon. Maxie did not start to feel alarmed until she realized that Robin was going to the stables behind the house.

Before she could stop him, he had slipped in by a side door. Maxie followed into the dimly lit stable, where horses whickered sleepily at the human presence. Mindful that there might be a groom sleeping on the upper level, she kept her voice low, but still managed to get a full measure of outrage into it. "What the devil are we doing here?"

"Finding transport." Completely nonchalant, Robin walked the length of the center aisle, studying the box stalls on each side. Most of the horses were for fieldwork, but there were several very tolerable hacks as well. Leading out the two best, he rapidly saddled them, ignoring Maxie's fuming silence.

"Probably advisable to lead them to the estate boundary," he said. "Do you have a preference for which one you want?"

Maxie planted herself in front of him, arms akimbo and fire in her eye. "Blast it, Robin, I don't want to be a party to horse theft. Or do you intend to turn these loose a few miles down the road, like you did with Simmons' nag?"

He gave her a smile of infuriating calmness. "Not this time. We're going to need the beasts for the rest of the journey. But don't worry, I'll let the groom know what happened to them." He pulled a piece of paper from his pocket and hung it on a nail that protruded from a vertical post. Several words were scrawled on the surface, but it was too dim inside the barn for Maxie to read them. More seriously, he said, "Truly, this will get us into no trouble. I know the owner of the estate. If you insist, I'll tell you the whole story, but I would prefer to leave that until a later date."

Maxie stared at him for a long moment, intensely uncomfortable with his cavalier appropriation of two valuable horses. Last night's feeling of closeness had evaporated; once more her companion was the man of mystery. Given his background and former career, it was quite possible that he knew the estate owner; it was equally possible that he was indulging in a bit of pragmatic freebootery.

Lightly he touched her cheek. "Trust me just a little while longer?"

After a moment when the issue wavered in the balance, she took the reins of the smaller horse, a bay gelding, and walked to the stable door. In for a penny, in for a pound—but Robin was certainly testing her faith.

Their luck held through the quiet half-mile walk across the park to a small gate in the estate wall. Once outside Ruxton, they spent a few moments adjusting stirrups, then mounted and headed south.

They rode in silence for a time, Maxie feeling the back of her neck prickle in anticipation of pursuers yelling, "Stop, thief!"

With distance her apprehension diminished; Robin made thievery seem easy. "Will we be able to reach London today?"

"Yes, though it will be late when we arrive."

Maxie sighed. It was now time to consider a topic she had been resolutely ignoring. "Do we have enough money left for a night's lodging?"

"Not really," he admitted. "We can afford tolls and food for the day, but there won't be enough for a decent room in London. Much less two rooms."

She glanced at him askance.

"Don't look at me like that," Robin said ruefully. "I don't like the idea any better than you do, but things will have to change in London. In the eyes of respectable folk you are quite horrendously compromised, but it doesn't count, since nobody knows. In London, however, we will rejoin the real world. At the very least I imagine you will want to visit the aunt you mentioned, and we are going to have to behave with a semblance of propriety and make sure that our lies about the journey match."

"What has that to do with separate beds?"

"You know the answer as well as I do," he said with amusement. "If any of your relations—or mine, for that matter—discover that we have been traveling together, there will be a loud outcry demanding that we marry immediately. And if they knew we've been sleeping together every night . . ." He rolled his eyes in mock horror. "*Le beau monde* has a suspicious mind. From the point of view of the respectable world, you would be ruined."

"Why should you be so concerned about that?" Maxie asked dryly. "I thought marriage was what you wanted."

He grinned. "I can think of nothing that would make you cry off more quickly than being told you had to marry me."

Maxie blushed, thinking that Robin had taken her measure rather well. "I am quite capable of resisting social pressure, particularly from people I don't know and needn't live among."

"So am I, but I learned a long time ago that superficial conformity simplifies one's life enormously."

"When in Rome, do as the Romans do?"

"Exactly. And that goes double for London."

Tacitly conceding the point, Maxie returned to practical matters. "Perhaps we should spend the night outside the city."

"We could, but there are fewer isolated barns in southern England, and hedgerows aren't as practical when we have horses. Even bartering entertainment is less effective in these parts; sophisticated southerners are more difficult to amuse." Robin's golden brows drew together in thought. "If you're willing, we could spend tonight with friends of mine in London. They have ample space, and they would be delighted to have you."

Maxie considered, her gaze resting absently on her mount's ears. "That would certainly be convenient, if you're sure they wouldn't mind receiving a total stranger."

"They wouldn't," he assured her. "And I can obtain money tomorrow during the day."

She started to make an automatic protest about accepting money from him; until now, their contributions had been roughly equal. Then she closed her mouth without speaking. A fortnight earlier such an offer would have roused her determined opposition, but now she could face the prospect with equanimity. Perhaps she was beginning to feel like half of a couple, able to share without worrying about protecting her own boundaries.

In spite of everything that had happened, Maxie was not quite comfortable with the thought of relaxing her hard-earned independence, and her unease showed in her acid question. "Dare I ask where you intend to get the money, Lord Robert?"

"From a banker, very boring and legitimate." His eyes twinkled. "Did you know that you always call me Lord Robert when you are disapproving?"

She thought a moment, then gave a reluctant smile of agreement. "I suppose that silly fraudulent title symbolizes everything I don't know and don't trust about you."

"Do you really distrust me?" he asked quietly.

They were entering a small village, and that gave Maxie time to think about her answer. After they had threaded single-file through the narrow high street and were on the open road, side by side again, she said slowly, "It's no credit to my good sense, but I do trust you, at least to a point."

"What is that point?" He didn't look at her as he asked, and his expression was cool and unforthcoming.

"I am sure you would not knowingly lead me into disaster and I believe you will always honor your word." Maxie sighed. "But perhaps I'm wrong. I can't help remembering the comment of a woman I knew in Boston. She said that being in love reduces one's intelligence by half and eliminates good judgment altogether." She stopped in sudden consternation, realizing what she had just revealed.

Robin turned his head swiftly, his blue eyes intense. Catching her horse's bridle, he brought them both to a halt. Then he backed his horse next to hers, so close their legs touched, and bent over for a long, fiercely emotional kiss.

As she responded, her arms reaching up to circle his neck, Maxie was startled by the depth of feeling her oblique declaration had unleashed. Robin might feel incapable of declaring love himself, but it seemed that her love was not an unwelcome gift.

When he released her, his eyes were grave and vulnerable. "Ask whatever you wish and I'll answer the best I can."

For the moment, it was enough to know that she could. Maxie smiled and flicked her mount's reins. "I can wait."

As they resumed riding, the strain of the early morning was gone and they were close again.

Desdemona's baggage from the damaged coach had been delivered late the previous night, so she was able to don a fresh gown. Unfortunately, it was as dreary as what she had worn the previous day. She really must do something about her wardrobe.

As one of the inn's maids fixed her hair, Desdemona thought back over the previous evening, not quite believing what had happened. After their mutual baring of souls, both she and Lord Wolverton had stepped back emotionally, and over dinner and through the evening the conversation had been general rather than personal. Even though he was the sort of rich landowner whom Desdemona often opposed politically, she had to admit that Giles' mind was both humane and tolerant—probably more tolerant than her own, if she was going to be absolutely honest.

As bedtime neared, she had tensed, wondering if he would attempt to persuade her to join him, but he had treated her with unexceptionable propriety. Except for one thorough good-night kiss, the memory of which made her lips curve into a daft, cat-in-the-creampot smile . . .

Hastily Desdemona rearranged her expression, bestowed a half-crown on the maid, and made her way to the private parlor to break her fast. She had prepared for some constraint when she met the marquess again, and was perversely disappointed that he was not down before her.

Her tea and toast had just been served when he joined her. After a warm greeting, Giles said, "I've been to the smith, and it doesn't look like your coach will be repaired before tomorrow at the earliest." Then, diffidently, "Would you care to accompany me to my brother's estate, Ruxton? After, I can either bring you back here, or take you into London. It would save you some waiting."

Desdemona was delighted to realize that he was as shy about how to proceed as she was. Not that she had really thought him a glib womanizer, but his manner confirmed that he was feeling some of the same trepidation that she was. "I'd love to. But do you think we will find our fugitives there?" She poured a cup of tea and handed it to the marquess.

He accepted the cup and settled into a chair opposite her. "I doubt it," he said wryly. "I'm beginning to think of them as wills-o'-the-wisp, eternally flitting away just over the horizon." He stirred milk into his tea. "Do you think your niece will attempt to reach you in London?"

She shrugged. "I hope so, though I wouldn't wager major money on it. All I can do is return home and hope for the best.

Will your brother go to Wolverton House when he arrives in London?''

"No, the place is closed and has no staff but a caretaker at the moment. I've been thinking of selling it, actually." He glanced up. "But now I think not. There is a chance I shall be spending more time in town in the future."

Desdemona liked the sound of that and found herself smiling again. Really, she was behaving quite absurdly, like a schoolroom miss suffering her first case of calf love. As she looked down at her plate and meticulously spread marmalade over her toast, she realized that she had never felt this way before. She had been a shy and bookish girl, slow to develop interest in the opposite sex; in her salad days she had been tormented by unwanted advances, and she had married young and without love. Surely she was entitled to a little folly. "Will you be able to locate Lord Robert?"

"Money must be high on his list of priorities, so I'll leave word with his bankers." He thought for a moment. "And I'll let some of Robin's friends know I'm looking for him."

The conversation brought Desdemona's fancies to earth. If Lord Robert had caused her niece harm, the repercussions would certainly affect the fragile feelings growing between herself and the marquess. Resolutely she reached for another piece of toast. Let the future take care of itself; for the moment, she intended to enjoy a day in the company of the most attractive man she had ever known.

The roads were muddy from the previous day's storm, and the sun was high in the sky when they reached Ruxton. The gatekeeper recognized the marquess immediately, but swore that Lord Robert had not visited. Unconvinced, they entered the estate and went to the steward's office.

The steward, Haslip, was frowning over his books when Giles and Desdemona entered, but the frown disappeared when he glanced up and identified the man who had hired him and supervised his work for years. "Lord Wolverton!" He stood. "This is an unexpected pleasure, my lord. Will you be staying for a time?"

Giles shook his head. "I just stopped by to see if my brother was here."

Haslip said cautiously, "He may have been, but I can't say for sure."

When Giles raised his brows questioningly, Haslip said, "No one saw him, but this morning two horses were missing and this note was in the stable." He handed a piece of paper to the marquess. "I'm not sure this is his lordship's handwriting. If it is, well enough, but perhaps this was written by a clever thief." The steward grimaced. "Took the two best hacks in the stables."

Giles scanned the note. It said only, "I need the horses," and was sighed "Lord Robert Andreville." The writing was his brother's distinctive back-slanting script.

"That's his hand." Giles handed the paper back. "So he was here last night. At what time was it noticed that the horses were missing?"

"About nine o'clock."

"I'd like to look in the house and see if he spent the night. If he arrived late, perhaps he didn't wish to waken anyone." Giles decided that there was no point in mentioning Miss Collins unnecessarily; the less anyone knew, the better.

Haslip obviously had questions, such as how his employer had entered a walled estate, why he had left without notifying anyone of his presence, and why he needed two horses, but the steward said only, "Of course, my lord. I'll fetch the house keys."

After being let into the manor house, Giles dismissed the steward. Then he and Desdemona spent some time searching the house, finishing in the kitchen.

"They were here, all right," Desdemona said after a prowl that led her to the stillroom, the china closet, and a tin bathing tub with a few drops of water inside. She held a newly washed and polished crystal goblet up to the light. "It appears they dined in some style."

"Oh, Robin has always had style." Giles glanced at his companion. "From the number of linens that were so carefully refolded, it also appears they slept in separate beds. Perhaps all our worries were for naught."

"Perhaps." Though her comment was noncommittal, Desdemona was prepared to believe that a couple could travel together without the man seducing the woman. A day earlier she would have disputed the possibility, but association with Giles was teaching her that a mature man did not invariably act like a lust-crazed youth. Perhaps Lord Robert really had offered his escort to Maxima from altruism. But even if there had been no misconduct, the questions of propriety and reputation remained, and only time would answer them. "Now that they're riding, they could be in London tomorrow. I suppose that is where we should go, too."

"Yes." The marquess gave her an encouraging smile. "In another day or two, this whole imbroglio should be cleared up."

As she led the way from the house, Desdemona thought wryly that the problem of Maxima might be on the verge of solution, but the problem of the marquess was a good deal more challenging. Still, it was the sort of challenge she could relish.

London was immense, noisy, and noisome, assaulting Maxie's senses so forcefully that Boston seemed like a market town by comparison. The journey had not been exceptionally long, perhaps seventy miles, but the muddy condition of the roads had slowed them and it was nearly dark now. Moreover, they were both travel-stained and thoroughly disreputable-looking.

At first she couldn't believe it when Robin pulled to a halt in front of the grandest mansion in a section of the city full of grand mansions. "We're stopping here?" she asked, dismayed.

He gave her a reassuring smile and a hand down from her mount. "This is where my friends live. The knocker is up, so they're in residence. Don't worry, they've seen me in worse case."

Her feet planted on the cobblestones, Maxie scrutinized the massive facade, feeling like a muddy, inappropriately dressed provincial. Pride came to her aid; she would be damned if she would turn coward now. What did it matter what a parcel of overbred English artistocrats thought of her? If Robin thought it fitting to bring her here, she'd not skulk in like a craven hound.

She held the horses while Robin wielded the knocker. Very shortly the door was opened by a livery-clad and bewigged footman whose expression might have been similar if he had found a barrel of long-dead fish on the steps.

Without giving the servant a chance to speak, Robin said, "Call someone to take care of our horses." He had made one of his instant transitions, this time into pure aristocratic hauteur.

The footman made a gurgle of protest, then subsided under his visitor's disdainful eye. Within a few moments, the butler had been summoned and the footman himself led the horses back to the mews.

In spite of her resolutions, Maxie was hard-pressed not to cringe when she set foot in a white marble foyer so vast that a cavalry company could have mustered in it. The vaulted ceiling soared two stories above, larger-than-life classical statues stood on pedestals around the edges, and a sweeping double staircase dominated the center of the room. Maxie was not unfamiliar with grand houses, but this one might have been a royal palace. In fact, for all she knew, the building was Carlton House with the Prince Regent carousing upstairs.

Unimpressed by the lavish surroundings, Robin was as nonchalant as if he were dressed in full London fig rather than like a tinker. "Is the duchess in?"

The butler, less easily intimidated than his minion, said loftily, "Her grace is not receiving."

"That is not what I asked," Robin said, arching his brows with palpable disbelief that a mere butler dared question him. "The duchess will see me. Tell her Lord Robert is here."

The butler paused, his face reflecting rapid mental calculations that weighed the visitor's accent and manner against his unsavory appearance. Reaching a conclusion, he bowed slightly and went off.

Duchess? Maxie wondered if the august lady would prove to be Robin's grandmother, and he the adored family black sheep or something equally appalling. She had decided early in their acquaintance that Robin was well-bred, but was he really from the highest levels of English society? With a sick feeling in her stomach, she admitted that it was quite possible, even probable.

Rigid with discomfort, she avoided Robin's eye, pulling in on herself in this strange and possibly hostile territory. Every muscle in her body tense, she prowled about the foyer like a cat investigating a new home; even her companion's air of command hadn't gotten them invited into a drawing room.

Maxie had reached the farthest corner of the foyer when she heard the sound of swift footsteps. Turning, she saw a glorious golden creature racing down the sweeping staircase. The woman didn't see Maxie; instead, she hurled herself at her visitor, ignoring his filthy clothing. "Robin, you wretch! Why didn't you let me know you were coming?"

Robin reached out, laughing, to catch her up in his arms. "Show a little care, Maggie! Think of the future Marquess of Wilton, if not of yourself."

In her quiet corner, Maxie felt a shock so profound that for a moment her vision darkened. She had thought herself prepared for what this house had to offer, but not this. God in heaven, not this! How could he have brought her to his mistress's house? How could he?

The duchess chuckled. "You're as bad as Rafe. It could be a girl, you know."

"Nonsense. You are far too efficient not to provide the requisite heir on your first attempt."

For a moment the two stayed loosely linked in each other's arms with the casualness of settled intimacy. Sharing the same blazing blond looks, they might almost have been siblings.

In all the long journey from the north, Robin had never seemed farther away from her. Her gilt hair shone in the lamplight, and even in his shabby, travel-worn clothing he was unmistakably an aristocrat. Not since her early childhood, when she had been taunted by white children, had Maxie felt so much a half-breed and an outcast, so irredeemably small, dark, and alien.

Letting go of the duchess, Robin said, "I want you to meet someone very special."

As he led Maggie across the foyer, Maxie was near paralysis from a volatile blend of anger and social confusion. What did one do in the presence of a duchess? In particular, what did a female dressed as a male do?

The answer floated up from a *grande dame* she had known in Boston: a citizen of the American republic bowed to no mortal, only to God, and only then if so inclined. That being so, the mistress of the man who had asked for her hand certainly did not rate a curtsy.

On consideration, Maxie decided that since she was dressed as a boy, removing her hat was appropriate, so she did. Doubtless her expression was one of ferocious hostility, for the duchess's eyes widened in surprise. She had changeable gray-green eyes, not blue like Robin's.

"Maggie, this is Miss Maxima Collins. Maxie, this is the Duchess of Candover." Robin laid a light, reassuring hand on Maxie's arm. "I am trying to persuade Maxie to marry me."

The gray-green eyes reflected shock, swiftly followed by brimming amusement as the duchess surveyed her visitor.

At the sight of that amusement, Maxie tilted toward explosion; doubtless the duchess thought Robin's declared interest in a grubby undersized tomboy was some kind of joke.

Her fury was allayed when Maggie stepped forward, her hand extended and genuine warmth in her voice. "My dear, how marvelous to meet you!" She clasped Maxie's unresponsive hand in both of hers, continuing with a conspiratorial smile, "I do hope you can bring yourself to accept him. Robin has a number of redeeming qualities, though I expect you want to murder him just now, don't you?"

The comment was so accurate that Maxie was thrown off-balance. "I am considering the best method, as a matter of fact," she said. Her teeth were gritted, but she was determined to match the duchess's aplomb. "Boiling oil seems too quick."

Maggie laughed. Close-up, her features lacked the symmetry of perfect beauty, but her glowing charm was far more potent than mere beauty could ever be. No wonder she haunted Robin's dreams. "I gather he just brought you here without explanation?"

"Exactly so, your grace." Maxie glanced at Robin, who didn't even look ashamed of himself. Instead, he smiled, as if these were perfectly normal circumstances. His hand was still rested on her elbow, and she drew comfort from his touch even as she wanted to wring his neck. "Robin made a vague reference to calling on friends, no more."

"The result of too many years spying, where the less one says, the better." Maggie waved her hand around her. "I was shocked myself the first time I saw this mausoleum, even though my husband had warned me that the house was designed to put Blenheim in the shade." She cocked her head to one side, a considering expression on her face. "Are you American?"

Apparently she shared Robin's ear for accents, as she had shared so much else with him. The thought did not improve Maxie's temper. "Yes, I am. My father was English, however. A younger son of Lord Collingwood." She was immediately ashamed of herself for feeling the need to mention her aristocratic relatives; her mother's kin had proved more worthy of respect than her father's.

The other woman's brows drew together thoughtfully. "Collingwood. The seat is in the north, isn't it? Durham?"

"Yes." That sounded too curt, so Maxie added, "I was visiting with my uncle through the spring."

Robin had given her a quizzical glance when she mentioned the Collingwood connection. Now he said, "Having just arrived in London with pockets to let, we were hoping Candover House might have room for us for a night or two."

"I'm sure we can find space," the duchess said with a smile. She glanced at Maxie. "Let me show you to a room. I'm sure you'll welcome a chance to relax and refresh yourself."

"If you don't mind, your grace, I'd like to have a word alone with Robin first." Maxie's voice was under control, but there was a dangerous glitter in her eyes.

"Of course." In response to some invisible signal, a footman materialized. The duchess said, "Please bring in Lord Robert's and Miss Collins' baggage." Then she paused, clearly considering Robin's peripatetic habits. "I should have asked first if you had any baggage, or if this is one of your more impromptu journeys?"

"We're traveling in relative style. We both have packs on our horses." Robin studied his companion's set features. He had guessed she would be startled and not best pleased at being brought to Maggie's house, but her barely suppressed rage was far greater than he had expected. "If you will excuse us for a few minutes?"

Then he escorted Maxie into the adjoining salon, bracing himself for the explosion.

13

Though smaller than the entrance hall, the salon was every
bit as grand, but Maxie was beyond being intimidated by
furnishings. As Robin closed the paneled door, she whirled on
him, every ounce of her small body quivering with fury. "How
dare you bring me to your mistress's house!"

Robin was more than ready to concede that he had made a
major error in judgment, but he doubted that confession would
do much to mitigate Maxie's anger. Deciding that the rational
reasons for his decision might help, he said mildly, "Maggie
hasn't been my mistress in some years. She is still, however,
my friend, and she and I have been in the habit of relying on
each other. Since we needed a place to stay, it seemed natural
to come here."

He crossed the salon to the fireplace and leaned against the
marble mantel, wishing he felt as casual as he was acting. "I
knew I could trust her and Candover to accept two disgraceful
travelers without questions, outrage, or dangerous gossip. Here
you can make the transition back to respectable young lady with
no one the wiser."

He could see by the way Maxie's hands clenched into fists
that cool rationality wasn't working, but she maintained a
tenuous control. "You identified yourself to the butler as Lord
Robert, and the duchess referred to you the same way," she
said through clenched teeth. "I thought you said it wasn't a real
title."

"You are the one who said it wasn't real. I merely didn't
correct your misapprehension," Robin pointed out. "Apparently
your father didn't explain the odd minor quirks of the title
system. For example, the use of 'Lord' with one's Christian
name is the exclusive prerogative of the younger sons of dukes
and marquesses. Lord Robert Andreville is my correct, legal

name. Along with four or five other names in the middle,'' he added after another moment's thought.

Maxie's wide brown eyes narrowed as she assimilated his statement. She looked more exotic, and more dangerous, than ever. ''You said you weren't a nobleman.''

''I'm not. Lord Robert is a courtesy title. I'm a commoner, just like you. If my brother should die, which God forbid, I would be instantly ennobled.'' He shrugged. ''It doesn't make much sense.''

''Your father was a duke?''

He shook his head. ''The Marquess of Wolverton. One step lower on the ladder.''

''So you were on your brother's estate when we met.'' Maxie was staring at him as if he were a complete stranger. ''What kind of man are you? From beginning to end you've deliberately misled me, letting me think you were a homeless wanderer, a thief, or worse. How many other lies have you told me?''

''I've always told you the truth.'' As Robin shifted his weight from one foot to the other, his gaze did not meet hers. He was falling into the exaggerated coolness that was his reaction to nerves or guilt; even knowing it was a mistake, it was impossible to remove the calm detachment from his voice. ''Though I'll admit to a few falsehoods spoken to others in your presence.''

Maxie's anger exploded into pure, coruscating rage. She was standing by a delicate table, and in one smooth motion she seized the porcelain figurine standing there and hurled it toward Robin.

The statuette shattered on the marble fireplace inches from his outstretched hand. He didn't move, even when splinters of china struck him, but the fingers of his left hand whitened where they clenched the edge of the mantel.

''I don't care if every word you spoke was approved for accuracy by God Himself!'' she raged. ''You must have been educated by lawyers or Jesuits. Your intent was deception, even if you appeased your delicate conscience by manipulating the truth rather than outright lies.'' Her voice broke. ''What a fool I've been to believe you.''

Her raw pain cut through Robin's own defensiveness with the impact of a blow. Shaken, he took a deep, steadying breath.

"You are quite right. I was using the truth to create a false impression. But it wasn't to make a fool of you."

"Why, then?" Maxie was staring at him, the fine planes of her face tight, her vulnerability making him ache for having unintentionally hurt her.

There was a long silence while he confronted his motives. Finally he said, "I'm not very comfortable with Lord Robert Andreville, and if I don't like the fellow, I could hardly expect you to." It was a slow and painful admission. "And from the moment I met you, I wanted—very much—for you to like me."

Difficult though it was, he should have tried honesty sooner. Maxie's tense body eased as her fury dissipated, and their locked gazes held for an endless moment.

"I see." From the expression on her face, she did see, probably more than he would have liked. She crossed the room to lean her shoulder against the opposite end of the mantel, her arms folded in front of her.

Instead of referring to what he had just revealed, she asked, "Did you bring me here so Maggie could approve me?" Though anger might be gone, Maxie's expression was stark. "I don't suppose you meant to flaunt me, since I will hardly enhance your status. Of course, it would be very hard to find a female who was more beautiful or more aristocratic than your duchess." Her tone was an echo of Robin at his most detached. "It seems more likely that you want to horrify her with the depths you have fallen to since she left you. Producing a disreputable savage would certainly show her a thing or two."

"Good God, you can't possibly believe that I brought you here for any such reason!" Understanding now precisely why she had been so angry, Robin felt a little sick. He had been so involved in his own confused emotions that he had forgotten that under her sanity and self-possession Maxie had fears and scars of her own. Forcefully he said, "You are a woman of wisdom and character and would be a credit to any man lucky enough to win you. And even covered with mud and looking like you have been dragged through a bush backward, you are beautiful."

She shrugged, unconvinced, her eyes not meeting his. In an unconscious parody of Robin's earlier casualness, she stretched one arm along the mantel edge and stroked the carving, as if it was the most interesting thing in the world.

"I plead guilty to being an insensitive dolt," he said quietly. "To say that I brought you here for Maggie's approval has the wrong connnotation, but it is true that I wanted you to meet her. You are the two most important women in my life, and I think you might become friends."

"If she disapproves of me, as she surely does, what then? Do you try to pack me off to Boston?" Maxie's voice was brittle.

"She won't disapprove of you." He covered her hand where it rested on the marble. Her fingers jerked at his touch, but she did not pull away. "I think what you are really asking is if I would choose you over over her." He tightened his grip. "The answer is yes. Even if Maggie was wrongheaded enough to try to interfere, she would fail. You are the only one with the power to divide us."

Maxie's eyes closed and a quick spasm of emotion crossed her face. Giving in to instinct, Robin stepped forward and drew her into his arms. Unresisting, she buried her face against his shoulder as if exhausted. No matter what their verbal conflicts, on the level of physical touch there was always harmony between them. Robin held her close, hoping that the embrace was soothing her as much as it was helping him.

Because of Maxie's forceful character, he tended to forget how small she was, and he felt a surge of protective tenderness; her head barely reached his chin, and he was not a tall man. "Your head is heart-high," he said softly. With one hand he pulled the pins from her hair so that it fell down her back in a bright ebony cascade.

"I'm an incredible idiot, Kanawiosta. When we were traveling together, I wanted to block out the past and the future, because for the first time in years I was happy." He caressed the back of her head, burying his fingers in the silky tresses. "I knew that sooner or later I must explain myself, but I was a coward and preferred to put the reckoning off as long as possible. I didn't consider how unfair I was being to you."

"What other surprises have you in store for me?" she asked in a low voice.

He thought a moment. "Well, I'm fairly well-off. Among other things, I'm the owner of Ruxton."

That caused her to look up, a flash of amused exasperation in her eyes. "You mean you were stealing your own horses?" When he nodded, she exclaimed, "To think of the worrying I did!"

"I said we didn't need to worry," he reminded her.

"The duchess is right." Her voice was severe, but her lips twitched with suppressed humor. "You are a wretch."

He sighed, no longer amused. "I know. That's why it seemed such a good idea to be someone else."

Maxie looked directly at him, her expression grave. "We must talk more about that, but not, I think, tonight."

"Thank you." Robin smiled wryly. "I don't think I would be up to it just now. Any more than you are probably up to deciding whether or not to marry me." The words were said lightly, but he was holding his breath, needing to know if the events of the evening had give her such a disgust of him that marriage was not a possibility.

She shook her head, her face troubled. "I don't know, Robin. We are even further apart than I thought." Raising her hands, she fidgeted with his shabby lapels. "I don't know whether I can fit into your English world, or if I even want to try."

"We are closer than you realize, and not just physically." He brushed a kiss on her hair. "But now is not the time for talking about that, either. The important thing is that you are not saying no." He grinned suddenly. "Thank you for not hitting me with that china figurine. Perhaps you should have. I was being incredibly obtuse."

"I just wanted to make a point, not damage you." Her eyes stayed fixed on his shirt. "I'll admit that I've called you Lord Robert when I was exasperated. What does it mean when you call me Kanawiosta?"

Robin considered for a moment. "I suppose it means that I am speaking from the heart and hope you will listen the same way."

"That's not a bad reason." After a long silence, she glanced up with a trace of mischief. "If I married you, would I have a title? And if so, what would it be?"

"You would be called Lady Robert Andreville. Lady Robert for short. Or perhaps Lady Robin, more informally."

Her eyes widened. "Seriously? That isn't another one of your jests?"

"God's own truth."

Maxie threw her head back and laughed. "What an absurd system! No wonder the American founding fathers discarded it."

The door opened and the Duchess of Candover entered. Seeing her guests in each other's arms, she began to retreat. "Sorry. I guess you didn't hear my knock."

"No need to run off." Robin released Maxie without haste. "We've negotiated a truce."

Too wise to comment, the duchess said, "Rafe just sent a message that he will be leaving Westminster earlier than he had expected. Would you two care to join us for dinner in an hour or so? I would love to have you, but if you're too tired, you may prefer a tray in your room."

After glancing at Robin for confirmation, Maxie said, "We'll accept with pleasure, though I warn you, I have only one dress with me, and it will be considerably the worse for travel."

"No matter. My maid can brush and press it for you," Maggie said. Then her gaze fell on the fragments of broken china, and her face lit up. "How splendid! You broke that ghastly replica of the Laocoön."

Maxie's face flamed. "I'm sorry, your grace, it was entirely my fault. I will replace it as soon as I can."

"Don't you dare!" Maggie gave an impish smile. "It was a wedding present from one of the Whitbourne cousins who must have disapproved of Rafe marrying me. Three people being eaten by snakes is hardly an amiable gift, don't you agree? I've been leaving it on the edge of the table, hoping one of the maids would accidentally knock it off, but with no success."

Maxie chuckled. It took a real lady to make a guilty guest believe she was doing her hostess a favor. "If you have anything else you wish broken," she said gravely, "let me know and I shall be happy to oblige."

"Done!" Maggie turned. "Shall I take you to your room now? There is time for a bath or a rest if you wish."

With a touch of grimness, Maxie followed the duchess upstairs. If this was Robin's world, the sooner she learned whether she could live in it, the better.

* * *

After Maxie had emerged from a luxurious hot bath, the duchess sent her own French maid to assist. The maid, Lavalle, was well-trained; she did not betray disapproval of such an irregular guest by so much as a single twitch, though there was a pained expression on her face as she handed over the newly pressed gown. However, Maxie's fluent, if Canadian-accented, French soon won Lavalle over.

Maxie donned her plain white muslin gown philosophically, since the only other choice was her travel-worn breeches. The maid did an elegant job of twisting her dark hair into a chignon, and Maxie thought her appearance was presentable, in an unmemorable way. Nonetheless, she took one nervous glance in the mirror when a footman came to summon her. Then, head high, she followed him downstairs.

Robin and the duchess were talking casually, their golden heads close together. His clothing had also undergone refurbishing in the last hour, and a fresh shirt and cravat had been conjured up from somewhere, probably the duke's own wardrobe. While still hardly dressed to London standards, he looked so perfectly at ease in the grand salon that for a moment Maxie felt her qualms return.

Robin glanced up at Maxie's entry, then stood and stared a moment, his azure eyes glowing, before he came forward to bow over her hand. "You look absolutely delectable," he said softly.

Maxie colored, but his admiring gaze warmed her right down to her toes. "It's good of you to say so, but this dress would not be fashionable even in Boston, much less London."

"Believe me, men are much less interested in fashion than in the overall effect, which in your case is quite ravishing." He took her arm and guided her to a seat between him and the duchess. "Mind you, I may be prejudiced because that is the first dress I've ever seen you in."

Robin's appreciation and nonsense relaxed her, and she joined in the conversation without self-consciousness. The duchess was wearing a dress very nearly as simple as Maxie's own, another example of the other woman's exquisite tact. Robin must have also given warning of Maxie's eccentric drinking habits, because she was offered lemonade, even though her two companions were drinking sherry.

The duchess was just frowning at the mantel clock when the door opened. Maxie knew instantly that it was the Duke of Candover who entered. Just as Robin was a chameleon, capable of playing a thousand roles, the duke was unmistakably an aristocrat, incapable of ever being anything else. He was also quite staggeringly handsome, a fit mate for the glorious Maggie.

"Sorry to be late, my dear," the newcomer said, "but Castlereagh waylaid me just as I was leaving Westminster." Then he stopped, a broad smile on his face. "Robin, you rogue. What brings you to London?"

The two men shook hands with every evidence of warmth. Maxie watched, thinking that the duke had a pride and unconscious arrogance reminiscent of a Mohawk warrior. The resemblance was increased by his height and the fact that his hair and complexion were as dark as Maxie's own.

Then Robin introduced them, and as Candover bowed over her hand, Maxie saw that his eyes were a cool northern gray, with humor and friendly speculation lurking in the depths. "Collins," he said thoughtfully. "Are you by any chance related to the Durham Collinses?"

"The present Lord Collingwood is my uncle, your grace."

"Then we are cousins of some sort, the second or third degree." The duke gave her a smile that for pure, paralyzing impact almost equaled Robin's. "It is always a pleasure to meet a new cousin, especially an attractive one." Offering his arm, he continued, "Since I am unfashionably famished, perhaps we can go directly into dinner. I am a great deal more amiable when I have been fed."

She smiled and accepted his arm, thinking that, on the contrary, the duke could hardly have been more congenial, though his welcome had more to do with his esteem for Robin than for Maxie herself. As they went to the dining room, she felt dwarfed by his height; Robin was really a much more convenient size.

As the duchess had promised, it was a simple family dinner, with only three courses, though they were generous and superbly cooked. Maxie was grateful not to have to deal with the endless

rounds of food considered essential at Chanleigh; small wonder
that her uncle's womenfolk were on the well-upholstered side.

She had feared there might be some beastly London dining
customs that would show her for the ignorant provincial that
she was, but her concern was unfounded; she had seen more
forks and spoons in Boston. The conversation was superior,
flowing easily back and forth, with the three English people
all making distinct if unobtrusive attempts to make sure that
the American would not feel excluded. Maxie was touched at
the consideration, and a bit amused as well. Had she been so
obviously overpowered by Candover House when she had first
arrived? Apparently so, though not necessarily for the reasons
that the duchess thought.

The men forwent the pleasures of port to join the women for
coffee in the drawing room. Maxie was glad; even though the
duchess had been everything amiable, Maxie was not quite ready
for a *tête-à-tête* with Robin's mistress. Former mistress.

The Candovers became involved in a discussion of their
impending remove to the country, and the guests drifted over
to the French doors with their coffeecups. Behind the house was
a garden so lush that it was hard to believe they were in the
heart of one of the greatest cities in the world.

Maxie glanced at their hosts. There was a bond between the
duke and duchess so powerful that it was nearly tangible. "Even
if she married him for his money," she mused, "there is a good
deal more than that between them now."

Robin gave her a quizzical glance. "Where on earth did you
get the idea that Maggie married Rafe for his fortune?"

"From you." Maxie flushed; she had not meant to speak her
impertinent thought out loud, but having done so, she must
continue. "It was the morning we joined the drovers. You said
that your Maggie had gone to a man who could give her more
than you could." She gestured expressively at their surroundings. "All this, and a noble title, too—it is rather a lot. Still,
it doesn't ring quite true. The duchess doesn't seem especially
mercenary, and by your own admission you are also a wealthy
man."

Robin turned and looked out the glass doors, a strange
expression on his face. At length he said, "I didn't mean to

mislead you by that remark, but apparently I did. Your instincts are quite correct. Maggie is not a woman who can be bought, only won." He absently sipped his coffee. "When I said that she went to someone who could give her more, I meant emotionally, not financially. Money and position were never the issues."

"Is it still so painful, Robin?" Maxie asked quietly. "Now that I've met her, I understand why she is so hard to forget."

Robin shook his head. "I'm not thinking about losses at all. If I look odd, it's because I finally understand something Maggie once said to me." He gave Maxie an oblique glance. "The reason I understand now is because I have met you."

It was Maxie's turn to stare outside and sip her coffee. It occurred to her that they were progressing in a complex emotional minuet. One of them would find and share an insight, then they would swing apart and absorb what had been said before coming together again. Then there would be another moment of revelation, and another stepping back, but each time they moved together, they came a little closer. Given their pasts, perhaps it was necessary that they learn about themselves and each other in small steps; certainly she wasn't ready to comment on Robin's latest remark. She did not doubt that he cared for her, but the thought was almost as frightening as it was exciting.

She shifted her focus so that she saw her own reflection rather than the darkened garden. In her simple dress and restrained coiffure, Maxie could almost have been an elegant Boston lady. Her lips quirked into a smile. "Covered with mud and looking as if I had been dragged through a bush backward?"

"Not the most poetic of compliments, I'll admit, but true. The first . . ." Robin chuckled. "Or rather, the second thing I noticed after you jumped on me in the forest at Wolverhampton was how beautiful you are."

"I did not jump on you," she said indignantly. "I tripped. If you hadn't been lurking there like the serpent in Eden . . ."

He laughed outright. "I had best change the subject before I learn a few more unpalatable truths." After draining the last of his coffee, he set the delicate cup and saucer on a table by the French doors. "For someone who had misgivings about London society, you seem quite at ease."

She arched her brows. "Surely you don't expect me to believe that everyone in the *beau monde* is like the Candovers."

"No, they would be exceptional anywhere," he agreed. "But society is merely a collection of individuals, and London has great diversity. It is quite possible to choose a congenial circle of friends and ignore the rest. For that matter, one needn't even spend time in London."

"My experience of society has not always been so fortunate." Maxie heard the brittleness in her tone. For a moment she considered stopping there, but on impulse she continued. It was time for another step in the minuet. "Though America is a republic, there are those who are fascinated by the aristocracy. As the son of a lord, with considerable wit and education, my father was welcome in the homes of many of what are sometimes called the 'better families.' "

Her smile was acid. "Max was considered eccentric, of course, because of being a book peddler, and he had no money. But even so, during the winters when we lived in Boston, we were invited out to dinner two or three times a week. Clergymen, professors, wealthy merchants—they all welcomed the Honorable Maximus Collins."

She finished her coffee and set it aside, then stared into the garden again, unconsciously crossing her arms in a self-protective gesture. "It was one such evening when I was about twenty that I overheard Mrs. Lodge, my hostess, talking with some bosom bow of hers. That's when I learned that Max wouldn't accept an invitation unless I was invited also. Mrs. Lodge was willing to tolerate that in order to enjoy dear Mr. Collins' charm and breeding, but if the little half-breed cast any lures out to the menfolk, Mrs. Lodge was fully prepared to cut the connection. Standards must be maintained, you know. Hard to believe that a gentleman like Mr. Collins had actually married a savage, but men were helpless victims of their lusts."

Robin swore under his breath. "No wonder you think poorly of society, if that has been your experience." He laid a light hand on her shoulder, and the comforting warmth of his touch made it easier for Maxie to shrug dismissively.

"Not everyone was like that. In some houses I was welcome in my own right rather than as an inconvenient necessity. I never told my father what I had heard—Max was doing the best he could for me. And he enjoyed those evenings so much, it would have been a pity to take some of them away from him.''

Robin's hand tightened. "Mrs. Lodge was surely a bigot, but she may also have been speaking from the cattiness that some aging women feel toward young, attractive females.''

"You really think so?" Maxie asked, surprised and intrigued by the thought. "I never thought of that.''

"I think it quite possible. I doubt if Boston beldames are substantially different from London ones. Take away the race prejudice, and what is left is exactly what any jealous matron might say about a lovely young girl.''

Maxie gave a wicked smile, suddenly amused by an incident that had been a secret pain for years. "Perhaps you're right. Mrs. Lodge had three muffin-faced daughters with not a waistline among them.'' She cocked her head to one side. "Why is it so much easier for us to be clear-sighted about another person's problems than about our own?''

"It's a law of nature.'' Robin dropped his hand, since his companion had recovered her humor. "Like the sun rising in the east, and apples falling down from a tree rather than up.''

An arrested expression crossed Maxie's face. "Would it be possible to visit the tree that Newton was sitting under when the falling apple started him thinking of gravity?''

After a startled moment, Robin said, "I don't see why not, if it is still alive. I'm not sure where the tree is located—Lincolnshire, perhaps—but I can find out.''

Maxie sighed, serious again. "Later, perhaps. There are more important things to do first.''

"I suppose that tomorrow we will go to the hotel where your father died?''

She was going to nod, then stopped as she was gripped by sudden panic. Disgusted with herself, Maxie acknowledged that she had come the length of England to find answers, yet now she was afraid of them. Afraid of what she would learn, or afraid that when the mystery of her father's death was resolved, she would be faced with a decision about Robin? She loved him, he wanted to marry her . . . It should be simple, but it wasn't.

Yielding to cowardice, she said, "Rather than go there

directly, perhaps I should call on Aunt Desdemona. She saw my father several times before he died. She might be able to tell me what his activities were."

Robin frowned. "It was suspicion of your uncle that sent you off to investigate. If he is guilty of some villainy, might your aunt be involved also?"

Maxie considered, then shook her head. "I doubt it. They are not close, their lives are completely different. Besides, from her letters, Desdemona doesn't seem the villainous type."

"Fair enough. Do you want me to accompany you, or would you rather ask Maggie for a maid?"

Maxie wrinkled her nose in distaste. "Respectability is such a tedious business. Since a frail flower like me can't cross town in a carriage without a companion, I would rather have you. Besides, if Aunt Desdemona is villainous, you would be far more useful."

"For which vote of confidence I am duly grateful," Robin murmured, his eyes twinkling. "If you don't mind waiting until the end of the morning, I'd like to pay early calls on my banker and my tailor. Luckily I was having some new clothing made up and it should be ready now. I just hope it hasn't been sent to Yorkshire already." He cast a jaundiced eye on his frayed sleeve. "I shan't miss this coat."

"May I have it?" Maxie asked. "I've some very fond memories of that coat."

"You may have it with my blessings." Robin hesitated. "Don't bite my head off for the suggestion, but would you let me have another dress or so made up for you? Having only one might prove a nuisance here in London."

"I suppose you're right," she said without enthusiasm, but also without taking umbrage at his offer. "But I don't want to waste time on fittings."

"No need. Maggie's maid can take the measurements from this dress." His gaze flickered over her figure. "It's simple, but very well-cut and -fitted."

"Thank you. I made it myself. Lack of funds makes one wonderfully versatile." Maxie raised a hand to cover her yawn. "I'm ready to retire. It has been a long day, and tomorrow is likely to be taxing."

Robin nodded. "I'm going to feel very alone in that bed tonight."

"So will I." Maxie found that her eyes dropped before the warmth of his gaze. Now that they were in conventional social roles, what had been so natural on the journey made her a little shy. Not that she wouldn't be bundling with Robin still if they were in different circumstances. Then she frowned as a thought struck her. "You won't have nightmares if you're alone, will you?"

"If I do, they won't be as bad as the ones in the past." He touched her cheek in a gesture as intimate as a kiss. "You were right—burdens are lighter for being shared."

As Maxie had thought earlier, she and Robin were drawing closer and closer together. It was a warming thought to take to her lonesome bed.

It was very late when Lord Collingwood reached the Clarendon Hotel, and if he hadn't been a lord, it was unlikely that accommodations would have been found for him.

For all his fatigue, Collingwood had trouble getting to sleep, and after a half-hour of tossing, he reached for the traveling flask of spirits he had had the foresight to leave on the bedside table. In the dark, he drank directly from the flask while he contemplated his mission. From Simmons' reports, Maxima might be in London already, possibly even found the truth about her father. And if that wasn't bad enough, there was the blond mountebank whom she had taken up with. Lord knew who the fellow was, but if he was still with the girl, he meant trouble.

Collingwood gloomily took another swig of brandy. A scandal would do his own daughters' marital prospects no good. Of course, there were measures that could be taken, but family, after all, was family. Beyond that, he liked Maxima, in spite of her irregular upbringing and ancestry. If he hadn't liked her, he wouldn't be going to all this effort to spare her.

The flask was half-empty when he lay back to rest again. The first thing to do in the morning was try to locate that scoundrel Simmons. As he buried his head under the pillow, his lordship decided that family was the very devil.

* * *

The Duke of Candover was brushing out his wife's long wheat-gold hair, a task he enjoyed far too much to relegate to the abigail. Margot, also known as Maggie, leaned back against him, a smile of contentment on her face and her eyes half-closed. "What do you think of Robin's friend Maxie?"

"I was wondering how long it would take you to bring up the subject," he said with amusement. "Did Robin tell you how they came to turn up on our doorstep?"

"Not in any detail." After a moment she added, "He wants to marry her."

"Really!" Rafe's hand stilled in surprise. "Surely he can't have known her long."

"How is that to the point? I wanted to marry you the first night I met you."

"You never told me that before." He felt absurdly pleased as he resumed brushing.

"You are quite conceited enough," his wife said, then jumped with a squeak when he tickled her ribs.

"She's not at all in the common style," the duke mused. "Intelligent, unconventional. Not unlike Robin himself. And very lovely, in a very individual way."

"I thought you would notice that," the duchess remarked rather dryly.

Rafe grinned. "I prefer blondes myself." Setting down the brush, he began to massage her temples. "Does it bother you to see him with another woman? I find it a little surprising that he brought her here."

"On the contrary, I would be surprised, and hurt, if Robin didn't feel he could come to me." Margot made a rueful face. "In answer to your question, I suppose every woman, in some selfish corner of her mind, would like her former lovers to remember her with a heartbroken sigh and the words, 'What a woman she was. If only things had been different . . .' But I want to see Robin happy, not pining for the past or marrying some vapid chit because he is lonely and there is no one better to be found."

She closed her eyes again, relaxing under her husband's expert ministrations. "I've been a little concerned about Robin ever since we left Paris. Even though his letters were always lighthearted and amusing, something felt wrong about them. But tonight when I saw him''—she tried to define the change—''he was his old self again.'' After another moment, she added, ''No, better than that.''

She laughed suddenly. ''Maxie was bristling like an angry cat when we were introduced. Robin hadn't bothered to explain where he was taking her. I do like her, though. In a world full of nobodies, she is very much somebody.''

''I suggest you go slowly with your overtures of friendship,'' Rafe replied. ''Miss Collins may look upon Robin's friendship with another female with something less than enthusiasm.''

Hearing between the lines, Margot tilted her head back to look up at him. ''Surely you know that you needn't be jealous of Robin? I had thought that you and he had become friends.''

Rafe gave a wry smile and ran a caressing hand down her slim arching throat. He had learned to accept his wife's relationship with Robin, but it had not been easy for a passionate and possessive man. ''Not jealous. Envious, perhaps, for all the years he had you and I didn't.''

She shook her head, her solemn gray-green eyes fixed on his. ''He had Maggie, the spy. But the circumstances that created her are done, and so is she.''

''I know that. You are Margot now.'' Rafe leaned over and gave his wife a slow, possessive kiss. ''And Margot is *mine*.'' Then he scooped her up in his arms and carried her to their bed and proved it, in the most profound and satisfying of ways.

14

Desdemona entered her sunny parlor, reveling in the fact of being home again. It was not a large house and had a staff of only four, but it was her own. Now that she was back in her mundane world, she could almost believe that the last mad weeks had been her imagination, the result of too much lobster or too many late political dinners.

At the sound of a carriage stopping outside, she peered out the window, then grinned. There was nothing imaginary about the broad athletic figure of the Marquess of Wolverton, who was now mounting the steps. He had said he would call this morning at the unfashionable hour of eleven, and the clock was chiming as he knocked. Desdemona liked a man who could be relied on. As she waited for him to be shown in, she rang for coffee.

After greetings had been exchanged and coffee poured, Giles got down to business. "My brother is in London. In fact, I missed him this morning at the bank by no more than a quarter of an hour."

"Splendid. Did they have any notion where he was staying?"

"Unfortunately not, but at least we know now that he has arrived in London and that he is making no attempt to avoid detection. I should locate him in the next day or two, and surely he will know where your niece is."

She was about to reply when her parlor maid entered. "Miss Maxima Collins and Lord Robert Andreville to see you, my lady."

Desdemona was so startled that her jaw dropped as the object of her long pursuit walked into the parlor. She had been told that her niece was small, dark, and attractive, but that description did not do justice to the reality. The ebony-haired young lady who swept into the room was tiny and self-possessed, with a face as striking as her perfectly proportioned figure.

The girl's muslin dress was demure, but nothing would make Maxima Collins seem like a butter-wouldn't-melt-her-mouth miss. She did not look much like her father, she did not look English, and she most assuredly did not look like anyone who would be easily victimized by life. "I hope you will forgive this unannounced intrusion, Aunt Desdemona," she said politely, then gestured to her companion. "This is my friend, Lord Robert Andreville. Robin, my aunt, Lady Ross."

Rising to her feet, Desdemona spared a glance for her niece's ecsort, then another, understanding instantly why the girl had been willing to go off with him. The golden Lord Robert looked like a gentleman, not a rogue, and he was handsome enough to turn any girl's head.

He bowed gracefully to his hostess and murmured, "Your servant, Lady Ross," at the same time offering a smile that would have given palpitations to a more susceptible female.

Not being susceptible, at least not at the moment, Desdemona favored him with a darkling look and a brief nod of acknowledgment, then offered her niece her hand. "My dear girl, I'm so glad to finally meet you. I've been very worried."

The two women studied each other as they shook hands, and from her niece's expression, her tall and titian-haired aunt was as much a surprise as vice versa. They must have looked like two cats touching inquiring noses, Desdemona thought ruefully, which was why Giles was chuckling. He had risen to his feet and gave every evidence of enjoying the situation hugely.

Lord Robert hadn't noticed his brother's presence, but at the sound of laughter he glanced around the room, then raised his brows in surprise. "Giles! This is a coincidence. I didn't know you were planning on coming to London this spring."

Wolverton shook his head, still chuckling. "I wasn't. You're entirely responsible for my being here."

"Indeed?"

"Lady Ross and I have been haring across England for the last fortnight, separately and together, trying to find you two," the marquess explained. "And now you walk in, bland as butter, as if paying morning calls on an elderly aunt."

"Aunt Desdemona is not elderly," Maxima pointed out.

"Thank you," the unelderly aunt muttered, feeling that the

situation was rapidly getting out of hand. But to be fair, it had never been in hand.

"I was speaking metaphorically." Giles glanced at Desdemona with a mischievous smile. "I have, in fact, noticed that she is not elderly. Miss Collins, since confusion seems the order of the day, let me introduce myself. I'm Wolverton, elder brother of your scapegrace escort."

"Ah, yes," she said thoughtfully, "the one who, if he died, which God forbid, would cause Robin to be instantly ennobled."

Wolverton blinked while he sorted that out, then nodded. "Exactly so."

"I think it is time that we all sat down and had some coffee," Desdemona said in a voice of heroic restraint, ringing the bell for more cups and another pot.

Maxima sat opposite her aunt. "Why were you worried, Aunt Desdemona? You didn't even know I was coming to visit you."

"I arrived at Chanleigh shortly after you decamped. Under questioning, Cletus and Althea admitted that you had left unexpectedly and probably had little money. I deduced that if you were indeed coming to visit me in London, it must be the hard way." Another tray arrived, and Desdemona poured coffee for the new arrivals. "A lone young female, attempting to walk hundreds of miles across a strange country filled with rogues and robbers and Lord knows what—of course I was worried. So I decided to come after you."

"That was very good of you, but you needn't have been concerned." Maxima's wide brown eyes showed mild surprise that anyone should have been anxious. "It was a very pleasant trip and nothing of note happened."

A choking sound came from Lord Robert, and Maxima abandoned mildness to direct a dagger look at him. Her escort assumed a look of unreliable innocence, then glanced at his older brother. "How did you become involved, Giles?"

"Lady Ross was told that her niece had been forcibly abducted by my womanizing brother," was the succinct reply.

"Oh, really, Giles," Lord Robert said with amusement. "Womanizing? What had I done in my blameless months in Yorkshire to deserve that?"

"It is what the villagers told me," Desdemona said stiffly. "So I went to Wolverhampton to make inquiries."

"Lady Ross fails to do the occasion justice," the marquess interjected. Clearly he was having the time of his life. "In fact, she swept into my library like an avenging fury, slammed her parasol across my desk, accused and convicted you *in absentia* of all manner of crimes and moral turpitude, threatened you with the full might and majesty of the law, then swept out again."

Turning a fiery red under the interested gazes of her niece and Lord Robert, Desdemona scowled at the marquess. She had perhaps acted a bit intemperately that day, and it was most ungentlemanly of him to mention it.

"Womanizing *and* moral turpitude?" Lord Robert gave his hostess a sympathetic look. "Having heard that, of course you had no choice but to try to rescue your hapless niece from me."

His statement elicited an eloquent sniff from Maxima. "Your fears were understandable, but quite misplaced, Aunt. In fact, Lord Robert insisted on accompanying me solely out of concern for my safety." A note of exasperation entered her soft, well-bred voice. "Like you, he assumed that I was a helpless incompetent who would never survive the trip."

Lord Robert gave her a smile of obvious affection. "That misapprehension didn't last long, Maxie."

"Maxie?" Desdemona repeated. "What a vulgar nickname."

Her niece bristled. "It is what my father called me, Aunt Desdemona, and it is what I prefer."

"Your father called me Dizzy, and I didn't much like that, either," Desdemona said dryly. "However, if it is your preference, I shall endeavor to become accustomed to it." She surveyed the small, composed figure sitting opposite. "Perhaps you should stop calling me aunt. There are only a few years between us, and I don't seem to have done a very good job of aunting. Perhaps it is better if we simply try to become friends."

Maxie gave a shy smile. "I would like that very much."

Desdemona sipped more coffee, then sighed. "This is an awkward topic, and probably an auntly one, but I cannot help but be concerned for your reputation." She glanced at Lord Robert. "Doubtless things are somewhat different in America, but surely you are aware of the English proprieties?" The lift at the end of her sentence was accompanied by a pious hope that she would not have to become more specific.

"If you mean what I think you mean," Maxie said in a tone whose frostiness would have done credit to a patroness of Almack's, "I assure you that Lord Robert has behaved as a perfect gentleman." The effect was spoiled when she added something under her breath that sounded like, "Unfortunately."

Desdemona stared at her niece, sure that she had misheard, but Giles, who was closer to the girl, suddenly had a fit of coughing that sounded like a doomed attempt to stifle hilarity.

Deciding that abandoning the topic was the better part of wisdom, Desdemona asked, "Where are you staying? I would be delighted to have you here."

Maxie glanced doubtfully at her escort, who was watching with a gleam of wicked humor in his blue eyes. "That is very kind of you, but I don't know. . . . We are staying at Candover House. The duke and duchess have been everything that is amiable."

That fact startled the marquess. "You're staying with Candover and his wife?" he asked in disbelief.

"Yes." It was Lord Robert who answered, a hint of challenge in his voice. "And why not?"

"Why not indeed?" Giles murmured, in command of himself again.

Desdemona wondered curiously what that was about; perhaps Giles could be induced to explain privately later. Turning back to her niece, she asked, "Why did you come south so suddenly, Maxie? Was Althea plaguing you?" She grimaced. "My sister-in-law can't abide anyone disagreeing with her, which is why she and I have never gotten on."

Her niece hesitated, weighing her answer. "That was much of the reason," she said finally. "And I wanted to meet you before returning to America."

"You'll be leaving England?" That was a possibility that had never occurred to her aunt, though it should have.

An opaque look came into the girl's rich brown eyes. "My plans are a little uncertain just now."

In a way, the news that Maxie might go back to America was welcome; if that happened, any indiscretions that had occurred might have no scandalous repercussions. Then again, Desdemona thought with a return to gloom, nature being what it was, perhaps there would be other kinds of repercussions.

Maxie set her coffee aside and leaned forward, her hands clasped tensely in her lap. "Please, Desdemona, if you don't mind, could you tell me about the times you and Max saw each other before he died?"

Looking at her niece's anxious face, Desdemona guessed the true reason the girl had come to London. Max had been devoted to his only daughter and obviously the feeling had been mutual. It must be very hard to know that her father had died alone, so far from her. "Of course I don't mind talking about it," she said gently, settling back in the sofa with a nostalgic smile. "It was so good to see Max again. I was just a child when he left for America, but he wrote the most wonderful letters . . ."

As the two women began talking, Giles gestured to his brother and the two men retired to the far end of the drawing room, where they could speak privately. "It sounds like Lady Ross led you a merry dance," Robin said with a grin.

"No more so than her niece did you. Since her ladyship was threatening all and sundry Andrevilles, I decided that it behooved me to find you first, in the hopes of heading off scandal or your incarceration." Giles sat in one of the wing chairs. "Tell me, did Simmons ever catch up with you?"

"Yes, in Market Harborough." His brother settled in the chair opposite. "How do you know about him?"

"I gave him a ride near Blyth. He was stumbling along, nursing his injuries and plotting revenge on the 'yaller-headed fancy man' who had jumped him from behind."

"Of course I jumped him from behind. The fellow is twice my size," said Robin with irrefutable logic. "If there is one thing I've learned over the years, it's that 'fighting fairly' is a dangerous luxury."

Ignoring the philosophical aside, the marquess asked, "Why was he pursuing you?"

"Collingwood sent him after Maxie to bring her back." Robin shrugged. "She didn't want to go with him."

"Simmons did say that your mort held a pistol on him."

"Maxie is a most capable young lady. In Market Harborough, she had to be restrained from knifing friend Simmons. Life in the forests of the New World is rather different from a London drawing room," Robin allowed, amusement lighting his eyes. "I had some difficulty persuading her that she should accept my escort, partly because she thought I looked useless."

"She is certainly not what I expected." The marquess smiled wryly. "On the overwrought occasion when Lady Ross and I met, I countered her charge that you were a vile seducer with the suggestion that she and her niece were deliberately plotting to entrap you."

That sent Robin off into whoops. "Oh, Lord, I wish I could have been there," he gasped. "No one who knew Maxie could possibly think such a thing. There isn't a duplicitous bone in her delightful body. Full frontal assault in broad daylight is her style, not sneak attack."

"If you had been there to hear it, none of this would have happened. I did rather wonder what had become of you."

"Surely you weren't worried?" Robin said, surprised. "Just that morning I had mentioned that I might wander off when something—or someone—interesting happened along. It must have been intuition on my part."

"I reminded myself of that." The marquess lounged back in his chair, resting one ankle on the opposite knee. "Given that neither vile seduction nor entrapment was taking place, just what was happening?"

"Coming the head of the family, Giles?"

"I suppose so," the marquess admitted. "I think I'm entitled to an answer. You did put me in a rather awkward position vis-à-vis Lady Ross, and although matters appear to be under control, your escapade could have caused a scandal that would have rebounded on the whole family."

Robin was silent for a moment. "You're right. I'm sorry, it has been a long time since I've had to think in terms of scandal and propriety. I didn't mean to cause you distress."

Giles grinned. "Actually, it did me a great deal of good to be dragged from my rut, but I would rather not have to defend your honor against outraged aunts again."

"Particularly since you may have had a doubt or two about my behavior yourself," Robin said with uncomfortable perception. A hint of challenge showed in his cool blue eyes. "To answer your earlier question about what was going on, I am attempting to persuade Maxie to marry me. Will you have any objections if I am successful?"

The marquess raised his brows. "Would it matter if I did?"

"If you mean would your disapproval stop me, the answer is no. But I would very much prefer that you welcome her into the family. She has not always been accepted as she deserves." Robin glanced down and made a minute adjustment to his elegantly tailored sleeve. "Besides, you are two of my favorite people and I would hope that you could be friends." After a moment he added, "You did suggest that it was time I settled down."

Giles glanced across the room, where the two women were conversing with a matching intensity that made it easy to believe that they were closely related. Maxima Collins was a pocket-sized hoyden with the courage to cross England on foot, attack a professional bruiser, and dine with a duchess. She should suit Robin very well. The corners of Giles' mouth quirked up. "I'm not sure that marriage to Miss Collins would best be described as 'settling down,' but for what it's worth, you have my blessing." He gave his brother an appraising glance. "You really think she might turn you down? You seem to be on very easy terms."

Robin's gaze turned to Maxie and his expression closed. "The issue is still in doubt."

Giles sighed; neither of them seemed to be having much success with the fair sex. Did the problem lie with the Andreville men, or with the independent and appealing Collins women? Then he chuckled and got to his feet; if the ladies in question weren't independent, they wouldn't be so appealing. "Lady Ross and Miss Collins have a great deal to discuss, and we should probably leave them to it. If you like, I can give you a ride in my carriage and you can leave yours for Miss Collins."

"An excellent notion."

As they took their leave, the marquess found himself hoping fervently that the chit accepted Robin. It had been obvious as soon as his brother entered Lady's Ross drawing room that he was himself again, and if it took a dark-eyed dazzler with a temper to make Robin look fully alive again, Giles was more than willing to welcome her as a sister-in-law.

Desdemona and her niece continued their conversation over lunch and into the afternoon, discussing not just Maximus Collins but a wide range of other topics. After the younger woman left, her aunt subsided onto the sofa in a state of mental and verbal satisfaction. It had been duty that originally sent her after an unknown niece; now it was a pleasure to become acquainted with the real Maxie, who was far more interesting than the insipid imaginary miss whom Desdemona had thought needed rescuing.

In their hours of talking, Desdemona had recognized that her brother had found contentment in the eccentric life he had chosen, and that knowledge also pleased her. Perhaps it was being in London that had made him seem strained and unhappy on the occasions he had visited his younger sister.

Desdemona had also come to see a resemblance, both mental and physical, between Max and his only daughter. It was in her niece's face when she laughed, and in her eclectic education and lively mind. There were those who would think that Maximus Collins had wasted his life, but the daughter he had left was not at all a bad memorial to his mortal span. Desdemona also wondered, with regret that she would never know her, about Maxie's Mohawk mother; she must have been a remarkable woman.

Lord Robert had been a surprise, and a pleasant one. He was obviously more than willing to do the gentlemanly thing by Maxima, and the girl herself seemed not indifferent to him.

It would be a splendid match. Desdemona lay back on the sofa and grinned at the ceiling, chastising herself for having such an unprogressive thought. She was a modern, independent woman and had been fully prepared to support her niece if the girl didn't want to marry the man who had compromised her. But apparently such support would be unnecessary. In the last few days Desdemona had begun to think that marriage was not necessarily a bad thing, not when it was founded on mutual respect and affection, and not if Maxie was willing.

Most unworthy thought of all, Lady Collingwood would go purple with envious fury if her despised half-breed niece married such a supremely desirable *parti*. Desdemona allowed herself a few more minutes of beatific contemplation, then sat up and rang for her abigail.

Sally Griffin had been packed back to London from the Midlands when she come down with a bad cold, but she was recovered by now, and most intrigued by the goings-on in what was usually a too-quiet household. "Yes, milady?" she said when she reached the drawing room, her eyes bright with curiosity.

"I am dining tonight at Candover House, Griffin. My niece is staying there, and the duchess was kind enough to invite me so I could satisfy myself that she was in good company." Sally was interested to note that her mistress looked more than a little self-conscious. "We have only a few hours, but do you think any of my gowns could be altered to be more fashionable?"

Sally's eyes lit up. "Do you mean you're finally willing to show what the good Lord gave you? I've always said there's hardly a lady in London with a figure to match yours." While Lady Ross blushed, the abigail continued enthusiastically, "I've always thought that with a bit of altering the Devonshire brown silk would be quite smashing. But we must hurry, there's no time to waste."

Five years earlier, Sally had been turned off from her previous position without a character after a false accusation of theft. She had been only seventeen, with no friends or family to help her and had been facing the choice of starvation or working the streets when Lady Ross took her on. There were some who talked about helping the less fortunate, and that was all it was: talk. But Lady Ross wasn't one of them; she didn't help people just in big ways, with her politicking, but in little ways as well, like she had done with Sally.

Having discovered the kind heart under the brusque tongue, the abigail was most attached to her mistress and had often regretted that her ladyship chose to conceal her considerable assets under frumpish clothes. But now, unless Sally much mistook the matter, her ladyship wanted to look her best for that handsome marquess.

Before her mistress could succumb to second thoughts, the abigail seized her hand and tugged her to the stairs. Come this evening, Lady Ross would be fine as five pence, or her name wasn't Sally Griffin.

15

Maxie was relieved to learn that Robin had not yet returned to Candover House, for that meant their expedition to the hotel where her father died must be postponed until the next day. More and more she was concerned about what they would find there. According to Desdemona, Max had been tense and uneasy during his sojourn in London, and Maxie feared that he had been involved in something that had brought disaster on his head.

Desdemona herself had been a delight; finally Maxie had found an English relation that she actually felt related to. Her father had said once that his daughter reminded him of his little sister, and now Maxie understood why: under their superficial differences, the women were two of a kind. Her aunt might be a strong-minded eccentric by the narrow standards of English society, but Maxie didn't doubt that Desdemona would manage splendidly in the American backwoods.

Robin's brother had also been a pleasant surprise. Though the two Andrevilles had no obvious family resemblance, the marquess had a lurking smile and tolerant attitude much like Robin's. More, while he had been amiable from the first introduction, he had been positively welcoming after he had conversed privately with his brother. Perhaps that meant he would not object to having her among the aristocratic Andrevilles?

Having reached her bedroom, Maxie went to hang up the plain bonnet that the duchess had lent her, then gasped and stood with her arms akimbo while she studied the contents of her wardrobe. In the brief hours since Robin had suggested augmenting her supply of clothing, four gowns had appeared, with matching slippers neatly lined up below. In addition, accessories such as gloves, stockings, and shawls were folded on the narrow shelves that ran down one side of the wardrobe.

Bemused, she pulled out the most elaborate of the garments, a handsome silk evening gown in the precise shade of crimson that would best suit Maxie's coloring. There was no faulting Robin's taste, or perhaps it was more accurate to say that he had deduced the kind of elegant simplicity that Maxie herself favored. He had also known when to stop; too much largess and she would have balked.

Maxie didn't bother trying on any of the dresses. Given Robin's unusual talents, she had no doubt that everything would fit perfectly. Maggie would have helped; it was a fair guess that when a duchess requested prompt service, the request was honored. The duchess's abigail must have taken the measurements from Maxie's original dress when it was cleaned and pressed the previous day, then enlisted a dozen seamstresses to produce the new garments so swiftly.

As she closed the doors of the wardrobe, Maxie smiled wryly, realizing that Robin didn't even have to be present to distract her from brooding about her father. Her momentary levity disappeared; instead of brooding about her father, she could now brood about Robin.

It was incredibly tempting to grab his offer of marriage with both hands, before he changed his mind. But she could not escape the belief that her principal virtue was that she was available while the woman who was Robin's first choice was not. If Maxie wasn't in love with Robin, they might have been able to make a comfortable marriage, enjoying each other's company and bodies without major conflicts. They might not reach the highs of a love match, perhaps, but they would also avoid the lows.

But since she loved Robin and he didn't love her, the imbalance would be disastrous. It would be slow poison to live with him, always knowing that he had chosen her largely because she was an amusing diversion and she had been there when he had had a bad night. Even worse, Maxie suspected that the fact that she had seemed to be alone in the world had appealed to his protective instincts.

She shuddered at the thought and rubbed wearily at her temples. Well, she was not entirely alone in the world, and charity and dependence were not what she wanted as the basis of marriage. Unless Robin really and truly wanted to marry her, Maxima Collins, half-breed American and not at all a lady, she would be a fool to accept him. Once she went back to America, he would forget her soon enough. Then he could marry some vapid little chit from his own background, who was skilled at languishing and playing the helpless innocent. *That* should certainly please his protective instincts.

With a growl, Maxie decided that she had better find something to distract herself with before she started chewing on the furniture. She was willing to be wise and noble about turning Robin down, but being gracious as well was too much to ask of herself.

Unclenching her jaw, Maxie marched downstairs to the library. When she had gotten a brief glimpse of it the night before, Candover had observed the expression of delight on her face and invited her to browse to her heart's content.

The library was enormous, and uninhabited except for a ball of black fluff on one of the chairs. Maxie studied it a moment before deciding that it was either a sleeping cat or a misplaced fur muff. Then she began to prowl, randomly pulling volumes from the shelves to get a sense of what was available. Candover had books that she had always wanted to read but had never been able to obtain. There were volumes of poetry, history, philosophy, art, and everything else that might challenge or delight a mind. Best of all, these were books that had been read; this was not just a rich man's display library. Her opinion of the duke, already high, went up several more notches.

Deciding to be methodical, Maxie pushed the rolling library ladder to the far corner of the long room and climbed to the platform at the top. There, with a complete disregard for propriety, she hitched up her dress, crossed her legs under her, and pulled a volume from the top shelf. With diligence, she calculated happily, she might finish working her way through the library somewhere about the year 1850.

After an hour or so of browsing, Maxie's bad temper was entirely gone. Lost in *Persian Letters* by Montesquieu, she had almost forgotten where she was when the sound of someone entering the room caught her attention and she glanced up to see the duchess. Maxie wondered if she should announce her own presence, since the other woman didn't glance above eye level and must think she was alone.

After hastily closing the door behind her, the duchess swayed and sat abruptly on a long sofa, then leaned back. Alarmed, Maxie descended the ladder. "Are you unwell, your grace? Shall I call someone?" As she drew near, she saw that her hostess's lovely face was an interesting shade of gray-green that did not complement her eyes.

Registering Maxie's presence, the duchess attempted to smile. "Don't do that. The reason I slipped in here was to avoid alarming anyone. Candover has every servant in the house hovering nervously over me, and he's the worst of all." She sighed and closed her eyes. "There's nothing really wrong with me. I just haven't quite gotten the knack of breeding yet. Most women are ill in the morning, but for me it seems to be the afternoon."

"A-h-h," Maxie said sympathetically, remembering that Robin had mentioned an heir when he had greeted Maggie the night before. After a quick glance at the duchess's slim waist, Maxie decided that she must be quite early in her pregnancy. "Lie back and put your feet up on the sofa."

While her grace meekly obeyed, Maxie found a folded wool blanket on another sofa and spread it over her. "Perhaps you should have a little something to eat." When the duchess shuddered, Maxie said reassuringly, "Honestly, many women find that it helps to eat several times during the day. Nothing elaborate, perhaps something like tea and biscuits."

The duchess considered. "It might be worth a try."

A half-hour later, after the expectant mother had nibbled through two crisp little muffins, she was restored to her normal color. Leaning back into the corner of the sofa, she said, "Thank you for your advice. I feel amazingly better." She made a face. "At least, until the next time."

"Don't worry, your grace, the nausea disappears magically sometime after the third month."

"You're very knowledgeable." There was a slight question in the duchess's voice.

"Did Robin explain my background to you, your grace?"

"Of course not." The duchess gave her a stern look. "He

is the last man on earth to talk about another person's private business. Sometimes it is impossible to get him to say anything useful about anything. And I wish you would call me Margot."

"Not Maggie?"

"My real name is Margot and that is what I am called now. Maggie is a nickname Robin gave me, and it lasted through my spying days." She smiled. "I'm sure that to him I'll always be Maggie, just as I can't think of him as Lord Robert."

The duchess tilted her golden head to one side as if weighing whether to say more. Abruptly she said, "I know you are uncomfortable with me, but I am no threat to you. On the contrary, I would like to be friends."

Maxie blinked in surprise, then gave the duchess full marks for confronting an awkward situation. "I haven't meant to return your hospitality with churlishness," she said carefully. "But I must admit that I have trouble understanding the relationship between you and Robin."

"You haven't been churlish. Actually, I think you have dealt very well with a situation that would send most women into strong hysterics." Margot sipped reflectively on her tea. "I met Robin when he saved me, at considerable risk to himself, from a French mob that had killed my father. I had no real reason to return to England and a passionate desire to fight Napoleon in any way I could, so we decided to work together.

"We were young and had only each other to trust, and there was a great deal of caring between us. It was easy—and very rewarding—to become lovers. Nonetheless, I had been acquainted with Robin for a dozen years before I knew his real name, station in life, or was even sure of his nationality."

She set her teacup down and began to turn a ring on her finger absently. "It may be hard to understand this outside of the context of war. Robin would go off for months at a time, risking his life in ways I tried not to think about. Then he would show up, blithe and good-natured, as if he had just strolled around the corner. I think there is a great deal that he never told me, to spare me from worrying even more.

"In some ways we were very close. Yet there were other parts of our lives that never touched at all. Eventually, it seemed wrong to be lovers, and that ceased. But the friendship and trust remained, and always will.'' Her gray-green eyes were unfocused as she contemplated the past. ''Perhaps the outcome would have been different if I hadn't been in love with Rafe before I ever met Robin. It is impossible to say.''

Her manner changed, becoming brisk. ''That's another story. But perhaps now you can better understand why I would do almost anything to see Robin happy.''

Including baring her soul to another woman who was very nearly a stranger. Maxie's throat tightened. ''I appreciate your openness, Margot.'' Her voice was low, and to cover her uncertainty Maxie leaned forward to pour a cup of tea for herself. ''What you are doing is more than generous, to both Robin and me.''

Having had a moment to collect herself, she glanced up, her gaze meeting the duchess's. ''It is easy to understand why Robin is in love with you.''

Margot shook her head decisively. ''Robin was never in love with me. Not then, not now.'' She opened her mouth as if to continue, then stopped. ''I won't say any more. Perhaps I've already said too much.''

Margot had convinced Maxie that she was not in love with Robin, but there was nothing in her words that proved that Robin was not still in love with her. Quite unable to discuss the topic further, Maxie glanced away, her gaze falling on the fur ball on the adjacent chair. ''Is that a cat or a muff, Margot?''

''A cat, Rex by name,'' The duchess said, willing to accept the change of subject.

Maxie scrutinized the featureless black fur. ''Is he ill? He hasn't moved since I got here an hour and a half ago.''

''Don't worry, he isn't dead, just tired.'' Margot smiled mischievously. ''Very, very tired.''

As if responding to the attention, Rex stretched luxuriously, revealing a very large feline body, then rolled onto his back, four tufted feet aloft as he returned to his nap.

Any lingering tension in the room dissolved as the two women laughed together. Maxie decided that no matter what the future held, she was very glad to have made Margot's acquaintance. Then she refilled the two teacups and began to describe her life in America.

* * *

Wolverton would be calling momentarily to take her to Candover House, and Desdemona stared at her reflection in the mirror with blind panic. "Griffin, I can't possibly go out looking like this! When you said you would alter the gown, I didn't know you intended to cut it to the navel."

"Now, now, milady, you're exaggerating," Sally said soothingly. The abigail had expected this reaction and had not let Lady Ross near the mirror until it was too late for either gown or coiffure to be changed. "This is a fashionable neckline, but by no means an extreme one." After a moment's thought, Sally suggested, "Perhaps you should wear your pearls rather than the cameo? That will make you feel a mite less exposed."

The triple strand of pearls did fill in the vast expanse of bare skin better, though Desdemona still felt as if she was in one of those beastly nightmares where one is caught in public in one's shift. It wasn't just the dress's décolletage, low though that was. Griffin had also taken the silk gown in along the seams so that it lovingly hugged Desdemona's flamboyant figure. She stared at her image with horrified fascination. "I look like a Cyprian."

"But the very most expensive kind, milady," Sally said with a wicked smile.

Desdemona began to laugh. "I'm being absurd, aren't I?" She turned to the mirror and tried to look see herself objectively. Devonshire brown was a dark shade with reddish tones that did not suit many women, but it was perfect with Desdemona's vivid titian hair and creamy complexion.

Griffin had scorned her mistress's usual severe chignon in favor of a tumble of waves and curls threaded with gold beads. The abigail had also applied a few subtle cosmetics. Desdemona had to admit that if the image in the mirror belonged to a stranger, she would have thought the woman a dashing and not unattractive female. In an Amazonian sort of way.

The rap of the door knocker sounded through the house; the marquess had arrived and it was too late to change now. Desdemona put her shoulders back and straightened to her full height. Unfortunately, the action emphasized a portion of her anatomy that was quite prominent enough already, but the only

way she could survive the evening was by pretending that she
was comfortable with her own appearance.

Giles was waiting at the foot of the steps, and as Desdemona
approached him, he just stared at her, a stunned expression on
his face. Suddenly anxious, she stopped, clutching the railing,
convinced that she had made an absolute fool of herself. She
was a tough old fowl dressed up as a game pullet, and
Desdemona instinctively reached for her shawl with the intention
of drawing it around her shoulders.

Mercifully the marquess interpreted her expression. He
mounted the two last steps and took one of her hands in both
of his, effectively preventing her from hiding in her shawl.
"Forgive my stupefaction, Desdemona. I knew you were lovely,
but tonight you positively take my breath away." He lifted her
hand to his lips and kissed it.

Her hand tingling from his kiss, Desdemona exhaled the
breath of air she hadn't known she was holding. There was
absolutely no doubt about the sincerity of Giles' admiration.
Best of all, the warmth in his eyes didn't make her feel hunted;
it made her feel quite pleased with herself.

She smiled up at the marquess and took his arm. "Shall we
be off?" It was going to be an enjoyable evening.

The evening was more than enjoyable; it was wonderful.
While no great issues were debated or resolved, the conversation
and company were pure pleasure. There were just the six of
them: the Candovers, Maxima and Lord Robert, and Desdemona and Wolverton. Desdemona knew that she could never
be the equal of the stunning blond duchess, or of Maxie, tiny
and darkly exquisite in crimson, but Giles seemed pleased with
her even in a party that included two diamonds of the first water.

Even Candover had indulged in a little teasing flirtation with
her. Desdemona had met the duke in the course of her political
activities, but he had never flirted before. No one who saw the
way he looked at his wife could believe that he had any real
interest in another woman, and after Desdemona recovered from
her initial shock, she had accepted his words as a simple
compliment and flirted back. More than that, depraved creature
that she was, she had actually enjoyed doing it.

On the carriage ride back to her house, she and Giles had talked casually, in words anyone could have overheard, but his large strong hand enfolded hers and she felt quite preposterously happy. When they reached Desdemona's house, he escorted her up the steps, then rested his hands briefly on her shoulders, his expression intent. His grasp tightened for a moment and she wondered if he was going to kiss her, right there in Mount Street. Then her parlormaid opened the door and he dropped his hands, saying simply, "Good night," before turning away.

It was too early for this lovely evening to end. Desdemona said, "Wait," and the marquess paused. Suddenly shy, she said, "It isn't really late. Would you like to come in for a few minutes? Perhaps have some brandy?"

He hesitated, clearly on the brink of refusing.

Desdemona, amazed at her own temerity, smiled up at him. "Please?"

"For just a few minutes," he said after an unflatteringly long pause.

Desdemona sent the servants off to bed, then led Giles into the drawing room and poured them each a brandy. Sitting in opposing chairs, they talked idly for a while, but the earlier ease was gone. The marquess watched her with a dark, brooding expression that made Desdemona uneasy. He had not kissed her or said anything the least bit romantic since that strange, intense interlude in the inn at Daventry. Perhaps he was just going slowly; more likely, she thought with profound depression, his interest in her had been a momentary aberration.

Abruptly he finished his brandy in one quick swallow and stood. "I think it's best that I go."

Convinced that she had done something wrong, Desdemona was crushed, and it showed in her all-too-expressive face.

The marquess gave her a wry glance. "Don't look at me like that, as if I've just cast my vote against your apprentice protection law."

She looked away, feeling like an utter fool. A proper female would have learned not to wear her heart on her sleeve by the age of seventeen.

In two steps Giles closed the space between them, then put one finger under her chin and turned her to face him. His eyes troubled, he said, "If I stay I am going to have a great deal of trouble keeping my hands off you, which you will probably find upsetting and which will certainly raise havoc with the slow, genteel courtship I have been planning."

Courtship? Hearing him say the word made Desdemona almost dizzy with relief. "I don't think you are likely to turn into a lust-crazed savage. And if you do"—she gave him a dazzling smile—"it's a risk I'm willing to take."

Giles grinned but retreated, putting a safe distance between them. "Perhaps I'll manage to behave as a gentleman, but I can't guarantee it."

"Good!" Desdemona said recklessly.

He laughed, lines crinkling the tanned skin around his eyes. "Do you realize just how much you have changed in the last fortnight?"

"I hope it's for the better."

"I think so. You seem more relaxed, happier." He leaned against the fireplace mantel, his arms folded across his chest, his expression serious. "This may be too early for a formal offer of marriage, but I'd like you to consider the possibility."

Desdemona stared at him, her eyes wide and grave as her playful relief ebbed away. She had been drifting along, delighting in his company and his admiration, but now that he had actually spoken, painful reality closed in on her.

He raised his eyebrows at her expression. "Surely you aren't surprised. The idea of marriage first came up in Daventry."

"I guess I didn't believe that after you had a chance to consider, you would really make an offer," she said in a small voice.

He gave the wry half-smile she loved. "I'm not sure whether that shows lack of faith in me, or in yourself." His smile faded. "You are living proof that a woman doesn't need a husband to live a worthwhile life. Even if you do wish to remarry, I can understand that you might prefer more promising material. Just tell me and I will not raise the subject again."

His statement reminded her that she was not the only one to feel uncertain. She shook her head emphatically. "I have no doubt that you would make a marvelous husband. The problem is"—she swallowed hard—"I don't know if I would make an adequate wife."

He relaxed at her words and caught her gaze with his own. "You are honest, beautiful, have a kind heart, and do not suffer fools gladly. To me, those seem like excellent qualifications for a wife."

She had to laugh a little at what he considered important, but her eyes slid away. "I . . . I don't know if I can give you an heir. It is true that my husband and I did not share a bed for very long, so perhaps I am not barren, but I am past thirty now—"

He cut her off sharply. "That doesn't matter. I'm offering for you because I want you to be my wife, not a brood mare. I could have remarried years ago if an heir was that important." More quietly he added, "It wouldn't bother me to know that Robin or a son of his will have Wolverton after me."

Desdemona looked down to where her hands were frantically twined in her lap. The trouble with half-truths is that they were not much protection after they were demolished. She should have known that the real truth could not be avoided. Her eyes still on her hands, she said, "There is another, more basic reason why I fear that I would not be the wife for you." She forced herself to look at him. "You are a warm, passionate man, and surely you want a wife who is the same kind. But I don't know if I can ever be that kind of woman."

As she looked down again, her shoulders bowed and her voice broke. "My husband used to say that it was like bedding an icicle, that any trollop on the streets was warmer than I."

At that, Giles could no longer stay away from her. Crossing the room, he drew her up into his embrace. "Hush, love," he said, rocking her gently in his arms, his cheek against her hair. "Few women are passionate in a miserable marriage. Don't condemn yourself by the words of a selfish brute."

She clung to him, shaking, but he felt her begin to relax. He stroked the back of her head, accidentally loosening her hair so that it fell in thick waves over his hand. "You are so incredibly fair-minded. There is probably not another woman in London who would so conscientiously spell out her presumed failings when a marquess offered for her."

Desdemona leaned back in his embrace to look him squarely in the eye, her expression severe. "I'm not interested in marrying a marquess. I'm interested in marrying Giles Andreville, who is the nicest, most amusing, most attractive man in England.''

If he understood her fears, she certainly understood his. A slow smile spread over Giles' face. ''It seems that we both think marriage is a good idea, so when shall we do it?'' Then, before she could answer, he succumbed to temptation and kissed her.

''You don't kiss like a cold woman,'' he murmured. In fact, her response and the feel of her long luscious body against his triggered an explosion of desire that very nearly disabled Giles' considerable self-control. It took a major act of will to end the kiss and loosen his embrace, and a long minute before his breathing was steady enough for him to speak. ''I think that we can work matters out to our mutual satisfaction, don't you?''

She had been smiling up at him with dazed delight, but at his words her expression became grave and her gaze dropped to his cravat. ''Marriage is forever, Giles. It might be better if we don't do anything so irrevocable until we are sure. Or rather,'' she qualified, ''until I am sure that I can fulfill my part of the bargain.''

''There will never be any guarantees, Desdemona. I think it is enough to believe that love will carry us through.'' He kissed the top of her red head. ''And I love you, very much.''

She looked up at that, her gray eyes wide and vulnerable. ''I love you too. But I still don't know if I want to trust to that alone. I think it would be better if we made sure first.''

He stared at her, wondering if he had understood properly. ''Desdemona, are you propositioning me?''

She nodded, blushing, then ducked her head again.

Wrapping his arms around her, he drew Desdemona close again as he began to laugh. Before she could take offense, he said, ''Do you have any idea just how intimidating it is to tell a man that his whole future depends on one night's performance? The mere thought is incapacitating!''

His amusement broke the tension, and she looked up with a shy smile. ''It doesn't have to be just one night. We can take as long as necessary.'' Her smile turned mischievous and she pressed against him, wriggling with pleasure at the hard strength of his powerful frame. ''And if memory serves me correctly, you don't seem the least bit incapacitated.''

Giles gasped, his arms tightening, then whispered, "What a woman you are." His slate-blue eyes were so filled with tenderness that she thought she might melt into a happy puddle in the middle of her very respectable drawing room. His voice husky, he continued, "Shall we see if I can convince you that you will make the best of all possible wives?" Then he bent over for another kiss that left them both breathless.

As she guided them upstairs to her room, Desdemona might have fallen without his supporting arm around her waist. Somewhere in that last kiss, she had realized that he was right, that the powerful attraction that she felt for him meant that she really was capable of being a warm and willing wife.

When they entered her room, she pulled his head down for another kiss, more happy than she could ever remember being in her life. Just because she was sure he was right didn't mean that they had to skip the proof, did it?

The night was one of shyness and discovery, passion and laughter, too precious to waste on sleep. It was with the greatest of reluctance that Giles acknowledged the lightening sky outside Desdemona's windows. "A pity that it's high summer and dawn comes so early," he said softly, his breath stirring her tangled hair. "I don't want to leave, but it's time."

With a purr of contentment, Desdemona rolled over so she lay half across his chest, her chin resting on her crossed arms. There was no trace of the angry, defensive woman who had first invaded his life. Now she was all soft welcome. "Why leave? The servants will have already deduced what is going on."

"Except for my coachman, not necessarily." He chuckled. "I admit that for people of our advanced years propriety is not of first importance, but I prefer that there be no gossip around your name."

Smiling mischievously, Desdemona wriggled her lush curves against Giles to such good effect that he caught her tight and drew her down for another kiss. When it was necessary for survival's sake to stop for air, he asked, "Do you still think yourself a cold woman?" As Desdemona's fine white skin colored rosily, Giles observed with interest, "You have the most enchanting blushes, and they go much farther than I realized."

That made her blush even more, and by the time Giles had finished investigating just how far the blushes went, another half hour had passed. After, as they lay twined together, Desdemona murmured, "I didn't know it could be like this."

"Neither did I."

Desdemona raised her head in surprise. "Truly?"

"Truly." Giles nodded, mesmerized by the way her red hair glowed in the dawn light. "I suppose I've had the normal amount of experience, but—I've never before made love with my beloved. Nothing in the past has ever equaled this." Her smile was so radiant that he kissed her again, lingeringly. "Are you ready to make a decision about marriage, or do you need more time?"

She laughed and linked her arms around his neck, her gray eyes bright with happiness. "After last night, do you think I'd be fool enough to let you get away?"

16

The Abingdon Hotel stood on the street called Long Acre near Covent Garden. It was a small, unpretentious establishment, respectable but only just. As Robin helped Maxie from the hackney, her gloved hand clenched around his as if she was unconsciously preparing for battle. She was wearing her simplest dress, the plain muslin one she had made herself, and her hair was dressed severely under a simple straw bonnet; she wanted no one to be distracted by her appearance.

Maxie had been able to think of no better strategy than to simply go to the hotel and make inquiries. Surely it was unusual for a guest to die at the hotel, and the event would be remembered. And if she did not receive straightforward answers to her questions, well, that would give her another kind of information.

As the well-dressed young couple disappeared into the hotel, the owner of the tobacco shop next door peered through the grimy glass of his front window, squinting to confirm that they matched the description he had been given: a blond fellow handsome as a lord, and a dusky little pocket Venus. The old man nodded; aye, they must be the ones.

Turning to the lad who assisted him, the tobacconist said, "Go 'round the corner and tell Simmons that the folk he asked me to watch for are in Abingdon's now. Mind you hurry, and if he ain't there, go after 'im. There'll be a half-crown for you if 'e gets here in time."

And there'd be three quid, less the half-crown, for himself. Vastly pleased, the tobacconist treated himself to one of his own most expensive cigars.

* * *

Inside the shabby vestibule, Robin asked the spotty young clerk, "May we speak with the manager, please?"

The clerk looked up from the newspaper he was reading. After an insulting glance at Maxie, he said, "I can rent you a room, but you'll have to pay for a whole day even if you only want it for an hour."

"We do not need a room," Robin said in a voice edged with steel. "We want to speak to the manager. Now."

The clerk considered making a surly reply, then thought better of it; the visitor might be a swell, but he also looked like a man best not crossed. "I'll see if Wilkens'll see you."

Maxie clenched and unclenched her hands as they waited. If it hadn't been for the calming effect of Robin's presence, she would be ricocheting from the walls. She was grateful that he didn't attempt conversation; in her present mood, she might bite his head off.

As she paced the narrow confines of the entry hall, Maxie wondered why she was so inexplicably anxious. She had fought off wolves in an autumn blizzard with more composure than she was showing today. She had already faced the grim possibility that her father might have been murdered because of some nefarious activity, and the even grimmer one that her uncle may have been involved. Closing her eyes, she forced herself to breathe more slowly. Could her anxiety come from the fact that, at heart, she didn't really believe that anything so dreadful could be true, yet she might learn something today that would confirm her worst fears?

The clerk returned and jerked his thumb over his shoulder. "He'll see you. Down the hall, last door on the left."

Wilkens proved to be a stout, balding man with an expression of permanent wariness. Not bothering to rise from his desk, he glanced up and barked, "State your business and be quick about it. I'm a busy man."

They had agreed in advance that Robin would speak, since a man would doubtless be taken more seriously. "My name is Lord Robert Andreville," he said crisply. "I understand that about four months ago, one of your guests died unexpectedly, a Mr. Collins."

"The American gent." Wilkens' face, not very open to begin with, promptly shuttered down. "Aye, he turned up his toes here."

"Could you tell us something of the circumstances of his death?" When the manager didn't reply, Robin prompted, "Who found him, and what time of day was it? Was Mr. Collins still alive when he was found? Was a physician called?"

The manager scowled. "What business is it of yours?"

Unable to keep silent, Maxie said, "He was my father. Surely I have a right to know what his last hours were like."

Wilkens swung around to study her, his expression unreadable. "Sorry, miss." Glancing away, he said, "A maid found him. The physician said it must have been his heart and he went sudden like."

"What was the physician's name?" Robin asked.

Wilkens stood, his expression surly. "You've taken enough of my time. There's nothin' more to know—Collins died and that's it. If it hadn't happened here, it would have been somewhere else, and I wish it had been. Now get out. I've work to do."

Maxie opened her mouth to protest, wanting to know more, but Robin took her arm firmly. "Thank you, Mr. Wilkens. Sorry to have inconvenienced you."

As her companion steered them out of the office and closed the door, Maxie hissed angrily, "I want to ask him more, Robin. He wasn't telling the truth."

"No," Robin agreed, "and he wasn't going to, either. There may be a better way to get information."

Instead of following the hall to the front of the building, Robin turned the other way. "Servants always know what's going on and perhaps no one has persuaded them to hold their tongues."

The door at the end of the passage led to a cobbled yard with stables built around three sides. Maxie followed Robin across the court to a set of open doors. Inside the stable an elderly gentleman was oiling a piece of harness and whistling tunelessly between crooked front teeth. He looked considerably more congenial than either of the men in the hotel.

"Good day, sir," Robin said cheerily.

The ostler looked up, startled but not displeased by such

amiability from a well-dressed gent. "Good day to you, sir,"
he replied. "What can I do for you?"

"My name's Bob Andreville." Robin offered his hand. His
speech was different, and it took Maxie a moment to realize
that he was using a strong, distinctly American accent. "I was
wondering, have you been working here long?"

"Nigh on to ten years." After wiping one oily hand down
his trousers, the ostler returned Robin's handshake. "Name's
Will Jenkins. You an American?"

"That I am, but my father was born in Yorkshire. This is
my first trip to England. Would have come sooner, but for the
war." He shook his head. "Damned fool things, wars.
Americans and Britons should be friends."

"Ain't that the truth," the ostler agreed. "I've a cousin in
Virginia. You from that part of the colonies?"

The two men continued in that vein while Maxie fidgeted,
restless but realizing that Robin was right: they would learn far
more from the friendly ostler than from the hostile Wilkens.

After several minutes, Robin said, "A friend of mine, Max
Collins, came here for a visit a few months back. Then just
before I sailed over myself, I heard he'd died, but no one knew
exactly what had happened. I remembered he was staying at
the Abingdon Hotel, so I thought since I was here I'd stop by
to see what I could learn." He looked sorrowful. "We hear
stories about how dangerous London is. Did thieves set on him
or something like that?"

" 'Twas no such thing. Mr. Collins died right here in his
bed." Jenkins shook his grizzled head. "A sorry thing, that.
He was a real gent, very pleasant to everyone, even that
mawworm Wilkens. It was a real shock when he killed himself."

"A real shock when he killed himself . . ." The words hit
Maxie like a cannonball, with an impact so shattering that it
was beyond pain. "No," she whispered. "He wouldn't have
done that."

As Robin inhaled sharply, Jenkins glanced at Maxie. "Sorry
to be the one to tell you if he was a friend of yours, miss, but
there ain't much doubt. The gent tried to arrange it so's no one
would know, but he wasn't careful enough. Musta been upset

about somethin' and just decided he couldn't take it no more."
His expression was compassionate. " 'Most everyone feels that
way sometimes, it's just that Mr. Collins did somethin' about
it."

As a child, Maxie had once ventured onto a frozen pond
during a January thaw; even twenty years later she had not
forgotten her terror when ice she had believed solid began
breaking up beneath her. Desperately she had tried to retreat
to the shore, but there had been no hope or safety anywhere
as the ice splintered in all directions. She had plunged into the
frigid dark water and nearly drowned before her father heard
her screams and rescued her.

Her feelings now were similar to when the ice broke beneath
her, but a thousand times worse. What Jenkins said was
impossible, unbearable. "No," she repeated, burying her face
in her hands, her voice a thread of anguish. "He wouldn't have
done that. *He wouldn't have done that*!"

Maxie heard Robin speak her name, but his voice was distant,
of no importance. "No!" she screamed. Mindless with grief,
she lifted her skirts and whirled away, racing up the alley to
the street, then darting into the heavy traffic on Long Acre. She
collided with a man who smelled of onions, losing her bonnet
and almost falling, then regained her balance and kept going.
A hoarse shout sounded in her ear and someone grabbed her
arm, jerking her from the path of a horse that reared up in the
air, its pawing ironclad hooves barely missing her.

Without even noticing the face of her rescuer, Maxie broke
away and resumed running, as if somewhere there was a place
where the past was different, where she would not have to
believe that her father had killed himself. She tripped but felt
nothing when her knees and palms smashed into the cobblestones.

Scrambling to her feet, she was about to resume her flight
when strong hands seized her shoulders and Robin's familiar
voice said urgently, "Stop, Maxie, please! You'll hurt yourself."

She tried to escape, but he wouldn't release her. Blinded by
tears, Maxie balled her hands into fists and struck out heedlessly.
"My father would never have killed himself and left me!" she

cried, pounding on Robin's chest, trying to get free. "He loved me, he would never have done that!"

Robin clasped her to him, immobilizing her flailing fists by pinning her arms to her sides. He had never seen her cry, but now tears poured down her face as she continued to struggle against him. He gasped as one of her elbows caught him in the stomach, knocking the wind from him. He dared not use more force for fear of hurting her, but she was a dangerous woman to hold against her will.

"We still don't know exactly what happened, Kanawiosta," he said when he caught his breath again. "Perhaps the ostler was wrong."

Maxie's struggles ceased but the tears continued, and her small body trembled in his arms. He ached at the sight of her misery, knowing that she was in some private hell that he could not share, not yet, not unless she would let him. Ignoring the curious onlookers, he continued speaking to her in a low voice, his lips near her ear, hoping the sound would soothe her even though she seemed beyond absorbing the words.

Then some instinct developed in his dangerous years on the Continent made Robin look up. Half a block away, on the other side of the stream of traffic, stood Simmons, his face dark and threatening. Their gazes locked, and Robin saw fury in the man who had pursued them the length of England.

Swearing at the fact that Simmons had appeared now, of all times, Robin hailed a passing hackney. Mercifully it stopped and he lifted Maxie in his arms and pushed in front of a merchant who was trying to claim the same vehicle. "The lady is ill," he said curtly, then slammed the door in the merchant's face.

Simmons watched the hackney depart with a scowl. From the way the young lady was reacting, she had learned the truth, and taken it even more badly than her uncle had feared. He beckoned to a scrawny urchin who regularly worked for him. "Find out where they're going."

The lad nodded, then raced after the hackney. When he caught up with the vehicle, he leapt up and grabbed the back, then wriggled around until he found a comfortable spot to cling for the rest of the ride. When the lad returned, at least Simmons would be able to tell Collingwood where his niece was staying. It wasn't much, but it was something that could be salvaged from a job that had otherwise been a disaster.

Though Maxie was not unconscious, her body was chilled, showing all the symptoms of shock, and she seemed oblivious of Robin's presence. He held her on his lap through the ride back to Candover House, enfolding her in his arms as he tried to infuse her with some of his own body warmth.

When she first mentioned her father's death, Robin had immediately thought that suicide was at least as likely as murder, as well as providing a plausible explanation for Collingwood's secrecy. However, given the violence of Maxie's reaction to the news, she had never considered that her father might have killed himself, had completely blocked out the possibility because it was literally unthinkable.

Back at Candover House, Robin carried her inside past the startled butler, stopping long enough to order that warm water, towels, and salve be sent to her bedchamber. Then he carried Maxie upstairs and laid her on her bed. His hands gentle, he undressed her, removing her ruined muslin dress and stockings. After all, he had seen her in her shift before, and at the moment he didn't give a damn about propriety.

When the basin of warm water arrived, he dismissed the maid, then carefully washed away the blood and grit on Maxie's knees and palms. None of the injuries was deep enough to warrant bandaging, though they must have stung like the very devil when he spread salve on her raw flesh.

Maxie didn't resist, cooperate, or show any discomfort at Robin's ministrations, and her eyes never met his. When he was done, she rolled away and buried her head in the pillows, and he wondered if the way she was turning inward was an aspect of her Mohawk heritage. Not that the reason was important; what mattered and hurt was that she was shutting him out.

When Robin had finished, he pulled a blanket over her, then covered her curled fist with his own hand. "Is there anything I can do?"

She gave her head an infinitesimal shake.

"Kanawiosta, when I was drowning in grief, you told me that a burden shared is lighter," he said softly. "Is there nothing you will accept from me?"

"Not now." Her muffled voice was almost inaudible. "I'm sorry."

"Do you want me to leave?"

She nodded.

Heavy of heart, Robin stood. In spite of her petite frame, she had never looked fragile, but now the slight form under the blanket looked diminished and vulnerable. He did not try to define his feelings; he only knew that he would have willingly given everything he possessed to alleviate her misery. Needing to express some of his tenderness, he touched her raven hair in a caress too light for her to feel or to retreat from.

Having heard from her servants that there was trouble afoot, the duchess waited outside in a chair, her hands patiently folded in her lap. "What has happened?" she asked quietly, standing and coming over to him.

Robin sighed and ran his hand through his blond hair in frustration. "Apparently Maxie's father committed suicide."

"Oh, dear Lord," Maggie whispered. She had also lost her beloved father under tragic circumstances, and she could understand the younger woman's feelings all too well.

"If only I could do something." His mouth twisted. "But all she wants is to be left alone."

"Give her a little time to absorb the shock," Maggie advised. "Grief is a solitary affair, and one must go inward first and come to terms with it before comfort from others can be accepted."

"I'm sure you're right, Duchess." He tried to smile. "But it is very hard to see her like this."

"Love hurts, Robin." Then, in a deliberate attempt to lighten the atmosphere, she added, "So does hunger, and I find myself hungry very often now. Come and have tea with me." Taking his arm, Maggie marched him off to the morning room. Tea wasn't much, but it was better than nothing.

They had finished a silent tea when the butler entered and presented a card to the duchess. She raised her brows at the sight, then passed it to Robin. "Lord Collingwood is here."

Robin scrutinized the card, his expression thoughtful. "Shall we receive him together? You are Maxie's hostess, but I have a vested interest in anything he might have to say."

"Of course."

The butler left, then ushered the visitor in a few minutes later. Lord Collingwood was a tall man with a thin, tired face. If one looked, there was a faint resemblance to his sister, but he was a drabber, more conventional creature than Lady Ross.

Collingwood made his bow to the duchess. "I am sorry to call uninvited, but I have reason to believe that my niece, Miss Maxima Collins, is visiting you. I would like to see her."

"She is here," Margot admitted, "but unwell and not receiving visitors. Would you like to leave a message for her?"

Collingwood hesitated, and while he thought, his gaze fell on Robin, who was standing unobtrusively to one side of the room. The visitor's eyes narrowed. "My niece was traveling with a man of your description."

Robin inclined his head but kept his distance. "I am Lord Robert Andreville."

That rocked the visitor. "Wolverton's brother?"

"The same."

Collingwood shook his head in disbelief. "And here I'd been worrying that the girl had been taken in by some rogue."

"Noble birth is hardly proof against villainy," Robin said. "However, as it happens, my intentions regarding Miss Collins have been honorable. We met by chance. Having some experience of the dangers of traveling, I offered my escort to ensure that she reached London safely." His tone was dry, but he liked what he saw of Collingwood, who seemed very much the English gentleman, definitely not the sort to have his brother murdered. No wonder Maxie had doubted that her uncle could be a villain.

A glint of humor showed in Collingwood's eyes at the oversimplification. "You certainly protected her from the Bow Street Runner I sent to bring her back to Chanleigh."

"Good Lord! Simmons is a Runner?" After a stunned moment, Robin had to laugh at himself. "I should have guessed. Maxie and I thought he was some kind of villain."

''There are few superficial differences between Runners and the villains they pursue,'' Collingwood agreed. ''Ned Simmons might have turned criminal when his boxing days were done. Instead, he is one of Bow Street's best. He helped me investigate my brother's death, and since he was near Durham when my niece ran away, I asked him to find her.''

Deciding it was time to intervene, Margot said, ''Please take a seat, Lord Collingwood. I gather that we are all concerned with Miss Collins' welfare, so we might as well speak frankly.''

''From what Simmons said, apparently my niece heard something very upsetting at the Abingdon Hotel.'' There was a questioning note in Collingwood's voice as he sat down.

Robin nodded. ''She learned that her father killed himself. The manager didn't talk—I assume that you or Simmons had gotten to him—but one of the servants told us, and she is taking the news very badly.''

Collingwood sighed, his face troubled. ''I knew she would be upset: she was devoted to Max. That's why I didn't tell her and tried to prevent her from reaching London, where she might learn what happened.''

''It was your attempt to conceal the truth that sent her off to investigate,'' Robin said acerbically. ''Maxie overheard a discussion between you and your wife that implied there was some kind of foul play involved in her father's death.''

''So that's what happened,'' Collingwood said as realization dawned. ''At first I thought she had decided on impulse to visit my sister, Lady Ross. It wasn't until my sister appeared in Durham that I realized something was amiss. Then, with every report Simmons sent back, I became progressively more alarmed. I'm grateful she didn't run into disaster.'' He looked gloomy. ''Now that I am not concerned for her life, I can begin to worry about her reputation.''

''There is no reason anyone need know how she reached London,'' the duchess pointed out. ''The real problem is her reaction to the news of her father's death.''

''Something has happened that may cheer her a bit.'' Collingwood studied Robin. ''I gather that you have constituted yourself her defender.''

''That is as good a term as any,'' Robin agreed.

"Then I suppose I can tell you that Maxima is something of an heiress. Not a great sum, a mere independence of five hundred pounds a year, but quite enough to keep her comfortably either here or in America." The baron looked at Robin hopefully.

Amused, Robin decided that Collingwood hoped the legacy would make his niece a more desirable matrimonial object. At least the man wasn't coming out and insisting that Robin must marry Maxie for having ruined her honor; Robin was no more fond of such pressure than Maxie herself. "From whom is she inheriting?" he asked. "She said her father left nothing."

"That's true enough. Max was absolutely hopeless about money." Collingwood grimaced. "It's rather complicated. Our aunt, Lady Clendennon, was my brother's godmother. Her Christian name was Maxima, and my brother and his daughter were both called after her. She was always fond of Max, even though she considered him totally unreliable. Once or twice a year she would receive a letter from him, and it would put her in a good mood for weeks. She went around complaining about what a wastrel Max was, but with a smile."

The baron smiled ruefully. "If Max had had half as much prudence as he had charm, he could have been prime minister. Still, he seems to have enjoyed his life, at least until the end. Who am I to say that he should have done differently?

"At any rate, Aunt Clendennon thought that giving Max money would be a complete waste, so she decided to make Max's daughter one of her heirs instead. She died last winter and her lawyer wrote my brother in Boston, which is the main reason he returned to England when he did. Since the lawyer had been vague and uncooperative about the terms of the will, Max decided to go to London to talk to him personally."

"Why wasn't Maxie told any of this? I gather that you were informed, yet you are not her guardian."

"I am the head of her family, and she had no one else to stand for her. My brother told me of the legacy when he first reached Durham, but he forbade me to tell Maxima until the matter was settled. He didn't want to get her hopes up if it wasn't going to work out." Collingwood looked gloomy. "The legal issues were complicated. She could not inherit before her twenty-fifth birthday, and the money was to be held in trust after that for as long as Max was alive; apparently my aunt was concerned that my brother would waste Maxima's inheritance.

"After Max died, that was no longer an issue, but the present Lord Clendennon was influencing the lawyer to look for reasons to disqualify Maxima, because the income would revert to him if for some reason she didn't inherit. I have to say he's a greedy devil, even if he is my cousin," Collingwood said as an aside. "When he found out her mother was a Red Indian, Clendennon suggested that perhaps Maxima was illegitimate, the product of a casual liaison, or perhaps not even Max's daughter."

Robin whistled softly. "I don't blame you for not wanting to tell Maxie that. She would have been furious."

"And who could blame her? I put my own lawyer to work and he wrote to a colleague in Boston. Just this week I received a copy of my brother's marriage lines. He and his wife were married by an Anglican priest, and Maxima is entirely legitimate under English law."

Collingwood gave a faint, satisfied smile. "Even if there hadn't been a Christian ceremony, I was prepared to argue that her parents were legally married under the laws of her mother's people. For that matter, illegitimacy would not necessarily have invalidated the bequest, but Clendennon might have used it as an excuse to cause legal trouble that would take considerable time and money to resolve. This is much simpler."

"You've gone to great effort on your niece's behalf," Margot observed.

"Of course," Collingwood said, raising his brows. "She's family. Besides, I'm fond of the girl. I wish my own daughters had some of her spirit." He rose to his feet. "I'll be staying at the Clarendon for several days, and I'd like to see Maxima before I return to Durham. Will you tell her I called?"

"Of course," Robin said. "Do you want to explain about her inheritance yourself?"

Collingwood thought a moment. "Use your judgment. If she will see you and not me, tell her if you think it might cheer her up. I've made a muddle of the whole business, I'm afraid."

"Maxie is fortunate to have such a conscientious uncle,"

Robin said. "Given the constraints you had, there may have been no resolution that wasn't muddled."

"Thank you." Collingwood looked a little happier as he took his leave. "Lord Robert, your grace."

After the baron left, Robin turned to look at Maggie. "Did you catch what I did in Collingwood's story?"

She nodded, her gray-green eyes gleaming. Drawing conclusions from sketchy data was the essence of the spy's art, and they were both very, very good at it. "But is there any way to prove it?"

"Not definitely, but with more information I could make a convincing case. Absolute proof isn't necessary." Robin felt a surge of satisfaction that came from knowing there was something useful he could do for Maxie. "And I know just the person who can help me."

It was well-known among certain elements of society that Ned Simmons could often be found at the tavern called Noah's Ark, and that is where he had gone to ground, sitting in a corner and scowling at his tankard. He had failed badly in the Collingwood affair, and he did not forgive failure lightly, especially not in himself. Finishing his drink in one long swallow, he looked up for the barmaid to ask for another. Then he froze, staring in disbelief at the blond swell sauntering toward him across the taproom, looking entirely at home among the assorted riffraff in spite of his elegant tailoring.

"Mind if I sit down?" Taking silence for assent, the newcomer pulled out the opposite chair. "I think it is time we were formally introduced. My name is Lord Robert Andreville."

Simmons glowered. "Well, I'll be damned."

"Very likely," Andreville agreed cheerfully.

For a moment Simmons wavered between being amused and diving across the table and putting his hands around the rogue's throat. Amusement won, and he accepted the proffered hand with a rumbling chuckle. "I've heard of you, your lordship. You and I are in related lines of work."

"I've retired now." Andreville didn't flinch at the bone-bruising handshake Simmons returned. "If I concede that in a fair fight you would mop the floor with me, and that in an unfair fight the winner would be whoever went longest without making a mistake, can we go directly to conversation without proving who is the fiercest?''

Simmons chuckled again at the tactful way Andreville threw a sop to his pride. It had hurt to be bested by a pretty fellow half his size; it was much easier to accept defeat from a man who was something of a legend to those few who knew of him. Besides, Andreville was right: in a proper mill, Simmons would be the master. Knowing that, he no longer felt the need to prove it. "I've heard of you. We've a mutual friend at Whitehall."

"I know. Not all the spying was done on the Continent—a good bit was needed right here in London." Andreville signaled the barmaid and ordered another round for Simmons and one of the same for himself. When the wench was gone, he continued, "Lord Lattimer said you were invaluable to him."

"He told you that?"

"Yes, and he is not a man to give praise lightly." Andreville took a swig from the tankard the barmaid set down, and a pained expression flickered across his face.

Simmons hid a smile in his own tankard; porter was not a drink everyone appreciated.

His expression grave, Andreville continued, "I've also talked to Collingwood, so I understand now why you were so hellbent on stopping Miss Collins from reaching London."

"Aye." Simmons' amusement faded. "Would have succeeded if it weren't for you. I saw the chit after she found out about her father. Wish she could've been spared that. I've a daughter myself. Wouldn't want her to know something like that about me."

"Miss Collins thought there might have been foul play involved in her father's death, and she was determined to learn the truth." Andreville sighed. "I think she would have found out, no matter who tried to stop her."

"Daresay you're right," Simmons agreed, thinking of the way the little vixen had swung a knife at him. Not at all a milk-and-water sort of miss. "Now, did you come by just to pass the time of day, or do you have something else in mind?"

Andreville pushed his tankard aside, ready to talk business.

''I want to hire you. Max Collins committed suicide, and I want to know the whole reason why, as soon as possible. You are already familiar with the story, and London is your city. Will you tell me what you know, and help me learn the rest?''

''You can indeed.'' Simmons leaned back on the oak settle, vastly content. Not only was he getting the chance to offset his earlier failure, but he'd be paid for the privilege. And if he was any judge of men—and he was—Andreville was the sort who would pay well. Maybe there was some justice in the world.

17

Maxie felt as if she were wandering in a shadowland of evil dreams, but knew that there would be no awakening. Her father had taken his own life, and the knowledge was a pain more devastating than she could have imagined. Burrowed into her pillows like a woodland creature seeking refuge, she lost track of the hours. The pattern of sunlight slowly shifted across the floor, then disappeared as clouds obscured the sky. Someone entered and left a tray of food, then left without speaking. The room darkened, and eventually the sounds of the household faded as night deepened.

When a distant clock struck midnight, Maxie forced herself to sit up and take stock. She couldn't spend the rest of her life hiding in a bedchamber, and with grim humor she wondered just how much time would have to pass before her hosts would feel compelled to coax her out. Twenty-four hours? Three days? A week? Or would Margot's superb hospitality allow Maxie to stay here forever, a mad mourner served by silent maids?

Even if the duchess would allow that, Robin wouldn't. Maxie buried her head in her hands, wondering dully what would happen next. As she had told Robin at Ruxton, she had been unable to sense her path beyond London, and now she knew why. She felt suspended, unable to go forward, unable to retreat, too numb to imagine anything resembling normal life.

Wearily she slid from the bed and found her dressing gown, one of the garments that had magically appeared in her wardrobe the day before. She stopped and thought. Had she really been in London only two days? It seemed a century since she had arrived, met Margot, had that rousing row with Robin, met her aunt. Belting the robe around her narrow waist, she slipped out the door and went barefoot through the silent house to the library. Books had never failed to make her feel better, and perhaps being surrounded by them would help clarify her dazed mind.

There was a desk at the far end of the library, and she fumbled through the drawers until she found flint and steel to ignite a candle. Even that small amount of light hurt her eyes after so long in the dark, and she turned away as she settled into the leather upholstered chair behind the desk.

The room was cool, and occasional raindrops spatted against the windows. Myriad volumes lined the room in friendly ranks, their titles reflecting dull gold in the candlelight. As she inhaled the pleasant scents of leather bindings and furniture polish, mingled with a faded tang of smoke, the knot in her chest eased a little.

A walnut box of pipe tobacco stood on one side of the desk. Moved by dim memory, she opened the box and put a large pinch of tobacco in a shallow china bowl used for ashes, then set the shredded leaf afire. The pungent scent carried her back to a ceremony she had attended in her childhood. Among her mother's people, tobacco was considered sacred, and it was burned to carry prayers to the spirit world. Her mother had believed all the faces of God should be honored, whether Iroquois or Christian, and had raised Maxie to believe the same.

As she watched the smoke twine and dissipate into the blackness, Maxie was not even sure what to pray for.

Candover House was dark when Robin returned. The principles of investigation were the same everywhere; with Simmons' help and his own expertise, it had not been difficult to reconstruct the last days of Maximus Collins.

He let himself in with the key Maggie had given him. After closing the massive front door, Robin stopped suddenly as the instincts developed over a dozen perilous years sounded a cautionary note. After a moment of intense stillness, reaching out with his senses, he recognized what had disturbed him: though the household slept, there was a distinct, fresh scent of burning tobacco here on a floor that had no bedchambers.

Probably it meant no more than that a servant had smoked a pipe while checking that the doors were locked, or that Candover himself was up late. Nonetheless, having an over-

developed bump of curiosity that had saved his life more than
once, Robin followed the scent to the library, where faint light
showed beneath the door.

When he quietly opened the door, he saw that Maxie sat at
the far end of the room. Her ebony hair spilled over her
shoulders, shining even in the dim light, and her eyes were fixed
absently on a spiral of fragrant smoke. He was grateful to see
that she was once more alive to the world, though her expression
was still bleak and infinitely distant.

She looked up, unsurprised by his presence, her eyes
shadowed. "'Have you been skulking about London?''

Taking that as willingness to have him near, he walked the
length of the room and took a chair several feet away from her.
"Exactly. As you can see, I'm wearing my skulking clothes:
it seemed best where I was going.'' He noticed that she was
barefoot, wearing only a light robe over her shift, and thought
she might be cold. "You asked for this coat when I was done
with it, so perhaps this is a good time to give it to you.'' He
peeled the coat off and offered it to her.

After a slow moment, she took the garment and draped it
around her shoulders, then leaned back in her chair again,
looking very small in the folds of dark fabric.

"I've learned some things I think you'll find interesting,''
Robin said. "Can you bear to listen now, or should I wait?''

She made a vague gesture with her hand. "It doesn't matter.
Now will do.''

In her passivity, she seemed almost another woman, and it
hurt to see the dimming of her spirit. Perhaps what he had
learned might rekindle her essential flame. "Your uncle
Collingwood was here today. He is very concerned for you.
As you probably have guessed, he sent Simmons to prevent you
from reaching London so that you would not learn what you
learned. It turns out that Simmons is a Bow Street Runner.''

She dropped another pinch of tobacco on the smoldering
mound. "What is a Bow Street Runner?''

"A thieftaker. Primarily they work for the chief magistrate
of Westminster, whose office is in Bow Street, hence the name,''
Robin explained. "Bow Street has become the center of law
enforcement for a wide area, and Runners can be hired by

private citizens for special tasks. That is what your uncle did.''

Maxie nodded, not over-interested in what he was saying. She still had not met his eyes.

''What I am going to tell you may be painful, but I want you to hear me out.'' Robin scanned her perfectly cut, immobile profile, hoping what he had to say would make a difference. ''Collingwood was puzzled by your father's death, and he hired Simmons to investigate what had happened. Without going into all the details, it seems that your Great-aunt Maxima had left you five hundred pounds a year, but you could not receive it until you were over twenty-five and your father had died.

''Though he may have concealed it from you, your father's health had apparently been deteriorating for some time. When he came to London, he not only called on your aunt's executor to learn the details of your legacy, he also visited two physicians. I've talked to both, and they agreed that your father's heart was failing. Neither could guess how long he would last, but they were both sure he was dying. It was just a matter of time.''

Maxie's head came up at that, her brown eyes meeting his, but she didn't speak; she scarcely seemed to breathe.

Robin continued, ''I've talked to a number of people today, including an old friend of your father's, a woman he had known before he went to America, and whom he visited again. There is no way to prove a man's state of mind, but based on his actions and some of the things he told the woman, I would be willing to swear that your father decided to end his life so that you would inherit quickly and not have to go through the grief of nursing him through a slow death. Perhaps he himself did not want to die that way, weakened and waiting for the end. You would know that better than I.''

Maxie was trembling, and her tongue licked out to moisten her dry lips. ''How did he do it?''

''With a massive dose of digitalis, a heart medication that is a poison in large quantities. Both physicians had given him some, warning him to be careful how much he used because it can be fatal. It seems likely that your father thought he would have time to dispose of the bottle, but the medicine overcame him quickly. If he had had a little more time, no one would have realized that he hadn't died naturally.''

Robin stopped for a moment, then finished quietly, "Your father didn't abandon you carelessly, but because he cared so much. I think he wanted to give you with his death what he was unable to give you in life. He was wrong not to know that you would rather have had him for whatever weeks or months were left, but his action sprang from love. I hope that knowing that makes a difference to you."

Maxie's brown eyes came alive then, and as she buried her face in her hands, she whispered, "It does. Dear God, it makes all the difference in the world."

This time her tears were not of devastation, but of healing. "With the wandering life we lived, my father and I were everything to each other. No matter how insulting strangers were, no matter how much I was despised for my Mohawk blood, I was always sure that my father cared for me. When I heard that he had killed himself, with no word or thought for me, it felt as if my whole life had been built on a lie."

It was as Robin had guessed: even strong, resilient young women had their Achilles' heels, and needing to believe in her father's love was Maxie's. This time she did not reject the comfort of his arms. Instead, she accepted his embrace as easily as in all of the nights they had spent together, her body pliant and trusting.

Her tears ended quickly, and when she leaned back in his arms, she was herself again. "Thank you, Robin," she said softly. "My father's failing health was something that we both knew but never spoke of. He hated being weak. To take his own life in one quixotic gesture, knowing that I would benefit—it is exactly the sort of thing he would do, but I would never have been able to see it for myself."

"The most important things are always the hardest to see." Desire flared with stunning intensity now that it was not suppressed by protectiveness, and Robin released her immediately, backing away before she could sense the change in him. Maxie had been through an emotional maelstrom today; it would be unfair of him to take advantage of her vulnerability. Perching on the edge of the desk, he swung one leg casually, as if he wasn't acutely aware of her nearness and her utter, unselfconscious desirability. Looking for distraction, his gaze fell on the smoldering tobacco. "Is there any particular meaning to this?"

"Tobacco is sacred to my mother's people, and it is burned to carry prayers and wishes to the spirits."

As Robin had said before, he believed in making sacrifices to the gods of luck. He took a pinch of dried leaf and added to the mound, blowing carefully so it would continue to burn.

"What did you wish for?" Maxie asked.

He glanced at her. She was recovering with remarkable speed, only the faint trace of tears on her smooth tan cheeks bearing witness to her earlier emotional desolation. She had such strength. "If I tell you, will that prevent the wish from coming true?"

She smiled. "I don't think it makes a difference."

A moment ago, he had told himself that it was not the time to speak, but when he saw her irresistible smile, Robin threw caution to the winds. "I was wishing you would marry me."

Her levity faded and she leaned back in the chair, tugging the coat around her. It was still warm from his body, with a faint delicious masculine scent. She had wanted the garment because in the future, when she was alone, it would remind her of what it was like to be in Robin's arms. Her voice light, Maxie said, "That's a dangerous habit you have, offering marriage. If you aren't careful, I might accept."

"Why won't you?" Even in the dim light, his eyes were vividly blue as they met hers.

She sighed and glanced down at her linked hands. While the question of her father's death was unresolved, she had avoided this discussion, but she no longer had an excuse. It was best to speak; tomorrow would be no easier.

Looking up, she studied him. Robin was only an arm's length away physically, yet his blond handsomeness, casual confidence, and bone-deep aristocratic elegance represented a chasm too wide to bridge. "Because I think marriage would be a mistake," she said bluntly. "We are too different. I am the child of a wastrel book peddler and a woman considered a savage by your countrymen. You are born of centuries of wealth, breeding, and privilege." She swallowed hard, trying to make her voice steady, as if her conclusion was an easy one. "I think, in time, you would regret our marriage."

"Would you regret it?" he asked softly, his gaze holding hers.

"I would if you did," she replied, knowing that her simple words were the essence of the dilemma. Loving him, she would be unable to endure his regrets; no matter carefully he hid discontent under politeness, she would feel it.

"You're wrong, you know. The differences between us are superficial, but the similarities are profound." Robin's flexible voice was taut with conviction. "We were both born outsiders, Maxie. In your case, it was because of your mixed blood, never wholly belonging with either your father's or your mother's people." In his white shirt sleeves he looked lean and strong and overpoweringly attractive as he lounged against the desk, his hands loosely curled around the edge. "I know something of what you endured because I, in spite of wealth, privilege, and endless noble ancestors, was a natural misfit, no more at home in my world than you were in yours."

He smiled without humor. "Perhaps it would have been different if I had had a mother, if my father had been able to bear the sight of me, but perhaps not, perhaps I was born perverse. Every generation or two the Andrevilles throw up a black sheep, and my keepers were convinced I was one before I was out of leading strings. Something had only to be forbidden to attract me. Everything I did was wrong, proof that I was naturally incorrigible. I questioned things that should not be questioned, disobeyed commands I disagreed with, made up stories that were seen as wicked lies.

"My nurse even thought I was left-handed just to spite her. Sometimes she tied my left hand behind my back so I must use the right; other times she beat my left palm with a brass ruler until it bled." His mouth twisted. "When my brother found out, he put a stop to that particular cruelty even though he was just a lad himself. I don't know what I would have done without Giles. Gone thoroughly to the bad, I suppose. He was more truly my parent than my real father."

He lifted one hand dismissively. "All that is no longer important, though I am probably one of the few boys in England who thought that public school was an improvement on life at home. At Winchester I was considered an eccentric, but I became a more successful one. Then, by chance, I found a calling that suited me very well, that enabled me to use my unholy talents productively.''

Give a dog a bad name and watch him bite. His words painted a very different picture from the life Maxie had imagined. How had he survived such a childhood with his humor and sanity and kindness intact? Still . . . ''Granted that neither of us grew up believing that we belonged,'' she said slowly, ''is that enough of a bond to hold us together? Are we defined by our weaknesses?''

''Not by our weaknesses, but by our trust.'' He stirred restlessly, then stilled. ''Trust is the foundation of closeness, because we dare show our weaknesses only to those who we hope will understand and accept us in spite of them. Even when I scarcely knew you, I found myself speaking of things I have told no one else, had barely even admitted to myself.''

''That is what worries me, Robin,'' Maxie said, matching honesty with honesty. ''I wonder if you want to marry me because I was there when you were hurting. Because you needed to talk and I listened, have you come to think I am special, when in truth, any woman would have done as well?''

''Do you think so little of my judgment, Kanawiosta?'' He smiled with a sweetness and intimacy that melted her heart. ''No other woman would have been the same. I knew you were special from the moment I met you, and it was your wisdom and caring that helped me begin to heal a wound that threatened to destroy me. I will carry my guilts and regrets for what I have done until I die, but because you shared them and made me face them, they will no longer disable me.''

Just as she would never cease to mourn her father's untimely death, but she was no longer paralyzed by the pain of it. She and Robin had helped each other through dark nights of the soul, and perhaps that was a foundation for a lifetime. But perhaps it was not; normal life was made of dailyness, not high drama.

Maxie bit her lip miserably. ''I don't know if I can be happy here, Robin. England seems a far more congenial place since I left Chanleigh and met you, but . . .'' Her voice trailed off as she thought of the forests and mountains of her homeland, the blunt honesty of her countrymen. "I don't know if I could bear it if I never saw America again."

"The one true advantage of wealth is the freedom it gives. Marrying me won't make you a prisoner, Maxie. After all of my years of wandering I would like a permanent home, and perhaps, if you are willing, it could be Ruxton. But I want to visit America, see the land that shaped you, meet your mother's people. We can create any life we please, either here or in America. The choice is yours."

Robin stopped, his gaze holding hers. "You said that I had something to learn, and you were right." Every syllable distinct, he finished softly, "What I learned is that I love you. And because I do, my true home is in you."

Maxie gasped as she heard the words she had never expected. "You said you were not very good at love."

"I didn't think I was," he said wryly. "I believed that I loved Maggie as much as I was capable of, and that she left me because it wasn't enough, because there was some subtle deficiency in me. Now I know it was not that I was incapable of loving more, but that I had not met the woman I could truly fall in love with. Maggie tried to explain that to me once, but it was beyond my understanding." He was silent a moment, searching for words. "I love Maggie, but there were always limits. With you, Kanawiosta, there are none." His knuckles whitened as his hands gripped the edge of the table. "I don't know if you can love me the same way, but if there is even a chance that someday you might . . ." He stopped, painful uncertainty on his face.

Maxie was awed by his willingness to make himself vulnerable. It was impossible to disbelieve such transparent honesty; for whatever miraculous reason, he loved her, and the knowledge was shining joy that filled her like the sun's radiance. "Lord, Robin, of course I love you," she said, her voice catching. "All my talk of our differences, my doubts about England—they were only smoke. My true fear was that I loved you too much to marry if you didn't love me."

She stood and opened her arms, and Robin walked straight into them.

From the beginning, their bodies had known that it was utterly right to be together, and now that doubts were gone, desire exploded, fierce and compelling. How could she have ever thought him cool? Robin had been right when he said passion was easy; it was the easiest, most natural thing in the world. She gloried in the resilient tension of his lean, supple body, pressing against him in wordless response to his mouth and hands and intoxicating nearness.

Even more than fire, there was tenderness and understanding and mirth, all woven together into an emotion far greater than the sum of its parts. When it seemed that she might expire from sheer bubbling happiness, Maxie leaned back in his arms and gazed into his eyes, laughing. Somehow they had arrived on the sofa, where she lay across Robin's lap. His coat had long since fallen from her shoulders, and her robe had joined it on the floor. "How on earth did we manage to spend so many nights together and behave ourselves?"

Robin smiled with a sweetness that took her breath away. Maxie realized that he had dropped the teasing and tales and verbal obfuscation that he had used as a barrier against the world. Now he was allowing her to see him as he really was, and she loved him all the more. Robin was right: the differences between them were superficial, the similarities profound. They belonged together, and nothing in the future could ever separate them.

"Hard to believe we were so very, very good, isn't it?" His voice bright with laughter, Robin stroked her from neck to hip. Through the thin shift Maxie felt his touch like a brand of fire. "The principle behind bundling is that one must maintain mental walls because it is the wrong time to give into desire. When we were traveling, it wasn't the right time for us and we both knew it."

"Times change." Burying her hands in the silky gold of Robin's hair, Maxie drew his head down for another kiss. Just before their lips met, she whispered, "Let the walls come tumbling down!"

Robin and Maxie were delighted when the Marquess of Wolverton announced that he and Lady Ross were also to marry. Privately Robin told his older brother that the marquess was now responsible for getting his own heirs. A gleam in his eye, Giles murmured that he knew what his duty was.

Lord Collingwood was profoundly pleased when his niece married so well. Being a prudent man, he didn't mention his satisfaction in front of his vexed wife and daughters.

The canal-boat captain, John Blaine, had no proof of the identity of the anonymous donor who gave him his own barge, but privately he was sure. That's why he named the vessel *Maxima*.

Simmons was shocked speechless, and secretly touched, when he and his wife were invited to the nuptials of Lord Robert Andreville and Miss Maxima Collins. Privately, he offered the highest of compliments: if Lord Robert hadn't had the misfortune to be born a gentleman, he would have made a damned good Bow Street Runner.

The Duke and Duchess of Candover were equally delighted by the marriage, Margot with a pure, unselfish pleasure in the fact that Robin had found the same kind of happiness that she had. Rafe was also genuinely pleased for Robin and Maxie, but less altruistically, he was secretly gratified that his wife's handsome, charming former lover would now be kept busy by his dazzling American wife.

Before settling at Ruxton, Lord and Lady Robert Andreville took an extended wedding trip to America that included a visit to her ladyship's maternal relations. Maxie was not surprised that during a month with the Mohawks, her husband acquired a very decent command of the Iroquois language: by this time, nothing Robin did could surprise her.